ALL

F O R

MONEY

GLENN KAPLAN

ALL

FOR

MONEY

A NOVEL

ST. MARTIN'S PRESS
NEW YORK

Design by Judith A. Stagnitto

Library of Congress Cataloging-in-Publication Data

Kaplan, Glenn.
    All for money / Glenn Kaplan.
      p.   cm.
    ISBN 0-312-08759-4
    I. Title.
    PS3561.A557A79   1993
    813'.54—dc20   92-41838
                                        CIP

First Edition: April 1993

10 9 8 7 6 5 4 3 2 1

For Alec.
For every good reason.

ACKNOWLEDGMENTS

Because writing is such a solitary occupation, the few people who penetrate the author's bubble matter enormously. I would like to thank them.

First of all, George Rohr for the inspiration. Alice Lichtenstein and Jim Berkovitz, who gave me the validation I needed to get beyond page ten. Joy Sliwa, who lent me media contacts. Chip Block, who lent me publishing expertise. Peter Model, who led me to the steadfast and indomitable Robert Ducas. Charlie Hayward, who was once again friend and ally. Victoria Hamilton, Barry and Karen Mills, and Joyce Greenberg, who were interested readers and patient friends. Maureen Baron for taking the risk. My editor Bill Thomas for taking the trouble and providing such clarity of vision. Also, three magical vacation places where I was able to work like crazy: Coccoloba Plantation in Anguilla, Biras Creek in Virgin Gorda, and Dick and Adrienne Munich's barn in the Berkshires.

Finally, as always, Evelyn.

ALL

F O R

MONEY

JANUARY

CHAPTER ONE

We're getting close to the big moment. So far, Levine has taken me through what he calls the "broadstroke preliminaries" in an effortless dance. I am prepared to be bought out? Yes, one-two. And I would stay on to run the magazine for a year? Why not, three-four. Getting half up front and the rest at year's end? Of course, one-two. Levine and I move together like Fred and Ginger.

We agree, one-two. We agree, three-four. We agree to agree to earnings targets for my year under contract. If *Elixir* makes them, I get the full price. If we exceed them, there are bonus formulas. If *Elixir* falls short, there are penalties. Stiff penalties. I could lose the second half of the money. Or even all of it. Okay, fair is fair. The music is building to its crescendo. Levine leans forward on the conference room table, hands clenched together.

"Our offer, Bob, is ten million dollars." The music stops. I am alone on the dance floor.

"Ten million," I repeat tonelessly. This is not only more than I expected. It is over two million more. *Two million*. Inside me, a little cartoon man is bouncing off the walls, howling with joy and astonishment, "Yeee-oow! Wow! Whooop-whooop! Yip-pee! Ka-zoweee!" He is not someone you bring to a meeting like this on the thirty-sixth floor of the headquarters of American Communications Corporation. I struggle to immobilize any twitching muscle, any pulsing vein, that might betray me. I want to look impassive, maybe even a little bored. I hope the effort doesn't show.

"Ten million," I say, staring out the window to see if the icy morning rain has let up, as the radio predicted it would. "Yes," I mutter, half to myself. The sun is trying valiantly to poke through the clouds. It could well turn into one of those mild winter days that feel like a preview of spring. I repeat the number thoughtfully, "Ten million."

It's hard to believe this is happening to me. *Me*. An average-looking guy of thirty-five, average height of five-ten, with average blue eyes and sandy-

1

colored hair. All right, maybe my looks are a *little* better than average. But I'm just a middle-class kid from a dumpy nowhere town in New Hampshire. All right, *lower* middle class.

"Yes indeed," snaps Tim Conover, the pale, patrician investment banker who must be about my age, "ten million. That, Mr. Macallan, is not merely a generous offer; it is American's best offer." Look at him, acting like the master of all he sees. I can just imagine paterfamilias Conover sitting him on his knee: "Son, we expect you to move mountains. We expect you to make millions. And here is a head start on everyone else in the race. Take this road map, use these connections, and if you slip up, you can always fall back on your trust fund." Yes, Conover acts like he was born to be here, ingesting millions without so much as a hiccup. Like it's some kind of goddamn birthright.

"I'm on record," he lectures, infatuated with the sound of his own voice, "as recommending that American's first offer for your magazine be lower. Substantially lower. But Ted wants to close this deal quickly and has decided not to let his investment banker engage in the kind of hardball that could get him a lower price. Remember, Bob, we at Hale Hadley are bringing a number of magazine properties to American's attention. A number. So I would advise against the poker face and say the words 'ten million' with more of the enthusiasm they deserve."

Conover is a fine one to talk about posturing. Since he first telephoned his way into my life eight weeks ago, inquiring if I might be willing to be acquired by a major media company "that must remain anonymous for now," he has done nothing but assume poses. The Great Investment Banker. The Great Keeper of Publishing Insights. The Great Arranger of secret meetings where I hand over financial statements I must smuggle out of my own company. And, of course, the Great Negotiator. Conover is working feverishly to show the world he can make the big jump from mere vice president to managing director and partner of Hale Hadley, the most prestigious and haughty of Wall Street firms. Surrounded by perfect English hunt prints in his perfect office of industrial ersatz Chippendale, Timothy Evans Conover keeps on his desk, facing himself, a photo framed in gold-tooled leather. Not of his perfect blond family in Connecticut, but of his perfect blond self. Just himself. Square-jawed, Hermès-tied, and confident. Still, he cannot be pissed off merely because his client won't let him chisel me down to a lower price. He earns a straight 2 percent fee. The more American pays, the more he brings back to the Hale Hadley bonus pool.

"Let's go easy, Tim." Chubby, balding Ted Levine pats the legal pad in front of Conover. "That's an awful lot to think about." Levine certainly doesn't look like he was born to be here. But he has the aura inner city kids have when they grow up poor but savvy, so he fits. Where I come from, being part of a meeting like this is beyond anyone's imagining.

"I understand you, Bob," Levine says, soothing and avuncular. "You've spent five years building *Elixir* up from nothing into a great, a really outstanding, book." No one in publishing ever calls a magazine a magazine.

2

It's always a "book." There are fashion books, life-style books, business books, women's service books, shelter books, girlie books, trade books, a thousand kinds of books, and no magazines.

"*Elixir* is not just his company," Levine says. "It's his baby. But Tim is right about one thing: this is our best offer. I want to cut through all the back-and-forth bullshit. We want *Elixir* and we want it now. We want you to run it for at least the transition year and maybe a lot longer. We want you to be happy, completely happy, so we can go on to the next acquisition. I'm committed to having the new magazine group assembled and running by the end of this year. We're working seven days a week with our investment bankers at Hale Hadley and at, uh, at Seligssohn Brothers to line up all the books we want."

Conover snaps to attention in midsulk. Of course. So the rumors are true. Hale Hadley's fifty-year grip on American's investment banking business is slipping. And on Conover's watch. That can't play well back at the firm. Conover scribbles something on his legal pad.

"It's a very good offer, Ted," I say, praying that my face is still expressionless. Negotiate, Macallan. Maintain your cool. "But I would like to sleep on it."

"Twenty-four hours?" Levine asks.

"Forty-eight. I'm a heavy sleeper."

"Agreed."

We stand up together and shake hands. As we head toward the elevators, I am hoping I can finally relax and let myself react when the elevator doors close. Maybe whoop and holler or jump up and down a little. No such luck. Conover is on his way back to Hale Hadley; he joins me. Once outside the arena of the Great Negotiator, he becomes the Great Salesman again. He must be thinking of the bonus pool.

"You know, Bob, in today's market you'd be hard-pressed to find an offer better than this one. When Ted first described his strategy for the new group, I told him that *Elixir* should be his cornerstone, the first property to acquire. The niche you've carved for yourself in the medical market is unique."

The elevator doors open after only a couple of floors. A clerk with a mailroom wagon and a gum-cracking secretary in spike heels enter. We fall silent.

No one at *Elixir* knows about this meeting. I told Marie I was at the doctor's this morning. For the past two months I've been slinking around like some secret agent, calling Conover from home or from pay phones, carrying documents to meetings on street corners. If word leaked out prematurely, it could upset my advertisers or my key employees and upset the deal. These people must be handled with care and delicacy. Especially Leo. Leo is convinced that he ought to own the book, that he *is* the book, that it is nothing without him. But I will deal with Leo later. Right now, it's time for yet another shrouded call from a pay phone. I've got to let Wendy know about the offer before I go back to the office. Ten million dollars. Take roughly 40 percent off the top for Uncle Sam, New York State, and New York City taxes. That leaves about six million and change, free and clear, for Wendy and me. Six million worth of freedom and independence. Our chance to stop—me at thirty-three, Wendy at thirty—and decide what we would do if we could do just about anything we wanted to.

As the elevator doors open on the ground floor, I fish into my pocket for change. All I have is a dime, three pennies, and a subway token.

"Tim, uh, I've got to make a quick phone call." I put my opened hand in front of him. "Sorry, but—"

"No problem." Conover reaches for his change and deposits a quarter onto my palm. He pauses, then extracts the subway token. "My secretary uses them," he explains as he smiles and pockets it. "You know, Bob Macallan, you're a very lucky man." And he is gone.

I take Conover's expensive quarter to the bank of pay phones and call Wendy's office.

"Truedale and Wolfson. May I help you?"

"Is Wendy in, Iris? It's Bob."

"Oh, hi. No, she went flying out the door with Liz about an hour ago. Client in a panic."

Let's see. That could be the no-cholesterol gourmet restaurant on Second Avenue. Or maybe Paint It Black, the SoHo boutique that, for a couple of thousand, will outfit you in black from head to toe, to assume the pose of the Bohemian capitalists who pose as contemporary artists.

Truedale and Wolfson is a tiny marketing consulting firm, consisting of Iris, the secretary, and a couple of former brand managers, refugees from the snakepit politics of an international toothpaste and hair-care products giant. Truedale is Liz, the imposing beakish redhead with the Harvard MBA and stress-induced hemorrhoids. Wolfson is Wendy, the not at all imposing brunette with the Columbia MBA and the infinite capacity for surprising me, her husband.

"Is the panic at Paint It Black?"

"No. Bradfordco. Wendy said she'd meet you at the party at like eight-thirty or nine." Oh yes, I almost forgot. The party. Three people we know, two business types and one art world denizen, have given up on New York life and are about to defect to simpler parts. Tonight they are throwing their "Quitting the Rat Race Forever Party" in the arty one's downtown loft.

"One more thing, Iris. I've got a number for her."

"A number?"

"Uh-huh, tell her it's ten."

"Ten?"

"That's right. Ten."

Pause. Pause.

"I won't ask."

"Good. When she calls in, tell her I hope she'll be up for dinner and a movie tonight, because *I* will be." Dinner and a movie is our private code

4

for a roll in the hay. It started after we had been dating for a few months. I called Wendy late one afternoon. . . .

"Dinner and a movie?" she had asked. "You haven't phoned for over a week and a half. And now, on the spur of the moment, you ask me if I'd like dinner and a movie tonight, all very la-di-da." In the early stages of building the magazine, I had a one-track mind, a one-track life, one subject of conversation, and almost no patience for anything or anyone else. I was a pretty good company builder and pretty awful company.

"Is dinner and a movie really what you want, Macallan? You know, when most guys call and ask you for dinner and a movie, what they really want is to jump on your bones *after* dinner and a movie. But you're not most guys. At least to me you're not. Are you 'most guys' to you? Well, are you?" I had no answer. "You know I'd love to have dinner and a movie with you, but I don't think dinner and a movie is what you should be calling me for. Don't you think it's time we got beyond dinner and a movie?" Then her voice turned low and gentle. "You do understand? Don't you? Robert?" Another long silence from me, then she hung up.

That really shook me. I had been smitten with Wendy right from the start. Spunky, savvy, startlingly honest, and so pretty I found myself having lusty dreams about her night after night. She was the first native Manhattan woman I'd met who was truly down-to-earth. Her father a Wall Street lawyer, her mother an art history professor, Wendy had inhaled all the chaos and sophistication of this city and was not in the slightest bit impressed—not with herself or anything else that couldn't pass her very stringent "Real Test." I called her back immediately, told her I loved her, and asked her to marry me. She said no thank you, but said she would, under the circumstances, consent to dinner and a movie and, maybe afterward, dinner and a movie. It took another year for her to say yes to marrying me.

Iris is concerned on Wendy's behalf. "You let your wife slave away at Bradfordco till all hours, after which you drag her to some downtown party, then you expect her to be up for dinner and a movie? When is she supposed to get any sleep?"

"Oh, I thought you knew. She has people who do that *for* her."

"Good-bye, Bob."

As I hang up and turn to leave the marble mausoleum that is American's lobby, I see a man I remember from somewhere coming toward me, waving.

"Hey! Bob Macallan. Hi. It's Ken Atwood. From *Stone Age*. Last year? MPA convention? Princess Hotel. Bermuda." His left hand on my shoulder, the right hand pumping away.

"Why, sure, Ken. It's nice to see you again." Atwood is publisher of the number one trade book of the rock and gravel industry and vice president of the Mackey Magazine Group, which also publishes *Bronze Age, Wood Age, Cement Age, Plastic Age,* and a few more industry *Ages.* All incredibly dreary, incredibly profitable "bibles" of their respective fields.

"You know, Bob, I heard a rumor that Phil Congdon is still down there in Bermuda, sleeping it off. Remember how he passed out, Scotch in hand, right there at the pitch 'n' putt contest. Just went to sleep in the middle of it all. Ha, ha, ha, ha!" Atwood laughs in short, piercing bursts, machine-gun style. He is a slight, obsequious ferret of a man, with a foot-long shock of hair dyed Grecian Formula black and combed unconvincingly over his bald head. Of course he knows me from the Magazine Publishers Association convention in Bermuda. He knows all the other delegates, too, their wives, kids, caddies, and chambermaids.

"Bob, I've got a proposition I'd like to pass on to you. Can I offer you a lift?" He motions toward a silver stretch limo waiting outside at the curb. A big, bloated Lincoln with windows tinted almost black. The car must be half a block long.

"Sure," I say. "An investment banker just collected his fee, and now I can't even afford the subway."

"Huh?"

"Never mind. I'd love a lift. You headed in my direction?"

"Absolutely."

He escorts me to the steel dinosaur at curbside. The rain has let up completely now; you can feel the air trying to warm up to near fifty. Once inside the car, Atwood turns toward the uniformed hulk in the front seat: "Ricky, we're going to Twenty-fifth and Park." To me: "That's right, isn't it?" There's a streamlined panel of controls sloping down out of the ceiling. He pushes the red switch in the center of it. The window between Ricky and us hums up into place.

"Drink?" Atwood gestures toward the limo's bar, a row of cut crystal decanters in a cabinet of genuine walnut-grain Formica. It also holds the TV, telephone, and what appears to be a fax machine.

"No thanks," I say.

"Right. Only eleven o'clock. Sun isn't over the yardarm yet. Listen, Bob. It is Bob, isn't it? I mean, Bob's okay?"

"Sure. Everyone calls me Bob." Except Wendy, who, when she's very serious about something, calls me Robert.

"Bob, we at Mackey have tremendous admiration for the job you've done building *Elixir*. We've been keeping close tabs on your progress."

"Evidently. How did you happen to find me in the lobby just now?"

"Mr. Mackey pays me to know these things. Do you mind if I . . . ?" He reaches for the decanter with the little silver necklace marked "Bourbon" and pours himself three fingers' worth. "I'm gonna get right to the point. If you're thinking of selling out to American, hold on. Don't sell *Elixir* to anyone, and certainly not to those stiffs at American, until you talk to us. Mr. Mackey has an offer he wants to make."

Elton Mackey is known in some circles as "Wacky Mackey," a tough guy who dreams up big, off-the-wall gestures that produce results. Legend has it he acquired his first magazine twenty-five years ago. Mackay was, and still is, one of the biggest printers in Cleveland. When *Stone Age,* the floundering number two book in the gravel game, couldn't pay its printing bills, Mackey took it over.

Stone Age, the story goes, was being killed by another Cleveland operation, *Gravel Weekly,* which happened to be housed in a building that had a big billboard on the roof. Now the magazine business runs on rumors. Whenever there are whispered half-truths and innuendo afloat about a publication, facts always take a backseat. Once rumors start about a book, it's hard to stop them. So Mackey rented the billboard on the roof of the *Gravel Weekly* building. He did it anonymously, through lawyers of his lawyers. And the sign he put up said in twelve-foot block letters: IGNORE THE RUMORS. That's it. Right above the sign that said: "Gravel Weekly, Voice of America's Bedrock Industry." IGNORE THE RUMORS. What rumors? Suddenly, rumors began, planted by Mackey operatives around the industry. At the office, the paranoia the billboard was meant to create ran rampant. "Is it true the circulation numbers are slipping?" "Are ad pages really down?" "Is the editor going to jump ship?" Soon, everyone from *Gravel Weekly* found himself in the position of the guy who's asked, "When did you stop beating your wife?"

Into that climate of fear and uncertainty Elton Mackey jumped. For every ad a company placed in *Gravel Weekly* Mackey gave away the same space in *Stone Age.* Free. For a year Mackey gave away every ad page in his magazine, while using the orchestrated paranoia at *Gravel Weekly* to rob it of most of its key executives. At the end of two years, *Stone Age* was the indisputed number one, *Gravel Weekly* was in receivership, and Mackey bought the billboard company from whom he had rented the fateful sign. "It really pays to advertise," he said. That, at least, is the story.

"Mr. Mackey wants to meet with you personally," Atwood says. "At your earliest convenience. Tomorrow, if possible."

The overgrown statusmobile waddles around the corner of Forty-sixth Street and begins the descent downtown along Park Avenue.

"I'm certainly flattered by all the interest, but I don't remember telling anyone, first of all, that *Elixir* is for sale. Or, second, that I'm about to sell it to American."

"Bob, we're in publishing. Come on. This is the information business. But okay. *If* you were planning to sell *Elixir,* you could not have picked a better time. The magazine game is going to be played by a handful of major players, and if you're serious, and I assume you are, the question is whose team you're going to play on. I'm here to tell you it ought to be Mackey's team."

"I see."

"But I don't want to steal Mr. Mackey's thunder. If you're close to a deal with American—and mind you, no one is saying you are—but if you are, you owe it to yourself to talk to Mr. Mackey. If you can swing it, tomorrow. In Cleveland. Mr. Mackey's got the corporate jet parked out at Teterboro just waiting for you to say yes. How about if Ricky picks you up tomorrow morning at eight? You'll be in Cleveland before ten. There'll

7

be a car waiting to take you to Laurelwood, where Mr. Mackey can lay it all out for you. Whaddya say, Bob? You've got nothing to lose by listening. And it might even be the smartest decision of your life."

Atwood lives up to his title of Publisher, a job that has little to do with publishing and everything to do with selling.

"Sure. What have I got to lose?"

"You betcha, Bobby. Besides, Cleveland is beautiful this time of year." Atwood emits another machine-gun burst of laughter. I hate being called Bobby.

The gray brontosaurus is approaching Twenty-fifth and Park, headquarters of General Insurance, a shabby relic of the days when office buildings tried to look like Gothic cathedrals. I housed *Elixir* there, not because it's close to the trendy district of ad agencies and publishing houses, but because the space is cheap. I have observed the entrepreneur's cardinal rule: keep your overhead low. With its vast population of non-English-speaking immigrant clerks, General's building and the real estate immediately around it are in little danger of ever becoming fashionable or expensive.

We're saying good-bye in front of General's gaping cathedral doors. "Bob, I hope we can soon welcome you to the Mackey family." He's patting my shoulder and pumping the arm again. "Ricky will be waiting for you tomorrow at eight sharp. Outside One-eleven Riverside Drive. Right?"

I nod respectfully at the depth and accuracy of the research he's done.

"The information business, Bobby"—he taps his left temple sagely—"the information business." He fires off a round of farewell laughs, jumps back into the fat gray beast, and vanishes into the traffic. Leo loves big limos like that, too. *Loves* them. Limos to and from the airport. Limos to sales presentations. Limos everywhere around conventions. Limos for clients. Limos for himself. He calls them "vital sales tools" and "instruments of credibility." Limos and high-priced hookers. Vital tools of the trade.

Entering the *Elixir* office today gives me a jolt. It's the same spartan, unglamorous place—sixty-year-old corridors tiled with thirty-year-old linoleum, offices updated with nothing fancier than paint, cheap gray industrial carpeting, and the eclectic collection of office furnishings, much of it bought secondhand, that I've acquired as the company has grown from its start in my rented studio apartment on West Ninety-fourth Street. For the first time, it all feels separate from me. I am indeed going to separate from it. For five years, it has been an extension of me. Every new employee, every stick of furniture, every telephone, every computer, represented an enlargement of me. Suddenly, the magazine has its own life. And my life will go elsewhere.

Things are quiet. I duck into my office and close the door. I inspect the top of my desk, looking for any stray notes or reminders that might clue someone about my meeting at American. Nothing. I review my calendar for telltale entries. None. I open drawers and ransack a bit. Any scrap or scribble? Not a one. That I can find.

I go down the corridor where my salespeople sit. It is eleven-thirty. They are all out, on the way to fancy lunches where they will tell the *Elixir* story for the umpteenth time to marketing and media types who've heard it all before about every magazine ever published. Like the twenty-five-dollar expense account Dover sole they will dine on, presentation is what makes the meal. How to serve up the same old story of audience loyalty, the skads of money they are dying to spend on your product, and how they'll read every word of your ad because they read every word of the magazine. How can you dress it up, make it amusing, surprising, more relevant? Medallions of audience demographics, lightly poached in white wine, served on a bed of braised costs-per-thousand, with a light saffron reach and frequency sauce.

I check the offices one by one looking for I don't know what—a memo or calendar entry that says: "Next Tuesday: Be sure to discover Macallan's plan to sell company to American Communications. Call Mackey to generate a second offer." There's nothing in Roni Kessler's office, nor in Mike Carmody's, nor in Wayne Crosby's. Nothing that I can see.

That leaves the big office at the end of the hall. The office that is bigger than mine. Leo's office. Leo Sayles. "Hi, I'm Leo Sayles," Leo always says, extending his oversized baseball mitt of a hand. "That's S-A-Y-L-E-S. But my friends call me Mr. Sales. That's S-A-L-E-S." A wink, a pat on the shoulder, and Leo has turned the stranger into a co-conspirator and confidant. Funny thing is, he can really do it. Leo *is* Mr. Sales, the most competitive, relentless persuader on earth. Leo isn't merely out to beat other salesmen. Leo wants to beat the entire world into submission. Leo will do whatever it takes. Charm you, drink you under the table, dazzle you with loop-the-loops of reason, seduce you with friendship, embarrass you with praise, lavish you with gifts, or scare the shit out of you. Whatever it takes to turn your head, win your heart, weaken your resistance, pummel your will into jelly, and get you to say yes.

The only times I've ever seen Leo looking tired and limp are when he's sitting alone at his desk with no target for his persuasion. But let the phone ring or any human prospect appear in view, and Leo's chubby, round face fills with life. The gray beady little eyes turn to happy smiling slits, like the ancient mask of Comedy. On the wall behind his desk you see a dozen or so framed photos of Leo's happy mask posed with golf pros, politicians, corporate VIPs, celebrity speakers at conventions, and an occasional movie star. Leo is their friend and companion—graceful and portly, jovial and smooth, with meticulously tailored suits and a gleaming silver ring of hair around his bald head. He grins into the camera, revealing nothing. Alone, Leo does not exist; he is an empty vessel. Paired against a potential victim, Leo is the most vibrant of men. The motto etched on his bronze paperweight is: "You don't need a rest. You need a win."

Leo was a very important catch for *Elixir*. He was the top salesman at Becker Publications; he led the charge for three of their technical journals, plus their consumer health magazine, *Vitality*. A very important guy, but vulnerable to a better offer. Leo had been passed over too many times; all the young bucks he trained now wear the title of Publisher or Advertising Director and he was still just a salesman. I was happy to let him wear the titles of Associate Publisher and Advertising Director. I would have let him call himself just about anything he wanted. Why? Because Leo has *connections*.

Leo knows everyone who has drug and medical services to advertise. Everyone. He has known them since they first had a dollar in budget to approve. He's taken them to lunch to celebrate their first promotion and every one after that. By the time they have real power, Leo has them in the palm of his hand. Brand managers, marketing managers, group vice presidents, media directors, executive vice presidents, and, whenever they have risen from the marketing ranks, presidents and chairmen of the board.

"I know this business like nobody else," he said on the day I hired him. He held up a little black pocket notebook with gold-edged pages and his monogram on the cover. "I know because I wrote the book on it." He sat across from my desk, flipping through his magic book. He stopped randomly at one page. "Hoffman?" he asked, looking at the entry. "Ron Hoffman. Has he been hard to get?"

Hard? More like impossible. That SOB senior vice president at Steiner-Rochelle had instructed his secretary to cease even the courtesy of saying that he would return my phone calls. "Yeah," I had to admit, "Hoffman is a real ball-buster."

"Really?" Leo oozed with delight. He reached across my desk, took my phone in hand, and dialed Hoffman. "Peggy, love," he cooed to the secretary, "it's Mr. Sales. Is Ron in today? . . . Uh-huh. San Francisco. . . . Next Tuesday. Great. Well, I've got to take him to lunch to catch up. I've got a new book I'm repping. When is he available? . . . Wednesday the fourth. Fine. . . . The Grill Room, twelve-thirty. Perfect. And how's little Jenny?" He's reading farther down in the Hoffman file. "Sixth grade? No! So soon? Seems like everyone around us is getting older. Good thing we're not." Laugh, laugh. "Oh, the name of my new book? I don't think Ron's ever heard of it. Ta-ta, love." He hung up, closed his book, and replaced it in his suit jacket. "There now, young man, I think we're gonna be just fine. Mr. Sales is here."

Leo cost *Elixir* more than it could really afford at the time. One hundred fifty thousand a year guaranteed, with generous kickers if he exceeded sales targets. At the time, I was thirty-one; Leo was fifty-three. He feigned a paternal indulgence in my shortcomings, about which he would lecture me at length.

Whenever I question his lavish expense reports (he cheats in all sorts of ways, big and small), he gets very high-and-mighty: "I am your credibility in this industry, I should remind you." He turns in mammoth bar bills, tabs for sumptuous lunches and dinners, stretch limos galore, and, of course, hookers, billed under a host of ingenious covers, all paid out in cash: health clubs, emergency audiovisual equipment, and tips to hotel managers. Thousands and thousands of cash tips to hotel managers. Using his limitless accounting imagination, he pays for clients' wives and girlfriends to attend conferences they have no business attending, when they're held in places like Barbados or Palm Springs. And on birthdays, he is always at the door with a case of Dom Perignon.

Once, when we were going over receipts following a big convention in Las Vegas, Leo let me thumb through his little black book. He listed all sorts of information under the names of his executives. Names of secretaries, wives, children, grandchildren, favorite restaurants, golf handicaps, birthdays. Every so often an executive's name would appear along with an ethnic designation that didn't seem to belong. Frank Mead was listed as "French"; Harvey Whitman was "Greek"; Arnie Dietz was "English." These, Leo explained, referred not to their ancestral homelands, but to their sexual tastes. Harvey Whitman the Greek had nothing to do with the land of Aristotle and Euripides. When he attends a convention, he likes to be set up with a hapless girl his daughter's age and ram his aging dick into her asshole. Dietz, who is listed as "English," had great-grandparents from Germany. But his delight, when he's away from the Scarsdale colonial with the second mortgage, is to be tied up naked by a dominatrix in leather skivvies and a chrome-studded dog collar. To be spanked, insulted, and abused. Getting harder the more abusive the mistress becomes, Dietz will finally come unassisted when she squats over him, pulls her G-string to one side, and pees on his face. Or so Leo says.

Leo is their procurer, their confessor, their gatekeeper to the world of secret, dirty desires. Leo relishes the role. He is a lusty male madam, all-knowing, all-forgiving. It is part prurience—he never passes up the chance to tell raunchy stories, usually with punch lines about excreta or female odor—and part power. Leo has the goods on his clients. He is invaluable to them, and, as a result, to me.

Leo's desk is neat and fussy. In front of the blotter is a pretentious marble "executive" pen stand, two pens held aloft as if awaiting the signatures of Prime Ministers on a treaty, instead of requisitions for advertising space. Tucked into the corner of the blotter is a stack of business cards. No one special. Except the bottom one. It comes from Ken Atwood, publisher of *Stone Age*. The last four digits of his telephone number have been crossed out and four new numbers handwritten in. His new number? His personal line? I pick up Leo's phone and dial the number.

"Hello." It is Atwood, all right. He must have gone straight back to his office. No secretary screening the call. It must be his personal line.

"Hello," he says again, starting to sound annoyed. I say nothing.

"Hello, who is this, anyway? Hello. Who are you trying to reach?" I hang up.

Leo's phone reeks of his cologne. He's quite fond of the stuff and uses far too much of it. It smells like rotting flowers mixed with cinnamon and clove. I've seen him in the men's room slathering it on. It comes in a silver-topped bottle with a phony-looking royal crest. "House of Lords," the label proclaims in ornate letters. "The aristocrat of scents. For the man born to power." One thing about Leo. He leaves behind a trail you can smell. Literally.

CHAPTER TWO

I finish the day at my desk, pretending that absolutely nothing has happened. I go through papers, answer correspondence, even make a few phone calls. I manage to concentrate so completely that I even forget momentarily that I have just agreed to change absolutely everything about my life. I keep my office door three-quarters closed to discourage visitors. It works. So far as I can tell, no one suspects a thing. As for my suspicions about Leo, he does not come back to the office; his afternoon appointment was at his favorite drug company in New Jersey. The one near his home, the one that he always manages to see right after lunch.

At sevenish, I am the last one to leave. Finally, just as I finish locking the outside door, I give in to the euphoria I have felt since the conference room table this morning. I spin around and slap my back against the wall. "Yes! Yes! Yes!" I shout to myself in a hoarse whisper. I raise one fist in victory and pound it repeatedly into the palm of my other hand. "Yes! Yes! Yes!" Back still against the wall, I let my legs fold slowly underneath me as I slide down the wall. "Yes! Yes! Yes!" I am on the floor for I'm not sure how long, pounding my hand and muttering my one-word victory cheer, when suddenly I hear a woman speaking.

"Hey, mista? What'samatta?" Her accent is thick, its origin unrecognizable. "What'samatta? You seek, mista, huh?"

It is the cleaning lady in her gray shift and rolled-down nylons. She is standing over me holding her wagon loaded with brooms, mops, dust rags, and oversized plastic garbage bag bulging with office detritus.

"You gotta pass, mista? Gotta haffa pass." She has one hand on the handle of her broom, ready to strike in case I turn out to be violent as well as loony. "I call security, mista, hey?"

"No, ma'am, that's okay." I pull myself up to a standing position slowly, careful not to scare her. I brush my topcoat down and give my necktie a little hitch to try to restore my dignity. See? I'm really a gentleman. I belong here. I pay rent here. I just made ten million dollars behind that door there. See? But she does not see. She grasps the broom handle tighter and shoots me an even angrier I-don't-need-this-kind-of-shit stare.

"It's okay, ma'am. Really." I start walking past her. Very slowly on padded feet. The way you walk past a sneering watchdog tied to a chain whose length you cannot gauge. "It's okay. I'm just going to the elevator."

I take a few steps past her. "Say, where's Rose? You know, Rose. Rose usually works this floor on weeknights. You must know Rose."

No response.

"I've known Rose for years. Isn't Rose on the night shift anymore?"

"I new onna job." I see her relax her grip on the broom handle as I disappear around the corner toward the elevators. I decide to walk downtown to the party. The cold night air is probably just what I need. Goddammit. Why does Wendy have to be in a closed-door meeting today of all days? I really need to see Wendy.

I can hear rock music blaring out on the street in front of the old cast-iron loft building. After my thirty-block hegira, I am chilled to the bone but composed. A walk through the city's anonymous, impersonal busyness usually has a calming effect on me.

Lights flashing in the third-floor windows signal where the party is. There's an official greeter in the tiny vestibule of the building, a guy wearing a dark pinstripe suit, white shirt, regimental striped tie, and brightly colored running shoes. His face is covered by a hard plastic Halloween mask—the face of a rat. Not the cute, white laboratory kind, but the mangy gray-brown kind that crawls up out of the sewer. The button on his lapel reads: "I'm quitting the rat race." He holds a clipboard with the guest list.

"Your name, please?"

"Bob Macallan."

He scans the middle of the two-page list, finds my name, and checks it with his pencil. "Welcome," he says, inviting me in. "Coats go over there. Elevator's back there to your right. You may have to ring for it a coupla times. Pretty noisy up there."

He is almost shouting. It's pretty noisy down here, too.

"Has Wendy Wolfson arrived yet?" I ask in just under a holler.

He checks the end of his list.

"Nope." Three couples in business attire appear at the door behind me; he turns his attention to them. I hang up my topcoat on the already crowded pipe rack.

The guy running the freight elevator is also dressed in business suit, running shoes, and rat mask. "Want one?" he asks, indicating the box of "I'm quitting the rat race" buttons at his feet.

"No thanks."

The elevator doors open like a giant mouth onto the party. "Have fun," the rat says as he closes the steel jaws behind me and descends for another trip. The loft is a vast, dark, noisy cave. The racket is awful; at least three different kinds of recorded music are competing for attention. Pools of light here and there reveal clusters of people, some dressed for business, some expensive artsy casual. They populate the stand-up bar, the snack table, the dance floor, and the conversation nook furnished with old couches and folding chairs. At the far end of the loft is a towering video wall—twenty-five big TVs stacked five high and five wide, projecting a single image fractured like an electronic mosaic. It looks like a rock video playing on it now.

I hear a voice over the din and feel a hand on my shoulder. "Hey, Bob, glad you could make it." It is Pete Romanos, one of tonight's hosts. "Is Wendy coming?"

"Yeah, she's on her way," I answer. Tall and handsome, black-haired and athletic, nearly perfect Pete was the senior lending officer for all of North America at Citizens Bank of New York.

"Great," he says. "I'm glad you're both gonna be here. Barb and I are gonna miss you guys." At thirty-six he was a genuine banking wunderkind. Until two months ago when he was fired. Due to politics, not performance.

"Likewise, Pete. Likewise."

Romanos became the fall guy for Citizens' troubled real estate portfolio. In fact, he had inherited the bad loans, but his boss, supposedly his mentor all those years, used the bank's crisis as an excuse to kill off his younger colleague turned competitor. He went to the credulous and very nervous management committee blaming Pete for the real estate headaches. Eager to find a scapegoat, the committee bought the story. Then he had his lie accidentally leaked to the press. After fourteen years as a model for success, Pete Romanos was finished in banking. At least in New York.

"Quite a party, eh?" he says in a genuinely amused tone.

"Yeah. And how."

"The rat race theme was Morowski's idea," he explains. Ron Morowski is the art world denizen of the trio of soon-to-be ex–New Yorkers. A failed artist, then failed art critic, and now a failed art dealer, Morowski is responsible for the party's downtown location. This is the loft he is leaving behind. "Ron got Wang Chu to do the video wall," Pete says.

"Wang Chu?" I ask.

"You know, the video artist. Heavy into anarchism."

"Oh yeah," I lie, "Wang Chu. Of course."

Pete shrugs at the scene around us. "Maybe the rat thing is a little much." I nod.

Waiters pass us carrying trays of tidbits. They are dressed like the greeter and the elevator operator—in business suits, running shoes, and rat masks.

"Tell me, Pete; have you made up your mind where you're going?"

"Pacific Northwest, and I almost don't care what I do as long as it's not banking. Maybe I'll do capital equipment leasing; maybe I'll open a hardware store. I'm actually kinda grateful I got booted the way I did. It woke me up to the kind of assholes I was surrounded by. That bastard Davis," he says, referring to his erstwhile mentor, "pillar of the community, chairman of the American Banking Association ethics committee. Ethics committee! Talks like a scoutmaster out of one side of his mouth and spits poison darts out of the other. Funny thing is, he believes in the scoutmaster crap and pretends it's somebody else doing the killing. Sonofabitch goes home feeling pure and superior no matter what he does all day. Now, *that's* what I call an aptitude for corporate life."

14

Pete snatches a cheese concoction from a passing tray, pops it into his mouth, and chews it with a little frown. Pete the gourmet is under-whelmed. "He used me the whole time. When he needed to look progres-sive in the go-go years, he promoted me as his rising star. When things got tough, he needed a symbol of the bad old days to blame." Pete yanks an imaginary noose above himself and cocks his head to one side. "No, I'm happy to be getting out now while I'm still young enough. Spend your life with that kind of people, you end up being just like them. I wonder how a guy like that can look his kids in the eye?" Pete stops for a second, then laughs as he answers his own question. "No problem! He teaches 'em how to be a rat just like him. That's why I'm getting my kids the hell outta here."

He grabs another hors d'oeuvre and pops it in his mouth. "In the meantime," he says, his eyes lighting up with surprise and delight, "let's enjoy what this evil, oversophisticated burg does have to offer. I don't think it'll be easy to get fresh porcini mushrooms in . . ." He grabs another one from the tray. ". . . Tacoma." Someone calls to Pete from the far side of the loft. He waves back. "Listen, Bob; Barb and I definitely want to have dinner with you and Wendy before we leave."

"Absolutely; say when. We're not going anywhere."

He grabs a third passing mushroom and disappears into the crowd. I would stand here by the elevator to be sure of catching Wendy when she arrives, but there is a giant stereo speaker blasting nearby. I decide to head for the bar.

Halfway across the floor, someone in the crowd grabs me by the arm and turns me around.

"So, Bob? You're going to sell out to American." It is Bruce Marcus, angry and a little drunk, his face jammed up against mine. "And through Hale-fucking-Hadley, of all firms." Marcus is the third of our trio of hosts. He, too, is abandoning New York, closing down his failed investment banking boutique after fourteen frustrating months without completing a single deal. Short and wiry with a large, round nose, scruffy black mustache, and pointy receding chin, Bruce has been shoving his face up against everyone else's for as long as I can remember. Eager as a puppy and mean as a jackal, that's Bruce. He pushes everyone and everything too hard. His aggression has always been too raw, his ambition too naked, the kind of pushy New Yorker they warn you about when you grow up in small-town New England. "What makes Brucey run?" he used to joke self-deprecat-ingly, fully aware of the impression he was making.

"After all the time I invested in you!" he says with boozy breath all over my face. "I deserve a percentage from one of you bastards, you or American or Hale Hadley. I'm the one who got you primed to sell. There'd have been no goddamn deal without me. It's not fair," he sneers. He hounded me for months, trying to get my consent to let him peddle *Elixir* to all sorts of companies I would not touch with a barge pole. He did not take my refusals seriously until I finally screamed at him, "Marcus, stop it! Now fuck off, eat shit, and die!" That he understood.

"I taught you everything you know about this goddamn city," he says. Marcus and I were neighbors in the same shabby West Side rental building when I first came to New York. "I took you under my wing," he says. "You didn't know a thing. Why, you fell off a goddamn watermelon truck from, uh, Vermont, wasn't it?"

"New Hampshire, Bruce. And I think the truck was hauling cabbages."

Marcus had been fresh from a poor childhood in a shabby, declining neighborhood in the Bronx and four years on scholarship at NYU. An intern in a third-tier Wall Street firm, he was desperate to conquer Manhattan. He made a big show of tutoring me about the realities of New York living. In fact, I did learn a lot about street smarts from him. But I would never admit it to him, not then or now.

"What on earth makes you think I'm selling my company?" I ask innocently. I have complete confidence in my poker face by now.

"Good, good." He pats my shoulder with fake pride. "Flat tone, no visible excitement. Very convincing. I almost believe it."

I shrug casually as if I'm about to walk away. Actually, I'm racking my brains for a ploy to get him to reveal the source of his intelligence. He is only the second or possibly third person today who is not supposed to know but does.

"Don't you want to know how I know?" he asks. "Don'tcha? Huh?"

"Bruce, I'm going to get a drink. You want to join me?" I shrug again and take another step toward the bar. I couldn't care less, I am saying. No, I couldn't care less. *Tell me, you bastard. Tell me!*

"Information is my business," he says with a smirk. "You should know that." He flicks away a piece of lint that may or may not actually be on my lapel. "I'm in the information business, Robbie. Like you."

Just then, the screech of microphone feedback fills the loft. It is coming from the video wall. I turn to face the racket. Marcus takes a couple steps toward the bar, then turns around for a parting shot.

"Just remember, Macallan!" he shouts over the racket. "You owe me! I taught you everything you know about this town! And I plan to collect!" He makes a gesture with thumb and pointed index finger that could be a gun firing or might just be "so long."

"Friends!" the voice on the microphone bellows. "Friends and revelers!" It is Morowski standing on a chair in front of the video wall. In his black jeans, black silk shirt, little ponytail, and closely trimmed beard flecked with gray, he could be SoHo's answer to Hamlet. Except for the bald crown of his head and incipient paunch, which are pure Friar Tuck.

"Friends and . . ." *Screeeeeeeeeeeeeech!* The mike does it again. A guy runs from the amplifier to Morowski and the mike. He makes an adjustment and Morowski begins again. The crowd begins to gather around the video wall.

"Friends," he announces, "Pete and Bruce and I are delighted that all of you could make it tonight to help us say good-bye to New York. I think this is going to be a very memorable party. As you know, my two co-hosts come from the world of finance. So in the spirit of each contributing that which he does best, I have allowed them to contribute the money which is paying for our food and drink. And I, coming from the world of art, am contributing the style, culture, and sophistication." The crowd laughs. "No offense, boys, but it's true. And this is still my loft until the end of the month. Don't worry; they'll have their chance for rebuttal a little later." More titters.

Morowski has everyone's attention and he knows it. He milks his moment in the spotlight with desperate pleasure. "I want you all to know that tonight is not merely an important moment for this city—just look at the three talented men it is losing—but an important moment for the cultural continuum, which is, after all, the only thing that lives beyond us." Morowski must be preparing the rhetoric he will need in his new job as associate professor of something in the fine arts department at Bennington College.

"I am talking, friends, about the premiere of a work of art. Here. Tonight. My dear friend and colleague Wang Chu has created a video wall that, I think, captures the essence of what tonight stands for. The rejection of, expulsion from, and, ultimately, the existential realization of the essence of New York City. As we've come to expect from Wang, it is a dangerous work—a work of irony and wit, with undercurrents of the fearless intellectual terrorism that made him first a premier performance artist and now a trailblazer in video art. I'm sorry Wang couldn't be here tonight to share in this premiere. But he is in Peru, thanks to a grant from the Irving Bruckheimer Foundation. He is at this very moment with the Shining Path freedom fighters at an undisclosed location, creating a video record of actual executions of real-life traitors. I know it will be an important artistic statement we'll all be eager to see. But now, it gives me great pleasure to premiere Wang Chu's video tribute to New York, created especially for this celebration."

Morowski hops down off the chair and signals to the guy by the amplifier. The twenty-five TV screens jump to life, and all the speakers scattered about the loft start blasting the familiar orchestral opening of the song "New York, New York." The huge single image on the television mosaic is helicopter footage of the Manhattan skyline at sunrise. Travelogue stuff rich with "breathtaking" triteness. The vocalist is Liza Minelli, whose original cornball, really-big-shoo rendition of this song is the most cornball and really-big-shoo of all. She belts out one line after another as the camera in the helicopter soars and dives around the tall buildings. So far, Wang Chu has not spoofed the big-screen "Big Apple" show they feed to out-of-towners on bus tours; he has duplicated it. Or more likely borrowed it.

Then, just as Liza and the adoring panoramas start to become truly tedious, something happens in the bottom row of TV screens. The skyline is replaced by pulsating brown images of something. Then, as the next-to-the-bottom row of screens turns brown, the new image becomes clear. It is rats. Swarms of rats all mashed together so close they can hardly move, except to quiver and snap at each other with cramped little movements.

The third row of screens adds another line to the growing rat image. There must be hundreds of them packed together in what appears to be a bizarre scientific experiment; the video has the gritty, flat look of laboratory film.

Liza bellows about waking up in the city that never sleeps as the rats overtake more of the skyline, one screen at a time. Most of the rats at the bottom of the heap are by now dead or dying, their only motions death twitches and gasps. As the last skyline screen turns to rats, three rats leap and snap at each other on top of the body pile. One stumbles and the other two attack him and tear at his throat. Blood spurts onto the three of them. The injured rat collapses onto the heap, quivering and dying. Liza is winding up for her really big finish. The two surviving rats fly at each other. Then, just as Liza tells us that if she can make it there, she'll make it anywhere, the bigger rat jumps on the back of the smaller one and starts mounting him (or is it her?). At this moment, Wang Chu's true video artistry kicks in.

As Liza wails the big finale, "It's! Up! To! You! New! York! New-ooo! Yo-o-o-rk!" the larger rat, in slow-motion replay, thrusts in and out of his victim's behind perfectly in tune to the music. "New-ooo-York!" she sings one last time. As the orchestra comes down from Liza's crescendo with the "dum-ta-ta-da-da, dum-ta-ta-da-da" closing, the scene dissolves away to reveal an elegant shot of a white stretch limo outside the Plaza Hotel. It is nighttime; the street is wet, reflecting the glitter and glitz of the setting—the gleaming hotel canopy, the gilded fretwork on the building, the shiny, extravagant car. It could be a commercial for perfume or designer fashions or anything expensive and exclusive. As the next-to-last "dum-ta-ta-da-da" sounds, the liveried chauffeur opens the back door of the limo. An elegant couple steps out, he in a tux, she in a sequined evening gown. The doorman nods respectfully as they pass. They are perfect in every detail. Except for the rat masks that cover their faces. The music dum-ta-ta-da-das out. The picture fades to black.

An awkward silence follows. The crowd seems to be trying to make up its mind about how to respond to the video. Are they hesitating because it was strange and hostile? Or because it is a work of art—not a TV show—and nobody in culture-savvy New York would ever think of applauding a Rembrandt or a Matisse? Morowski has no doubts about what to do. Standing on his chair by the video wall, he is applauding like mad. Slowly, the crowd begins to follow suit. The applause builds and then subsides. Once again, competing flavors of rock music start to pound out of the speakers. The crowd starts to disperse; it's back to the party.

I feel unsettled. I don't really want a drink, but I head for the bar anyway. As I pass through the crush of bodies, I suddenly hear a voice behind me from the other end of the loft. A little scratchy, sort of husky, but in a very female way, it's the voice that can cut through the din of the noisiest party and reach me. Not because it is loud, because it is Wendy's.

"Ro-bert! Ro-bert!"

I turn around. She is standing by the closing jaws of the elevator, waving. I wave back and head in her direction, excusing myself left and right as I snake a path through the people. She is signaling as I approach. With both hands open and palms out, she flashes all ten fingers and silently mouths the word *ten* with a little question mark at the end. I nod in return. She flips her palms back inward as if to inspect their contents and gives her fingers a wiggle, counting off one to ten. She stares at her hands with astonishment, then looks up at me. "Wow!" she mouths soundlessly.

The blare of the party evaporates as I finally reach her. We blur together in a hug. This is what I've been wanting to do since this morning in the thirty-sixth-floor conference room. This is what I craved. Wendy's delicate narrow shoulders and back, so easy for me to scoop up and hold, her arms reaching up to surround me with all five-feet-three of her. Wendy with raven black hair—shoulder-length, thick, and wavy, just starting to show streaks of gray—where I can bury my face. Her bright eyes of crystal blue that see the world with more confidence than I do. Her baby face, lineless and pale, her not quite beakish nose, and delicate rosebud mouth.

"Oh, Robert," she whispers between soft little kisses, "you really did it. You really did it." I feel my spring unwinding. Finally. I nod and nuzzle, easing her down off her tiptoes. We slide apart a little, arms still locked. We smile. The noise and racket around us returns. We are not alone anymore.

"Did you just get here?" I ask.

She shrugs a small apology. "Clients." The volume of the party noise seems to be going up, widening the distance between us. A rat-masked waiter stops beside us with a tray. Wendy shakes her head no.

"No thanks," I say to him.

"Yuck," she says with a little wince. "I hate rats. Just the thought gives me the creeps."

"Then you missed the video."

Our arms drop apart.

"I guess so. What was it about?"

"More rats than you can imagine." I tilt my head backward in the direction of the video wall. "Twenty-five TV screens' worth."

"Ugh, gross!"

Another rat waiter appears before us and offers us a tray. Wendy gives a little involuntary shiver.

"You want to get out of here?" I ask.

"Love to."

Out in the cold street, snow is falling. Big flakes spaced far apart and drifting slowly, almost hanging in the air. They cast a quiet over the narrow street of old loft buildings and make the sky feel close, a soundstage with a ceiling just overhead.

Wendy locks onto my right arm as we walk. "It's really ten?" she asks.

"That's right. I resisted the temptation to tell them that I'd have been happy to accept eight."

"Whatta hardass, Macallan. That's why I love you. Such a brilliant negotiator." She stops and lets go of my arm. She is pondering something.

"Ten million?" she asks the air and shakes her head. She rolls the number around in her mouth, trying it on in different ways. *"Ten* million. Ten *mill*-ion. Ten mill-*ion."* She stamps her feet up and down, ra-ta-tat-tat, ra-ta-tat-tat. "Wow!"

"Uh-huh. Ten million dollars."

"Ohhh, Robert. Ohhh, Robert." She hugs me, then lets go. "We're really rich. I mean not *really* rich, like billionaires, but we're really actually rich, you and me."

"I'd say so."

"What kind of terms is American offering?"

"An earn-out. Half the cash up front. I stay on for a year to run *Elixir.* If we make our target earnings, we get the rest of the dough. Maybe even more if we go off the charts. But *Elixir* can't do worse than this year. If we fall below that number, the second payment could be reduced or, if it falls below eighty percent, canceled. There are terms and specifics for the penalties, a couple of disaster provisions, you know, scenarios where they could demand all the money back. But I can't imagine how that could happen. Should be straightforward and simple. All we have to do is not screw up. Then, I'm out the door. And you and I go do whatever we feel like doing."

"That's my favorite part of the story." She reaches around me with a gentle hug. "Oh, Robert, you did it. You really, really did it." She lets go and takes my arm again, very excited. "Oh, sweetie, we can do everything now. Everything. Let's plan it all out, okay? We can have our first baby by the end of this year, if we start trying now. Then, we can buy a company, maybe, and run it together. You and me. And have another baby, then maybe three? And maybe sell that company and buy a bigger one? Work and love, love and work. Just like Freud said. Wouldn't that be great? We have to decide where we want our baby to be conceived; that's very important, you know. And we ought to be trying to figure out what are going to be the coming growth industries—for the company we buy."

"Hey, hey, wait a second. I haven't even finished this deal and you're already running a business empire and an army of kids. What about a little time just to digest today's events first?"

"Sorry, sorry. I get a little carried away." With thumb and index finger together, she zips her mouth shut. Pause. Smile. "Want to walk a little more?"

"Sure." We kiss and begin strolling lazily uptown toward Greenwich Village. I reach for a snowflake in the air, grabbing it like a baseball player snatching a foul ball. "I figure taxes will take fortyish percent off the top. That should leave six million or so net to us."

Wendy leans in and out as she walks, using her armhold on me as balance, taking big, scuffing steps like a kid. "That's what I figured, too," she says. She pauses, then clears her throat. A sure sign that something touchy is coming.

"Yes?" I ask, trying playfully to make whatever it is a little more difficult.

"Well, Robert, now that we're, uh, now that we're, uh, sort of, uh . . ."

"You want a mink coat?"

"No! Are you kidding? Me? A mink? No way. You can't check them in restaurants, muggers pay extra special attention to you, and they make me look, well, matronly. But you're sort of in a related area."

"Jewelry?"

"No, cold weather."

"Do tell."

"You know our vacation next month?"

"Yeah, the last week in February. Same as last year and the year before and the year before that. Room two-twelve at the end of the pool, Charter Beach Hotel, Antigua. Best value in the Caribbean, *mon.*"

"Well, I thought a change might be a little fun. And then, when those negotiations with American began in earnest, I figured there was a better than even chance we might end up, you know . . ."

"Go on, you've already said the 'R' word."

"Well, I thought it might be a real gas to go someplace where the real R-I-C-H go."

"And so?"

"So I changed our reservation from Charter Beach to the one and only Bangle Bay."

"Never heard of it."

"Well, you would have, if you ever read those issues of *Vanity Fair* I leave around the bedroom."

"It's a silly, inane magazine."

"It is not. It's fun. And very well written. A lot of the time."

"Okay, okay. Now what's so special about Bangle Bay?"

"It's the ultra-exclusive resort that's strictly for very quiet, very classy money. Been around for years and years. No rock stars, no gold chains, no gambling, no glitz. Really, they grill your travel agent about you before they'll book you. They won't let just anybody come. It's got the best beach in the Caribbean, surrounded by mountains and set on three hundred untouched acres of nature preserve. All for sixty lucky guests. The facilities are grossly underutilized. Intentionally. All the time. There are four or five deck chairs for every guest. Empty tennis courts, unused towels. No hassles, no noise. Just pure peace and beauty completely removed from the world of mere mortals."

"And where is it?"

"British Virgin Islands. Way at the very farthest tip of Virgin Gorda."

"And how much is it?"

"Well, uh . . ." Meekly she peeps, "A thousand dollars a day."

"Including meals?"

She shakes her head no. Sheepishly.

"Wendy, it's the same sky and ocean and sand at Charter for only three hundred a day."

"I'm perfectly happy to pay my fair half of everything, just like we always do. I just wanted—"

"No need to explain." I am amused. This is something I would never think of doing. "What the hell? Let's christen our good fortune by showing ourselves that we can waste some of it. It'll be more fun than lighting cigars with ten-dollar bills. And I'll pay the whole tab this time."

"Now you hold on a minute, Robert Macallan. I'm not so sure about that. You know, you're not the only successful person in this family. Truedale and Wolfson is having its best year ever. No telling how big a bonus I'll award myself. Who knows? Maybe McKinsey or Arthur D. Little will buy *us* out for a few million. That kind of thing does happen, you know."

"So I hear." We walk holding hands; our conversation fades away. The magical silence of the snowflakes fills the vacuum. At the next stoplight I ask, "What time today did you get my message?"

"About noon. I ducked out of the meeting to use the john."

"Something else was happening at that very moment. Do you have any idea what it could be?"

"You were bouncing off the walls."

"I was getting a second offer for *Elixir.*"

"No?" She stops dead and lets her arm drop from mine. "Who from?"

"Wacky Mackey, king of the rough-tough trade books."

"Who's he?"

"Big player. Out of Cleveland. Industrial nuts 'n' bolts books. Like *Stone Age, Plastic Age,* that sort of thing. Just as I'm walking out of American headquarters, Mackey's man Atwood walks up to me and says he has an offer for me. He's got the limo waiting there to take me back to the office. Not only did he know I had been upstairs; he knew exactly what I'd been doing. 'Don't sell to American,' he says, 'until you talk to Mr. Mackey.' "

"How did he know? You told me the negotiations were secret."

"I thought they were, too."

"So how much does Mackey want to offer you?"

"I'll find out tomorrow. He's flying me out to Cleveland on the corporate jet."

"Sounds classy."

"Believe me; it's not. Mackey's guy Atwood rides around in this ridiculous stretch limo with a bar and a TV. He's an old-fashioned publishing glad-hander with a drinking problem, bad suits, and a dyed mop of hair he combs over his bald head like this." I place my hand just above my left ear and sweep it across to the other ear.

"Ick."

"He feels sleazy, too. I think maybe Leo leaked the American deal to Atwood. But I can't figure out how Leo found out. Conover wanted to keep it hush-hush. Levine would never want a second bidder. I swear I didn't leave any clues at *Elixir.* I don't know how he knew. Then, the capper is Bruce Marcus. He comes up to me just now and says how he deserves a commission from me or Hale Hadley. Even Marcus found out, the little worm. I have no idea how. None."

"You're always telling me that there are no secrets in publishing. Not as soon as more than one person knows."

"Yeah, twice today I've heard that. 'The information business. We're all in the information business.' "

"Well, I guess there's no harm done. You did get a second offer, after all."

"Yes. I suppose."

"Ooh, a second offer." Wendy rubs her hands together in anticipation of a higher bid.

"You want to get a cab?" I ask. We have reached Houston Street, where cabs are flying by in both directions.

"Coming right up," Wendy says. With one hand still fast on my arm, she leans way out over the edge of the curb, one stockinged leg extended far out of her coat and into the air. She gives a little kick, and a cab slams to a stop beside us.

We settle into the broken-down backseat for the seventy-block trek uptown. The driver is listening to unidentifiable folk music on an ancient cassette player on the seat beside him. The plastic partition is closed and so scratched it is almost opaque. The effect is as private as New York cabs get.

"So how was your day?" I ask. I motion for her to lean back. I pick up her left leg, remove the shoe, and start massaging her foot. Wendy loves to have her feet rubbed at the end of the day.

"Ahhh, thank you, sweetheart." She throws her head back with a sigh as I press and knead the bottom of her foot. "It started out as one of the crappiest business days I've ever had. My client was a jerk. My client's boss was an even bigger jerk. And the biggest boss was the biggest jerk of all. It had all the corporate garbage: hierarchy, ass-kissing, lying, scapegoating, misguided decisions, and, of course, fear. Fear, fear everywhere." She pauses and sighs, "Mmm, lovely."

The cab rattles and bounces us through pothole after pothole. The shaking becomes part of the massage; it jolts my hands to different areas of her foot. "So Liz and I are caught in the middle with our marketing study. I got really aggravated, really pissed off. Then, I came back from the phone call. And poof. Like magic. These idiots couldn't touch me. They don't care what happens to their company. So what? They don't care about our recommendation. So what? All they care about is the little office wars they're playing with each other. And then, as soon as I stopped caring, I became incredibly effective."

As the cab reaches Fiftieth Street, I switch to the right foot. "Ooh, thank you; that feels so good. Do you think you'll hire someone to do this in the future, or will you keep your hands-on management style?"

"Hmm, I haven't thought about it yet."

"That's really what I married you for, you know. Hands-on management."

"Then I guess that's not something I can delegate."

"It's not even the teeniest bit negotiable."

"We'll put it in my employment contract. So what happened next?"

"We sat there till eight o'clock arguing the merits of whether Bradfordco should enter this new market. It was a real mess. But you know what? I brought them all around. Macallan, you should have seen me. I convinced the product guy, the group vice president, even the senior vice president of the division. I showed them how they could convince Mr. Muckety-Muck not to go ahead, without making him angry and bringing down the political roof on their heads. They insist I come back for the big presentation. I was awesome, Macallan. Awesome. And it was fun. Amazing what a few million can do for your outlook."

"To say nothing of your consulting skills."

The cab pulls up to our building at Seventy-eighth Street and Riverside Drive, a 1920s apartment building that has been semi–spruced up since becoming a co-op in the late seventies. One of these years, the building's board will get the doormen uniforms that fit.

"Know what I could go for right about now?" Wendy coos as we enter the empty elevator.

"No, what?"

"Dinner and a movie."

"I thought you'd never ask."

Our two-bedroom apartment, with just a tiny slice of river view from our bedroom window, is no showpiece. It is a refuge. When Wendy and I first moved in, our decor might have passed for poor man's English country, thanks mostly to the middle-budget chintz couch and love seat and the two Sheriden antique reproductions Wendy inherited in battered condition from her grandmother. Since then, our additions of furniture, pictures, and lighting have all been eccentric and accidental; the only effect we were going for was to make the place comfortable for us. The design world would not be impressed. All it is is our home.

Tonight, Wendy makes it look even homier, as she leaves a trail of hastily shed clothes from the front hall foyer back to our bedroom. This lovemaking is talky. We talk through fantasies of what we might do, not so much with the money, but with the independence it will buy. Wendy comes with a quiet shudder in the middle of the farmhouse in Tuscany fantasy. I come with a little groan during the beach shack in Bora Bora. Wendy is now curled up under the sheet, face half-buried in the pillow.

"Of course, the castle in Périgord has a lot going for it," she muses, her tongue thickening with sleep. "D'you like the musty taste of black truffles?"

"I like the musty taste of you, don't I?" I feel a gentle kick. "I still can't figure out how the hell Atwood and that shit Marcus knew about my meeting at American."

"Gossip. Everybody gossips in your business. Doesmmatter." She is drifting away. I relax and listen to her breathing turning deep and rhythmic. Suddenly the telephone lets out its cheerful electronic chirp.

"Arrrggh." She wraps the pillow around her ears. The answering machine kicks in. I reach across the night table and turn up the playback volume. After the beep the caller announces, "This is your father callin' from Bayport." Unmistakable New England twang—broad *a*'s, dropped *r*'s. It sounds like "Yah fahthah cawlin' from Baypott." I pick up the phone, Wendy lifts her head from the pillow, wrinkles her nose, and drops back into the burrow.

"Hey, old man," I say.

Wendy mutters into the pillow, "Again?" Dad has been calling with uncharacteristic regularity over the past few weeks. In fact, never before has he taken such a keen interest in my career. I can't decide whether living alone is finally getting to him or if this is his indirect Yankee way of showing fatherly pride. This is the first time he has ever asked for a blow-by-blow account of my adventures in the world beyond Bayport. A world that, up to now, he has made it clear he does not approve of. And while I tell myself it is silly, a part of me still craves the old man's approval.

"Hi, Son. Howya doin'?" he asks.

"Great. How're you?"

"Pretty fair. How's that pretty wife a yours?"

"Oh, she's fine." Face still buried, Wendy raises one limp arm straight up into the air and lets it drop, lifeless. "Wendy says hi," I say.

"Did you have your big meetin'?"

"Yes, they made me a very nice offer. They would like to make me a moderately rich man at the ripe old age of thirty-five. They seem so intent on it, I may not have the heart to turn them down."

"Just remember; don't count the money until it's in your hand."

"I know; I know."

"How much they wanna offer you?"

"Ten million. Works out to six and change after taxes. But I have to stay on for a year to collect it all."

Silence.

"Dad? You there?"

Another silence. He seems to be searching for his voice. Finally he manages to speak, but only in a whisper. "Ten million, Son. . . . Geez. I can't imagine that much money." He clears his throat. "Geez, Son, you really done it." His voice is almost back to normal. "You really done it. I wish your mother was here to see this. She always said you were gonna be a big shot."

"She would have cracked my head open if I wasn't. You know, there's no motivator like terror."

He takes a deep breath, still recovering from the shock of the big number. "That woman put everything she had into you. From the day you were born." He pronounces it "bonn."

My mother worried herself into an early grave shortly before I finished college. She never had any faith that things would work out well. And for her, they never did. She worried about everything and converted her worry into pains and ailments of every type. She worried about my father and the business failures he suffered, one after the other. She worried about me; she worried about my little brother Jimmy and the friction between us. She worried about basic things like would we lose our modest house. And then, when that disaster didn't happen, she worried about our inability to keep up with our increasingly prosperous neighbors. She worried about her boys not getting more out of life than she and Dad did. And, with goading and guilt, got results out of me. Although she could never do much for my father or Jimmy except to worry more and make herself sicker. Then, when she went to work at the insurance office to pay for what my dad scornfully called "that fancy college," she worried about preserving his breadwinner's self-respect. The one thing she never worried about, however, was her crutch, her consolation, her killer, cigarettes. At the end, as she lay at home in bed, shriveled and bald from the cancer treatments, a wheezing sack of bones, she would whisper through cracked, blistered lips, "You know, I'd still like a cigarette."

"Son," my dad goes on over the phone, "things are sure workin' out for you. Better 'n' they ever did for me." Pause. "Or your brother. You know Jimmy's goin' through another hard time. Looks like that job of his isn't working out."

"I thought he was up for a promotion?" Jimmy has lately been assistant manager of a big Toyota dealership outside Boston. "I thought he was in line to become general manager. Isn't that still on?"

"No, he says the owner's jerking him around. The more he helps 'em make money, the madder they get at him. Showing up the old man's sons for the bums they are. You know how your brother is."

"Yeah, I know." I know my brother Jimmy, angry and hostile, scornful of my good grades and college scholarship, mocking my cosmopolitan ambitions and my "phony, uppity airs." Fat, potbellied Jimmy ran in the opposite direction from me and made himself even more defiantly lower class than our already defiantly lower-class father. "Are they going to fire him?"

"No, he's gonna quit 'fore that."

"What's he want to do next?" Jimmy's been in this spot before. In several crummy, marginal sales jobs that never really led anywhere.

"I think he wants to move back home and see what he can find here in Bayport."

"Really?"

"He already knows people here, and they know him. And I sure got enough room here in the house. Bayport'd be good for him, after all the shit he's been through. Maybe he could get some help starting his own business. Maybe his rich brother from the big city could give him a little help in getting started."

"Dad, I've offered him help in the past and he's always—"

"I know; I know. I guess I taught him to be proud 'n' independent. Like me."

"I guess so. Between the two of you it's like the New England Chapter of the John Wayne Real Men Don't Accept Help from Anybody Society."

"Your brother's a fine boy."

"You *know* that I'm willing."

"He's had it real tough, Bob. Real tough. It'll be good for him to get back home."

"Well, let him know I'm here for him, if he wants help."

"I will." Pause. "Son, do you mind if I ask you a question?"

"Shoot."

"You remember, when you got outta American, you said they, were treatin' you awful bad. Awful bad. I told you back then to watch out for that buncha four-flushin' Ivy League bastards." He pronounces it "bah-studds." "They were nothin' but slick phonies. Especially that guy Wood-man."

"Woodcock. Harry Woodcock."

"Yeah, him. I warned you about those kinda people when I took you to college. Remember? Now you're gonna go back and work for them again? After being your own boss? I mean, if they're willin' to pay you all that money, don't you think maybe somebody else might, too? I mean, Son, I never been in a position like that, but do you think you ought to jump at the first offer? Shouldn't you get an offer from somebody else?"

"Funny you should mention that. It looks like I might be getting that second offer tomorrow. A guy's flying me out to Cleveland on his private jet."

"He is?"

"Uh-huh, a fellow named Elton Mackey. Owns a bunch of trade magazines, a printing company, a billboard company, a theme park, a restaurant chain, I think. A real empire builder. They call him Wacky Mackey."

"Mackey?"

"EMC is his holding company."

"Mackey. Hmmm. I think I saw an article about him in the Bayport paper. Said he built the whole thing up from nothin'. Dropped out a school, didn't he? Started workin' as a printer. Sounds like a fine man. Real fine. Salt a the earth. Now that's a man you oughtta be proud to do business with."

"Well, I'll tell you after tomorrow."

"Son, I'd give this man a good listen. Those bastards at American screwed you good 'n' plenty. You said so yourself."

"That was five years ago. Besides, there's a new guy running magazines now. Levine. He comes from outside American. So it's a whole new crew. And I don't know where Woodcock is. I'm sure they got his number by now. He's probably running the audit department. Or maybe building maintenance."

"Sounds like Mackey's the kinda guy you oughtta hook up with."

27

"I don't know. I've only met one guy from EMC and I might be willing to spend a few minutes with him—but only if you held a gun to my head."

"Whaddya mean by that?"

"I mean that if this Atwood is representative of the Mackey organization, and I'll betcha he is, I wouldn't care to get in bed with them."

"Why not?"

"He's a sleaze, that's why. An old-time, hard-drinking, glad-handing sleaze in a bad poly-blend suit and Grecian Formula hair that he combs over to hide his bald head."

"You mean he didn't go to a fancy college like yours where they taught him to be some kinda snob that thinks his shit don't stink."

"It's got nothing to do with that. He's not my kind of guy."

"Is Harry Woodman your type a guy? You said he was good-lookin' and dressed real fine. Is Woodman what you're lookin' for?"

"It's Wood-*cock* and he's not my type of guy, either. I'm just looking to make the best deal I can and still be able to live with it."

"I'm just tellin' you as your father that you don't always have your head screwed on straight. Couple a weeks ago you were gonna be at your magazine for the next twenty years. Now all of a sudden you're gonna make millions sellin' it off. I don't want to see you run off half-cocked and take the first offer. I know, things have a way of falling into place for you. But a chance like this won't come along twice, even with that shit luck an' ignorance a yours."

Ever since I can remember, he would say it was "shit luck an' ignorance" whenever something of mine came through and something of Jimmy's didn't. It always hurt when he said it. Now, for the first time, that phrase has lost its sting. I smile at him and his simple view of the world.

"Come on, Dad," I say.

"Son, all I'm sayin' is I don't want you to blow it."

After all the ones *you* blew, I can't help thinking: the auto parts business, the roofing business, the siding business, the photo booths in the shopping centers, the delivery trucks that the bank repossessed. That idiotic mail-order scheme. The job at Walton's coat hanger factory. A year ago I would have been yelling at him by now, but something in me has changed. Is it my newfound wealth or am I finally growing up? "Come on, Dad, let's change the subject," I say. Suddenly it feels as if *I* am the parent and *he* is the child.

"Just hear me out," he insists. "I'm thinking about what's best for you. All I'm asking is that you give this Mackey a real good listen. He's gotta be a better man than anybody at American. I know you're a big shot down in New York, but you're still Clint Macallan's son. I'm tellin' you to stick with the kinda people you belong with. I'm telling you what's right for people like us, Son. I learned the hard way."

"That's right, Dad, you did." The poor guy did get beat up all his life. But his life and mine are worlds apart. Worlds apart. "Thanks for the advice, Dad. I appreciate it."

"Now you take your time makin' up your mind, y'hear. Don't jump just for the sake a jumping. Think about what I said."

"I will, Dad."

"Good night, Son."

"Good night, Dad." I put down the phone and switch off the light. Wendy is asleep beside me. I drift off into unconsciousness thinking it just might be that money, lots of money, has the power to heal and make everything all right.

CHAPTER THREE

Next morning, Ricky, the driver, is waiting outside in the gray whale.

"Mr. Mackey wants you to make yourself at home," he says, ushering me in, acting the gracious host. "You got your TV back there, your bar, your phone, and your fax. To call, just push 'Send' after you dial and 'End' when you're through. If you wanna use the fax, lemme know; that's a little more complicated." Ricky turns around, closes the window between us, and we're off, watching the daily commuter logjam on the other side of the road as we whiz by on the empty northbound route.

At the airport, we're rushed through the gate with hardly a stop. Ricky drives right onto the tarmac where the $12 million Beechjet is waiting, engines howling and ready to go. The door is open, the copilot standing by. He opens the limo door and beckons me to take the three steps to the airstair. In a matter of seconds, the plane is sealed, taxied, and airborne. I'm alone in the compartment, with seven other leather easy chairs arranged around the perimeter of the cabin. It's just tall enough for a man of average height to stand. The EMC logo is everywhere: on the seat backs, on the pebbly plastic wallcoating, in the carpeting, on the medallion in the center of the coffee table that's bolted to the floor. There are phones, a fax, a videocassette player, a CRT screen with our flight data flashing and changing from moment to moment. The rack of magazines contains the whole lineup of Mackey publications: *Stone Age, Bronze Age, Cement Age, Plastic Age,* plus some others I hadn't been aware of. *Rubber Age, Dry Cleaning Journal, Laundry News, Indianapolis Business, Car Wash Journal, Tire Times,* and more. They are dense, turgid, technical, full of heavy, ugly graphics and boosterism for "our industry." Somehow, I pull myself away from the rack, resisting the temptation to read every word they contain, and collect my thoughts for my meeting with Wacky Mackey.

While I like the idea of a second offer, I do not like the way in which Mackey has gotten it rolling, and I resent the ease with which he lifted the veil of secrecy I'd been working so hard to maintain. But the "how" of this moment is far less important than what he has to offer. And, since it seemed to work so well yesterday, I decide to use the impassive poker face here, too.

As New Jersey turns into the hills of Pennsylvania twenty-five thousand feet below, I come back to what, in talks with Wendy and with myself, I've decided I really want.

The offer from American taught me that I want out. Out of *Elixir*. I'd never imagined that the magazine would be salable so soon. I figured another four or five years in the saddle. But when I stopped to consider selling now, it was really the first moment I'd stopped to consider anything since the day, five years ago, when Harry Woodcock squeezed me and my idea for reaching the medical market out of American. The offer has made me realize that I am tired. Not tired of working, but tired of the particular niche of the particular business I am in. Tired of thinking about doctors and how to "serve" their needs and interests, tired of telling the same sales story to the same advertisers and ad agency people. I'm getting tired of my baby *Elixir*. It is now almost grown-up. Certainly, taking it to the next phase of growth and expansion would require more capital than I could ever muster on my own. No, I realize that what I loved about *Elixir* was the "me" part of it. And to take it to the next logical step would, in one way or the other, mean turning it into an institution, which would mean negating the vital importance of "me." A year spent reporting in to American will be like sleepwalking. Then I'll be free. To invent myself anew. To start a new chapter, throw all the cards up in the air and see where they fall.

The plane lands in Cleveland and taxis over to the private air terminal. Another fat limo is waiting, practically at the wing tip, with a Cleveland clone of Ricky holding the door. He, too, has his limo hospitality rap all set. "Help yourself to the bar. There's the TV, cassette machine, and the phone all right here. Sorry, but the fax is busted. We're supposed to get it fixed this week."

"No problem, I got all my faxing done on the plane. How far is it to the office?"

"I should have you at Laurelwood in half an hour max. You know, that's Mr. Mackey's home. Laurelwood. The office is downtown on Euclid. He owns the whole building. Thirty-one stories. His office is on the top floor. Got a view of the lake that'll just blow you away. I tell my girlfriend next time the wife's outta town, we'll sneak up to the roof. And I'll fuck her brains out above Lake Erie." Ricky's midwestern counterpart has that extra touch of friendliness New Yorkers so often lack.

Soon we're off the expressway and in the middle of horse country. Behind bare winter trees and hedgerows are mansions surrounded by immense brown lawns dotted with patches of snow. Everywhere there are riding rings and magnificently maintained barns. We slow down at the stone gates with "Laurelwood" carved in Old English lettering and turn in. Above, at the crest of the gentle hill ahead, sits a turn-of-the-century Tudor mansion only a little smaller than a Boeing 747. We glide past the empty rolling lawns and stop under the *porte cochere*.

Before I can reach for my door handle, Ricky's twin has bounded out of the car to let me out. I stand for an instant to stretch my legs and take in the fresh air of this unusually warm winter morning, the first breath of the day that has not been processed by a moving metal transportation machine. Above me I hear what sounds like a symphony orchestra playing Neil Diamond's elevator music classic, "Sweet Caroline." I look up into the roof of the carriage shelter. There, embedded in one of the giant timbers, is an outdoor stereo speaker. "Swe-e-e-e-t Car-o-line. Dum-dum-dum."

Beyond, in front of the four-car garage, sits a champagne-colored Mercedes 500 SL, the ninety-thousand-dollar two-seater that in Texas they call a "mistress car." The license plate reads: SHOPPER.

The wrought-iron handle on the mansion's massive front door clangs as the door swings out to reveal Elton Mackey himself.

"Bob Macallan." He surges forward and grabs my hand with a bone crusher grip. The hands are thick and powerful; they have known hard manual labor, although the calluses have been pampered into distant memory by armies of manicurists. He smiles. "Bob Macallan, founding genius and chief cook and bottle washer of *Elixir* magazine. I'm glad you could make it. Welcome, buddy; it's good to see you."

Mackey, about sixty, is shorter than me and about twice as thick, a small refrigerator with stubby arms and legs. His considerable paunch is cement solid; he could use it to break through walls if any ever dared to get in his way. He's wearing a textured white shirt, open at the collar, gabardine slacks, and expensive Italian slip-ons with tassels. His fat cheeks are scarred and pitted with pockmarks; the pores on his fleshy nose are deep and wide like moon craters.

"Travel arrangements suit you?"

"Fabulous, Mr. Mackey. Just fabulous."

"Hey, none of this 'Mr. Mackey' shit. It's El to you."

"Right, El. Great trip."

"It's the only way to fly. It makes you realize that there's no first-class on commercial airlines, no matter where you sit. Costs me a fucking fortune, but it's worth it." He pats my shoulder, then squeezes, giving just a hint of his strength. "Atwood tells me you guys had a good meeting yesterday. A good meeting. Come on in, lemme show you around."

He guides me into an entrance hall big enough to be a train station. Towering, vaulted, timbered ceilings, marble floors, chandeliers, Tudor balustrades, the works. Everything short of Charles Laughton in Henry VIII costume tossing mutton joints over his shoulder, for Elton Mackey is king of this castle.

"Whaddya think?" He sweeps his arm across the interior panorama. He's not listening for a response. "You know how I got all this?"

"Well, I've heard some of the legends, but I, uh . . ."

Mackey barges ahead, oblivious.

"I did it by figuring out what the score really is in every business I've gotten into. *Exactly* what the score is. Know what I mean?"

I nod.

31

"You know all the bullshit that companies wrap themselves in? Higher purposes, advancement of the state of the art, industry standards, pursuit of excellence? Crap like that. Well, when I took over my first magazine, I was a printer."

"Yes, I've heard."

"To me, a magazine is a printing job. The more pages, the more I make. So when I take over *Stone Age* because those schmucks can't pay their bills, I realize I can sell my pages a second time to the advertisers. And a third time to the readers." He laughs with a big bellow, not unlike Charles Laughton's King Henry. "How many guys get to sell their product three times? *Three times*. I was in love with this business from that moment on."

I hear the string section winding up for a big finish on "Sweet Caroline." I look up toward the source. One of the rosettes in the hand-carved ceiling has been ripped out and replaced with another round speaker. Mackey notices me noticing.

"I got the whole place wired for sound, inside and out. I'll show you the control panel later." He leads me to a vast white dining room. The walls and ceilings are a riot of sculpted fruit and harvest symbols, framed in intricate architectural borders, all hand-carved, all painted white. Mackey waves at the unduplicatable work of craftsmen long dead. "When we bought this place, all this wood was the color of dark red shit. Cherrywood or something. Like a fucking funeral parlor." The entire room is white. White lacquer floor, walls, and ceilings. White chairs surround the endless dinner table, whose surface is clear glass, to show off the white shag carpeting beneath. We keep on walking to a small den. Mackey sits us down on facing black leather couches. In the corner is a three-tiered booze wagon of chrome rails and smoked glass shelves, altar for the dozens of carefully arranged bottles.

"So I'm looking at this business that can sell its pages three times and it's still losing money, and I ask, 'What's the problem? What's in the way?' I look at the editorial. Mind you, this is not the *Atlantic-fucking-Monthly*. It's news about rock crushing. Looks okay to me. The editorial staff are the same frightened little weenie English majors who just have to work"— Mackey affects an English accent and raises his pinky finger while holding an imaginary teacup—"who just have to work as *writers*. Even if they get paid in a dark room. No, they're not the problem. I look at the sales reps. They're the same boozy, glad-handing assholes who fell out of jobs in plant management and ad agencies and can't make a living anywhere else. But they're not the problem. The problem is the competition. *Gravel Weekly*. That's the problem. I ask the reps, 'Why are our numbers down?' They tell me that it started as a crisis of confidence. That we've slipped in lots of little ways and suddenly the industry starts to whisper about you. Rumors begin. And after a while, the rumors turn into the truth. 'Rumors?' I ask. 'You mean rumors can make or break a magazine?' They say, 'Not exactly.' But I heard all I needed to. I say fuck trying to figure out how to change the editorial or repackage the sales pitch. I knew what to do. You see, there was this big billboard."

I can't help sputtering with laughter and surprise. "So the story really is true!"

"You bet your ass." Mackey holds out his hands, indicating the big, wide billboard of memory. " 'Ignore the Rumors.' That's what it said."

"Geez, so it's really true. That's brilliant." It's also scary as hell.

Mackey is giving advice now. "You figure out what the score really is. Then you move. And you don't give a shit what anyone thinks. Because once you get the results, they'll all come kissing your ass. You know that from your own experience."

He leans forward and pats me on the knee in a kind, almost fatherly way. Even in this subdued light, his gold Rolex shines. It's the top-of-the-line President model. A ring of diamonds around the face, diamonds on all twelve numbers.

"That's the same satisfaction you must be getting with *Elixir*. You get squeezed out of American because of politics, and now those fuckers come kissing your ass to buy you out. To buy the idea they said was no goddamn good." He pauses, pleased with himself, letting me consider the depth of his intelligence gathering. "I know all about it, Bob. And I know all about you." He sits back triumphantly to tell me all about myself. "Just about the time you left American, your apartment building went co-op. You bought your apartment for thirty-five grand, sold it for two hundred the next day. You started the magazine with that money. That was goddamn lucky. But you knew it and you didn't blow the opportunity. You took a little shithole of a place with a sofa bed, a phone, and a typewriter and started your magazine. You got it off the ground with your own capital. You got that blood specialist from Harvard to publish his paper in your special issue underwritten solely by Ames Pharmaceuticals. Then you were off and running. You even managed to hire Leo Sayles for more than he's worth. I assume you're overpaying him; everyone else who ever hired him did. And now American wants to buy you out. Not bad for a guy from Bayport, New Hampshire. You've come a long way from that dead little mill town. Just like I've come a long way from downtown in Hough, the roughest, meanest hellhole in Cleveland. You know, compared to Hough, Bayport is fucking Beverly Hills."

He gets up and starts pacing around, turning to face me when a point needs reinforcement. "I know all about you, Bob Macallan. And you're the guy I'm looking for. That's why I brought you out here like this. I could lead up to my offer with a lot of flattery. I could slobber all over you and tell you what a great property *Elixir* is. But you know that and we're both too smart to waste time on that horseshit. So let's get to it. How much is American offering?" He is pretending not to know. "Eight? Nine? Nine and a half? Ten?"

"Somewhere in that neighborhood."

"Well, you tell me what neighborhood you'd like to be in. Go ahead; tell me. Is ten-five your neighborhood? Maybe eleven is your magic number? Is eleven-five better than, say, ten?" Mackey closes the deal in his mind and clicks on the mental calculator. "Let's see, after taxes that would give you about seven million. Let's invest it in tax-free munis and you get about three hundred thou' a year for the rest of your life. For just sitting around on your ass. Not bad."

"No, not bad at all."

"Of course it's not bad. But is that what you really want?"

"I don't know. I could try it out and see."

"You want twelve? I'll give you twelve. That's a good two and a half to three million more than it's worth, strictly speaking. But never mind. You can get your little pile. A nice medium number with six zeros after it. And you'll get used to it so quick you won't fucking believe it. And then you know what? You'll discover what the game is really about." He stops pacing and sits down beside me again.

"You know what it's really all about?" The question is rhetorical. "It's about this." He makes a goose egg with thumb and forefinger. "Zero. It's about getting another zero. You got your number with six zeros and you realize what a different league you'd be in if you were up there with the guys who've got seven zeros. Ten, twenty, thirty million. And don't you think the guy with seven zeros is thinking, *If only I had another zero.* And if you can get to a hundred million, well, why can't you get another zero yet? I tell ya, the game isn't about the houses and the jets and the cars and the broads. They're just the toys. Don't get me wrong; they're good toys. But the game is about the zeros, watching the little dot go farther and farther back into the horizon." He waves to the vanishing decimal point way down at the tail end of his net worth figure. "Me, I gotta lotta zeros in me. And more zeros to get. And, Macallan, I'm convinced you've gotta lotta zeros in you. A lot. *Elixir* is great, but, frankly, you're not going to get any more than six little zeros out of it. To get that extra zero, you've got to move to a bigger playing field. And that's what I want to offer you." An interruption. Mackey looks up at the doorway.

A tall, sixtyish woman with hair bleached into straw has appeared. "So this is the young man with the doctor magazine." She has a loud, self-consciously social voice. "I'm Vera Mackey." I stand as she walks over with extended hand. "El's told me all about you." The hand is a bony claw with perfect pink talons; it wears a mammoth ring with a teardrop emerald surrounded by diamonds. Bulging veins trace road maps to the wrist and the Lady President Rolex, diamond-encrusted like Mackey's, but with the mother-of-pearl watch face.

"I think your magazine sounds wonderful. It sounds like just the thing to help dress up El's other publications. And looking at you now, I can see you're such an interesting young man." She has sustained the handshake long beyond greeting. "You know, most of El's magazines are run by such *un*interesting men. Have you ever sat through dinner with the publisher of

34

Car Wash Journal? Well, all I can tell you is don't." There's no question whose Mercedes it is with the SHOPPER license plate. Vera sports a Louis Vuitton bag, Hermès scarf, Chanel blazer and Chanel gold chain belt loaded with big double-C logos, Ferragamo pumps with legible hardware, and white slacks that look like they've never been sat in. Her face has the death-mask tautness of many visits to the plastic surgeon. "I certainly look forward to you joining our little family." She finally lets go, but not without a last little squeeze of my hand.

"Where are you off to?" Mackey asks vacantly.

"The new line from Escada. Private showing at Tower City. Not that you'd care."

"Yeah, have fun."

"Oh, you can be sure I will, dear." Then peering right into me, "And it was a pleasure meeting you, Mr. Macallan. I do hope to see more of you around here. El, I hope you give this young man everything he wants. I know I certainly would." She jingles her car keys, turns, and leaves.

Mackey follows her with his eyes, his look a combination of fascination and contempt. Like the chicken-wing ladies who rule New York society, Vera Mackey starves herself thin. There's no ass or thighs on her. I shudder to think how what little flesh there is hangs off her aging bones.

"Hmmph." He snaps back to attention. "Drink?" he asks, moving toward the chrome and glass booze cart.

"No thanks."

Mackey pours himself a good-morning Scotch and spells out his proposition. He will pay me as much as eleven million five for *Elixir*. To be paid over three years. But that's not what he's really after. Mackey wants me to build him a new magazine group. Classy, high-gloss magazines directed at upscale male audiences, starting with *Elixir*. He wants to catch lawyers, architects, stockbrokers, all the prosperous professional and executive types. He wants me to create the books or acquire them, and whatever categories we enter, he wants me to clear the field of the serious competition.

"It's what I learned when I put the screws to *Gravel Weekly*. There are only two things you can do to competitors. You buy 'em or you break 'em. Buy 'em or break 'em. You've got the smarts and the balls to do it, and I've got the capital to back you up. You throw in with me, and in five years or less I'll see to it that you've got zeros. Lots of 'em. More than you'll ever see from American."

"That's quite an offer. Really quite an offer. I don't know what to say, El."

"You can say yes. That's what you can say."

Poker face, don't fail me now. "Well, it's so much to think about. I figured we were just going to haggle price and terms for *Elixir*."

"Nah, that's small change. Do you think I'd bring you out here if all I wanted was to buy your magazine? Do you think I'd send the jet for you? Bring you to my home? I don't have to go through all this song and dance to buy a magazine."

Suddenly, Mackey looks tired. He stops, lets out a big sigh, and stares at the floor. "I got nobody in this organization who can help me make this happen. I got a dozen guys like Atwood. They're fine at what they do, but they've topped out at *Stone Age* and *Car Wash Journal*. They're not going anywhere." He sits back, his body limp. "I got no sons. And my two daughters? They've got full-time jobs as world-class shoppers, just like their mother. And the guys they're married to? A couple of gold-digging jerks I wouldn't trust with the men's room key. I'm alone in this thing, Macallan. Alone."

He looks up at me with different eyes, no longer the all-conquering bully of a few minutes ago. "I can't pull this thing off alone. I can't. Look at me. Look at the books I publish. They're just like me. Hard-nosed. Homely. And common as dirt. This new upscale network? I can practically see it, feel it, taste it. But that's not enough. I can't pick the trendy designers. *You* can. I can't pick the hot editors and writers. You can. I can't front for it and make the important pitches. You can. But I can provide the muscle to back it all up. And *you can't.*"

The old Mackey is back again, more potent than before. "Macallan, you're like me, you from Bayport, me from Hough. You're like me because we're both outsiders. But the difference is this. When I show up at American Communications, I know I'm an outsider and they know it, too. But when you show up, you may know you're an outsider, *but they fucking don't.* You can pass for one of them. That's your secret. And our strength. Together, Macallan, we can turn the world of upscale publishing upside down. You know we can."

He leans back on the couch. "I'm a guy who operates on gut." He slaps his hard, fat belly with both hands. "First, I feed it information. Lots and lots of information." He strokes the belly, admiring its girth. "I feed it everything there is to know about the business, about the players, about their strengths and weaknesses and what I can get out of 'em. I let it all digest. Then," he jumps to his feet, "I go where my gut tells me to."

In this case, it leads him to the hooch wagon for a refill. "Macallan, I'm not making you a better offer for your magazine." He swills back a big gulp of whiskey. "I'm making you the best offer of your whole fucking life."

I am winging back to New York in Mackey's jet. We discussed at length his terms, his strategy. I listened carefully to his promises, weighed his arguments, and calculated the possible gains. If all goes well, Mackey will indeed make me a richer man than American will. He will make me a much bigger shot than I am now, far bigger than American will make me. I will have his jet to fly around in, his limos awaiting me everywhere. In return for helping him realize his very shrewd magazine network idea, Mackey will fulfill for me every fantasy of avarice, power, and status. He will heap on me the rewards that are the wet dreams of every middle-management desk jockey doomed to spend his days crushed under corporate bureaucracy and choked by drab-colored neckties.

Mackey has it all figured out brilliantly. Except for one item. I am not interested.

This is not what I want. At least not now.

And even if I did want it now, I would not want it from the hand of Elton Mackey. I don't like him. I don't trust him. I don't want to work for him. I don't want to work with him. I don't want him in my face or anywhere in my life. A few years ago, I would have viewed Mackey as one of those distasteful but necessary compromises. For the sake of money, hold your nose and endure. But not today. Mackey does not understand that the bonanza I most look forward to is not money. It is *freedom*. Not just freedom from want and worry. But freedom from greed. Freedom from status. Freedom from the endless one-upmanship, freedom from the senseless ringing of cash registers, drowning out the ability to distinguish between "I want" and "I need."

I want to claim my independence. From the tyranny of bosses and employees and clients and suppliers and everyone in business with the power to hold my fate hostage.

Even more, I want to claim my independence from the specter that has haunted me since my first moment of memory. Fear.

All my life, I've been running scared. Scared that yet another of Dad's business ventures would fail, scared that we'd lose our home, scared that we'd be poor and suffer indignities that only proved how unworthy we Macallans really were. I ran scared all through school, and because I ran scared, I ran extra hard, hoping to stay ahead of the demon that would unveil me to be the phony I was sure I was. I ran scared and got good grades, a scholarship to a prestigious college, a job at the top-rated magazine company, and finally, after a temporary setback, a thriving magazine of my own. And I never stopped running scared. I worked frantically at my charades of competence, my pantomimes of success. But I knew that no matter what robes I heaped on, it could never change the awful truth within. That I did not deserve any of it and at any moment the relentless demon that had been pursuing me all along would catch up and expose my unworthiness to the world.

I think I may have finally outrun that villain.

I will collect half of the money from American in a month or so. I will slide the company into their empire with grace. I will play the role of the good corporate soldier. I will collect the rest of the money and slip away, leaving it all behind.

I will start again, answering to no one I do not choose to answer to. I won't do anything I do not choose to do. Wendy and I will wallow in the luxury of choice.

I will bury the demons of fear and failure that broke my father and killed my mother. I will make it right. All of it. I will take what I have earned by running scared and hard. I will let myself admit that I deserve it. I swear, by all my struggles, I will let nothing stand in the way.

FEBRUARY

CHAPTER FOUR

I am fishing through my tie rack, trying to figure out which one I feel like wearing tonight. Wendy is pottering around the apartment, barefoot in her nightgown, humming to herself. She's collecting magazines, her two new books on pregnancy, and the week's collection of *New York Times* life-style sections she's been too busy to read. Along with two rented videocassette movies, she's arranging a little fortress of entertainment around her favorite spot on the living room couch, to pass the evening alone while I attend to the final ritual in the selling of my company to American. The closing dinner at Le Roi Soleil, a medium-overpriced businessman's French restaurant.

I am standing in my closet doorway, running my hands along the strips of colored silk, still ambivalent. Wendy joins me.

"How about this one?" She holds out a particularly bright, peacock-green paisley she bought me a few months ago.

"Don't you think that's a little too vivid for someone who's about to be reinducted into the ranks of a big corporation? Don't forget the middle manager's motto: *Semper Mediocritus.*"

"You are in no danger of ever becoming middle management." She looks up at me. "Something bothering you?"

"I just saw this huge question mark flash before my eyes. They handed me the check yesterday morning. I signed the papers. The company belongs to them now. I have turned over the company bank accounts to them. I am a subsidiary. I have terminated our relationships with our accountants and lawyers. Their lawyers have been through every stitch of my corporate underwear, so to speak."

"So to speak."

"And I just wondered if I've done the right thing. Made the right decision."

"Of course you did."

"How can you be so sure?"

"Because my husband told me so and my husband is always right about these things. Just ask him." She gives me a little squeeze.

"I'll have bosses to please now, people I'm supposed to be afraid of."

"You've got some earnings numbers to hit, that's all. Numbers you negotiated, numbers you know you can make. Then, in a year, you can say, 'Good-bye, American. Hello, other half of my bankroll.' Do you think maybe you're just the tiniest bit sad at giving up the company?"

"Yeah, maybe that's the twinge. And it is, after all, American I'm going back to."

"And how would you feel about going back to those antediluvian days before Hale Hadley called?"

"No way."

"There's your answer. You couldn't stand Wacky Mackey, could you?"

"You mean Tacky Mackey."

"So there it is." She yanks the peacock tie off the rack. "You should damn well look like the brilliant success you are."

I reach for a muted gray tie with faint blue stripes. "But shouldn't I try to resocialize myself for the role I'll play for the next year? Loyal gray soldier?"

"Not on your life, Macallan." Wendy starts tying her chosen tie around the collar of my white shirt. This lady ties a mean four-in-hand; she always manages to get the little cleft below the knot centered perfectly. First try.

"There now, that's my man. Fiercely independent."

"Indifferent to the tyranny of corporate life," I chime in.

"And totally loved."

I wrap my arms around her. She nestles.

"You know, Macallan, now that you've got half a small fortune bulging out of your pocket, you'd better remember something."

"What's that?"

"I am the best woman you ever had." She is stroking me.

"Absolutely," I agree, "the best." She is getting noticeable results.

"And the last."

"Absolutely. The last. The best."

"It's you and me, Macallan, heading into the brave new world of the nineties." She is humming what sounds like the theme from "Star Trek." "Married sex," she whispers, "the final frontier." She starts covering my face with tiny kisses. "These are the voyages of the couple Macallan. Their lifelong mission—to seek out new worlds, to explore new universes of delight, to boldly go where no couple has gone before." She hums more "Star Trek," plants more kisses. "Now close your eyes and put your hands behind your back." I do as I am told. "Let your last, best woman show you how a night of triumph begins."

I hear a zipper being opened.

It is mine.

★ ★ ★

As I cross the lobby of our building, I prepare for the walk up to West End Avenue to find a cab. Riverside Drive is a great place to live, the very edge of the city. Beyond is space and expanse, the Hudson, the Palisades, the rest of the country to which Manhattan Island is nominally connected. The Drive is the best place to live and the worst place to get a cab. I look down Seventy-eighth Street. Nothing. I peer up and down the Drive, then across the mighty river at the lights of New Jersey. The wind is cold and dry.

Suddenly, a stretch limo pulls up in front of me. The rear window is open; the passenger sticks his head out, dog-style. It is Ken Atwood in the gray whale.

"Hey, Macallan! Need a lift? Cabs are a bitch to find in this neighborhood."

"Geez, Atwood, you are some piece of work."

"So happens Ricky and I are on our way to midtown. To Fifty-first Street. Right past Le Roi Soleil." He exaggerates his phony French, "Le rrrwah solay."

Atwood flashes me a major-league wink, motions me in, and slides across the seat to make room. I get in. He grins smugly. I nod respectfully at his little victory.

"I know," I say, "the information business."

The beast pulls away from the curb and heads toward midtown.

"Drink?" Atwood motions toward the bar.

"No, thanks. I'm sure there'll be plenty tonight."

"I'm sure there will be. Cocktails, wine, brandy, port. Champagne toasts saluting the future of *Elixir,* American's newest acquisition." He raises an imaginary glass to toast me. "I can't believe you went for their deal. I guess we really had you pegged wrong." Atwood's comb-over hair has been mussed by the wind. He wets his fingertips on his tongue and mats the hair back into place, pressing it firmly against his cue ball head.

"I went for the deal that was right for me. I made that clear when I talked to Mackey."

"Mr. Mackey was disappointed. Hurt and disappointed."

"That's funny, when I spoke to him, all he did was call me an asshole and hang up."

"He's too proud to show it, but believe me, you really hurt him when you turned him down."

"Sorry, I didn't realize Mackey is so vulnerable. He doesn't exactly come across as Mr. Sensitivity."

"You know, Bob, it's still not too late. The closing was only yesterday. Their check probably hasn't even cleared yet. There isn't anything that can't be undone."

"Ken, I made my decision."

"And ten from American is better than eleven-five and more from Mackey."

"I've got my own plans, my own agenda. American suits it better."

"I see. So there's no talking you out of it?"

"Sorry."

"Okay." Atwood turns pensive. He leans forward to get the bourbon decanter. "Sure you won't join me?"

"No thanks, go ahead."

We ride for a long time in silence, Atwood nursing his drink.

"I think I should tell you, Bob, that Mr. Mackey's plans for the upscale network will go ahead full-steam. With or without you."

"I would imagine so. It's a good idea."

"Mr. Mackey is going to make it work."

"I'm sure he will. Tell him I wish him all the best."

"Macallan, I think you're an okay kid."

"I think you're swell, too, Ken. What are you driving at?"

"I'm saying that Mr. Mackey is going to make his idea work."

"Good for him."

"He could start out with a book in any category he wants to."

"It's a free country."

"You've been a very lucky kid, Macallan. You built *Elixir* in a competitive, in a competitive, uh, vacuum. You were really the only contender from day one."

"That was the whole idea."

"Right. And you're harvesting the fruits of that now."

"So?"

"I think it's only fair to tell you that Mr. Mackey has decided to begin his network with a new book. In the medical category."

The limo has arrived in front of Le Roi Soleil. Ricky shifts into park but makes no motion toward getting out to open the door. I lean forward for the handle and let myself out.

"You can tell Mr. Mackey that I wish him the best of luck in his new ventures, whatever they may be."

"That's okay, Bobby. Better keep that luck for yourself. You're gonna need it. All of it." I shut the whale's door. The passenger window is closed; the reflection from the streetlight blots out any view of Atwood. I turn toward the canopy of Le Roi Soleil. I hear the beast grumble away behind me.

Le Roi Soleil is the kind of old-fashioned French restaurant the unsubtle men of Wall Street love. Everything is heavy-handed: the thick, buttery sauces; brazenly overpriced clarets; tufted red velvet banquettes; arrogant, servile waiters who take pride in knowing how to light a gentleman's cigar without letting the flame touch the precious leaf.

The restaurant is Conover's choice because the dinner is his treat, Hale Hadley's symbolic payback to the deal participants who have wrestled together for a month and finally wrested an agreement.

Our private room is down the travertine stairway to the left of the bar just before the main dining room. I am the last to arrive.

"Bob, Bob, Bob." Conover's greeting is warm and effusive. He pats my shoulder and squeezes the back of my arm as if I were his dearest friend from childhood. "Gentlemen," he announces to the other eight men, who are broken up into little klatches, "the man who made the big killing is here. A champagne for Bob." Conover hands me a tulip glass. "A toast," he says, "to the whiz kid of medical publishing who just wrote himself a prescription for ten million worth of the best medicine there is. Now, Bob, if we can negotiate a bigger cut for the rest of us here tonight, we can promise that the truth about what your magazine is *really* worth will never leave this room."

A big laugh all around. We clink. We drink.

After the toast, the lawyers go back into their huddle. The four of them, two of mine, two of American's, can finally, after a month of playing adversaries for their respective clients, get comfortable with each other. As hired guns, they have more in common with each other than with their clients. Representing American, there's Jonathan Wylie and Tom Pierce from the old-line WASP firm of Dunlop, Buchanan, and Ames. Representing *Elixir,* Peter Dennison and Mark Bateman from the equally old-line firm of Curtis and Hastings. I used them instead of *Elixir*'s less prestigious regular outside counsel because of their reputation in handling friendly acquisitions with Fortune 500 giants like American. They are the ones who have hammered out the terms. We principals have only pointed them in the directions we desired. How much of the struggle they deliberately prolonged to rack up billable hours for their firms we will never know. At a closing dinner, though, you can always count on the two sets of opposing lawyers to form the single tightest clique.

Conover pats me one last time and leaves to pollinate the lawyer cluster. *Elixir*'s treasurer, Joe Bartolo, is in the corner talking to Levine. I join them. Facing Levine, I lean into Joe with a tone of mock conspiracy. "So! How do you size up our new boss?"

"He's got good taste in publishing and a financial reporting system that is . . . okay. But if he was to ask me, I'd tell him it's a system I could improve with a few of my own personal refinements."

"Do you think he'd ask?"

"I dunno. You told me he's pretty damn smart."

"Then I'll betcha he asks."

Joe breaks the kidding with a laugh and a phony punch into Levine's shoulder. Joe's social patterns are more at home in a muffler and tailpipe shop than Le Roi Soleil. But his natural warmth and intelligence make people overlook a lot. He's an uncomplicated man who wears his working-class origins on his sleeve. He reminds me of my father, or at least a talkative Brooklyn-Italian version of him. Like my old man, he calls guys like himself "salta the earth" and invents malaprop expressions like "the flaw in the ointment." The difference between him and my father is competence. Joe is very smart at what he does. My dad never got that far. Joe was *Elixir*'s outside accountant when the magazine needed only an hour or two of bookkeeping every month. As it grew, I needed more and more of Joe, and he saw a better opportunity with *Elixir* than with his small practice. Joe's contract with American was a specially negotiated point. I made sure of that. If they insist on moving him out after I'm gone, it will cost them a lot of money. The same for Jerry Greenstein, the managing editor.

What's more, I am awarding special acquisition bonuses of 50 percent of annual salary to all employees with more than one year of service to *Elixir*. It comes out of my first $5 million check. Some friends and advisers said I am being a schmuck, that I am giving away more than I have to. Maybe it's guilt money or just conscience, I can't tell. But I want them to feel like they have benefited from the sale because they contributed to building the company. And besides, I need them to perform at full force for another year to get the other $5 million. So I think of it as a good investment.

And then there's Leo. I negotiated a very special status for Leo. His inflated salary, for one thing, which the personnel types at American referred to as "celebrity wages." It really stuck in their craw. No matter. Leo above all required special handling. The day I told him I was selling out to American, I guaranteed him his current salary, with built-in raises under a three-year contract, plus the continuance of his lavish expense allowance and healthy bonus kickers if he exceeded sales targets. I never mentioned anything about Mackey or his offer. And neither did he.

Levine turns to me.

"Bob, I suppose it's my job to welcome you back home to American. But since I've been with the company less than a year, it seems a little presumptuous. You had, what, seven years with company?"

"Six. I got into the Henderson Program right after college." The Henderson Program was a special publishing internship, started by American's founding genius, Andrew Henderson, as a fast track to management. Exclusively for Yale graduates like himself.

"The old Henderson Program. I've heard stories about it. You must have been in one of the last groups."

"Next to last. It stopped the year the old man died."

"I didn't realize you went to Yale."

"I didn't. I, uh, finagled my way into the program. I went to Baldwin College." Baldwin is a smallish New England school with an undeservedly prestigious reputation. It's not quite a second-string Dartmouth, an imitation Amherst but far more provincial.

"That's a good school. I went to NYU. When it was still up in the Bronx. I guess that'll give you an idea of how much American has changed. Back when you were here, I wouldn't have been able to get a job in the mailroom with that on my résumé." Levine was hired in as a group vice president from Seligssohn Brothers, the high-powered firm he has since turned into Conover's rival for American's investment banking business.

"My Baldwin degree wasn't exactly something to be ashamed of," I say, "but I knew enough not to talk much about it, either."

"Well, I dunno about you guys," Joe interrupts, "but I was valedictorian at my school. The School of Hard Knocks. And that paved the way for me to go to night school in accounting. While I was studying advanced food technology at my uncle's bakery." He cackles and heads for the tray of hors d'oeuvres on the sideboard.

Levine laughs politely.

"I can only see hints of what American must have been like back then. But I can tell you it's a different company today. And I'm part of the proof. The days of the Yale men taking the train home to Greenwich every night at five, congratulating themselves on the magazines old man Henderson created, are gone. After the bath the company took on *American Fitness,* they did a lot of soul-searching. They knew there was something wrong, something in the culture that was preventing good ideas from coming to the surface. Imagine, a company like American, with the biggest stable of consumer books in the world, and in the past fifteen years it can't launch a single successful new project. It's incredible."

"Maybe not. If you were here in those days."

"What counts is the future. And it's a future we're buying. You're part of that new wave, Bob." Levine starts in about his mission, his plans, his strategy, all the whiz-bang synergistic acquisitions American hired him to do. I've heard it before and it's a good rap. I can nod in the right places, knit my brow thoughtfully when called for, and think back to the days at American Levine never knew.

"I have two pieces of paper in front of me," I remember Harry Woodcock telling me. It was five years ago. It feels like yesterday. "One of them is going Upstairs today." Upstairs means to the forty-eighth floor, where top management sits. *"I* can sign this one." It was my annual employee evaluation. "Or *you* can sign this one." It was my letter of resignation from American, all typed for me.

This was the first time I had ever seen Harry so direct and confrontational. His usual mode was diplomacy in the extreme—gracious, courtly, roundabout. The victim never saw the knife going into his back and, even in his dying moments, never suspected Harry of the stabbing. Little wonder. Harry Woodcock was the perfect corporate creature. Square-eyed, lantern-jawed, a former Yale lacrosse star. He had thickened and grayed gracefully in middle age. Handsome in a hearty Saxon way, Harry Woodcock had merged his entire being and identity into the mighty corporation he served.

"I have a responsibility to this company," he told me, "and to its values. Bob, you just don't seem to understand how things work here. This is a great corporation, an institution with traditions and our own way of doing things. Yet you seem to think that you are smarter or superior or something. The people who are above you in this corporation are there for a reason, and if you don't believe in their judgment and leadership, you don't belong here."

That was Harry's way of saying I would not kiss his ass.

Harry sucked up to authority shamelessly. He worked his corporate superiors with flattery and groveling. He wanted whatever those in power wanted. His antennae were tuned upward, and to those below him he

44

transmitted whatever signals he received from above. He had no content of his own, no opinions, no passions. He was always unquestioningly in favor of whatever it would take to win his next promotion.

As the number-three executive in the magazine development group, he expected the same behavior in the people below him, including me. I was one of three "kids" charged with studying and developing new ideas under Harry's tutelage. I thought the drill was about developing new ideas for magazines. Harry thought it was about developing relationships with powerful men Upstairs. I was wrong. Harry was right. Harry's boss's boss wanted to develop a magazine for the fitness craze. Harry saw the job of his minions as going out to gather all the confirmation the big boss required, being careful to omit and suppress anything contradictory. My colleagues played Harry's game and pleased Harry. I didn't. My colleagues did a lot of spadework that later helped launch American's biggest magazine failure. I tried to push an idea for a doctor magazine that combined professional content with life-style features, and ended up with this meeting in Harry's office.

He handed me my evaluation. He had marked my performance as "Below Average" on almost every category of behavior except "Attendance." And on the most important category of all, especially for one who had entered American as an intern in the hallowed Henderson Program, Harry sank me once and for all. The final item was "Publishing Judgment." The phrase had been old man Henderson's and was the magical career-maker or career-breaker at American. Harry said essentially that I had none, and if promoted further, I might prove dangerous to the company's future. It was as good as a death sentence. Paternalistic American didn't fire people in those days. But if that evaluation had gone into my file, I would have been permanently exiled to a job in coupon collating or truck fleet maintenance.

"I enjoy working with young people like yourself," Harry explained, trying to be, if not friendly, at least decent. "I try to give them the benefit of what I've learned, to incorporate them into what we believe here at American. It doesn't give me pleasure to write an evaluation like this, Bob. But I believe it is my responsibility to be as frank and objective as I can be."

In truth, I had become something of a wiseass. The more Harry wanted me to rig my studies to agree with management's preordained conclusions, the more independent I became. The more he tried to make me abandon the idea that ultimately became *Elixir*, the more stridently I promoted it.

"Bob, the resignation I have here is simple and straightforward. It says you are leaving to pursue other interests. I think it is the best route. For you and American. Sign it and I will tear up this evaluation right here and now. That's as far as I can stretch the rules for you and still stay within the guidelines of my conscience." He smiled. Kindly and generous in triumph.

My brain went blank. I should have expected this. But I was shocked. Outraged. My chest ached. My gut recoiled as if I'd been kicked. Fuck you, Harry, and your whole smug corporation. Suddenly I was scared. Scared because I was being rejected. Scared because I was going to succeed in this job by being right. Right about what the job was *supposed* to be about. I was scared because this felt like failure. And failure was the one thing I feared more than anything else. But fuck you, Harry. And fuck you, Failure. And fuck you, Father, who taught me that failure was what I had coming. I told myself I would do something. I just didn't know what.

I signed the resignation and walked out of Harry's office. The noise in my ears blocked out the world around me. The only sound I heard was my own breathing. I glided silently to the elevator on padded feet and descended to the lobby. My eyes filled with water, but no tears fell. The teeming crowds on midtown sidewalks parted magically to make way for me. No one touched me. No one saw me. I was in a trance. I walked the forty blocks north to my little apartment. Alone.

"Bob, you are the start of a whole new chapter in the rebirth of creative publishing at American." Levine is winding up his spiel and getting ready for another toast. "Let's get some more champagne. Over here, please." He indicates my glass and his to the waiter.

We drink.

"Oh, by the way, Bob, we're both getting a new boss. Actually, he's my boss. You'll still report to me, but that's a technicality, really. Most of the time I'm going to be off with Conover and the boys doing deals. So you should look to him to be your operational contact, the link between you unit heads and top management. He's been in Hong Kong for a few years running ad sales and circulation for our Asian editions. Done a hell of a job, I hear. The boys Upstairs love him. *Love* him. And he thinks the world of you. He says you are the next Andrew Henderson. You guys worked together way back when. Says he can't wait to see you again. He should be moved back from Hong Kong in a couple of weeks."

"I worked with a lot of people at American. What's his name?"

"Harry Woodcock."

CHAPTER FIVE

I was ten years old when my father's storm window business failed. Just before the creditors moved in, Doug Macallan, his partner and cousin, took most of the company cash and left town with no forwarding address. One night that spring, a few weeks before they closed my dad down, I was awakened by the sounds of a fight going on behind my parents' bedroom door.

"Well?" my mother shrieked. "Are we going to lose the house or aren't we?" Her voice was angry and cracking.

There was no reply.

"Answer me, goddammit! Are we or are we not going to lose the house?"

Dad mumbled something. It sounded like, "I don't know yet."

I sat bolt upright in the dark. Little Jimmy was asleep across the room, unbothered, undisturbed. Land mines could have been exploding on the front lawn and Jimmy would have slept through it.

"If we lose the house," Mom asked in a voice gone quieter but even more desperate, "where are we going to live? In the street?"

No reply. I had heard my parents fighting about money before, but this time it sounded worse. I got out of bed and moved to the doorway of my room. I sat on the floor, leaning back against the doorjamb, watching the crack of light beneath their bedroom door. The shadow of footsteps paced nervously behind it. I knew they belonged to my mother; my father never moved that fast.

"Answer me, Clint!" she said. "Where will we live?"

More silence. More pacing. Finally, he spoke.

"I said I don't know." Dad's tone of voice hardly ever varied, whether the occasion was Christmas morning or a funeral. He offered every spoken word grudgingly, like a miser being forced to part with a few precious dollars.

Words, on the other hand, gushed from my mother in such torrents that they lost all meaning. You saw the wave coming; you closed your eyes and ears and let it wash over you. It knocked you around a bit but did no real damage. This time it was different; her every word mattered. And stung.

"Where are we going to live?" she howled. "On Danforth Street?" That was a block of shabby triple-decker apartment houses. The bad part of town, where kids grew up poor and dirty and got in trouble with the police and their parents didn't care. I was afraid of Danforth Street. "Have you thought about it, Clint? Have you thought about *anything*? Have you?"

No reply. The pacing stopped. The bed creaked. My mother must have sat down. I heard the crackle of a match as she lit a cigarette.

"I could have married Larry Hughes." Her voice was lower and calmer. Harder to hear. "I could have been a lawyer's wife living in a big house on Walton Street. Larry was dying to marry me. Dying to. Or Ed Coyne. Look at him today. He's a cardiologist. A professional. With an education. With standing in this community. He provides for his family. I could have married him. Instead I fell in love with Clint Macallan, who told me that college was for chumps and office jobs for sissies. Clint Macallan who said to be a man you had to be your own boss. Well, where are the chumps and sissies now? Living up on Congress Hill. And what about you? Huh? What about *us*?"

The bed creaked. Shadows moved under the door. She was on her feet again.

"Aren't you even going to ask me where I'm going?" she asked.

Pause.

"Well, aren't you?"

"Okay, where you goin'?" Dad mumbled.

"Downstairs to the kitchen. While we still have a downstairs and a kitchen." She opened the bedroom door a few inches and held it there. A big slice of light poured out into the hallway. I scrambled back into the darkness of the room Jimmy and I shared. "You might as well go to bed," she said, still behind her door. "I want to think for a while." She closed the bedroom door behind her, leaving it ajar just enough to light her way toward the staircase. Then she went down to the kitchen.

I sat on the floor in the darkness, trying to imagine what life would be like if we lost our house. It was scary. Who would come to throw us out? Would we really have to move to Danforth Street? Would the kids at school laugh at me? Or, even worse, stop talking to me altogether? I felt like I was about to be branded publicly with a horrible crippling shame. I felt naked and helpless against enemies I did not know or understand. All I knew was that they had the power to ruin my life and destroy my family's home. And there wasn't a thing that I—or my dad—could do. I felt scared and vulnerable and frustrated. Why couldn't my dad be like other dads and just make enough money? He did not have to be rich. All we needed was enough money so that money was not always a big problem. But it always was. I got angry. Not at my dad. But at money. Because it was such a problem for Dad. Because it hurt him and us. And because of the awful things it did to Mom. It made her sad. It made her nervous. It made her get sick. It made her yell at Dad.

Dad turned off the light and went to sleep. In a few minutes, I could hear his deep, regular breathing. Jimmy lay sleeping on the other side of me. The two of them could sleep through anything. Mom and I were different, I told myself. I decided to go downstairs.

I scampered silently down the narrow stairway, turned the corner, and saw Mom seated in the darkened kitchen, looking out the window. The room was lit by the distant gray glow of the streetlight on Munjoy Street, on the far side of our backyard. I stood in the darkness of the doorway, waiting for her infallible maternal radar to pick up my presence. I waited, expecting to be detected instantly. But all she did was sigh deeply, put out one cigarette, and light another. She kept her gaze straight ahead.

Finally I whispered, "Mom?"

She jumped and turned around. The cigarette in her mouth lit her face with an eerie glow. It magnified the lines around her eyes and folds of skin that had just begun to sag. "You did this to me!" she used to scream at Dad during big fights. "I was beautiful once and look what you did to me!" It was true. She had been beautiful. Jimmy and I had seen the photos from her teens and early twenties. Her blond hair looked pure silver in the black-and-white photos; her face made us think of movie stars. We saw her posed with friends on the beach. They all looked happy, but Mom looked happiest of all. In every group picture, Mom was always the most beautiful woman, clearly the center of attention with her long blond hair and va-va-voom figure. Now, even though she was only thirty-six, she was jowly, with a second chin and a waist that had spread out to the same width as her hips. She grimaced with pains in all parts of her body and scratched her nervous skin rashes and smoked and smoked and smoked.

"It's me, Mom," I whispered.

"Robert, what are you doing up? Do you know what time it is?"

I walked into the kitchen and stood beside her. She smelled faintly of the perfume she wore every day and strongly of cigarettes.

"Have you been up very long?" she asked.

"No," I lied, "I just got up."

"What's the matter?" she asked, placing the palm of her hand against my forehead to test for fever. "Don't you feel well?"

"I feel okay. I just couldn't sleep, that's all."

She did not ask why I had decided to come downstairs to the kitchen. She wrapped her arms around me and hugged me against her.

"Are we gonna be okay, Mom?" I thought I could hide the fact that I had eavesdropped with very general questions.

"What do you mean, sweetheart?"

"You know, is everything gonna be okay?"

She sighed.

"I hope so, Robert. I really hope so." She loosened her hug but did not let go. She stared straight ahead and said nothing for a long time.

Finally she spoke. "Robert?"

"Yes, Mommy."

"I want you to promise me something."

"Okay."

"I want you to promise me that you'll study as hard as you can. You're gonna go to a good college and get a good education and be successful. Do you understand?"

"Yes, Mommy."

"You've always been the smart one. You've got the knack for school, and you're a good talker." She added under her breath, "I guess you got it from me 'cause God knows it doesn't come from your father." She returned her focus to me. "Robert, someday you're going to live in one of those big, beautiful houses on Walton Street. I just know you are."

I nodded, afraid to ask if we weren't going to be forced to live on Danforth Street before that wonderful someday arrived.

"You're my special boy." She hugged me tighter. "Promise me you won't make the same mistakes as your father." I had no idea what she was talking about. "Promise me you'll study hard."

"I promise."

"Promise me you'll get a good job and not be afraid to wear a tie and look respectable." Dad never wore a tie to work because he always worked with his hands. He used to sneer at men who worked in offices and did not get their hands dirty. He said what they did wasn't work. "Promise me you'll always show the world you're a gentleman. Respectable."

"I promise."

"You're going to be a big success and make your wife very happy and me very proud. Promise me you'll do it, Robert. I know you can."

"I promise."

She let go of me and sighed once more. "Now back to bed." She gave me a kiss on the top of the head and a pat on the rear end. I went back upstairs and got into bed. I lay there in the dark for what seemed like forever. I worried about being thrown out of the only house I had ever known. I fretted about moving to Danforth Street and fantasized about living on Walton Street. Finally, I fell into dreamless sleep.

The next day, a bright spring Sunday with trees just beginning to blossom, the Macallans piled into the car to visit the Paynes, friends of my parents who had a boy my age, a boy Jimmy's age, and a new baby girl. The Paynes had just bought a small ranch house in the nearby town of Cape Bette. We had to drive through the crumbling old center of town and along Danforth Street. We had gone this route hundreds of times before. But this time, I shuddered. I studied the shabby tenement houses through the car window. They appeared more dingy and horrible and shameful than ever before. They seemed to be threatening me. Were we really going to move here? I looked to the front seat for some kind of comfort or at least a reaction. Nothing. My parents rode in silence, looking straight ahead. Jimmy sat beside me, playing imaginary baseball games with the plastic Roger Maris doll that had once been mine.

"Let's go up Congress Hill before we head out to the Cape," I heard Mom say. "It's so pretty there."

Dad mumbled something and took the next turn up the steep grade to the enclave of Bayport's ruling elite. We had taken this detour on previous Sunday drives, always at Mom's urging. The turn onto Walton Street never failed to produce the same miraculous effect. Suddenly above this grim little city of modest wood frame houses was a noble street of magnificent, sprawling homes, all set back on glorious, expansive lawns. Dating from the late 1800s to the 1920s, the houses were traditional, usually English in style, or sometimes antebellum, made of red brick or fieldstone. The only wood on Walton Street was used for pillars and porticoes and decorative shingles. Beneath the slate roofs there were too many bedrooms to count, plus servants' rooms, dining rooms bigger than the whole downstairs of our house, ballrooms, sunrooms, mudrooms, winter dens, summer porches, sewing rooms, libraries, butler's pantries, back stairs, grand foyers, and who knew what other wasteful, extravagant, conspicuously underconsumed space.

So this is where I am destined to live, I thought, as I drank in the lush scene. Mom told me so last night. This is where she says I will belong. Someday.

I could not imagine where the wealth to build these houses could have come from. Certainly not the Bayport that I, my parents, and their forebears came from. Everything I had learned from my elders taught me that the splendor on Walton Street was not merely unattainable, but unimaginable.

No matter that a dozen or so families had actually attained it (usually through inheritance) and claimed it as their everyday reality.

"I love that English Tudor," Mom said as we passed her favorite house on the street. "Look, boys; look at those big timbers. Hand-hewn, I'll bet. Must have cost a fortune, even back then at the turn of the century when it was built." She never sounded jealous when we did this fantasy tour. She was full of innocent admiration, as if she were at a museum. I looked at the back of Mom's head and watched her gazing at the big houses. I felt a rush of pride, as if I were one of the owners. I felt proud of what would be our achievement, Mom's and mine.

Dad muttered something under his breath.

"What did you say, honey?" she asked.

"Nothin'."

"Come on; what did you say?"

"I said that's where old man Couri lives." Dad sounded subdued as usual, but a little more angry.

"Oh," Mom said, still wrapped up in the house, "that's nice."

Dad had stopped the car to accommodate Mom's gawking. Suddenly, he gave it the gas and the car lurched forward, away from the Tudor mansion.

"What's the matter?" she asked.

"Old man Couri is the guy who owns Bay Shore National Bank."

Mom went white. "Oh, I didn't know that." That was the bank that was threatening to foreclose on us. Jimmy made Roger Maris hit a home run and circle the imaginary bases around the backseat.

"Let's go," Jimmy urged, pounding the armrest with Roger. "Let's move this hunkajunk!"

"Jim-mee!" Mom protested his rude words but was clearly upset about other things.

"Know who lives over there?" Dad asked, pointing an accusing finger at the red brick Georgian looming ahead. "Do you, huh? Do you?"

"No," she said meekly.

"That's Jotham Eaton's house. He's the *bah-studd* sold us the truckload a cracked storm windows." That was the unsalable inventory that finally sank Dad's company. The price had seemed too good to be true. It was.

Mom sat speechless. Shattering his customary silence, he ranted on. "And there!" He pointed to the gray fieldstone manor house across the street. "That's Georgie Roth's fancy house. He's the one bought the land out from under my father's used car lot on Broad Street. Bought all the land out from under everybody. Made like he was doin' everyone a favor. Except he knew the highway would be goin' through right there and those guys from Price Cutter would want a put up a big new store. *Bah-studd* lied through his teeth to everyone. They're all *bah-studds* and four-flushers up here. That's how they got here. That's how they stay. *Bah-studds* and four-flushers. Biggest ones in town."

Mom reached across and touched Dad softly on the shoulder. "You're right, honey. I'm sorry. Let's get out of here."

51

He grunted and hit the gas. My reverie of living on Walton Street was exploding in a fireball of guilt. Guilt that confused me. The car jerked forward and Dad retreated into his fortress of silence. Mom turned around to face us in the backseat. "Your father's right, boys," she told us. "People who make that kind of money have to do terrible things to other people." I looked up at her imploringly, to try to remind her of our secret promises and the dreams she told me would come true. Nothing. She looked away for an instant, preoccupied with something beyond me. She shivered to herself, then returned her attention to my brother and me. "Rich people do terrible things. Bad things."

I kept looking up at her for some kind of recognition of the vows she had made me take. But the gaze she returned was formal and distant, like a teacher facing a classroom.

"Bad guys! Bad guys!" Jimmy shouted and pounded the seat back with Roger. Angry and frustrated at Mom, I slugged Jimmy in the ribs to shut him up and get the spotlight back on me.

But Mom went on with her lecture. "We may not have a lot, boys, but your father and I have our conscience. And our decency. No matter what happens. Just remember that. We've got something all the money in the world can't buy. A clear conscience. And *that's* the most precious thing we can pass on to you. Treasure it and keep it."

She gave a nod of the head to emphasize the period at the end of her final sentence, then turned around to face forward. Lovingly and soothingly, she began to pat the back of Dad's neck as he drove us away from Walton Street.

I looked back at the utopia she had promised me last night. I watched it disappear in the rear window. I looked to the front seat for some shred of reassurance from her. All I saw was the back of her head.

CHAPTER SIX

The first thing that a few million dollars changes is my sleep. It is troubled by visitors. Lots of visitors.

The tycoons of Bayport come to parade before me. Couri, Roth, Eaton, Baxter, and the others. The men with the big houses on Walton Street, who squeezed something even more amazing than blood out of the dull gray granite of New England—gold. They were not capitalist visionaries who expanded the horizons of prosperity. They were mean, cunning jackals who connived, cheated, chiseled, stole, and misered their fortunes out of the misfortunes of others.

"Old man Couri," I remember people saying, "he's rich." The last word always colored with a mixture of awe, jealousy, resentment, and self-righteous superiority. Yes, superiority. No mention of "the rich" would be complete without a smug reference to the special affliction that always seemed to accompany the big bank account. There was always a pox on the rich man's life that somehow evened the score for the rest of us. Sure, they'd say, old man Couri owns half of downtown and holds mortgages on the rest, but since his stomach operation all he can eat is graham crackers.

Couri appears in my dream, laughing at me, cracker crumbs and spittle dribbling from his wrinkled lips. "You, kid? You think you can be rich? No, not you, boy. You haven't got what it takes."

Georgie Roth sneers in his thick accent, "So, Meester Macallan, you tink you know from making money? You got lucky. *Vunce.* But you don't know nuttink. Nuttink."

And Ned Wiggins, who hired my father to run his factory when he knew Dad's luck was at an all-time low. Ned Wiggins, who humiliated Dad, then fired him, the way he humiliated and fired everyone who ever worked for him. He, too, comes to visit. "So you're Clint Macallan's boy. Well, the apple never falls far from the tree, does it? You won't last. You're not tough enough. You're not smart enough. No, not Clint Macallan's boy." Then he laughs that haunting bone-chilling belly laugh of sadistic delight that used to echo up and down the halls of his sooty factory. "No, not you, Macallan. Not you."

As the parade of Bayport tycoons passes, I realize that I am naked and covered with slime. A crowd of people stands around me, howling with laughter. They taunt me, sneering that I will always be a poor relation, a have-not, an undeserving second-class citizen. A chorus of old women shriek, "Bobby Macallan dared too much. Little Bobby's bit off more than he can chew. More than he can handle. Bobby thinks he can get more than he deserves. But he can't. No, he can't. No, he can't. Not little Bobby!" Then an explosion of light. It blinds me and burns me and leaves me in total darkness. I feel a man hulking over me. I cannot see him, but I know that I know him. I know his shape, I know his voice, but I cannot tell who he is. He laughs and bellows down at me, "You will lose it all. You will lose it all. I will make you lose it all. There is no safety from me. I will make you lose it all!"

I yank myself up in bed to escape the dream. I am sweaty and cold, exhausted and wide awake. I sit staring into the dark for stretches of time I cannot measure. The dream is just a dream, but it exposes a fear that is all too real. That I really am inadequate, that I am just faking it, that everything will be taken away. Not so much because of what I do, but because of what I am, who I am. Clint Macallan's son. I cannot bring myself to believe that what I have will last.

Wendy has more courage in the face of good fortune than I do. Since the deal happened, she has been bubbling over with plans. Plans for new apartments, better vacations, bigger career horizons, and babies. Plans and more plans for babies. And I find myself clutching inside every time she mentions children. *Not yet,* my gut tells me, *please, not quite yet.* I still fear in heredity an enemy, a deadly guerrilla hiding in the hills waiting to strike me down the way it struck down my father and all the Macallans of memory. The thought of losing everything is not nearly as terrifying as the thought that I might be passing my doom on to a child of mine.

"What if we conceived our baby in, say, Paris or Maui?" Wendy asked the other day. She has been conspiring with Chris, our travel agent, bringing home new brochures nearly every night. "It's gotta make a difference to the kind of person the baby becomes. I mean, one of those places would make a whole different baby than Peoria or the Bronx or Tierra del Fuego."

"Tierra del Fuego? You want to go to Tierra del Fuego to make a baby?"

"No, I just said that to get your attention. I was thinking of something more like this hotel outside Siena. Look." She stuck the folder in front of me. "It's a six-hundred-year-old former Carthusian monastery. See the arches in the courtyard. That's where they serve dinner. The swimming pool is surrounded by olive groves. *Olive* groves, Robert."

It did look like an extraordinary place. "And what if we end up not conceiving there?" I asked. "What would that mean for our baby?"

"I can't say. But look at this shot of the bedroom. Wouldn't it be a great place to try? I mean, what's the worst that can happen? Downside is we come back home and make a baby like normal people. With thermometers and calendars and me peeing in a little plastic cup in the morning to see what color I turn the vial in the chemistry set. But wouldn't it be a lot more fun to be diligent lovemakers in a place like this?"

I agree with her and smile, trying all the while to forget my feeling of dread. I can't help clutching inside whenever she mentions babies.

The first hint of dawn brings reason back into the bedroom. No, I reassure myself, I am not my father. Yet I can't help wondering just exactly how much of him is in me.

Wendy stirs in bed beside me, half-awake and trying to focus on me. She touches my arm across the pillow. "Up again?"

"I'm okay."

"Whenja wake up?"

"Not too long ago."

"You feel okay?" She is trying to act conscious without losing the thread of sleep.

"I'm fine. Go back to sleep. I'll wake you when it's time to get up." I pat her.

She drifts back into her cocoon. "Don't worry," she mumbles as her breathing deepens and slows. "I love you. And our babies."

This morning, the day before Wendy and I leave for her fabled Bangle Bay, my mind is not on the meeting taking place in front of me. Fortunately, Joe Bartolo and his financial records are the focus of the two guests who have become permanent guests since American bought the company—Tim Halas and Dudley Townsend. "Tweedledum" and "Tweedledumber" Joe calls them when they're out of earshot. A pair of officious young MBAs from Corporate Staff at American, sent to peer into every file and data base at *Elixir*. Now that American owns us, they're here to confirm that everything we said about the business is true. It's an unfriendly little exercise called the "postclosing adjustment."

Joe remains bemused throughout. He lets them know that *Elixir* has nothing to hide and that they have a lot to learn. He has even taken to singing at climactic moments in meetings. Leading them to the end of a column of figures, Joe turns on his Louis Armstrong voice and sings, "Whoa-oh-oh-oh-oh-oh and it comes out here," as he points to the bottom line. This confuses the boys to no end.

Today, Joe is patiently explaining the cash management implications of *Elixir*'s subscription monies. I'm thinking about my eleven o'clock appointment uptown at American headquarters. Harry Woodcock is back from Hong Kong and installed on the forty-eighth floor. He finally made it to corporate heaven, the sacred floor of top management, where the double-thick carpeting is bought in stadium-sized rolls to cover the extravagant stretches of empty space, where there is always silence, a handsome security guard, and a tall, leggy receptionist with a British accent. American may be a publishing company, but the corporate home of the men who run it is as far from the ink-stained chaos of *The Front Page* as Van Cleef & Arpels is from the dirt and sweat of a diamond mine. Tweedledum and Tweedledumber provide a daily reminder of the pretense that world stands for.

Harry's secretary set up the appointment late last week. She made a point of adding in her message that "Mr. Woodcock wants you to know he's delighted to welcome you back to American and hopes you can stay for lunch."

I get up from the table. "Gentlemen, please excuse me, I have another appointment to make on the forty-eighth floor." I look directly at Dudley, trying to see if I can get a reaction from the fishy blue eyes behind his round tortoiseshell glasses. I remember the thrills and awe that would have given me when I was starting out at American. I hope it impresses him as much.

Dudley is unfazed. He merely repeats his two annoying habits. He flips back the lock of straight blond hair that is forever falling over his forehead and wrinkles his nose as if he's smelling a bad odor. "Oh, yes," he says, squinting a little. "Mr. Woodcock mentioned that he'd be seeing you today. Let me give you a little tip for the dining room. Stick with red meat or chicken. They cook the fish to death."

"Yeah, Bob," Joe chortles as I make my exit, "watch out for the fish."

I have to walk down the corridor where the salespeople sit to get to my office. At this time of the morning, they should be at their phones setting up appointments. But Wayne's office is empty, as are Roni's and Mike's. As I approach Leo's open doorway, I hear them all inside having a meeting.

"I don't know what you're talking about, Leo. None of my accounts has said anything like that." That's the voice of Wayne Crosby, the handsome one with fraternity-boy good looks. He may be losing his hair, but not his touch with the girls.

"Me neither. I haven't heard a thing about any rumors," says Mike Carmody, the star sales trainee Leo raided from Becker Publications shortly after I raided Leo. "That young man reminds me of myself thirty years ago," Leo had said. I still find it hard to see much of a resemblance between the two. Mike is an uncomplicated plodder, a straightforward young man with no apparent taste for the corporate high life that is Leo's lifeblood.

"Honest, Leo, I haven't heard anything, either," I hear Roni Kessler say. She is the "princess" from the south shore of Long Island, whose obsessively perfect nails, gold jewelry, and frosted hair mislead some people into thinking that she is not a serious businessperson with remarkable native intelligence and unstoppable drive. "I know my accounts," she says, "and I'd know when they were picking up rumors about us."

"I understand," says Leo, "and I appreciate what you're saying. But you haven't been in this business for thirty years like I have." That's what Leo tells me all the time, especially when he thinks I'm wrong. "We're in a very delicate position at a very delicate moment, so far as this book is concerned. I've seen this kind of thing happen before, and if you don't take care of these rumors early, they can destroy your credibility. Believe me, it's better to put it on the table with your accounts and clear it up. Now."

"Seems alarmist to me, Leo," Crosby says, "going into an account and saying, 'Gee, in case you've heard any of these nasty rumors about *Elixir*, they're not true.'"

"Well, sure, Wayne, if you do it like that it is. But that's not how you do it. Think of it as a chance to make the client feel like you're taking him into your confidence, that you've got a special relationship. I'm not talking about being alarmist or defensive. I'm talking about being smart."

"But we're not sure that these rumors are for real. If what you heard is just an isolated—"

"Jesus, Mike, listen to me. If anything's going on out there, *I'll* be the first one to pick up on it. I've got more sources, more contacts, more goddamn years in the business. And I'm telling you there's a problem. We can beat it *and* save our year-end bonuses. But we've gotta act now."

I stick my head in the door. "Hi, guys. Problem?" They look up and greet me.

Leo retakes center stage. "Nothing I haven't seen before, Bob. Nothing we can't handle."

"Guys, can I have a word with Leo?" Wayne, Mike, and Roni adjourn to their offices. I close Leo's door and take the chair directly facing his Presidential pen caddy.

"We have a rumor problem?"

"It's nothing we can't handle. Nothing I haven't seen before."

"What exactly are you hearing out there, Leo?"

"Pretty much what I expected. Especially since the acquisition happened so quickly, with no warning. We had no chance to lay the groundwork. Everything was so hush-hush. Then boom, it's a done deal. It's what happens. People don't know the real story. They jump to the wrong conclusions. They talk to other people who don't know. Together, they jump to more of the wrong conclusions. You know how it goes. It's nothing we can't handle with a little genuine forthrightness."

"*Genuine* forthrightness?"

"Uh-huh, most of the time phony forthrightness is what this business demands. But at a time like this, we got to haul out the genuine item and level with people. I could have told you this would happen. But you never bothered to ask me."

Since the day I told him I was selling the company, Leo has surprised me. I was expecting more resentment, more backlash. I know he thinks that he is responsible for whatever success *Elixir* enjoys. But that Friday morning, his only reaction was a little twitch around the mouth. . . .

"So, you're selling to *American?*" he asked.

"That's right," I said, "American."

"Did you get them into a bidding war with someone else?"

"No. No bidding war. They were pretty much the only contender."

He took a deep breath and fondled the buttonholes on the cuff of his English suit jacket. The calculations were clearly clicking away in his head; I just couldn't tell what they were adding up to. A pause. Another breath. Then the old winning smile returned; the eyes vanished into their usual happy slits. Leo became paternal again, fond and slightly condescending. "Well, young man, you've done very well for yourself. You should be proud of what you've accomplished."

"Thanks, Leo." Quickly, I told him of his contract, his salary, bonuses, expense account, all the details of his prenegotiated privileged status. He listened carefully, weighing and measuring, weighing and measuring. It seemed to net out acceptably. We meandered out of Leo's issues back to the acquisition itself.

"Bob, you should have told me what you were up to. You should have let me in on what was happening. I could have found you other bidders, maybe even gotten you a better price. You know that I know all the players. Why, just off the top of my head," he gives a proud sweep of the hand over his Rolodex, "I'd say I could have gotten nibbles from, uh, Becker and, uh, Rainier. There are a lot of guys on the prowl." He flips through a few letters' worth of address cards. "I hear NewsCo is in the market for trade books these days. And the Mackey Group, too."

"Mackey?"

"Yeah, Mackey. You know, *Stone Age, Plastic Age*. The Cleveland operation."

"Yeah, I know." Leo's mention of Mackey was offhand and completely deadpan. It was just another of his many contacts. At least that was all he was prepared to let me sense. Then. And since. Not a sign or a signal of any kind that can let me connect Leo with Ken Atwood and his amazing ESP.

"So tell me about the rumors."

"Oh, people are saying that you sold *Elixir* because you had to, that it was about to go down the tubes. That the editorial independence we've always promised the contributors is kaput. With American now in charge and all those millions in over-the-counter drug advertising they have in their consumer books, we're going to be nothing more than a shill. The big pharmaceutical advertisers in American's books will call the shots on the papers we publish. It's crap like that. I could have told you it would happen."

It bothers me that Leo is the only one of my salespeople who seems to be hearing this stuff. I can't help thinking of Mackey and the way he blew *Gravel Weekly* out of the water with rumors. The memory of Atwood's threats is still disturbing. I must figure out a way to investigate any possible rumors myself.

"You don't think, Leo, these rumors could have a single source?"

"What do you mean, a single source?"

"A single source. Someone who would want to cause us some trouble."

"You mean like a smear campaign?"

"Yeah, like a smear campaign."

"Bob, Bob, Bob." Leo is shaking his head with affectionate exasperation, my Dutch uncle, setting me straight about the ways of the world. "This is a tough business, and it's very competitive and all that. But I don't think there's some evil genius out to get us. No need to get paranoid, Bob. I told you, this stuff is no surprise. It's natural. People love to talk about what's new. And *Elixir*'s purchase is new. They don't have the facts to go on, but they want to talk just the same. So they make it up. What people don't know they make up. After all, this is the *information business,* Bob."

"The information business?" I ask, having more unpleasant thoughts of Atwood.

"Sure. The information business. People are gonna get their information and enjoy it, even if it's wrong."

"So you recommend that our reps go out on a special campaign to explain what's really going on here."

"I recommend that *I* spearhead a special campaign, with me leading the kids on visits to the accounts. And while we're at it," Leo winks, "we write some extra orders. Just to help, uh, reconsecrate *Elixir*'s continuing commitment to excellence."

"Leo, you are incorrigible."

"That's why I'm worth at least twice what you pay me."

"Can you really put this stuff to rest once and for all?"

"Am I Mr. Sales or am I Mr. Sales?"

"Don't you think I should issue a statement? Or go along to visit the accounts? If there's a horse's mouth in this case, it's me."

"No. You're the last person who should go. That *would* look alarmist. Overkill. It'd make people think the rumors might actually be true. We want accounts to focus on the future of the book. And frankly, Bob, you represent the past." He leans forward, now more intimate. "Bob, I'm not trying to put you out to pasture prematurely or anything. But a year from now, chances are you'll be gone. Cashed out. Another millionaire on the

French Riviera surrounded by hundreds of jiggling titties on one of those topless beaches. The rest of us are still gonna be here writing orders for ad space in *Elixir*. You've got a lot of transition work to do here at the office. Leave the sales to us."

A little guy in the back of my head says I do not believe Leo completely. And a little guy in the front of my head says that he is making perfect sense and to take him at face value. The guy in front suggests that Leo may even see himself as the man to run the company when Macallan finally leaves.

As I get up from the chair, Leo says, "Listen, I'd like to meet this Harry Woodcock sometime soon. I mean, he is going to be our boss, right? Young Townsend tells me he's a helluva guy. Sooner or later, American ought to see where the leadership in this place really comes from." Leo laughs just enough to telegraph that he's kidding, but only just enough.

This unabashed display of ambition makes the guy in the front of my head feel pretty good about Leo. The guy in back still isn't so sure.

"Bob."

"Yes, Leo."

"Don't worry. I'll take care of everything. I'll make sure you get everything you've earned in this deal. Everything. I promise you."

"Thanks, Leo."

That's precisely what the little guy in back is worried about.

The leggy British receptionist on the forty-eighth floor looks up from the phone. With heartfelt condescension she gives me the bad news: "I'm terribly sorry, but Mr. Woodcock is on a call right now. To the Orient. Won't you please have a seat. I'm sure he won't be too much longer."

I peer over her desk to get a glimpse of the telephone console. Where I think I can see the labels "Woodcock 1," "Woodcock 2," and "Woodcock Sec" beside three phone lines there are no little lights glowing. I retire to the bank of couches and prepare myself for a good long wait.

Fortunately, there's an ample supply of magazines at hand: *American Week*, the news magazine and company flagship; *American Faces*, the celebrity gossip book; *American Enterprise*, the business book; *American Sports, American Woman, American Man*. These magazines, especially *American Week*, are what suckered me into this business in the first place. When I was a twelve-year-old growing up in a grim lower-middle-class household in grim, withholding Bayport, *American Week* was my secret passport to the unimaginably rich and stimulating world beyond. I inhaled it totally week after week.

It let me forget my dour, quiet father, always on the verge of financial disaster. It let me tune out my noisy, controlling mother, a woman who was angry and frustrated at her lot in life, yet who could never admit it to herself or anyone else. Through the magical magazine I could escape my relatives and schoolmates, who all seemed to feel that a trip to Boston once in a lifetime was more exposure to the outside world than one probably ever needed.

In the pages of *American Week* I found dispatches from Paris and Tokyo and Timbuktu, reviews of books that no one would ever read in Bayport, reviews of plays not just from Broadway, but from the West End. I, Clint Macallan's son, actually knew what was current on the London stage, or at least as much as *American Week* wanted me to know. To me, *American Week* was a personal message from the great, wonderful world I would someday get to know. Every page inflamed my imagination and taught me, not just facts, but attitude. *American Week* was the voice of sophistication and mastery. What's more, it was a recognizable male voice that was not my father's. Unlike my father, who let it be known that the only truly masculine behavior was stoic silence, this magazine gushed wonderful words and rich, eloquent responses. And it did it in a style so confident it could turn the grammatical rules of my schoolteachers upside down and still sound flawless. Such feats of compositional derring-do! Predicates preceding subjects, adjectives transformed into verbs, brazenly made up words that instantly communicated their new shade of meaning.

But it was not just the articles. To my adolescent sensibility, the ads were just as essential a source of information. The shark-face grille on the new Buick Riviera was as important as the Nobel Prize winners, probably even more important. To me, the airbrushed numbskull fantasies of the ads were documentary pictures of a world that actually existed. Somewhere out there were people who wore those clothes, lived in those houses, drank those drinks, possessed all the right toys and badges, and, as a result, walked around in a state of palpable, photographable bliss.

That wonderful magazine and I were the brainchildren of Andrew Elliot Henderson, the first and only bona fide publishing genius ever to inhabit the halls of this company. There behind the reception desk is Henderson's portrait, the white-haired hawk, crusty and impatient, scowling at everything that's less than "top-drawer." Henderson believed in the God-given right of Yale men to rule, not just publishing, but the world. And he left them a very influential chunk of world to rule. He named it American Publishing; later it became the vaster and more diversified enterprise called American Communications Corporation.

Imagine my astonishment when, as a sophomore on financial aid at Baldwin College, I first heard about the Henderson Internship Program. American had regular training programs for regular mortals in all its assorted departments, but the Henderson Program was something altogether different and infinitely more special. It was a fast-track inside track to success at the world's most prestigious publishing company, designed to create nothing less than Renaissance men of the magazine game. Henderson interns were rotated through every facet of the business, from the edit floor to the composing room, from the printing plants to circulation clearinghouses to ad sales. The Program was designed to provide a well-stocked pipeline of appropriately bred heirs to the Henderson legacy. However, only Yalies need apply, and only the prep school team-captain types among them, thank you. This, the Yale co-ed at the party assured me, would never change, not so long as Henderson was still alive and donating millions to old Eli.

But I would not be daunted. I made up my mind to get into the Henderson Program. Somehow.

I began writing letters to Avery Sterling, vice president of something like corporate protocol and keeper of the Henderson Program. I had a local stationery shop make up the classiest, most screamingly understated of letterheads on grayish linen stock. I made friends with a secretary in the Admissions Office who let me use the IBM typewriter on her lunch hours. I wrote letters about my admiration for American and Mr. Henderson, letters about articles in *American Week,* letters about the future of publishing, letters about my accomplishments on the Baldwin paper, even letters comparing Baldwin to Yale, postulating that provincial Baldwin was actually more like the Yale Mr. Henderson loved and remembered than the Yale of today because it had escaped the liberalism that had tainted the Ivy League mainstream. "Dear Mr. Sterling: Just a note to let you know that . . ." Once every six weeks, like clockwork.

I invented a character in those letters I thought worthy of American and the Henderson Program. He was active, confident, eager (but not too), poised, charming, worldly, and ever so well bred. He was a far, far cry from the anxious, uncertain striver I really was, the boy-man who covered his insecurities and ignorance with glibness and supercilious wit he hoped would pass for sophistication. But the more letters I wrote, the more real the character seemed to become. This fellow was more than the "airs" my mystified family had always accused me of putting on. Or so I hoped.

I waged a postal war of attrition from the middle of sophomore year onward. Letter after letter. Mr. Sterling's office would occasionally send me cold, polite responses, but nothing to give me hope that I might be considered for the Program. Finally, in the spring of my senior year, I took a bus to New Haven to try to meet Sterling during the annual interview marathon for Henderson candidates. Grudgingly, he consented to see me. I put on the truly authentic rep tie I had just purchased at J. Press. (The ties from the Campus Clothier at Baldwin seemed feeble imitations by comparison.) I did my best to live up to the character I had invented in my letters. Sterling was exquisitely courteous in the session but gave nothing away. For the next two weeks I held my breath. The purpose and validity of my entire life was suspended in the air, hanging by a single thread. Then, the letter arrived. "Dear Mr. Macallan: In what I must admit is a departure from tradition, I would like to congratulate you . . ."

Fifteen minutes pass with Woodcock tied up on what is likely a nonexistent phone call. I make a bet with myself that Harry will keep me cooling my heels for a full half hour. Then a matronly woman of the Barbara Bush school appears in the reception area.

"Mr. Macallan? Mr. Woodcock can see you now." She is as much vintage American Communications as Legs the Receptionist. The forty-eighth-floor greeters always remind you of James Bond bimbos. The forty-

61

eighth-floor secretaries always remind you of elderly den mothers from Greenwich, Connecticut.

"Hello, Mr. Macallan." She gives me her hand. "I'm Miss Boardman. Sorry about the wait. Hong Kong called all in a panic." She smiles and looks me right in the eye without flinching. "Things have been very hectic, frantic really, since he arrived. I'm afraid it's going to take a while to get Mr. Woodcock properly organized."

"No problem." I smile.

We arrive at the door to Harry's office. I can hear him talking. I look at the phone on Miss Boardman's desk. This time, the "Woodcock 2" line is definitely lit up. The call to the Far East was a lie.

"Please. Go right in," she says.

The office is grander than anything Harry ever had when I knew him. Enormous desk, two vast leather couches, real Barcelona chairs, a large Chinese screen, and wraparound view of Manhattan's mighty corporate aeries. The effect is diminished only by the stack of mover's boxes in the corner, still unpacked. Harry stands at his desk, riveted to his telephone. It must be someone important.

"Uh-huh. I agree. . . . Yes. That's right. . . . Yes, I couldn't agree more. . . . I agree; you're absolutely right." Now I *know* it's someone important, someone important and above him in the corporation. This is the Harry I remember. "Uh-huh. You bet. I absolutely agree. I've always felt that way, too. Always. . . . Right. . . . Of course. . . . Sure. I agree; you're absolutely right. Bye."

He hangs up, looks me over, and smiles warmly. "Bob Macallan. We-e-e-ell, Bob Macallan." His tone is pure admiration, a father at commencement exercises. "Welcome back, Bob." The handshake is firm, the pat on the shoulder very fond. "I'm delighted to see you, just delighted. Come; let's sit down." He steers us to the Barcelona chairs in the conversation area.

"Bob, I want you to know that I'm very proud of you. What you've accomplished is great, fantastic. And we're lucky to have you back. Very lucky indeed. I always knew there were great things in store for you."

"Thanks, Harry, you look great." I'm not just making chatter. Harry does look marvelous. Central Casting could not send over a more distinguished gray-haired, Yale-by-way-of-Exeter corporate executive.

"Well, Bob, it's been a long time." Uncomfortable pause. "I guess we've, uh, all grown and changed. I know I certainly have. I, uh . . ." Another awkward pause and the smile vanishes. Harry peers solemnly into my eyes. "Bob, I'd like to start by clearing the air." He leans forward, puts a hand on my knee. "What happened when you left American is history. Ancient history. I want to put it behind us. I was wrong about you. Dead wrong. I want you to know that I know it. It was one of the biggest mistakes of my career. Believe me; I knew it the minute you walked out the door. I realized when I, uh, I mean, it didn't surprise me in the least when you, uh." He cuts off his stumbling and takes a deep breath; he's swallowing something big. "Bob, what I'm trying to get at is, I'm sorry. I'd like to apologize for what happened five years ago. You were right and I was wrong. That's the long and short of it. You proved it. In spades. I just hope there are no hard feelings. I want us to be able to work together, not just as colleagues, but as friends. Please, Bob, accept my apology."

His glance is unwavering, his tone deadly earnest. He offers a handshake. "Fresh start?"

"Sure, Harry. Fresh start." I almost believe him.

"Wonderful. Let's go to work." He leaps up from the Barcelona chair and returns to his seat of power. I take the Visitor's Chair opposite the Big Executive's Desk. "I've got the *Elixir* file right here," he says, producing a thick dossier.

We go over the basic financials, the structure of the company, the key employees, the major advertisers, editorial plans. The talk is impersonal, strictly business. But when we get to the earnings targets over the coming year, Harry breaks form. He looks up from the paper with a big smile.

"And, if you make your earnings, on or about January thirtieth next year, you get, give or take a bit, another check for five million."

"On or about, give or take."

"That's a pretty good haul, young man."

"I'm not complaining."

"Ten million dollars." He rolls the figure around in his mouth and stares out the window. "For a book we thought had no potential. A person could argue," he says to the air, "that I brought this deal about. That I'm the one who made it happen. Go-betweens get a percentage of the deal all the time, for doing a lot less than I did. When I sent you packing, I was just trying to do the right thing. I've devoted my life to this company and what it stands for. The idea of the big payoff never entered my mind." He turns his gaze from the window and examines me quizzically, as if I were an exotic zoo animal. "But I guess that's what drives you guys. The big cash-in. Or do you guys call it 'the big cash-*out*'? That's what makes you guys tick, isn't it?"

"Us guys?"

"You entrepreneurs."

"Harry, when I started *Elixir* I had no idea or intention—"

He isn't listening. "I never even thought of starting a company. Guess my ego isn't oversized enough. American has provided me with all the excitement I've ever craved. I've spent my life trying to do what's best for this company. Whatever this company needs me to do . . ." His voice trails off as he stares out the window again. A moment of silence, then he snaps back to attention. "It's American's future that counts now. And thanks to new blood like Ted Levine, we're recognizing that we can learn from people like you." He looks directly into my eyes again. "Macallan, there's a lot we want you to teach us."

"Teach you?"

"Absolutely. About this entrepreneurial spirit. You know, we got burned pretty badly on that fitness book we were working on when you left. It was a bit of an embarrassment."

That's a mild way to put it. The biggest publishing farce of the century is more like it. American's first new magazine since Henderson's death, *American Fitness*. Between $35 million and $50 million poured down the drain in less than four months. In a magazine that no one ever wanted or cared about. No one except Dillon Edwards, the current chairman, and Walt Drummond, the current vice chairman, the two men Harry has followed up the corporate ladder, licking their heels like a loyal puppy dog.

"I guess we read the tea leaves wrong. We had so much momentum behind *American Fitness,* we completely overlooked the message you were trying to give us about the medical market. Maybe if we'd had more appreciation for your renegade spirit things might have gone differently. Now don't get me wrong. I'm not going over the past with regrets and shouldas."

Of course not. Everyone connected with the launch of *American Fitness* has since been promoted: Dillon, Walt, Harry, and all their loyal staff people. Everyone except the dozens of writers, designers, salespeople, and other workaday types who had the misfortune to pull that assignment. They were fired in the cost slashing that followed the decision to admit defeat.

"Bob, you've got something this company needs. And I don't just mean *Elixir.* I mean the entrepreneurial spirit. We need you to share it with us, to teach us how to get it, how to nourish it, how to make it work for American."

"Sure, Harry, whatever I can do." I want my money. Then I want out.

"That's what I knew you'd say. Good man." He fishes a fat binder out of his top drawer and passes it to me. "This is the training plan for the magazine group. It's a great program that Drummond's staff people have put together for rejuvenating the spirit of the group. We need you to be a part of it. An important part. We need you to pass on some of that entrepreneurship to our managers. Ted Levine is out there acquiring it for us. And I'm in charge of making it grow back here at home. I need your help, Bob. I need you to think of this program as your program."

I flip through the document. It is packed with schedules and course descriptions: Managing Change, Defying the Corporate System, The Entrepreneur versus the Intrapreneur. It is a compendium of all the rallying cries to which companies have been giving lip service ever since the publication of *In Search of Excellence*.

"This stuff looks great, Harry. But I don't know what it has to do with me or *Elixir.*"

"It has everything to do with you and *Elixir.* Your spirit, your success. American hasn't just bought your company; we've bought you. And we want to make the most of you while we've got you. Before you take your millions and go off to build your next empire."

"Harry, this training schedule looks like a full-time job. I've got a business to run."

"We do, too, Bob. We all do. It's going to be a busy year for all of us. But this is American's future we're talking about. And you are a key player in it."

He's got me by the earn-out; there's not much that's worth saying right now. I can always be too busy later.

"So we can count on you?"

"Sure, Harry. If only for old time's sake."

"Splendid. Now in the spirit of American changing to integrate with you, we need to ask you to make a few changes to integrate with American." He reaches for another document, a two-pager. Whatever it is, this part is carefully thought out and scripted. "To begin with, you really ought to have a liaison person at *Elixir,* someone to manage the relationship with corporate. I think Townsend is the perfect guy for the job."

"Townsend?" That's Tweedledumber. Insufferable stuck-up little snot-nose number two.

"Absolutely. Townsend. He's a little young, but he's smart as a whip. Top of his class at Wharton. Published a brilliant article on the theory of global magazine expansion—that's why we hired him—*and* he's already fully briefed on *Elixir's* inner workings. I'd like you to put him on staff starting immediately. He's a little expensive. His base is one hundred thousand, but he'll earn it, believe me."

Oh shit. Tweedledumber. In my face and on my budget for the next year.

"Now, as a company of American's, *Elixir* needs to get in line with corporate policies and procedures. For instance, we have a corporate purchasing department. We need you to work through them now. They can help you with everything: insurance, paper clips, typewriters, messenger services, you name it. It's pointless for you to duplicate what's already being done. Making the crossover is one job that Townsend can take off your hands."

Sure. And watch my overhead costs go through the ceiling. The way American shops it makes the Pentagon guys who buy five-hundred-dollar toilet seats look like bargain hunters. Low overhead has been *Elixir's* life-blood. A move like this could cost me a lot more than Townsend's inflated salary.

"What's more," Harry continues, "that space you occupy downtown is fine for a start-up operation, but it just won't do for a company in the American family. I've already put Townsend to work to find you more appropriate office space. I've heard there's a chunk of the fifth floor right here that might be open soon, but in any case, there's bound to be a more fitting address for *Elixir* somewhere near here in midtown."

"Harry," I say, trying to interrupt as politely as possible. "Harry, hold on just a minute. I'm afraid that's just not in the cards. When I negotiated this deal, we all agreed that *Elixir* would stay completely independent of corporate. Completely independent."

"You did?"

"We did."

"That's funny; I've gone over the contract of sale here, and I don't see anything like that stipulated anywhere." Harry gives me a look of pure innocence. What on earth could I be talking about?

"It's what Ted and I agreed to," I say, hearing my voice get a little strident. "We negotiated it in good faith. Levine has this mission to build, to create this entrepreneurial laboratory. That was the whole purpose of acquiring a book like *Elixir*. To let it function outside the corporate environment."

Harry gives me a broad smile. "Well, Bob, I've discussed these plans all the way up the line. With Walt Drummond and Dillon Edwards." He pauses to let that sink in. Then he smiles again, a sly dagger of a smile. "Ted's been out of town a lot lately, but I can't imagine that—"

"That was my good faith agreement, Harry! Good faith! No, it's not in the contract. But, Jesus, when you sit down with the most respected media company in America and they offer you a deal in good faith, then, Jesus Christ." I'm blowing my cool. I've got to calm down and think. I pause. "Harry, what I'm talking about is—"

"This *is* good faith, Bob," Harry cuts in. He is completely unruffled, still the happiest, friendliest man on earth. "Very good faith. It's good faith in what's best for this great company, American Communications."

I lose my cool again. "But Ted Levine negotiated for American and he promised me—"

Harry tries to be patient with me the way you are patient with a petulant, unreasonable child. "Ted Levine is still very new here. You know that. He's got a lot of interesting ideas, but he's also got to learn how we operate. Drummond and Dillon and I have discussed it at length. It's going to be a give-and-take process. It'll take a little while. In the meantime, you're like an old member of our American family, so the transition for you . . ."

Harry drones on, but I stop listening. I'm thinking about the end run Harry did around Levine by going to the chairman and the vice chairman. I'm trying to calculate the damage Harry can do to my bottom line and, as a result, to my earn-out. Harry's intention is clear. He wants to kill me with corporate politics, smiling and pretending to do the right thing all the while. He hasn't changed a bit, only gotten more powerful and more dangerous. He wants to finish the job he thought he finished five years ago.

I'm looking at gracious, ingratiating Harry talking at me. And I see my earnings goal recede further and further out of reach. I'm thinking about where I'll raise the revenues to pay for the changes Harry is dictating. About where I'll find the time to work on Harry's bullshit seminars. I'm thinking about Mackey's new medical book, Atwood's threats, Leo's rumors, Harry's man planted in my office.

"Bob, I want to welcome you back to American." Harry is winding up.

I can barely hear him over the noise in my brain. "Now how about I buy some lunch for the prodigal son." He couldn't be more cordial, more genial.

As we get up to leave, an image flashes before me. From my dream. The explosion of light, then blackness. The looming figure. The voice I know but cannot recognize: "There is no safety from me. I will make you lose it all. I will make you lose it all."

CHAPTER SEVEN

"Aaaa-choooo! Ah-ah-ah-chooo!"

Fortunately, Wendy has a box of Kleenex on her lap, courtesy of the stewardess.

"I can't fly when I have a *code,*" she says, blowing into her Kleenex. The cabin pressure suddenly changes as we begin our descent into San Juan. "Ayeee! My ears!" she cries and cups her face in her hands, chewing even more emphatically on the sugarless gum the sympathetic stewardess also provided.

"Bradford gave this to me," Wendy says in a half-whisper, trying to fight the pain. "The bastard. He breathed all over me, coughed right in my face. 'Come sit here,' he said, 'my favorite consultant. Right at my side.'" She sniffs. "Some privilege. The contagious bastard."

I rub her back gently in a vain effort to ease her discomfort.

"Clients," I mutter, trying to sound sympathetic. She really is a mess. Her cold came on overnight and was raging by the time we got to the airport early this morning. "They make it possible to take a vacation like this, then make it impossible to enjoy."

"That supposed to be some kinda philosophy or something?" she snaps back through the Kleenex.

"Hey, come on. I'm on your side."

"I'm sorry." She blows her nose.

"We'll get you some more O.J. when we land and some hot tea. You'll be better in a couple of days."

"You really think so?" She sounds pathetic. Tragic.

"Guaranteed."

"I had such big plans for this vacation."

"Don't worry. It'll be great." I hope my tone of confidence convinces her; it is not convincing me.

At the San Juan airport, we leave the big jet and the package deal vacationers with their overflowing plastic suitcases and legible T-shirts. We go from the cool modern terminal to the old terminal, where it is steamy and open to the tropical air. Here the small planes depart for the more exclusive secondary islands. Gone are the "I'm with Stupid" and "I lost mine in

67

Minneapolis" jerseys in the waiting areas. In their place are sleek women in linen travel dresses and men in preppy madras shorts or, occasionally, khaki slacks and tropicweight blue blazers.

Our twenty-passenger prop plane shakes and sputters and roars deafeningly all the way to Virgin Gorda. It makes a harrowing, miraculous landing onto a tiny airstrip carved from a barren cliffside overhanging the ocean. Wendy is too preoccupied with coughs and sneezes and daggers in her ears to notice much of anything.

The airport is a small cinderblock structure with a corrugated tin roof, more like a well-ventilated equipment shed than a terminal. After a brief ritual with the one-man customs bureau, I spot a jitney driver holding a clipboard and a sign with the names "Macallan" and "Cope."

"Hi there," I say, leaving Wendy a few steps behind with our bags. "Mr. and Mrs. Robert Macallan. You're here to take us to Bangle Bay?"

"Yes." He nods a little solemnly and checks his clipboard. "I've got one other couple coming along. You can go sit in the bus, please. I'll bring your bags over." He motions to the little Japanese pickup truck with back end outfitted with bench seats and a canopy. We climb in and wait.

The early afternoon sun is blazing brilliant; the air is heavy and dry except for an occasional light breeze off the water. The arrival of our flight has created a flutter of activity among the drivers and airport personnel. But the buzzing, milling about, checking of papers, carrying, and loading seem to be happening in slow motion. This is the Caribbean, I start to remember, and I feel myself relaxing a little. The second couple hops in the back of the jitney and takes the bench facing us. I did not notice them on the plane.

"Hi," she says with a tentative smile. "I'm Arlene Cope. This is my husband, Sid." Sid nods.

"Bob Macallan and Wendy Wolfson," I reply with a nontentative smile. Wendy smiles politely from behind a fistful of Kleenex.

Arlene and Sid are in their late fifties, healthy, trim, overgroomed, and overdressed—she in a beige pantsuit outfit, he in powder blue trousers and white textured shirt with an obnoxious pattern. They sport lots of gold jewelry and expensive Italian street shoes. "This is our first time on this island," Arlene says as the driver finishes loading the bags. "We heard about it from friends over on St. Thomas. That's where we go every year. I like to shop; Sid likes to gamble." The driver starts up the engine, and we lurch ahead, making our way out of the airport.

"Where you from?" I ask.

"Cleveland," Arlene says. "Shaker Heights." I wonder whether I should ask Sid about a certain publisher from their neck of the woods. He seems uninterested in talking, instead studying his exceptionally gold watch, star sapphire pinkie ring, and the gold buckles on his loafers. "And you?" Arlene asks.

"New York City."

"Oh, really. My sister Ciel lives in Freeport. On Long Island." I nod with the recognition that Freeport exists, is indeed in New York, and that there's a very remote chance I might even have run into her sister Ciel. "This your first time here?" she asks.

"Uh-huh."

"Ours, too."

Suddenly, the jitney is climbing almost ninety degrees uphill, going around an utterly blind curve. The gears are mashing and straining; the driver sounds his horn a few times in warning. As we struggle up the side of the barren mountain, a panorama of blue-green Caribbean and parched rocky island unfolds beneath us. At the top of the incline, we look across at more dry, rocky peaks yet to come and resorts below at the shorelines. The jitney starts heading downhill, again at almost ninety degrees. The gears burn and grind, this time with the effort to slow down the force of gravity.

The changing vistas and the racket of the little truck create welcome interruptions in the flow of conversation with Arlene, but eventually we get back to their decision to vacation on Virgin Gorda. "Some friends of ours bought one of the condos at the resort. And I tell you they just rave about the place, rave. They say they've got the two restaurants there, the marina, two clothing shops, and the cutest little English pub with a big-screen TV, all right there at the foot of the condos."

Wendy and I exchange looks of confusion.

"Really?" I say as the jitney grinds its way up another cliffside. "I didn't realize the facilities were so complete."

"Absolutely," Arlene assures me, talking over the transmission noise. "Captain Bob's Landing has everything. That's what our friends say. If we like it, we're thinking we might buy one of those condos ourselves. It's just a quick flight over to St. Thomas whenever Sid wants to gamble or I want to shop. Right, Sid?" Sid grunts something indecipherable. "Did you sign up for the hillside condos or the main building?"

Wendy blows her nose.

"We're not at Captain Bob's," I say, trying to hide my relief. "We're at Bangle Bay." Suddenly I feel grateful that Wendy reads *Vanity Fair*.

"Oh," Arlene says, a little put off. "That's the place next door. We heard about Bangle Bay."

"Nothin' to do there," Sid finally chimes in, his gold ID bracelet glinting in the sun. "And way overpriced." All right, Sid baby, maybe I will pose my question, after all. We start up another hill; the transmission racket goes up several decibels.

"Tell me, Sid," I shout, "you know a Cleveland company called EMC?"

"AMC? Manufacturers, aren't they?" he shouts back, cupping his ear. "Athletic equipment and stuff like that?"

"No, no. *Eee*-em-cee," I articulate over the noise, "Elton Mackey Corporation."

Sid sits back on the bench and cracks a smile of recognition. "Sure, what about 'em?" The truck levels off, the gear noise subsides.

"You know Mackey himself, the head guy?"

"Not personally."

"You know *of* him?"

"Doesn't everybody?" He grins again and reaches his hand into the air. He grabs an imaginary something in his fist, squeezes it, and twists it with a look of sadistic pleasure. "That's Mackey," he says as he drops his hand and winks at me. I get the message. Those were a man's balls he grabbed, squeezed, twisted, and tore off.

"Thanks," I say and let our conversation evaporate as we descend through a scruffy village of cinderblock houses painted brilliant pastel colors. Children and goats wander between the houses. Mothers hang out laundry; a group of teenage boys tinkers with a broken-down pickup truck. The driver waves; the villagers wave back. At the bottom of the hill, the road ends at a dock, where two boats and a group of local men are waiting. There's a sleek fiberglass Chris-Craft cabin cruiser of chocolate brown, with smoked glass windows and tufted vinyl upholstery. Beside it is an old but well-kept wooden launch, clean and freshly painted white, shaped like the lobster boats I knew from childhood but longer, outfitted with long benches and a canvas roof.

Sid and Arlene are ushered into Captain Bob's cabin cruiser. We wish each other a happy vacation. As their brown bomber roars away from the dock, Wendy and I are escorted into the white launch. With a much more modest clink-clink-putt-putt, our boat starts up and takes us out past the finger of land where the bay unfolds. The bay is a circle enclosed on three sides like a lake, perhaps two, maybe three miles at its widest point. Mountains descend along the far right shore to a peninsula that is all forest and scrub, with no signs of man. Our boat heads in that direction. After a few minutes, we can see at the foot of the mountains, on a smaller hill, the tower of a gray stone sugar mill. It has been expanded into a sort of castle. Terraces landscaped with flowers and shrubs descend from the castle to the dock, where an impressive collection of yachts, sail and motor, sits rocking in the sun.

"That's Bangle Bay!" the pilot shouts at us from the wheel.

No other structures are visible. Just tropical forest running uninterrupted along the peninsula, forming the outer edge of the bay. Then, on the last hillside, the virgin forest stops just before the land's end, where the bay opens onto Sir Francis Drake Channel. There sits the condo complex, cabins on stilts overlooking the water and the busy beachside village.

The pilot sees us looking in that direction. "That's Captain Bob's Landing!" he shouts. "You can always go over there, if you want to! Though most guests don't!" Satisfied that we are oriented, he returns his attention to the wheel.

Wendy blows her nose loudly and pokes her head out from under the canopy. She gazes up at the sun. "Macallan," she says through a sniffle, "I think I've got an idea."

★ ★ ★

70

Bangle Bay truly is another world. They call the guest quarters cottages. Transplanted to the Beverly Hills Hotel they would be called bungalows. Big bungalows. Spaced far apart, they all command ocean views, although some are closer to the beach than others. They are not merely uncottage-like; they are gracious houses of stucco and stone and terra-cotta tile with easily a thousand square feet of living space, including shaded terraces, discreetly walled-in outdoor showers open to the stars, step-down living rooms, and cathedral ceilings lined in rattan. The wicker and canvas furniture is big, generous, and comfortable, very simple and very expensive.

The assistant manager, an obsequious fiftyish Brit with sunken, boozy eyes, gave us the whole Bangle Bay drill as he was registering us. There are no phones in the rooms. Instead, beside each cottage is a flagpole about fifteen feet high. They tell you to run up the blue flag when you want room service, the yellow flag when you want the chambermaid, the red flag if you should have an emergency, the white flag when you want to be left utterly alone. The staff gets around on bicycles and in golf carts. Meals are served in the dining room at the top of the castle, on the terrace overlooking the bay and the yachts. The bar is on the opposite side of the castle, overlooking the Caribbean lagoon where the beach and the pool are, and beyond, on the far side of the peninsula, the open Atlantic. The surrounding three hundred acres of untouched forest and shoreline protect the property from even the slightest hint that the outside world still exists.

"See what I mean?" Wendy says after the bellman, a handsome black man with proud, noble posture, leaves us. She spins around on one foot and collapses into the overstuffed canvas sofa. "This is Bangle Bay." She rests for a minute in an odalisque sprawl. "And I have the cold of the century." A wet sneeze brings her to her feet again. "Dammit, I'm going to do something about this," she says and dashes over to our suitcases to fish out a bathing suit. "I'm going to bake it out of my system."

I go back to the manager's office in the lower level of the castle to try to raise Ted Levine in New York. Making the connection is no hassle. Finding Levine is. He's in meetings. No, they don't know where he is. Yes, they do know where he is, but he won't be back until tomorrow. Finally, I give up and put his secretary on notice that I expect him to be at his desk awaiting my call tomorrow morning at ten o'clock sharp. I am just as unlucky with my call to *Elixir*. Leo is out, it seems, with almost the entire staff. It must be one of his famous morale-building lunches, where he treats everyone to a senselessly expensive lunch, with himself at the head of the table. The climax of the show comes when Leo asks for the check and makes a big ceremony of signing it, all to a chorus of "Thank you, Leo" from the grateful table. I tell Marie to tell Leo that I will expect a full report on the status of sales calls tomorrow morning.

"So where did Leo take them?" I ask.

"Taos."

I wince. Taos is the hottest, priciest new restaurant in midtown. Leo had to have made those reservations at least a month ago. "Thanks for holding down the fort, Marie."

"It's all right, Bob. I don't like roast chili peppers, anyway. And somebody sane has got to be here when you're out. God knows what it'll be like when you're gone."

"I told you; that's not necessarily going to happen." I am not lying, I tell myself. I might stay on after my year. It is possible. In the meantime, I cannot afford to let them see me as a lame duck.

"Uh-huh," she says skeptically, "whatever you say. Tell me, how is Bangle Bay?"

"Oh, it's gorgeous. Just gorgeous."

"Would you say it's lush and luxurious?"

"Definitely."

"Would you say it's perhaps the last refuge of the rich and famous to have escaped the vulgarity and excess that has sadly polluted the rest of the world's exclusive hideaways, from Cap Ferrat to Papeete?"

"I guess so." Very puzzled, I ask, "What are you talking about?"

"That's what they say in this write-up in *Vanity Fair.*" I make a mental note to glance at the next issue Wendy gets. "So are you going to give me a complete description of everything when you get back?"

"You bet."

"Everything?"

"Everything. I promise."

"Then why are you sitting at a desk indoors talking on the phone? Go out and enjoy yourself. For both of us, you hear."

"Yes, ma'am."

Our first night at Bangle Bay is a disaster. We miss the elegant dinner in the castle; we miss the dancing under the stars. We stay in our cottage rubbing salves and ointments all over Wendy. She tried to bake the cold out of her system and gave herself a painful sunburn. Less than an hour in the Caribbean sun was all it took. Now she suffers on the outside as well as on the inside. I barely sleep. Wendy does not sleep at all. The creamy soft Porthault sheets are like scorching sandpaper to her; the gentle rustle of ocean breezes in the palms merely torments her; the salty perfume of the air is lost on her.

Finally morning comes and Wendy can begin to stand the touch of expensive linen against her skin. "This is too much, Robert," she sniffles then sneezes, "aachoo!" She reaches for the box of Kleenex on the night table. As she extends her arm, she winces in pain. "Ugh, I can't breathe, I can't sit, I can't lay down. I can't go outside. This is the perfect vacation. Just perfect. We can't even make love."

"Yes we can."

"Not unless we can do it without touching."

"I mean in a day or so."

"Listen, why don't you just go out by yourself today. I'll stay in the cottage. I've got ointment, Kleenex, antihistamines, a big pitcher of mango-orange juice, three books, and a view of the ocean." She sniffles with irony and a little self-pity, "What more could a girl ask for? Go on; get outta here. Go enjoy." She looks so sad, so defeated.

I turn to put on my nylon windbreaker over my black boxer bathing suit. There's no need for a shirt underneath. "I'll come back just before lunch," I say as apologetically and sympathetically as I can.

Her lower lip juts out with disappointment. "I don't think we should try to make a baby here, Robert."

"Why not, sweetie? You'll be fine by tomorrow, I'm sure."

"No, no. I've been thinking about it all night. I've decided it's just not auspicious."

"We can still do it," I offer consolingly, but she is not listening.

"I wanted us to make a baby *here,* where everything is so beautiful."

"We can still do it here, honey. Don't feel so sad."

"No, the signs just aren't right." She shakes her head and smiles, making a supreme effort to overcome the forces conspiring against her. "I'm sorry to be so heavy. I'll get over it. I'll be better soon. Really I will. Damn sunburn, damn cold. Now you go have fun this morning. We'll wait. We'll start trying to make a baby next month."

"You bet," I say, blowing her a kiss. As I leave, knowing that baby making is delayed into the future, I find myself breathing an enormous sigh of relief. No baby. Not now, please. I'm not ready. Not yet. Not yet.

Because the eastern Caribbean is one hour ahead of New York, I have some time to kill before my phone appointments. I walk uphill from our cottage through the shady woods toward the castle. Once out from under the trees, I see a world drenched in morning sun of pure lemon yellow. The sky is cloudless; the air is clear and coolish thanks to a breeze off the Atlantic.

The pool sits a few spectacularly landscaped levels down from the castle, overlooking the white crescent beach and the perfectly still lagoon. Wendy was right about the facilities being underutilized. Along the beach there are a dozen of the hotel's padded reclining chairs outfitted with sun tents that fold up and down like the hoods of gargantuan baby carriages. Only two are in use. It seems wherever you go at Bangle Bay, employees outnumber the guests. Perhaps twenty of the hooded recliners are set up around the pool. Three are occupied. Yet I count the towel man at his stand, the bartender polishing glasses under his canopy beside a busboy with a load of crushed ice, two maintenance men making the final morning checks on the pool's chemistry, another maintenance man mopping the deck surface of hand-painted Portuguese tiles, and two maids wiping off the cushions of empty chairs.

I get a couple of towels, slip out of my sneakers and windbreaker, and jump in. I start swimming laps. Not disciplined competitive laps, just back and forth. On my stomach with slow, arching, overhand strokes and quick flutter kicks. On my back with slow-motion arm pulls and frog kicks. Back and forth, back and forth. The water caresses me, soothes me, smooths me. Back and forth, back and forth. After a while, I become the water, the water becomes me, a fluid within a fluid glowing radiant in the morning sun. Back and forth, back and forth. This is the feeling of sensuous relaxation I discovered in myself in the Caribbean. It was born in the air, released in the water. What a shock to my Puritan selves. Robert Macallan of Bayport was never brought up to know a feeling like this. And Robert Macallan of New York never has the opportunity.

On my back now, swimming with eyes closed, I feel a force at once inside me dragging against the flow. My eyes open slightly to recapture my sense of body. Then I see where it comes from. A black shark fin cutting through the water, holding my bathing suit up. An erection. I thrash awkwardly. My legs sink beneath me.

Time to call New York.

"Ted," I say into the phone, "this is bullshit. Pure bullshit!"

I must be shouting. The effeminate Anglo desk clerk shoots me a look that says "tch, tch" and turns his back on me. He is pretending to file some papers so that I can embarrass myself in semiprivacy. I lower my voice to a half-whisper, even though I know he has seen much worse in this office. "This is bullshit, Ted. What about our agreement? What about the promises you made to me? Remember, your word? As a gentleman. As a representative of your goddamn corporation. I'm supposed to be independent. In-*dee*-pendent. That's what you said the whole point of this acquisition is. I've got lawyers, too, you know. You gave me your word."

"Bob, Bob, take it easy. Please." Levine uses the same soothing tone he used when Conover got into his haughty snit at the price negotiation. The difference is that Conover was merely posing; I am sincerely pissed off. "Bob," he says, his voice absolutely unruffled, "we *do* want you to be independent. And you will be independent. I mean you are independent."

I realize that I am at a fatal disadvantage trying to have this conversation over the phone. I cannot see his face; he is not forced to deal with my angry presence or my outrage. "Believe me, Bob, Harry has only the best interests of the company at heart. He just wants the chance to get his arms around his new job."

Yeah, I decide not to say, and his hands around my throat.

"*Walt* moved Harry into place for very strategic reasons," Levine explains, with the emphasis on the "Walt." Okay, I get the message. Harry is wired into the vice chairman. "It's true," Levine goes on, singing the official lies like a veteran flak chorus boy. "We're looking to change the culture of American. We really are. But intelligently. And with continuity. Walt trusts Harry to hold onto what's best about American just as he trusts me to bring in the right kind of new influences. Nobody's looking to squelch that spirit of yours. It's one of the things we acquired when we bought your book. So hold on to it, use it. Just temper it enough to play for the team. These are Harry's calls to make, and I'm in no position to second-guess him. Walt wouldn't stand for it." He adds, "Or Dillon, for that matter."

Okay, the chairman, too. "Nobody understands this company like Harry. Believe me, Bob; he's a resource we can all rely on."

I get the picture. Levine, the courageous, irreverent champion of the entrepreneurial spirit, is telling me—in corporatespeak—that Harry Woodcock is wired in directly to the top and that he, Levine, has his hands full covering his own ass. Welcome back to the big corporation, Macallan. All you've got to do is find a way to navigate through eleven more months of this horseshit. Then you can get your money and you're home free.

"Bob, I hate to cut you off, but I've got to run to a meeting. Have I given you the help you need?"

"Yeah, Ted. Thanks."

"Hey! Enjoy that vacation of yours. I wish I could get away like you." I'll bet you do, Levine. I'll bet you do.

I put the phone down quietly. I think I see the Brit smirk as he turns for an instant in my direction. I dial my office; he goes back to his filing. Marie is ready with a message from Leo.

"Leo says to tell you that everything is under control, that he and Wayne and Roni and Bruce are out squelching the rumors and writing more new orders than ever before."

"Well, where is he this morning?" I ask, trying not to sound peeved at Marie. "Didn't he understand that I wanted to talk to him?"

"Yes, Bob, I made that clear to him."

"So where is he?"

"He said to tell you that he's at a Publishers Council conference at the Hilton. There's a speech on magazines of the future. He says he knows you'd want him and the other salespeople to be there to hear the speaker and meet him."

"Okay, who's giving the talk?"

"Harry Woodcock."

"Thanks, Marie. Bye."

I slam the phone down. This time the Brit smirks openly.

I leave the office in the basement of the castle and stomp over to the empty bar at poolside. It is close enough to lunchtime, I tell myself, so I order a piña colada with Bacardi Black and sit down to kill some time.

Suddenly I hear a woman beside me. "So," she says, "you interrupted a beautiful swim to call the office. What a totally unrewarding thing to do."

"Huh?" I look up as she takes the stool beside me. She is as tall as me, thirtyish and American, hidden under a big straw sun hat, white cotton beach robe, and sunglasses.

"I'll have the same," she says to the bartender, pointing at my glass. She pulls off the hat and shakes loose tresses of shoulder-length hair the color of honey.

"There you were," she says, "swimming along happily. Letting your mind drift and your body relax in what is no doubt one of the most beautifully situated pools on earth. Then you thought about the office, got anxious, and went to the phone—destroying the whole moment." She removes the shades. "For both of us, I might add." She is not just tall and blond. She is also beautiful. Not bland-beautiful like fashion models and TV game show hostesses, but striking and handsome in a very individual way.

She has large ice blue eyes framed by thick, dramatic eyebrows. She wears no makeup and needs none. Her forehead and cheekbones are high and aristocratic. Her nose is longish and narrow, with a bump in the middle that makes it a bit crooked. Her mouth is sensuous and soft, with full lips that accentuate her angular jawline and pointed chin. "I could see you getting upset," she says. "Your stroke went to hell in the last two laps. I was sitting over there." She points to one of the deck chairs at the far end of the pool.

She unties the robe and lets it swing open, affording a glimpse of a trim body in a black two-piece bathing suit. "You know, you'll never get back that moment of perfect peace you were enjoying," she says, letting the robe drop off her shoulders. Her body is as good as the preview. Firm and athletic, yet softened by curves about the midsection. Strong yet utterly feminine. "Worst of all," she says, pointing an accusing finger, "I'll bet you didn't even resolve the thing that was bothering you." Casually she spins herself around on the bar stool, bare feet together, toes pointing outward, pretending not to show off her long legs. "You didn't, did you?"

I am not prepared for her or the situation. "Didn't what?" I ask.

"Didn't even resolve the thing that was bothering you." She leans forward toward the bartender and the drink he has just put before her. "Cottage number six," she tells him, making a scribbling motion in the air. Slowly and deliberately she puckers her lips around the straw, sort of kissing it before she sips. It is possible that the motion is unrehearsed.

"No, I didn't," I admit.

"Isn't it awful the things we do for money?" she asks rhetorically. "I hope you're getting lots and lots of it for your troubles." She takes another sip and gives her lips a coy little lick as she pulls away from the straw. "I love to talk about money," she says. "I don't think any subject makes people more uncomfortable. Especially at a place like Bangle Bay, where everyone pays through the nose *supposedly* to come and forget about it. But with so many rich people all together in one place, it's literally the only thing on everyone's mind." She turns suddenly and faces me, her breezy mood gone. She clutches my shoulder with one hand and gives me an urgent, concerned, imploring look.

"So, how much are you worth?" she asks.

My head recoils in astonishment.

"See what I mean?" she says. "Okay, let me ask you a different question. Which taste do you think women prefer—sperm or menstrual blood?"

"Well, I, uh, uh . . ."

"Didn't I tell you? You'll talk about sex but not money." She pulls her hands from the bar and gives her thighs a slap. "That's exactly my point. Sex as a subject is easy. Hell, everybody can talk about body functions." She takes another sip. "We all have them equally. But a million dollars? Or ten or twenty million? That's not handed out so equally. We have no polite, social way of talking about money. It's considered so personal, so secret, so . . . surrounded with *shame*. Yet there's no subject we're more curious about. Money. It's the last delicious taboo."

She makes a little show of adjusting her left bra strap. In the process she arches her back and stretches, giving me a long, slow look at her breasts in profile. They are round and firm and shaped like pomegranates.

"Take that Swiss arms dealer over there." She points at the fat bald man asleep in a deck chair on the far side of the pool. Mouth agape and snoring, his huge belly greased with suntan oil, he resembles a roast pig. "And that dewy young thing at his side in the microbikini," she adds. I check out the sleeping beauty with her hand resting gently on the roast pig's shoulder. She cannot be more than twenty-two. "That girl only *looks* like his daughter or favorite niece on vacation from school. There's probably nothing that would please him more than to tell you—in detail—just how many different ways he is having her on this vacation. But ask him how much he has in his numbered bank accounts in Zurich and he'll clam right up. Just the way you did."

"I guess that's probably true," I say.

"Of course it is. If you want the poop on someone, I mean the real inside story, would you ask about his sex life or his money?"

"I never thought about it that way."

"Of course you didn't. For most people sex is only a few minutes of grunting and sweating every now and then. Over the course of a lifetime, it doesn't amount to more than a few hours. But money? Now, *that's* an all-consuming passion. Whether you like it or not. Even trying to ignore it is a full-time job. Money defines absolutely everything about a person. Specifics, I'm afraid, are essential." She pauses. "So, I tell you what." She turns on the stool to face me again, arms at her side, legs slightly apart, toes wiggling in the air. "I'll show you mine if you show me yours."

"I beg your pardon?"

"Money, silly. I'll give you the lowdown on my money if you give me the lowdown on yours. Go on. Tell me about your money. How much you've got. Where it comes from. How you spend it. Come on," she says. "I'll match you." She gives her right bra strap a little snap. "Item for item."

"I, uh, work in the magazine business," I say, not wanting to go into my complicated résumé, "for American Communications Corporation."

"Then you must live in New York." She looks away for an instant, off into the distance, and says almost to herself, "Hmmm. I know lots of people in New York. Lots. I'll bet we even know some of the same people." She snaps back to attention. "Now, you say you work *for* American?"

"That's right."

She wags her index finger like a disapproving teacher and says, "Oh no you don't. Salary slaves don't come to Bangle Bay. They're not allowed. Everyone at Bangle Bay has to have money. Real money. They've got a test for it at the front gate, like a metal detector or something. You can't possibly just work for American. It must be more than that." She grabs me firmly by the shoulders and inspects me up and down. "Let's see? Are you the chairman? No, no, much too young. And definitely not corporate enough. Besides, the chairman wouldn't be staring at my breasts like that."

I cannot tell if my face goes red as I look away from her chest.

"So what is your *real* relationship with American?" She leans in close to me, her grip on my shoulders still tight. I can feel her breath on my face and smell the pineapple juice and alcohol. "Vee haff vays uff making you talk," she whispers in a German accent.

"Actually," I say, leaning backward away from her, "I'm only working for them temporarily. They bought my magazine and I'm under contract to run it for a year."

She lets go of me. "Oh goody, the big cash-out. Whew," she sighs with mock relief, "for a minute there I was afraid I was going to have to call the bouncer and have you sent over to Captain Bob's Landing with the rest of the upper-middle-class riffraff." She takes another sip. "So you sold your company to American Communications. That's great. Did you get a good price?"

"Good enough."

"See what I mean! You just proved my point about secrecy and shame. Or is it fear? Primitive superstition? If the fates hear how well you're doing, they'll take it all away from you."

"Not really." I am trying to stall.

"But I'm not being fair," she says, "asking you to go first. Here." She inserts the top of one index finger into the waistband of her bathing suit bottom and gives it a little snap. "I'll show you mine. As an act of good faith." She crosses her legs, takes another sip, and puts her glass back on the bar.

"I am worth," she says, "given daily fluctuations in world markets, approximately fifteen million dollars. Almost all of it inherited. Now, I know that's not a huge or even an interesting fortune these days. But it's enough to permit me to go wherever I want and do exactly as I please. I used to feel terrifically guilty about having all this money. Having a lot of money, it's what I call the big injustice."

"The big injustice?" I ask, a bit incredulous.

"Absolutely. The big injustice, maybe even the biggest of all. An injustice doesn't have to be a horrible cruel thing, like being crippled or being sent to a concentration camp. Why can't the injustice be a positive one? It's still the same case of too much of something being heaped, more or less by accident, on one person's plate. Living with a lot of money rubs injustice in your face every minute of the day. It's like an amputated leg; you can never get away from it. It's just not, you know, so obviously tragic."

"Oh, come on."

"No, I'm not asking for any sympathy or anything. I don't believe in that poor-little-rich-girl stuff."

I give her a skeptical look.

"For a long time, I tried to pretend my money wasn't there. I studied hard, got an MBA and a good job. I worked sixty-, seventy-hour weeks, did the whole young-achiever thing." She stops to take another sip and gives her head a shake as if trying to get rid of something caught in her hair. "I was just trying to please my father. He was disappointed that he had no sons. Dad was a real American businessman, a true Puritan. Every extra nickel he made was more divine proof of his innate superiority. Not that he was religious. Not in the least. He just had that self-righteous fire about money-making that Americans have. I tried hard to be like him, to be the way he wanted me to be. I tried, really I did. So I slaved away in this big, dumb corporation. What a joke. It kept rewarding me with stuff I didn't need. 'Great job, young lady, here's a fancier title and a bonus.' How idiotic! I didn't need a vice presidency to make me feel important. And I certainly didn't need more money, at least not in the little dribbles they handed out. They said, 'You've got a great future here.' And I asked, 'Filled with what?' Everything they had to offer was stuff I don't need more of. Then Father died, a final admission that he was actually human, just like the rest of us. What a shock. Especially to him. He left half his fortune to me and the rest to his foundation." She adds parenthetically, "He wrote Mother out of the will when they divorced." She pauses, brushes her hair back, and takes another sip. "So, I decided to keep the cash, securities, and real-estate holdings as his legacy and let the Puritan guilt go with him into the coffin."

She sips the last of her drink, exaggerating the hollow slurping noise in the bottom of her glass. "So here I am at Bangle Bay again. Just like the year before and the year before that, paying fifty percent more than this experience is worth to be sure I'm among friends. Correction—not among friends. Among peers. You, uh, know what I mean."

"Uh, of course." I am beginning to feel that I may be in over my head, at least socially.

She looks at me quizzically. Suddenly a light bulb goes on. "This your first time here?"

I nod. I wonder if I am about to receive a put-down.

"Your first time at a . . . you know . . ." She waves her hand in the air. "A place like this."

I nod again, cautious and cool.

"Tell me," she asks pointedly, "when exactly did you sell your company?"

What the hell. If she is some kind of snob, I'll get up and leave. "A few weeks ago."

"Then your money is brand-new!"

I don't quite know how to take that remark. "Not really. I, uh, I've been doing pretty well for some time now."

She charges past my defensiveness, very impatient. "Yes, yes, I'm sure you have. But your money—your *money*—is brand-new."

"I guess so." I am still not sure if she is making an accusation. Maybe they really do eject people who don't belong at Bangle Bay.

"Tell me, how did you grow up?"

"Huh?"

"Did you grow up rich?" She is speaking very fast; she wants her information and she wants it now. "Was your family a little rich? Upper-middle-class? Lower-upper-middle? Middle-middle? Lower-middle? Lower-lower-middle? Poor? Upwardly mobile? Downwardly mobile? Remember, we've left shame behind. Don't be shy. We're both grown-ups."

"Well, I guess, er, uh, middle-middle to lower-middle."

"Really?" She ponders for an instant, then races ahead. "But you always *felt* poor. Right?"

I nod slowly, confused but interested in where all this is heading.

She gives me a comforting touch on the arm. "And you grew up in a milieu that felt stupid and constraining and you couldn't wait to get the hell out."

"Yes," I reply without thinking. "Er, I mean not exactly. My family wa—"

"Yes, yes, yes. Your parents were wonderful, you love them, you're loyal to them, and their struggles on your behalf will always be an inspiration to you, and so on and so on. But the truth is, you outgrew them long before you were able to leave home. They never had a clue what you were about. And you grew up feeling like a prisoner not just in their world, but in their *view* of the world. Now, am I right or am I right?"

I nod in a way that I hope appears cool and casual.

"I knew the minute I saw you this was going to be—" She stops short as the bartender puts a fresh drink in front of her. Still breathless, she takes a long sip and starts again. "What's so wonderful is that your money is brand-new. I can't believe my good luck! This must be how a man feels when he finds himself a *virgin*. Oh, the things I can teach you . . . uh . . . Mr. uh . . ." She does not know my name. Still in high gear, she extends her right hand to shake, pretending we have just been formally introduced. I oblige. We shake.

"Bob Macallan," I say.

"Laura Chasen." She smiles. "Like the restaurant in L.A. But I'm not related and I've never eaten there."

I glance down at my left hand and catch myself flicking nervously at my wedding band with my thumb. I stop it. "Me neither," I say, referring to the famous restaurant.

"So tell me, Bob Macallan." She leans forward, putting both elbows on the bar, nestling her chin in her hands, her eyes intent on me. "How much did you sell your company for?"

I have not disclosed the number to anyone who is not related to me or being paid to handle my finances. What have I got to lose? I abandon my reticence. "Ten million," I say. I find myself smirking. All right, I am pretty goddamn pleased with myself.

"Nice," Laura whispers admiringly, chin still in her hands. She looks at me with total concentration. "Very nice."

"Yes, it is," I say. Her expression is a green light to bask in a little smugness. I bask. "Yes, it is."

A pleasant silence settles in between us. We smile.

She is the first to speak again. "It's not a lot of money as these things go. But it's enough. Oh yes, it's certainly enough." She gives my arm a friendly pat. "So what are you going to do with the rest of your life?"

"I, uh . . ." Oh, come on, Macallan, get real. *"We* haven't decided yet." She pretends not to notice the change in pronouns.

"You can do anything you want to now."

"I know."

"The rules that hold back the little people don't apply to you. Not anymore."

"I know that."

"No," she says, shaking her head. "Not yet you don't. But that's what *I* can teach you. That will be my role in your life. Unfortunately, I'm leaving for St. Barth's late this afternoon on a friend's boat. So that doesn't give us much time. Would you care to join me for a little lunch?" She motions toward the castle with her head.

"I, uh, I, uh." I know exactly what I should say, but not what I want to say. "I'm sorry, I can't."

She claps her hands together, sips the last of her drink, stands up, and puts on the white robe, straw hat, and sunglasses. "If you're interested in Lesson Two, I will be up on the cliffs after lunch on Nature Walk B." Standing face to face with me, she takes my left hand in hers and fondles my ring finger and the gold band around it. "By the way, I thought your hard-on was very handsome." Pause. "Mr. Bob MacMarried." Then she walks away.

CHAPTER EIGHT

"I'm feeling better," Wendy says. "Really I am." She pulls her bare sunburned legs off the wicker ottoman and crosses them under the robe she is wrapped in, the white terry one with the gold "BB" crest embroidered on the breast pocket. "Oooow!" She winces at the pain the movement causes but forces a chipper smile. "Just give me a little time, that's all." She still sounds stuffed up, but her cold symptoms have subsided to a mere runny nose, which she tends with the box of Kleenex in her lap.

We are sitting under the yellow canvas awning that shields our cottage terrace from the sun, finishing up the room service luncheon of sandwiches and fruit salad. "So?" she asks. "You want to see my lists? I mean *our* lists."

"Sure."

"Well, which one do you want to see first?"

"I don't know. Start anywhere."

"That's no fun. Which one are you most dying to see? This is practically our whole life I've got planned out here. It took me all morning."

I shrug.

She flips through the sheets of the yellow legal pad she had kept tucked under the cushion of her chair while we ate. "I've got babies' names rank-ordered. First names, middle names. Boys' names. Girls' names. I've got possible new career options for each of us as individuals, types of businesses you should run only by yourself, types of businesses I should run only by myself, types of businesses we could run together as a team. Let's see, I also did places we would consider moving to, places we wouldn't consider moving to. Where do you want to start?"

"You mean you didn't do retirement communities for our old age, broken out according to state, with subgroups for detached housing units, townhouse condos, and high-rise?"

"Ro-bert."

"You really are feeling better. I'm glad. Why don't you start with the page you're on now?"

"Okay, what do you think about Austin?"

"As a boy's name?"

"No, as a place to move to."

"Why on earth Austin?"

"I started with the A's."

"Out of the question."

"I agree."

"What's next?"

She gives me a sly grin, pauses for dramatic effect, and says, "Avignon."

I give her a puzzled look.

"You know how much I love France. You'd love it, too. We could have a farmhouse in the country. Up in the hills where they grow all the flowers for the perfume."

"What about your allergies?"

"Oh, yeah. I forgot." She looks moderately disappointed. "That'd never work, except in winter. Okay, then. Let me see." She flips through her lists. "How about Bart?"

"We don't want to live on St. Barth's. It's supposed to be the most overpriced island in the whole Caribbean."

"No, I mean for a name. A boy's name." Wendy is forever changing subjects without warning. I should know to expect it and even anticipate it, but it always catches me off guard. "What do you think? Bart." She says it low. "Bart!" Now high and chipper. "That's a guy who's strong, solid, bold, and—"

"Bright yellow and blue."

"Huh?"

"Bart Simpson."

"Oh," she says, her balloon burst. "Nix Bart."

Wendy leans forward and looks at me with a squint. "You don't look happy, Macallan. What's the matter?"

"Nothing. I'm fine." Not true. I have been working overtime trying not to think about Laura Chasen, the body she seemed to be offering me, and people like her who can afford to go through life doing whatever the hell they want. The more Wendy dwells on the subject of babies, the more I have to work at not thinking about Laura. The sensuous, languid air and the realization that I really am rich do not help. Maybe I am more of an escapist and a fantasist than I thought.

"You've been edgy all through lunch."

"It's nothing, honestly." Nobody really lives like that, do they? No strings? No responsibilities? No inhibitions?

"Don't tell me it's nothing. I can tell. What is it? Is it the bullshit with Levine and Woodcock? Do you want to do strategies together?" She flips to a blank page in her legal pad and raises her pen in readiness. "Come on. Action Plan A."

"No, let's not do that now." Even I can hear the whiny edge in my voice.

"Are you mad at me for getting sick? For giving myself this stupid sunburn? For ruining our vacation? I'm sorry." She sniffles and blows her nose. "But I didn't ask to get the cold. I got it in the line of duty. And as for the sunburn, I'm sorry. I'm sorry, I'm sorry. It was stupid of me. I admit it. But *I'm* the one who can barely move. Not you. And I was only trying to do something positive to make the goddamn cold go away and save our vacation." She looks as though she might burst into tears at any moment.

"No, I'm not mad at you. And you haven't ruined our vacation. I feel terrible about the cold, terrible about the sunburn. I wish I could make them go away, you know, just snap my fingers. I'm not mad, it's just that we're here on vacation trying to get away from responsibilities and you're hitting me with baby names, career planning, momentous life decisions—"

"It's the baby thing, isn't it?"

"No," I say, telling myself I'm not really lying. It isn't the baby thing exactly; it's everything the baby represents, everything I'd rather face sometime later. Exactly when I'm not sure. Maybe when I know better what my own possibilities are. But please not now. "Wendy," I plead, working hard not to spill what I am thinking, "this is supposed to be a vacation. Can't we relax a little? Just let go of reality for a bit?"

"You're right," she replies sheepishly.

"Honey, I don't care about being right or wrong." Suddenly, her flood of tears seems less imminent. I can keep our talk *away* from my deeper, darker thoughts. "I'm still pissed off about this Woodcock thing. And I feel bad because you've been cooped up here. And you've probably been going stir-crazy. And you feel disappointed. And I feel disappointed. So we're both on edge, so let's just—"

"Let's both just lighten up."

"Yeah."

She smiles. She is back in control of herself. "We could use a vacation from our vacation."

I smile back. "Yeah." I'm off the hook on the baby thing for the moment.

"All right then, Macallan. Go out and vacation for both of us. This is my one and only sick day. Tomorrow, I become fully mobile. You promise to go check out the delights of Bangle Bay for us. And I promise not to obsess about planning the future. No more pressure about babies or jobs or anything else while we're here. Deal?"

"Deal."

"Now get out of here. Get cruising. Just be back for cocktails at five."

"Don't worry." I have dressed for a walk, in sneakers, jeans, and hooded windbreaker.

"Where you gonna go?"

"Exploring. Nature Walk A goes up on the ridge overlooking the bay. Supposed to be a great view."

"Have fun, sweetie."

I turn to leave. "I'll try."

"Robert?"

I look back over my shoulder. "Yeah?"

"If you find another woman out there"—she smiles extra sweetly—"I'll kill you."

According to my map of the Bangle Bay grounds, Nature Walks A, B, and C all start in the woods behind the tennis courts. The forest is dry and scrubby but thick enough with spindly desert trees and overgrown cacti to shelter the walker from the Caribbean sun. The caption on the map tells me that Bangle Bay's gardener has worked on these plantings for twenty-five years, perfecting their random natural look. With its twisted branches and rocky outcroppings, this wood is what I've always imagined an olive grove in Greece or southern Italy would be like.

After a few minutes, I come upon a three-way split in the path, with three little wooden signs, "A," "B," "C," just as the map promised. I stop at the intersection and tell myself that my stated goal is to explore Path A. *Path A.* I stand at the crossroads in silent indecision. Inside me, Conscience wrestles with Curiosity. The contest is violent and bloody—but short. Curiosity wins. Conscience is carried away on a stretcher with possibly fatal injuries. I follow Path B.

The landscaper has placed slices of ledge into the steep hillside to serve as steps. What ought to be a rugged climb is just a walk upstairs in the cool shade. This must be the devil at work; it is too easy. Suddenly the ground levels off and the woods are behind me. I am in the open now, on the crest, looking down the peninsula, surrounded by an angry, dark blue Atlantic. The ocean is whitecapped to the horizon, the breeze strong and noisy.

My body tells me that an ocean wind like this should be cold, that I should hug myself against it. But this one is warm. The effect is at once confusing and seductive. The air blows inside my windbreaker and baggy jeans and puffs them up. It caresses my skin and fills my nose and ears. The scene is exhilarating. It wraps itself around me, picks me up, and holds me suspended inside it.

There is nothing man-made to be seen in any direction. Just cactus and bush, cliffs, waves, rocks, sunshine, mountains, and, above everything, the towering cloud-flecked sky. A path runs down the spine of the peninsula, in one direction toward jagged cliffs and the open sea, in the other toward the mountains on the far side of the resort. I walk toward the cliffs and crashing waves.

After a few yards, I see her sitting on the ground in front of a big gray rock, watching the waves and sky, white pants and white top blowing in the wind, floppy straw hat tied around her chin with a green silk scarf. Laura Chasen. The noise of the wind and waves covers the sound of my footsteps along the rocky path, I think. I come up behind her rock and stand. She does not turn around. I wait. She seems transfixed. I wait some more, then turn and take a half-step to leave.

"That's pretty antisocial," she says in a voice loud enough to be heard over the roar. I turn and look back. She is still facing forward in her meditative position. "It would be a crime not to sit down beside me and enjoy this moment, Mr. Macallan." She motions to me without looking in my direction, as if she were in the middle of watching a tennis match. I sit down beside her.

She pulls her sunglasses halfway down her nose and peers at me. "Mothers aren't the only ones with eyes in the back of their heads, you know." She pushes the shades back into place and assumes a more casual air. "Pretty nice, eh?"

I nod.

"You been up here at sunrise?"

"No."

"Definitely recommended."

"Duly noted," I say.

We sit in silence for a while, looking out. She takes off the hat and green scarf and lets the wind blow in her hair.

I do not know what kind of conversation to make, so I say what I'm thinking. "This is too easy."

"What on earth do you mean?"

"Well, usually, to get to someplace like this, you'd have to climb all day and go through hell. You know, really sweat for the privilege of getting this far away from it all."

She closes her eyes and holds her head back languidly. She nods to signal that she is still listening.

"But this is ten little steps uphill, on natural-looking, ergonomically designed stairs, no less. And just behind that hill is one of the cushiest resorts in the tropics. It doesn't seem fair to have all this pleasure so handy, so easy. The world doesn't work that way."

She opens her eyes and smiles at me. "Welcome to the world of the seriously rich. I really do have a lot to teach you, don't I?" She closes her eyes and drinks in the air. Another silence settles in.

After a while she sits up straight. "Looks a little like Cornwall on the Caribbean, don't you think? With the cliffs and the waves."

"I couldn't tell you."

"I could." Not snotty, just factual. "I could also tell you about the old thieves' quarter in Dar es Salaam, dawn over the golden temples in Burma, dinner beneath the Boromini frescoes in the palazzo of the Principessa d'Albano in Rome, and freezing my ass off trying to pee outside my tent in the howling winds of Tierra del Fuego. You name it, I've probably been there."

I think of Wendy's teasing remark about traveling to the tip of South America. "You really been to Tierra del Fuego?"

She nods. "That's what money means to me. Some people use it to buy power or houses or art collections. I use it to get around, to be wherever it's most interesting."

I have no response. That kind of life seems unimaginable to me, from every possible viewpoint—moral, practical, whatever—it is unimaginable.

"So, Bob Macallan," she asks, "what are you going to do now that you're rich?"

I shrug.

"Are you going to give yourself a shopping spree? You know, buy the big house or the sports car or the mink-lined trench coat you've always dreamed of?"

"Naah, that's not me."

"Good. It's so boring when people do that." She takes off her sunglasses, reaches across, and takes off mine. "Tell me, what *is* you?"

"I guess I haven't really figured that out yet. I suppose I'll do another business once I finish my contract with American. I don't know if I have the energy to start another company; maybe I'll buy one." I can see her eyes glazing over. "You know, build it up, sell it. I suppose I should stick to a media business; I don't know much about anything else. A lot of guys might feel they can go out and conquer any business now, but I just don't see myself in manufacturing or retailing." She stares out to sea, clearly bored, waiting for me to finish. "So the bottom line for me"—I am trying to wrap this up quickly and with minimal embarrassment—"is that I don't really know yet."

Pause. Yes, thank God, I'm done.

She jumps to her feet and marches toward the cliffs. "Time to begin Lesson Two," she says, beckoning me to follow. She reaches the cliffs a few steps ahead of me.

"I want you to stand here," she says, pointing to the very edge where she is poised, "right here." I comply. The drop beneath us down to the boiling surf and jagged rocks must be sixty feet. She nestles her body against mine. "Now close your eyes," she commands. I do. "Just feel." Her chest is pressed up alongside me; I feel a breast nestled against either side of my right arm. Her fingers brush softly across the contours of my face. "Feel the wind," she instructs. "Smell the air. Feel the sun on your skin. Now, open your eyes—but just for a second."

I open my eyes for an instant. The scene is as achingly beautiful as I remember. I shut my eyes again and hold the vision before me.

"Imagine," she whispers with warm breath in my ear and fingers brushing me like feathers all over, "imagine that you have ten minutes to live. You can spend nine and a half of those minutes grinding out a ten-cent boost in the quarterly dividend for Acme Industries and, as a reward, come here for your final thirty seconds. Or you can spend all ten minutes right here." Her fingers dance lightly over my crotch. "With me."

I open my eyes and step back to break the spell. "You're talking about a permanent state of vacation."

"Not at all." She wags her finger at me. "I'm talking about the only life you've got." She sits down on the edge of the cliff and dangles her feet. I sit down a few inches behind her.

"But this is a vacation," I say. "You can't live like this every day."

"You sound like my father. Tell me why not? Tell me—one free adult with ten minutes to live to another—why not?"

"Because, uh, because, uh, you've *got* to work at something. And this," I motion at our setting, "isn't work."

"Says who?"

Dumb pause. She jumps back in. "Your boss, that's who. Your employer. And *he* says it's not right because it doesn't suit *his* purposes."

"Yes," I protest, "but if everyone decided to live like this . . ."

"But *you* are not everyone. And *I* am not everyone. Don't worry. The rest of the world will show up for work at nine o'clock on Monday morning. Because they can't survive without their salary. That's what I'm trying to tell you. It's a problem *they* have. Not me. And now, not you. It takes courage to face that fact without feeling guilty."

I nod in silence, conjuring up unattractive images of the idle rich.

"The little people *have* to live by the rules. We don't. Just imagine. We could slaughter a goat up here, smear ourselves with its blood, and dance naked if we wanted to. No one would dare do anything about it." She looks at me wide-eyed and teasing. "We could even slaughter one of the local people passing by and probably get away with it. Yes. We could *buy* our way out of it. Remember? The big injustice?"

"That's an ugly thought."

"But true. Now I'm not interested in slaughtering goats or innocent island people. But I am interested in going wherever it's interesting and doing whatever the hell I please without looking for approval or acceptance from anybody."

She takes me by the shoulders and gives me a shake, looking deep into my eyes. "Don't you see? They don't have power over you anymore. Not your boss. Not your father. Not your mother. Not your *wife.*" She lets the last word sink in. "None of the authority figures who want to keep you toeing the line, living a cramped little life. Do you have children?" I shake my head no.

"That's good," she sighs. "They make life so fucking complicated." A hint of anger in her voice.

She lets go of me and lies back on the ground. She stretches her arms out and looks up at the sky. "Why on earth would you want to go back into business when you don't need the money?"

"What do you mean? Lots of people make a bundle and stay in business."

"Yeah, don't I know it." She sounds bitter.

"What's wrong with staying in business?"

"It's boring and bloodless, that's what. And you have no reason to. Are you one of those men who'd die without the wheeling and dealing? Like my father? The kind who love and cherish every extra nickel they make? Is that you?"

"No, not really."

"I didn't think so. And you're definitely not the sadistic plantation master type. Believe me; I can spot them. I was married to one. Briefly."

"I'm sorry."

"Don't be. They're kind of amazing, those guys. They simply have to have enslaved underlings around them at all times. Even at home." She laughs to herself. "It's the only thing that makes them feel important. Kind of pathetic. But not the most pathetic."

"Really, who's that?"

"The dopey little rich boys I grew up with. They simply lack the imagination to do anything else. For them, corporate life is an advanced form of baby-sitting. There they are with all this money. The power to make real magic with life. And what do they do? They piss their time away in this deprived nine-to-five existence."

"Deprived?" I think of limos, corner offices paneled with endangered tropical woods, power tables at overpriced restaurants, and all the other silly, coveted prizes of excess.

"Absolutely. Deprived. I know; I lived it. I married it and divorced it. Corporate life is nothing but deprivation. They start by depriving you of everything. Money, autonomy, identity, dignity, fulfillment, everything. Then they reward you in little drips and drabs. A trickle of money, a drop of autonomy, a dribble of self-respect. Always just enough to keep you hungry." She shakes her head with disgust. "Yuck! Wouldn't you rather go from one gorgeous experience to another, using your imagination and your checkbook to make life as interesting and fun as it can possibly be? Do you really need the headaches? The conflicts with stupid jerks? The compromises, the phoniness, the lying? It's all so goddamn negative."

I nod at her words, thinking and almost imagining letting go of . . . everything.

"Are you very social back in New York?"

"Do you mean do we go out and see people?"

"I mean *social*. You know."

"No. Why would I even think of trying?"

"Well, maybe you never had the right kind of introductions. I'm very well connected, you know. All over the world. I've got a magic address book. It can make amazing things happen. Ever seen a magic address book?"

Suddenly, I think of Leo's little black book, with its lists of kiddie birthdays and sexual kinks. I try to expel the distasteful image from my mind.

"I have a magic address book, with some very interesting New York entries in it. What's the name of your magazine?"

"*Elixir.*"

"In the phone book?"

"Yeah."

"Good. Expect an invitation or two. Maybe that'll help to open your eyes to some new possibilities. I have powers you can barely imagine, Bob Macallan. But you'll see, you'll see." She sits up suddenly and turns around on her knees to face me. "You want to make love? Right here under all this gloriousness? Right now? Come on." She holds her arms out at her sides, inviting me to open her like a Christmas present.

I bolt upright into a sitting position and look away before I can say anything. She reaches for my chin, cups it, and turns my face toward hers. She is smiling warmly, sympathetically. "Don't go fumferring on me. We weren't really about to have sex at this point in our relationship. I just wanted to shake you up and make a point. From now on, you shouldn't stop yourself from doing things because they're supposed to be wrong. We're not making love now *because it's wrong*. We're not making love now because it's not right *yet.*"

She takes my right hand in hers. "You have gotten rich at the peak moment of your life. Just look at the other men here at Bangle Bay. Yuck. You're not tired and flabby like the ones who made it when they were old. You're not soft and bratty like the young ones who've had it since birth. You are in your absolute prime as a man. You are in a position to do anything you want, take anything you want. You're old enough to really appreciate it and young enough to really enjoy it. Don't blow it. Don't become like," she sneers, "*like the rest of them.*"

She squeezes my hand and looks deep into my eyes. "I want you to promise me something. When you're with the people you're used to being with, doing the things you're used to doing, ask yourself: Is this really the way I want to spend my ten minutes? Ask yourself that five or ten times a day. If it doesn't change the way you live, you're a fool." She lets go of my hand. "End of Lesson Two."

She stands up and brushes off the seat of her pants. "Now, I've got to go finish packing. Come; walk me back as far as the path to the woods." We stroll side by side in silence. She carries her hat and scarf in her left hand. At the steps that lead down into the forest, she stops and takes my right hand. Not to shake it. To hold it.

"Listen, Bob Macallan, I think we should meet again in a few months for Lesson Three. I'll have been to some new and different places. And so will you. Unfortunately, we can't meet in New York. I can't stand New York. I'm sorry, I just can't. So where can we meet? Are you going anywhere interesting? Alone?"

I lift my sunglasses onto my forehead and look at her in amazement.

"You see? You can say anything. You can do anything. And look, no lightning. No thunder. No guilt. Nothing but what you choose." She lets go of my hand and cracks a grin. "Now listen, fella, I've got a yacht to catch. So where we gonna meet again? Huh?"

"Well," I hear myself saying, "I have a conference in London in June. It's just business associates."

"I love London in June! Love it! What are the dates?"

"Let me see, uh, twenty-six, twenty-seven, and twenty-eight." I did not realize I remembered the exact dates.

"Do you know where you'll be staying?"

"Grosvenor House."

"Perfect. I stay with friends in Chelsea. I'll be there. I'll even reschedule Thailand to do it. I'm putting you on notice. You are officially designated as my challenge for this year. You see? Everyone has their own kind of work to do, even people like me." She turns to leave, takes a step forward, then turns back. "Ooh, I almost forgot." She reaches into the pocket of her blouse, pulls out a folded envelope, and hands it to me. "A little something to make you think of me. A lock of my hair." She turns and dashes away down the stone steps, her long honey gold hair bouncing out of sight.

I unfold the envelope of buff parchment engraved with the Bangle Bay letterhead. I open it. Folded inside is a blank sheet of Bangle Bay stationery. It contains a little blue ribbon tied around some of Laura's hair. Coarse, curly, dark brown pubic hair.

MARCH

CHAPTER NINE

"Marie, give me my phone messages." I close the door of the little telephone cabin on the seventh floor, the corporate training floor, at American Communications. I am spending a lot of time here in Harry Woodcock's building. Much too much time. "Give me *all* my phone messages. Give me everyone's phone messages. Just please take a long time so I don't have to go back into that room."

"What's the matter, Bob? You sound kinda, kinda—"

"Kinda crazy, that's what. I'm on break from another management seminar—"

"Yeah, I know."

"We're going through a two-hundred-page manual of recommended procedures for cutting bureaucracy. This place is making me nuts! Tell me what's happening back in Sanity Land."

"Do you really want all your messages?"

"Sure."

"Including the ones from sales reps who read about the *Elixir* acquisition in *Inside Print*?"

"How many of those?"

"Like about two dozen. I count five insurance salesmen, nine stockbrokers, three financial planners, a custom tailor. You want me to go on?"

"No, just give me the real stuff."

"Harry from the printer called at nine-ten. He promises to have the new press on line Tuesday. He says there should be no problem with the next issue's timetable."

"Okay, we'll see what happens next week."

"You've got a message from some purchasing manager, Al Cleary, up at American headquarters, at ten."

"Send that one to Dudley and tell him I want a complete report on what they want from us. Next."

"You've got a message from Howie Marcus, ten-thirty."

"Howie, eh?"

"It's a long one. You want me to read it to you?"

"By all means. Was he calling from out of town?"

"No, he said he was here for the day."

"Let me have it."

"I'll read it just like he dictated it to me: 'Greetings from the hinterlands. Word has reached as far as Chicago of the awful rumors circulating about *Elixir*. It's a damn shame. I hope none of it is true. It's terrible how much damage rumors can do in this business. Whether they're true or not. As your friend and almost investment banker, you can be sure I'm doing everything I can to help put a stop to them. Next time you're in Chicago, let's do lunch. Your treat.' "

Pause.

"That it?" I ask.

"Uh-huh. Pretty weird, eh?"

"Yeah. Weird." Goddamn rumors. "Where's Leo this morning?"

"That's what's even weirder. After Marcus finished dictating his message, he asked for Leo. So I transferred him in. Then, I was looking for Leo just now on some old papers we had to file and Marsha tells me he left about quarter of eleven. Real sudden. Didn't tell her where, just said he'd be back after lunch."

Shit, that's all I need. Howie and Leo. Wait a minute. Howie? Leo? Atwood? Why didn't I consider that possibility before? My mind starts spinning out ugly scenarios.

"Bob, here's the one *I'm* interested in. A message from the office of Mr. Eugene Merritt. Eleven-oh-five. His secretary at the Merritt Foundation called. Would you and Wendy like to come to an informal brunch three Sundays from now up in Southpoint, Connecticut. She says she'll give me directions when you R.S.V.P."

"Eugene Merritt? Why does that name sound familiar?"

"Come on, Bob, don't you read *magazines*? Or Page Six? Gene Merritt. He's like this big society guy. Oldy moldy money. Related to all the Rockefellers and Vanderbilts and stuff, but his family's dough goes way back before them. His wife was one of those famous debutante beauties back in the thirties. I think she's dead now."

"Oh? *That* Gene Merritt."

"Yeah, that Gene Merritt. Pretty fancy people you're starting to hobnob with."

"What's he doing calling me?"

"His secretary says you have a mutual friend."

"We do?"

"Yeah. Lauren Chasen?"

"You mean *Laura* Chasen."

"Yeah, that's it."

★ ★ ★

92

"So you're going to watch Leo extra closely?" Wendy says, slipping off her pink panties and tossing them into the laundry bag.

"Like a hawk," I answer from the bed.

She shuts the closet door and turns to face me. The oversized T-shirt comes down to the tops of her knees. A silk-screened silhouette of Santa and his reindeer flying over the tops of buildings. "Christmas in Cincinnati," it reads. The only consolation Wendy got for being trapped in the Louisville airport last week by delayed connecting flights. It was half-price.

"Do you think Marcus could have—"

"I think anything is possible. He was pissed at me for selling the company without him. I'm sure he knows Atwood, too. And Leo? He knows everybody. So I'm giving Leo enough leeway to solve this rumor thing the way he says he can. But if I smell anything, he'll discover it was also enough rope to hang himself."

Wendy walks over to my side of the bed and motions for me to move my legs to one side to make room for her. I do. She sits down beside me and curls her legs underneath herself.

"Robert," she coos, "you know that conference of yours in London?"

"Uh-huh."

"If I'm not pregnant by then, I figured out a way for us not to miss the chance to try, if I happen to ovulate while you're in London." She leans forward and rests her elbows on my legs. "I just signed up for the big Euro-Marketing Conference in Geneva that same week. If the little chemistry kit turns blue, we've got twenty-four, maybe thirty-six hours to try. I catch the next flight to London. Two hours later it's wham-bam-thank-you-ma'am. You don't lose a minute with your big clients, and we don't lose the month of June. Isn't that great?"

I nod.

"Now, in case I don't ovulate while you're in London, I went ahead and made some more plans for us. You know, since we're both going to be over there." Pause. "You don't mind, do you?"

"More plans? No, I don't mind. It's just so unlike you to make plans. Do tell."

She looks happy and eager with anticipation. "Well, you know where Geneva is."

"Uh-huh. Switzerland."

"Of course, silly. But you know *where* it is."

"Yeah, uh, southwest of Zurich? North of Rome? Is this a quiz?"

"It's just across the French border from Divonne. You remember. Where I did that summer program when I was in high school?"

"Oh, yeah. Of course."

"You can meet me in Geneva and we can go to Divonne together."

"Aha. You want to go back and relive those thrilling days of yesteryear. You can show me all around."

"And we could stay in the Château de Divonne."

"Sure. Is that a nice hotel?"

93

"Nice? It's gorgeous. Beautiful old château with big rooms. I can't tell you the fantasies we girls used to have about being swept off our feet and taken to the Château back then."

"No, I guess you can't."

"And if I'm ovulating, we could make a baby *there*. It's so beautiful, Robert. You can see the Alps floating in the sky."

"Really?"

"Yes, and we can visit Nadine and Pierre, my friends in Vesancy. It's right next door." She cuddles up next to me. "I already called them and told them we're coming. We've got a picnic all planned. So how does that sound? Interesting travel, an elegant hotel, making babies, beautiful scenery, old friends, and me?"

"Sounds perfect."

"Can you take the extra days?"

"Sure. Harry Woodcock doesn't control my life that closely. At least not yet."

Wendy rolls over on the bed, legs flying momentarily in the air. She crawls under the covers on her side, takes a deep happy breath, and turns off the lamp on her night table. The room goes dark.

"Good night, sweetie," she says, giving me a little peck. I hear her burrowing into her pillow.

Pause.

"Uhhh, Wendy?" I say into the dark.

"Hmmm?" She is trying to fall asleep.

"We got an invitation today. To a brunch."

"That's nice."

"Up in Connecticut."

"Atsnice." She is still trying to fall asleep.

"Some fancy society guy. In Southpoint."

"Izzisforbusiness?" She is trying to shut me up so she can sleep.

"Not really."

"Cammwee talk about it in the morning." She rolls over to face the window and digs in deeper.

"The guy's name is Eugene Merritt. Ever heard of him?"

"Mmmm. Big society guy. Old-line." I hear her roll back a little toward me. She will converse but grudgingly. "Why's he inviting us?"

"Uh, well, he's a, uh, friend of a friend of ours."

She stirs a little. "Who?"

"Uh, you don't know her."

"I don't know her?" I feel the bed jump. Wendy's bedside lamp goes on. The room fills with light. She is sitting up in bed, leaning forward and looking at me. "I don't know *her*? Who is *her*?"

"The person who is our mutual friend of Gene Merritt."

"Is this another old girlfriend you conveniently forgot to tell me about? The last one embarra—"

"No, absolutely not."

"Well, who is she? Where do you know her from?"

"Her name is Laura Chasen. And I met her at, uh, Bangle Bay."

"What?" Wendy slaps her thighs. "Why didn't you tell me about her when we were there?"

"I just didn't see any reason to. Wasn't very important. You know how you just run into people at a resort."

"Something tells me Laura Chasen is not some sweet old dowager you met playing shuffleboard. I would have heard about her."

"No, I just never figured that—"

"What does she look like?" Rapid fire. "Come on, how old is she? Did she come on to you? Out with it, Macallan. What happened?" She shakes a fist at me.

"Nothing happened. Honest, absolutely nothing."

"What does she look like? How old is she? How's she built?"

"I don't know, I guess she's about your age."

"Je-sus!" She pounds her fist into the palm of her other hand. "What does she look like?"

"I guess she's, uh, sort of, uh, blond."

"Shit. A blonde. Is she married?"

"Divorced."

"Double shit. No, triple shit. A rich, blond, divorced friend of Gene Merritt, king of old-line society. That's some babe you managed to make friends with."

"Who else would you expect to run into at Bangle Bay?"

"Bangle Bay. Hmmph."

"Hey, Bangle Bay was your idea. That's the kind of people who go there. Remember Sid and Arlene from the jitney? I'd venture to say they're not friends of Gene Merritt. If we'd stayed at Captain Bob's like them, we'd probably be going to brunch at Arlene's sister Ciel's instead. At her tract house in Freeport, Long Island."

Wendy folds her arms across her chest and lets out a long breath. "Je-sus. What exactly did you do with this woman while I was a helpless invalid?"

"Chatted with her once. Saw her on the nature walk. Once."

"Once and once. That makes twice. What? Did you have a full-fledged relationship? How often were you running out to see her?"

"I didn't run out to see her. I just ran into her. Twice. That's all."

"How many days did you spend with her?"

"Look, she left Bangle Bay the afternoon of our second day. She had to catch a boat to St. Barth's."

"La-di-da. A boat to St. Barth's. You seem to know quite a bit about her personal life for someone you just ran into."

"Oh, come on."

"Did you tell her you're married?"

"She knows perfectly well I'm married."

"Is *she* going to be at this brunch?"

"No. I mean I don't know. No, I'm sure she won't be. She spends most of the year traveling. No, she won't be there. She just mentioned that it might be fun for me, I mean for us, to meet some of her friends here. A little taste of the unusual. You know, expand horizons and like that."

"What does she do, this Laura?"

"Nothing."

"What do you mean, nothing?"

"That's what she told me. She says she lives off her inheritance and travels around the world. Kind of an explorer."

"What did she explore with you?"

"Nothing, I tell you. Nothing."

"You swear?"

"I swear."

"You promise?"

"I promise."

"Robert, we're going to have a baby together. A baby. If you're going to play around with society tootsies, we'll have to call everything off. We've got to figure that out now. Do you understand me?"

"Yes, I understand. Nothing happened with this woman. Nothing will happen."

Wendy squints at me with laser eyes in one final attempt to burn through to the truth.

"Really," I say. "Really and truly."

She falls back against her pillow and lets out most of her tension.

"Look," I say, "if you don't want to go, we don't have to. I just figured it might be interesting, you know, amusing. Southpoint is supposed to be really incredible. And it's got to be an interesting group of guests. I'd only vaguely heard of this Merritt guy, but everybody tells me he's a real hot shit, socially speaking. These are people we'd probably never run into in our normal lives."

Wendy has calmed down but is still giving me a fishy look. "Why are you so interested to go?"

"I don't know. Change of pace. Something different. There's a world out there to explore. Who knows? Maybe there'll even be a good business connection or two. The people at Merritt's brunch have got to be potentially more useful than the people we'd meet at, say, Burger King."

Wendy is almost back to normal. I think she is as intrigued by our brunch invitation as I am but will not give me the satisfaction of admitting it. Yes, I think her interest has definitely been piqued.

"I've been to Southpoint, you know."

"Have you?"

She reaches over to her lamp and switches it off. The room goes dark again. "Oh yes. Southpoint is definitely a whole other world." I feel the bed jiggle as she shakes and fluffs her pillow back into position before burying her head in it. She drops into place and squirms for a second or two. Then she relaxes.

"Robert?" She is talking at the window.

"Yes?" I am talking at the ceiling.

"I just learned something about you that I never knew before."

"What's that?" I ask the darkness.

"There's a bit of the snob in you."

CHAPTER TEN

It was late on a rainy May afternoon near the end of my senior year in high school. My parents were at work. I was alone in the house, lying on the couch in the den, reading the Baldwin College catalog and daydreaming. Just a month before, I had survived an encounter with death. No, it was something even worse.

Harvard and Yale said no. In a flash, the unthinkable became the inevitable. I would have to go to my backup college.

For more than a year before the fateful letters arrived, I had spun elaborate fantasies about my magical life in the Ivy League. I would be one of a group of friends who would go on to run the world. They were waiting for me there. The next Jack Kennedy, the next Norman Mailer, the next John Kenneth Galbraith, the next Henry Luce, the next Linus Pauling. What a gang we would be. Nobel laureates, tycoons, famous artists—all of us honored and very rich. My grown-up life would be lived at the center of this awesome circle of power and achievement. I would share equally in the glory, thanks to my own brilliant but yet to be determined career.

To me, getting into Harvard or Yale meant being recognized as one of the true elite, the few chosen by destiny, family legacy, and admissions directors to lead the world. In my own case, I was forced to depend on only one of those forces.

And it let me down.

I was too proud show anyone at home or school how hurt I was. I busied myself with the job of rebuilding compromise fantasies about my magical life at Baldwin. It wasn't so bad, I tried to tell myself. Baldwin had offered me a generous scholarship. That was essential. If the Big H or Y had accepted me but without sufficient financial aid, I would have . . . no, I would have found a way, *any* way. Well, at least I would not have to attend the state university or, horror of horrors, the commuter college that Dad said would be more in line with our means. Mom overruled him and vowed that her salary from the insurance office would pay for a prestige education for me. Thanks to her, I felt I could still escape Bayport and become a gentleman of the world. Heartsick as I was, I knew that things could have been a lot worse.

Besides, I started telling myself, Baldwin was more or less like an Ivy League school. It was old. Chartered in December of 1799, it did date back two whole centuries, although just barely. It was rich—for a small men's college. It was famous, sort of. Two members of the class of 1831 had earned a place in the history books, a utopian essayist and a one-term alcoholic President. But most important to me, Baldwin had a gorgeous campus. It even looked a little like Harvard, with its quadrangle of historic brick buildings dripping with ivy, arched gateways, and towering elms—all the aristocratic trappings I hungered for. If only I could absorb a place like this, I told myself—even at a second choice like Baldwin—I would leave it feeling established and powerful.

I was flipping through the photos of the campus life, imagining myself in them, transformed magically from the awkward, uncertain high school striver I knew and loathed into a confident member of the intellectual and social elite. Hang on, Robert, I said, it will happen soon. Soon. I looked past the drizzle outside the window, the cramped little den, and the threadbare upholstery on the couch. I let the pictures transport me to a better world.

I barely heard the sound of the back door slamming and Jimmy coming into the house. But the angry footsteps pounding through the kitchen were hard to miss. They stopped at the refrigerator, paused, then continued in my direction.

"Hey, Brother," he mumbled as he stomped into the den and stood defiantly over me. My short, fat, fourteen-year-old brother Jimmy. All through our childhood, I towered over Jimmy. Not that I was so tall; he just stayed short. As he entered adolescence, Jimmy got heavy and tough. Lately, whenever he caught me sitting down he would sidle up close and stick his belly in my face, in order to look down at me when he spoke. This time he had a fistful of Oreos and a glass of milk. Because he liked to eat and because he knew it annoyed me, he was shoveling the cookies into his face in twos and threes, making a point of chewing with his mouth wide open. "You lookin' at that stupid Baldwin book again?" he asked, showing off a gooey black mouthful of half-masticated cookies.

I grunted, trying to ignore him.

After being subjected to my brotherly hostilities almost since the day he was born, Jimmy had developed a permanent chip on his shoulder. For most of those years, he was my handy in-house victim. I pummeled him at will. Mom howled at me. But I paid no attention. I beat him up physically and verbally whenever I felt angry or frustrated, which was often. But lately my little brother had begun to go on the offensive. He had started to pick the fights with me. And sometimes he would win, although I would pretend to be giving him the victory whenever he did.

"Did you have a good day at school?" I asked without looking up from my book.

"Skoooosucks," he muttered through the final mouthful of wet cookie mash. He glugged down the last of the milk and wiped away most of the white mustache and sticky crumbs with the back of his sleeve. "I hate school. It's for dorks." He slammed the empty Flintstones glass down on the table beside me. "Dorks like you."

"An attitude like that won't get you very far in this world," I said, not looking up. I turned to the next page.

"Dad says you're gonna put us in the poorhouse just so you can pretend to be some kinda college playboy."

I stared deeper into the photo of the Baldwin library reading room. It was a rich, tranquil, elegant place, with leather chairs, Persian rugs, mahogany library tables, and brass lamps. "We're already *in* the poorhouse," I snapped. In my tender injured state, I had taken to being even more condescending than usual. I looked up at him. "Or can't you see that?"

"Fuck you, asshole. I like this house."

"I don't." I flipped to the next page.

"I do. Asshole! Asshole!"

"Nice mouth, Jimmy. That'll get you far in this world." I turned another page, but I had stopped looking at the book.

"You don't like it here? Why doncha get out?"

"I *am* getting out," I said angrily. I tried to collect myself and go back into my book. "Next September I'm getting out of here. Believe me, once I'm off to college I'm gone. Forever."

"If you hate it so much, why doncha leave *now*? Huh?" He yanked the book out of my hand. "Why doncha leave right now? Make us all a lot happier."

"Because I have to get an education first, dummy. That's why." I grabbed the book back and tried to resume my relaxed pose, but Jimmy tore the catalog away again.

"You don't like it here, why doncha leave *now*?" He held the book behind his back and smirked. If I wanted to get it, I would have to get up and wrestle with him.

I sat up straight on the couch and sighed, the way you sigh at an annoying child. "I can't leave now, dopey. College doesn't start until fall."

"Who said anything about college? You're a big shot. Why doncha just go somewhere and be a big shot now?"

"Because I've got to get an education, that's why. So do you." I was always the perennial good boy in school. When Jimmy would follow four years later, the teachers made the mistake of comparing him to me. He was always Bob Macallan's little brother. Your big brother did this, your big brother did that, your big brother was so helpful, so diligent. As a result, Jimmy became the perennial bad boy.

"School's a buncha shit," he said. "I hate school. I can't wait to get out."

"That's not so smart, Jimmy. You should know better. You know what happens to people who don't get a good education."

"No, what?" he asked defiantly.

"They end up with stupid, crummy jobs. And stupid, crummy lives."

"Zat so?"

"You know it is."

"Oh yeah?"

"We've been over this before, Jimmy."

"Yeah? Well, Dad didn't go to college."

"Just look at him."

"What'samatta with Dad? Huh?"

I thought of Dad's business disasters, one after the other, his inability to make a good living, and what I felt it did to us as individuals and as a family. I said nothing.

Jimmy moved closer and looked down at me with smug disgust. "What's wrong with Dad? Huh?"

I stared at the floor.

Jimmy let go of the Baldwin catalog. It fell to the floor behind him with a thud I remember as deafening. "What's wrong with being like Dad?"

"Dad's a failure, that's what." I spit out my anger and frustration. "He can't make a living. We don't have any money. Nobody in town respects him. Nobody in town respects *us*. We live in this crappy, ugly little house. We're always on the edge of disaster. We can't afford anything. We have no status. Everybody looks down on us."

"They do not!"

"They do, too! I was there the day Ned Wiggins fired him. You were just a kid then. I'm older. I've seen all his businesses collapse. I know what people think when they look at him, when they look at *us*!"

"You don't know shit! You're just a stupid snob, that's all. You just wish you lived up on Congress Hill so you could look down your nose at everybody. But you don't. So you can't. So there!" He paused and looked around. "What's wrong with this house?"

"It's cramped and dinky and dark and shabby. We're all on top of each other. We have no room, no privacy."

"Lotta people live in houses like this."

"A lot of people don't know what a nice house is."

"I like this house just fine. Anybody else doesn't like it, he can go stuff it. It's good enough for Dad and Mom, it's good enough for me. Since when it's not good enough for you? Since when?"

"Since as long as I can remember."

"It's your house, too. Asshole."

"Stop calling me asshole."

"Stop acting like one."

Jimmy was clearly trying to provoke me into a fight. I vowed to resist.

"So what if you don't go to college? Dad didn't go to college. Didn't hurt him."

"Dad's a failure."

"Is not."

"He is, too."

"Dad didn't have to go to college. He went to work in the shipyards."

"Yeah, lot of good it did him."

"He says it made a man outta him. That and the Army."

"Yeah, some man."

"Don't you wanna be like Dad?"

"No, I don't want to be like Dad."

"You look like him. Just like him. Everybody says so." It was true. Every time someone mentioned our physical resemblance, I shuddered at the possibility that I would follow him in other ways, too. "Me, I look like Mom."

I could not resist the temptation for a cruel jab.

"Yeah, only shorter."

"Fuck you. Don't you want to be like Dad?"

"No how," I insisted. "No way. I want to be better. A lot better."

"Geez, Brother. You don't like this house. You don't like this family. You don't like Dad. You don't want to be anything like him. But you'll take his money to go to some stupid fairy college for rich kids that we can't afford."

"He's not paying for my college. *Mom* is."

Jimmy ignored me and went on. "You know something? If there's a guy I think's an asshole but I hang out with him 'cause he's gotta nice car or he's throwin' a party next Saturday, you know what I call that? Huh? I call it usin' him. Usin' him. Mom and Dad're killin' themselves so you can play candyass college kid. And you don't even like 'em. I think you're just usin' 'em. That's what I think."

I stood up from the couch. To be taller than Jimmy.

"They *owe* me an education. They *owe* me a chance."

Very slowly and deliberately, he bent down and picked up the Baldwin catalog. He held it open, clutched in both hands.

"They don't owe you nothin', Brother." Slowly and deliberately, he tore the book in two and let the pieces drop to the floor. Then he smiled at me, his teeth caked with black Oreo paste.

That did it. I lunged for him. I fell on top of him and knocked him onto the floor and started pummeling him. Over and over. Pound, pound, pound. He did not resist. He just lay there taking it. Unaffected, unbothered. He was hard. Surprisingly hard.

I stopped hitting him. He remained indifferent. He pulled himself out from under me and got up, looking like nothing had happened. He brushed his pants off and looked down at me on the floor. I was still panting and seething with anger.

"Just remember, Brother. Whether you like it or not, you'll always be one of us."

He turned and walked back toward the kitchen.

"You stupid phony," he snickered over his shoulder.

CHAPTER ELEVEN

"No way, Macallan," Wendy says insistently. "I would never want to raise our kids in a house like that. Ne-ver."

"Why not?" I bring the car to a stop. This Sunday morning is cloudless, bright, and chilly, with not a clue in the air that spring will arrive in just a few days. "It's just a big, rambling house," I say, "with gracious rolling lawns and lovely old trees. It's perfect."

"It certainly is big, I'll give you that."

"But it's not a stuffy mansion. It's a house-house, colonial frame style or whatever you call it. Look, no pillars, no porticoes. And it's probably got great little rooms up there where the roof angles in."

"Jesus Christ, Macallan, it's a fucking mansion! It must have seven bedrooms. And this isn't exactly Maple Street in Hometown, USA. It's Soundview Drive in Southpoint, Connecticut."

"But it doesn't look showy. It's not like those gaudy estates in Greenwich or Bedford. It has a homey, unpretentious feel to it—once you get used to the, uh, overall lay of the land."

"Right." Wendy sits in the car with her legs up, shoes off, and stockinged feet tapping against the dashboard. "Sure. Five-acre zoning and no house smaller than seven thousand square feet. It's just like Beaver Cleaver's homey little block—on steroids."

"But it feels kind of unpretentious, doesn't it? I mean, for such a rich neighborhood."

"That's because it's old money up here. New money goes in for the regal, formal stuff. Believe me, the unpretentious look you see in Southpoint is strictly a pretense. There's enough pretense around this town to choke a White House chief of protocol."

I take my foot off the brake and continue our five-mile-per-hour tour of Southpoint dream houses on the way to brunch with Eugene Merritt.

"I went biking through Southpoint with my girlfriends once," Wendy says.

"That's when you were here?"

"Yeah, summer between high school and college. We biked all the way up Long Island Sound to Newport."

"Sounds like fun."

"It was."

"So what happened?"

"We stopped at a lawn sale at one of these huge houses."

"You remember which one?"

"No, but it was somewhere along here. It had a front lawn on the water."

"And?"

"It was actually a pretty ordinary lawn sale, selling off their old junk. Toasters, record albums, old magazines, beat-up kitchen sets, the kids' old roller skates, stuff like that."

I nod.

"The lady of the house had this table full of little items. You know, can openers, costume jewelry, palm tree salt and pepper shakers from Florida."

"Yes?"

"And a box full of guess what?"

We pull up to the next gigantic but homey property, a fieldstone and shingle affair with a bluish slate roof.

"Her old worn-out bras! Can you believe it? Her dingy, sweaty, fraying old bras!"

"How much was she asking for them?"

"I don't remember."

"Waste not, want not, I guess."

"Come on, Macallan. She had the nerve to think that someone would want to buy her old bras. Do you know what that said to me about Southpoint?"

I shrug again.

"A combination of incredible arrogance and incredible cheapness. Makes me so mad when I hear cracks about Jewish people being penny-pinchers. Here was this high-WASP aristocrat, the product of all this privilege and so-called breeding, scrounging for spare change selling used bras."

"They say one woman's junk is another woman's trea—"

"My point, Robert, is that a place like Southpoint is no place to bring up kids. Things here are out of . . . out of proportion. I want our kids to grow up in an environment that's more, you know, regular. More normal. Don't you? You don't want a kid growing up thinking that the girl-next-door neighbor lives in a house like that." She motions toward the gargantuan Charles Addams–style house rolling into view before us, set back on a lawn big enough to be a golf hole.

"I don't know, honey. When I was growing up in Bayport, I always dreamed—"

"Those are dreams, Robert. I'm talking about our real life."

"But wouldn't you like to—"

"No, I wouldn't. And neither would you. Not really. I hate to say it, love of my life, but deep in my soul I'm middle-class."

"Ee-gad!" I protest, trying to sound arch and theatrically preppy. "I had no idea!"

"And I've got news for you."

"Yes, dah-ling dearest?"

"Whether you know it or not, so are you."

Number 1 Harbor Road is an authentic Greek Revival mansion from the 1830s, a white wooden structure dressed elegantly with Ionic columns on either side of the portico, floor-to-ceiling windows all around the ground floor. It is smallish by Southpoint standards, but beautifully proportioned. A gracious, perfectly preserved architectural gem. It sits at the top of a grassy hill overlooking just what you'd expect. A perfect half-moon cove sheltered from the waters of Long Island Sound, just right for expensive yachts. Only a handful of boats have been left in the water over the winter. There are a few launches and motorboats bobbing at the docks of the tiny marina and, moored farther out in the harbor, a lone lobster boat. I wonder aloud where in Southpoint a lobsterman might be able to afford a house.

"Do you think he commutes in from Danbury?" I ask Wendy as we approach the front door.

"I don't think there *is* a lobsterman. I'll betcha it's a Southpoint millionaire who likes to pretend he's a lobsterman. Remember those parties Marie Antoinette used to throw? Where everybody dressed up like peasants and pretended to be simple?"

"No."

We reach the front door. I push the doorbell.

"The French have a term for that kind of thing," Wendy explains. *"Nostalgie de la boue.* Nostalgia for the mud."

"I can't pronounce that. Is there another name for it?"

"Yeah. Lobster boat in Southpoint harbor."

The door opens to reveal a roundish, slightly stooped gentleman somewhere between his late sixties and late seventies. Gene Merritt is dressed in well-worn tweed and flannel, the same herringbone jacket and gray slacks a professor might wear, but nattier and clearly more expensive. He has a beak nose, clear hazel eyes, and wisps of silver hair surrounding his bald crown. Like Alistair Cooke from TV's "Masterpiece Theatre," but bubbling with life.

"Oh, the lobster boat?" he says, having heard Wendy's last sentence. "That belongs to Harland Tidwell. He's the only honest-to-God lobsterman left in Southpoint. In fact, he's just about the only honest-to-God Southpoint native left. Harland and I, that is. His family and mine have lived here since the 1700s. Everybody else is"—he gestures over his back in the general direction of the megahouses on Soundview Drive—"well, I guess you could call them immigrants."

He has a gracious, easy smile and just the faintest hint of lockjaw in his speech.

"Please, come in out of the cold." He motions us into the house. "You must be the Macallans."

"Bob Macallan, Mr. Merritt." I take his offered hand.

"Please. Gene."

"Gene, my wi—"

"Wendy Wolfson," she says, offering her hand.

"Delighted you could make it." He closes the door and ushers us into the front hallway. The interior of the house is open and flooded with late morning sunlight. The living room opens off to the left. There is a small group of people talking over drinks. The dining room, with table set for brunch, is off to the right. Original period furniture is everywhere. The rugs are antique Bokharas, worn through to the burlap in spots. It is like a museum recreation of the 1830s without the museum's velvet rope.

Suddenly, a small, round man in a striped gray houseboy's jacket appears beside Merritt. He could be the same age as his master. He reaches to help us out of our coats.

"*Grazie*, Carlo," Merritt says with a deadly flat American accent. Carlo nods a welcome to us, takes the coats, and heads for the back of the house. "Carlo and Silvana have been with us for thirty years. They more or less came with the farmhouse in Tuscany when we bought it. After my wife died, I started bringing them back with me for the months I spend stateside. They're a little bit the fish out of water here, but they like it better in Southpoint than in town. Silvana says Park Avenue is the ugliest street in the world." He hunches his shoulders in what must be an impersonation of Silvana: " '*Bruta, bruta.*' "

"Where in Tuscany is your house?" Wendy asks eagerly.

"A little village called Castelnuovo. I'm sure you've never heard of it. It's not even on the map."

"I adore Tuscany," Wendy says as she beams at Merritt, then back at me. He is living one of our fantasies, her look seems to say. This is turning out to be a positive experience for her, after all.

"You'll have to drop in when you're in Italy," Merritt says. "It's about twenty minutes out of Siena. Friends of Laura's are always welcome."

At the mention of Laura's name, Wendy takes my hand, ostensibly to hold it in a warm, wifely way. Instead, she digs her fingernails into my flesh. I look at her. She gives me a big smile.

"You know, Laura's father was the Merritt family lawyer. Much more than that, really. He was father confessor, friend, trust administrator, and bringer of bounty. He was single-handedly responsible for keeping the Merritt fortune healthy. You know how old money has a tendency to wither away into no money. Yes, Tom Chasen had a nose for making money. I'd say he was a true financial genius." He takes a look around his ancestral home, pondering something. "I watched his little Laura grow up from a baby." Wendy's nails dig in deeper. "I must say she's provided quite a varied and, uh, tempestuous spectacle. But she seems happier these days. I get postcards from all over. So? You met at Bangle Bay."

"That's right," I say, disengaging my injured hand from Wendy.

"Wonderful place, Bangle Bay. Emily and I went there for years and years. Last two weeks in January. Faithfully. We each kept a drawer of clothes just for that. Our Bangle Bay drawer. Come on into the living room and let's get you a drink. We're almost all here. Soon as Seymour Pinsky and friend arrive, we can sit down and eat."

At the mention of Seymour Pinsky, Wendy and I exchange surprised looks. Pinsky, the controversial writer of tormented literary fiction, is hardly the kind of guest we expected to meet here. He gained early fame with a brilliant collection of short stories, *The Novena Novellas*, and has spent the last twenty years releasing tantalizing bits and pieces of a still unfinished novel. His admirers are passionate about him; he is nothing less than the messiah of twentieth-century literature. His detractors call him a fraud, a lazy, clever manipulator of the voluble, jaded culture crowd.

Suddenly, the sound of a wild animal's howling fills the house. Merritt smiles at us over the din. "I hope you don't mind. The entertaining I do here in the country is a little more, shall we say, eccentric than in town." He leans toward us and whispers confidentially, "It's also a lot more casual and fun. You're friends of Laura's, so I'm sure you'll appreciate it."

He motions for us to follow him into the living room, where the racket is coming from. We join the group of five people. There's a tall older man holding a portable cassette player, a short young brown man, some kind of Asian in an ill-fitting suit, and a handsome white-haired American couple.

"That is the sound of a male hyena experiencing moments of, as it were, multiple ecstasy with a female hyena," says the reedy Englishman with leathery skin and the tape player. "I lay in the bush for an entire day waiting to get that on tape." He is well into his fifties but has a childlike aura.

Merritt pats him on the shoulder with one hand and snaps off the machine with the other. "St. John always brings back new animal sound effects from his safaris." He pronounces it *"Sin-jin."* "How do you know it's not the female experiencing multiple moments of ecstasy?"

The group laughs in response.

"Bob Macallan and Wendy Wolfson," Merritt announces, "St. John Morse-Reynolds, intrepid leader of African safaris for teenage boys whose parents have too much money and not enough sense. St. John tried to kill both my sons in the bush over the course of several summers. Despite his best efforts, they survived to manhood."

Carlo appears again at Merritt's side. "What can we get you to drink?" the master asks. "Champagne seems to be the order of the morning, but Carlo can fix you anything you like."

"Champagne sounds just right," Wendy says.

"Same," I say. Carlo, apparently conversant with English, goes to fill our orders.

Merritt continues the introductions with the Asian. "Jalang Gadja, special coordinator of an important research project between the University of Jakarta and Columbia." We exchange greetings. Carlo appears with our crystal tulip glasses of champagne.

"And Bill and Peggy Forster, Mr. and Mrs. retired U.S. Consul General in Florence, now of Porto Ercole. My dear old friends and touchstones of sanity in Tuscany." The Forsters nod and smile. "Bob and Wendy are friends of Tom Chasen's daughter. Bob's in magazine publishing and from what I gather has had some interesting goings-on of late."

Just then the doorbell rings.

"Aha!" Merritt exclaims. "The artistic contingent is here. Carlo, tell Silvana, *siamo pronti a mangiare.* Our literary lion is always hungry." Merritt excuses himself and heads for the vestibule.

Peggy Forster steps up to Wendy and me.

"So you're friends of Laura's," she says more to Wendy than to me. Wendy takes my hand again to pull me closer to the impending conversation. Once again, she digs her nails in. "How is she these days? We haven't seen her since her wedding to that young executive."

"Oh, she's doing great, just great," Wendy says through a smile of gritted teeth. "My husband, though, is closer to Laura than I am. How is she doing, honey?"

I manage to free my sore hand. "Laura's great," I vamp to the diplomat's wife. "We saw her just last month in the Caribbean. But briefly. There one day, gone the next. You know Laura."

"Yes," she says, looking thoughtful and troubled on Laura's behalf. "I do hope she's happier now."

An uncomfortable silence is about to settle in between Peggy Forster and us when Merritt appears in the living room with Seymour Pinsky and his female companion in tow. "I come bearing genius," Merritt announces. He begins introducing Pinsky and girlfriend Leandra Swerdloff around the room. St. John and Seymour, it seems, have met at Merritt's table many times before.

Pinsky is a tall, powerfully built man, only just starting to thicken and droop with late middle age. He has a full head of wiry gray hair and a thick salt-and-pepper beard. He is dressed like a writer in a corduroy jacket, brown winter turtleneck, and corduroy slacks. He has the fleshy, pock-marked face of a Russian Jewish peasant, with sad pale blue eyes peering out from shadowy sockets. But his most striking feature, just like the articles say, is his scar. A big ugly scar that runs from the center of his left cheek straight down to his jawline. You can even see it through his beard, a horrible skinny worm permanently stuck to his face. The mythology says that he got it as a teenager, defending himself in a fatal knife fight with his abusive alcoholic stepfather. He was arrested, tried for manslaughter, and acquitted. The history of mortal violence and a criminal record residing in a tor-mented Freudian intellectual has proved irresistible to the literary world. Pinsky has capitalized on it for years, reaping an unbroken chain of founda-tion grants and stylish dinner invitations.

Fortyish Leandra Swerdloff is his literary groupie, the perennial Benning-ton or Bard College bohemian who refuses to grow up. Gypsy print dress, oversized earrings and necklace from an earnest provincial crafts fair, black tights, long frizzy hair pulled back in a bun to frame her hollow, angular face.

"Come, folks," Merritt says cheerily. "Our bard needs sustenance." We head for the dining room.

Deftly, Merritt moves the talk from one person to another around the table. He sits at one end; St. John faces him at the other. The table is set with white linen and fine antique crystal, china, and silver. Hardly any of it matches. This is the tableware accumulated by generations of Merritts who

107

have lived here and eaten at this long, rather narrow table. I am seated at the far end of the window side, to St. John's right. Beside me is Jalang and beside him Leandra. Facing me directly is Pinsky, with Wendy at his side, Bill Forster next, then Peggy. Merritt admitted the seating was flawed but blamed it on the uneven number of guests (the famous gay architect canceled at the last minute) and his insistence on sitting next to Peggy, no matter what.

"So," Merritt asks Jalang at what seems to be the end of the Indonesian's conversational turn, "your conclusion is that the problem has to do with the students' sense of personal geography."

"That is right," Jalang says in his thick accent. "The Indonesian exists in relation to the location of his village. Even if I leave my village and go to Jakarta or Sumatra, I can still look on the horizon and see, in my mind's eye, where I have come from. But when I leave on an airplane and go to New York or Cambridge or Palo Alto, I have lost all frame of reference. I do not know where I am. It is a profound sense of disorientation that our students experience when they come here. That seems to be what affects their studies unfavorably."

"Fascinating," Merritt says. "How do you propose to help them overcome it?"

"I have begun by extending the terms of my grant for another year. So that I can stay in America and study it further." Jalang breaks from his deadpan academic sincerity and cracks a grin. "But I have arranged to finish the project in California, where the winters are much kinder."

A chuckle around the table.

Silvana emerges from the kitchen with another platter of frittata, the hearty open-faced Italian omelet loaded with artichoke, bacon, potatoes, peppers, and God knows what else. Silvana is short and round and almost indistinguishable from her husband Carlo, except that she has longer hair, large, flat breasts, and a white apron. She sets the platter on the sideboard and retreats into the kitchen.

Merritt motions for Carlo to serve Pinsky first. Pinsky has a gargantuan appetite. Every time you look up, his plate and glass are empty. The man is an eating and drinking machine. And he chatters away. For someone famous for writing about deep emotional pain, he is astonishingly charming and bubbly. With Merritt he is almost too charming and bubbly.

"Don't keep us so much in suspense," Merritt asks while the writer is in the middle of another mouthful. "Will we be seeing another installment of the novel sometime soon?"

Pinsky swallows his food quickly and drains his glass of Chianti. Without missing a beat, Carlo is there with a refill. "*Grazie,* Carlo," Pinsky says officiously and takes another swig. Suddenly his aura changes. Gone is the fluttery social charm. This is now the great artist talking. Very solemn. "I was working in the predawn hours this morning. As I do every morning. And I think I created the single passage that captures in metaphor the bottomless torment my main character feels." Leandra looks on adoringly. I can't help but wonder if she shaves her legs. My guess is she does, but not her underarms. "I want to create an art that is truly unbearable in the intensity of its pain. To make it hurt so much it becomes unreadable. This passage plumbs those depths, I think." Dramatic pause. "I hope." His face begins to brighten. "But I have to put it away to let it ripen and age before I can go back to it." He finishes off his glass. Immediately, Carlo refills him. He takes another sip. "It needs to ripen"—big smile at Merritt, glass in the air—"like our host's fine wines. I think in another year, maybe two, all the pieces will come together."

"True inspiration can't be run like a train schedule," Leandra pipes in from down the table. Pinsky smiles fondly in her direction.

"I saw a little piece you did in *Modern Shelter* the other month," Merritt says. "The one on Dotty Vanderbilt's townhouse renovation. I was very impressed."

Pinsky makes a dismissive gesture that looks like false modesty.

"No, really. I was very impressed."

"Thank you, Gene. Dotty really is such a dear heart. And she's been so good to me over the years. She truly is a gifted hostess. Uh, of course, no more gifted in hospitality than you. I jumped at the chance to do the article because I think I have a special insight into the new decor she's chosen. It's such a vibrant expression of her inner self. All of it, the colors, the fabrics, the irony of formal wedded to informal. It's all pure Dotty."

"Impressive," Merritt says, nodding. "Very impressive."

"Thanks." Embarrassed, Pinsky brushes away the adulation and rambles on about the historical bond between artists and the aristocracy.

I hear Merritt mutter something under his breath. I could swear it is, "Impressed that you finished it."

Finally, he gets to me. We go through a table talk version of the acquisition and what I do. "That's quite an accomplishment," Merritt concludes, "especially at your age. That's a fine company, American, a fine company." I give Wendy a look that says, If I could only tell him about Harry Woodcock and friends. "Yes, you've allied yourself with the best. I remember when I was at Yale, Andrew Henderson was the legend we all looked up to. Ten years out of the college and he had the biggest magazine in America. He created a company that stands for the best."

Wendy gives me a look that says, Don't you dare say anything.

"That's true," I start to say, "but American Communications today—"

Before I can finish the sentence, I feel a sharp pain in my shin. Wendy has kicked me under the table.

"Is even more dynamic," I say. "I consider myself very lucky." Now my leg and my hand hurt.

"I suspect," Merritt says, "there's not much luck involved in your case. I assume you've gone before the board of directors and met them."

"No." I smile. "My acquisition isn't that important."

"Really?" he asks quizzically, innocently unaware of how different his context is from mine. "I find it always helps to know the men in charge. Do you know Binkie Addison?"

"Binkie Addison? No, I'm afraid not."

"R. Bingham Addison. He's on your board. Binkie and I were roommates at Groton and Yale, ushers at each other's weddings, all that."

"Oh, him," I say. R. Bingham Addison is the former president of Blaine Consulting and one of the most powerful members of American's board of directors.

"I think you two would really hit it off. Binkie ought to see the kind of young blood they're bringing in. Laura was right when she told me you were a very interesting young man."

At the mention of Laura, I pull my legs back around either side of my chair to get them out of harm's way. I see Wendy's eyes narrow. Suddenly, Jalang, seated beside me, jerks his head back and winces. He looks around, puzzled.

"Something wrong, Jalang?" Merritt asks.

"No," he whimpers and offers the table a confused smile.

APRIL

CHAPTER TWELVE

Dudley Townsend is sitting in the chair across from my desk, as has become his all too regular habit. Joe Bartolo says the reason for Dudley's stiff posture and pigeonlike walk is the broomstick that the boy's mother stuck up his ass.

Dudley the superprep is a terrifying combination of the KGB and Junior Achievement. He is the eternal teacher's pet, the kid we've dreaded since grade school—smug, priggish, ever alert to the slightest infringement of the rules, and condescending to everyone except the Big Authority Figure, who in this case is Harry Woodcock.

Today Dudley is jabbering about plans for our new offices on the fifth floor of American headquarters. "There are several different designs we can choose from," he says. "I recommend this semimodular office cube configuration. It offers the most flexibility at the lowest cost, with minimal negative trade-offs in *Elixir*'s corporate imagery."

That is Dudley's endearing way of saying it's cheap and not bad-looking. He pulls an architect's plan out of a long cardboard tube and spreads it open on my desk, borrowing my stapler and pencil cup to keep it from curling up. "I think the key to this space flow is integration with separation. Integration with separation." That must be his big idea for today. Dudley always has one big idea every day. "We maximize the way the departments access each other with this large open space, while preserving their separateness with strategic areas of privacy defined by these partitions and cubicles. Executives retain these walled offices around the perimeter. Naturally." That includes Dudley. Naturally.

Dudley doesn't actually know anything about office design, or anything else for that matter. What he can do is absorb jargon and play it back brilliantly. No wonder he was such a hit in management consulting. To listen to him now, you'd think he'd spent his life in office design. In fact, he spent just enough time with the architects to catch the superficial drift of their ideas and pretend he invented them.

"You see," he says, leaning across the plans, "we put Joe's accounting people here in the center to act as the bridge, literally, between the editorial group and advertising sales. Church remains separate from state. Separate. But linked together by the one function essential to them both."

"Cash flow," I chime in.

"Precisely." Dudley nods approvingly.

The move will raise *Elixir*'s real estate costs from fifteen dollars per square foot here in the dowdy General Insurance building to thirty dollars per square foot in modularized, scientific, high-status American. Thirty dollars is not the actual cost; it's what corporate decides, through formulas more complex than atomic fission, to charge as *Elixir*'s share of corporate overhead. Once, when I winced at my soaring costs, Dudley sang me a perfect rendition of Woodcock's party line. I wasn't paying more, I was getting added value—the added value of being at corporate headquarters, the synergies (yes, he said that with a straight face) of residing amidst the other American magazines, and the incalculable addition to our prestige that American's address will bring.

According to Joe's calculations, *Elixir* will have to come up with an extra $200,000 in revenues to pay for the new real estate and deluxe furnishings. Plus an extra $135,000 to cover Dudley's overgenerous salary and benefits. Plus the moving costs, Dudley's modular cubicles, designer-label staplers, insurance, and everything else we'll have to "buy" from corporate at top dollar. Joe says the damage will come to somewhere around $500,000. Half a million dollars in new revenues I'll have to pull out of my hat or thin air to come in at plan and get the rest of the earn-out.

Wayne Crosby appears in the doorway looking concerned. "Bob, can I see you?"

"Sure, come on in." I start rolling up the blueprint, expecting Dudley to pick up the cue and get the hell out. He does not budge. Wayne takes the seat next to Dudley, pauses, looks at him, then back at me.

"It's, uh, a kinda delicate matter. About ad sales," Wayne says.

"Oh, please, go ahead," Dudley says. "I'm here to help in any way I possibly can."

"Thanks, Dudley." I hand him the blueprint and the cardboard tube. "Wayne and I need to talk. Alone."

"Well, I'm always available, no matter what the problem." Unfazed, Dudley gets up to leave. "Door open or closed?" he asks.

"Closed, please." The door clicks into place. Pause. "So, Wayne, how've you been? I haven't seen you in ages, I've been so goddamn busy." Busy with Harry Woodcock's endlessly time-consuming corporate bull-shit—seminars, training sessions, committee meetings, task force reports. It feels like I haven't had a full day at *Elixir* in a month. When I checked my calendar this morning, I discovered that I hadn't.

"It's this rumor thing," Wayne says.

"Leo tells me the problem is just about licked."

"I guess so. It's hard for me to say."

"Isn't that what he's told you?"

"Yeah. Sure."

"You don't sound convinced, Wayne. What's up?"

"I don't wanna sound like I'm complaining, but since Leo started this campaign of his, he hasn't let the rest of us go near our accounts without him in tow. I've got media directors, advertising directors, clients of *mine* that I'm not supposed to talk to without the go-ahead from Leo. Same for Mike, same for Roni. Now I know Leo's the senior guy, ad director, associate publisher, and all that. I can understand that you'd want him to handle this problem. But it's been a month now, and we're still in the dark. Leo says he's having meetings of his own with our clients' bosses and we're just supposed to sit still in the meantime. It's like we're all on hold until Leo makes everything all right again. Meanwhile there's shit going on out there that we oughtta be responding to."

"Really, what kind of shit?"

"Shit like Elton Mackey's party."

"Elton Mackey's party?"

"Elton Mackey's 'Party of the Century.' "

"His what?"

"That's what it's being billed as. It's the hottest invitation on the street, to say nothing of the weirdest."

Oh Jesus, Macallan, you are out of touch.

"Who is he inviting?"

"For starters, all our advertisers." Wayne pauses to let it sink in.

It sinks in. I remember my last conversation with Atwood in the gray whale.

"He's launching a new medical book, isn't he?"

"Not just a medical book. A medical life-style book."

"Shit. How soon?"

"No one knows. That's what the party is supposed to be about." Wayne reaches into his suit coat pocket and extracts a folded sheet of paper. "Here's a Xerox of the invitation. A friend of mine at Saatchi sent it to me."

Even through the rough photocopying, you can see that the invitation was printed on heavily textured paper. The text is in florid Spencerian script with so many ruffles and flourishes it's nearly impossible to read. It looks like a parody of a pretentious wedding invitation. With some difficulty I can make out what it says:

> Elton Mackey and the Mackey Magazine Group cordially invite you to come to Laurelwood in Gates Mills, Ohio, on May 6th to participate in a historic moment in magazine publishing. Here in baronial splendor, you will be served the rarest of delicacies for the palate and an even rarer delicacy for the marketing plan—America's physicians, captive and ready to buy your prod-

ucts and services. No elixir can cure what ails your media plan anymore. From now on, you will need the *Panacea*.
R.S.V.P. to confirm your seating on our private jets.

"Oh shit. When did these come out?"

"About a week ago. He's invited all the big guns in medical marketing, client types and agency people. Drug companies, instrument makers, radiological equipment, the works. All our advertisers. Even the guys from Jaguar and Mercedes, the ones I've been courting for months. He's chartered jets that will pick up the bodies at Teterboro in New Jersey, Midway in Chicago, Orange County Airport, Atlanta, all over. Supposedly he's tied up every rentable limo between Cleveland and Detroit to ferry everyone back and forth from Laurelwood on the day of the party. He's planted stories about having celebrity guests like Hippocrates, the Curies, Albert Schweitzer, and Jonas-fucking-Salk. No one knows what that's supposed to mean. It's created a shitload of interest, though. Mackey's books have never had any dealings with a lot of these guys, but he's sure managed to get their attention. Everyone's going."

"Everyone?"

"Hasn't Leo said anything about this?"

"Not a word. Are you sure he knows about it?"

"I heard him asking Ron Hoffman about it over the phone the day *before* the invitations hit the street."

"What's he said to you guys about it?"

"Keep mum and find out whatever we can."

"I think I should talk to Leo."

"Mike and Roni and I would appreciate it. We wanna get back to work and figure out what to do about this Mackey thing."

"Wayne, thanks a lot." I'm getting up and patting his shoulder as we leave my office. "Thanks a million."

Thanks five or six million is what I'm thinking.

I walk down the hall to Leo's office, pausing before stepping in front of the open doorway. I can hear him on the phone.

"Of course old Leo's gonna take care of you. Am I Mr. Sales or am I Mr. Sales? When we get our, uh, new management in place, you'll see how things are supposed to be run around here. You betcha. That's what I've been trying to tell you. This isn't just a golden opportunity for me, it's a golden opportunity for you, too."

I poke my head in the doorway and motion toward the empty visitor's chair. Leo snaps to attention. His tone changes. More formal, more public.

"That's right. Look for great things from *Elixir*. Great things. With resources we couldn't have even dreamed of a few months ago. We're part of America's mightiest magazine empire now, and you owe it to your marketing plan to come along with us. Every month. We can talk rates later. Just think about the concept; that's the key thing. The concept. I'll be calling you soon. Just remember the concept. Bye-bye."

Leo hangs up and beams a smile of welcome. I sit down.

"Mediplex Instruments," he says, motioning toward the telephone. "Helluva good prospect. One more call and I'll land him. One more call. What can I do for you, Bob?"

"How's the rumor campaign going?"

"You mean the *anti*rumor campaign? Couldn't be better. I think I've pretty well got the whole Western Hemisphere convinced that we are dealing strictly from strength and that we're only gonna be stronger as a result of being acquired by American. The past is behind us. There's nothing but futures ahead."

"So you can let Mike and Wayne and Roni get back to their accounts?"

Leo gives me a look that starts out puzzled, turns to slightly injured, then finishes with his familiar big grin. "I think I found out who started it all. The rumors, that is. Not that it matters now."

"Really? Who was the culprit?"

"It took me a while to put two and two together. But there always seemed to be one guy making calls and taking people to lunch just one step ahead of us."

"Who was that?"

"Your old friend. Howie Marcus."

"Marcus?"

"Absolutely. He was pissed because you didn't sell the company through him, right?"

"Right."

"Well, that was his way of getting back at you."

I decide not to ask, What about the call Marcus made to you in the middle of the rumor crisis? What about the meeting you dashed out to have with him?

"Listen," Leo says reassuringly. "It's all in the past now. Let me talk to the kids this afternoon. Everything's fine. Green lights, green lights." He picks up the yellow pad in front of him. "Here's a list of the extra orders I've been writing. I think the kids should get the full bonus credits wherever it's on an account of theirs. Full credits."

"That's big of you, Leo." You duplicitous bastard.

"Nah, that's leadership. Leadership. Listen, I'm preparing a list of suggestions for the business plan." He reaches into his top drawer for a yellow legal pad. "Not just sales ideas, either. I'm talking about management ideas, things I've been thinking about for thirty years in this business and never seen done. I've been bouncing some of them off young Dudley. He says that you and me and Woodcock and him ought to sit down together sometime soon. A bright kid, Dudley. Smart as a whip."

"Sure. Good idea." Pause. "Leo, is there anything else you want to tell me about?"

"I don't think so."

"You sure?"

"I told you it looks like December will set a new record for ad pages, didn't I?"

"Uh-huh."

"I told you I'm close to a contract with the Penulex brand manager."

"Yeah, I know."

"Then we're current."

"Nothing else?"

"No, nothing."

"Nothing about Elton Mackey's party? And all the advertisers of ours he's going to be hosting?"

"Oh, *that*?"

"Don't you consider that a significant event?"

"Naah. Word's been out for some time that Mackey's planning a new medical book. The party is just his way of making it official. Believe me, I've got us covered six ways to Sunday with our clients. I say let Mackey shoot his wad out in Cleveland. Let's see what he promises, then figure out our response. Till then, there's not much we can do. So why bother you? You've been so damned busy, I figured that was one thing you could do without."

"Listen, you've got to keep me on top of things, no matter how busy I look. I mean it, Leo."

"Sure, Bob, sure. Okay."

Marie sticks her head in the door. "Phone call, Bob."

"Please. Not right now."

"I think you might want to take it."

"Can I get back to them a little later? Leo and I—"

"He says you'll want to speak to him now."

"Who is it?"

"Elton Mackey."

"Jesus Christ. Can you transfer it in here?"

Marie disappears from the doorway and hollers back to Jeannie. Seconds later Leo's line rings. I reach across his desk and pick it up.

"Hello."

"Hello, Macallan. I knew I could get your attention. How's life in the big fancy corporation? You taking the five-oh-one home to Greenwich every night to brownnose with the Ivy League brass?"

"Not yet."

"Well, after you move uptown to the high-rent district you will. I can just see you there in the club car playing hearts with the Princeton and Yale boys, talking about your golf swing, and worrying about who we should let into the yacht club. It's gonna be a great life, Macallan."

"To what do I owe the honor of this call?"

"Just takin' your temperature. Seeing how life at American is treating you. You know I take a personal interest in your happiness."

"I'm very touched."

"For a while I was hearing some pretty grim rumors about your book.

Had me real concerned. But now I hear you've got a lot of big plans. Is it true?"

"Yeah."

"Glad to hear it."

"What is this call about, anyway?"

"Two important publishing figures keeping in touch. Happens all the time. It's a good thing the government has no evidence of this tête-à-tête of ours. They'd throw us in for collusion or monopoly or something. Aren't you glad there's no evidence; aren't you?"

"Yeah."

"Yeah, what? Aren't you glad there'll be no evidence?"

"Yes, I'm glad there'll be no evidence. What do you want?"

"Don't you figure I'd only call you if I had some kinda deal to offer? Why don't you ask me what kind of a deal it is?"

"Okay. What kind of a deal are you offering me?"

"I want to make you even happier than you are now. Ask me how I'm going to arrange it, go on."

"How are you going to arrange it?"

"Well, I want to hire you as a consultant for my new magazine. Your experience makes you the perfect man for the job."

"So I hear."

"Come on, Macallan, cheer up. You know what they say about imitation."

"Yeah, I'm deeply flattered."

"You should be. It isn't everybody who gets this kind of attention from me."

"Believe me, I appreciate how lucky I am."

"I knew you would. Tell me, would you rather have a book with controlled circulation or a book with paid circulation?"

"What?"

"Come on, just answer the question."

"Of course, I'd rather have paid circulation."

"Me, too. Say, have you heard about the little party I'm having next month?"

"Yeah, I've heard."

"Gonna be a helluva bash. I wish I could invite you, but if I add one more person to the list, the fucking caterer's bill is gonna clean me right out. You priced caviar lately? You know what those ten-pound tins of beluga go for? Personally, I don't know what the big deal is. The stuff tastes like stale pussy to me. But you gotta have it on hand. Know what I mean?"

"Yes."

"Anyway, we gotta lotta interesting people coming. Lot of folks you know. Advertisers, media directors. Gonna be a real good group. I'll rent you the guest list for a good price. It's a perfect list for *Elixir*. Go ahead, make me an offer for it, go ahead. Let's start at a dollar per name."

"Okay. I'll give you a dollar per name."

"Come on; you can do better than that."

"Two dollars per name."

"Good man. Tell you what; I'll get back to you after the party. You know, pretty soon you and I are gonna have a lot in common. The same kinda magazine. The same clients. The same ad budgets. You and I are gonna be just like two peas in a pod."

"I can't wait."

"Well, I guess I'll be seeing you around then. Say good-bye, Macallan."

"Good-bye."

"So long, buddy." Click.

As I pull the phone away from my ear, I am relieved to escape the overpowering, sickly sweet smell that seems permanently embedded in it. The smell of Leo's cologne, House of Lords.

CHAPTER THIRTEEN

More shit piles up on my desk, none of which I can resolve today. There's a problem at our printer in Kentucky. Half of his presses are down for two weeks during renovations; the overworked other half is not delivering the reproduction quality that has been one of *Elixir*'s trademarks. Worse still, our next issue may be late as a result. There'll be embarrassment, apologies, and make-goods to advertisers. Costs. Jerry has just submitted an impassioned request for additional editorial staff. More costs. Then there's Mackey and whatever he's got planned. And Leo. Was he holding back or was he really just trying not to bother me? And how the hell could I let myself get so busy with American to get so out of touch with the street?

I need a new plan. I need some fresh thinking. I need some distance and clarity. Clearly, I'm not going to get it sitting at my desk. So I decide to do what any red-blooded Fortune 500 executive would do under the circumstances. I will leave the office early to go home and make dinner for my wife.

As Marie dumps the day's last load of interoffice correspondence on my desk, she sees me writing out a shopping list on the back of a pink "While You Were Out" slip. She has seen the pattern before.

"Are you gonna fix one of those nouvelle things with hummingbird breasts roasted over mesquite twigs?"

"I've never roasted hummingbirds over mesquite twigs."

"You know what I mean. Like that stuff you brought in."

"That was duck and wild rice salad with pears and mango chutney."

"Same difference." Forty-seven-year-old Marie Padrone lives with her mother in Brooklyn.

"You said it was great."

"It was. But weird."

"Anyway, tonight I'm thinking pasta. Spaghetti à la carbonara. The way I learned on our vacation in Rome."

"Buono." She smiles approvingly. "Now, that can do you some good." Had she been born of a less protective mother and twenty years later, Marie might well have lived up to the promise of her surname, which means "big boss." I'm grateful for the luck of finding her three years ago and even more grateful that she does not quit for a job more in line with her native abilities, like running General Motors or the U.S. Army.

"Little pasta, little wine," she says, "nothing better for strategic planning. Why don't you get outta here before Balducci's gets too crowded. You hang around too much longer, the customers'll be lined up around the block and you'll end up ordering in Chinese."

"You're right. As usual."

I review my list one last time and head for the door.

"Anyone calls for me, you know what to tell them."

"You're unreachable."

"I'm in conference."

"With Andrew Henderson, Henry Luce . . ."

"And William Randolph Hearst."

Even in the crowding and jostling of Balducci's market, I begin to feel soothed. Choosing vegetables is much easier than choosing people. Vegetables reveal their flaws and true character more readily, and there's always a good selection in the bin. Still, there's inevitably that great-looking lettuce you scrutinize and scrutinize. It looks perfect in the store, but you get it home and discover it's got nothing but brown rot inside.

I fill my basket with varied, brightly colored salad greens. I don't know their names, except for the oak leaf lettuce and radicchio, but I do know how to dress them with a freshly made vinaigrette. It's a far cry from the tasteless hunks of iceberg lettuce I grew up with, glopped with that mixture of Miracle Whip, catsup, and pickle relish my mother called Russian dressing.

I complete my mission with fresh pasta, a hunk of aged Parmesan cheese for grating, fresh eggs, and *pancetta,* the thick Italian bacon. My carbonara has no relation to the cream sauce and ham concoction most restaurants serve. It is the real thing, cooked on the knife edge of disaster, with egg yolks, cheese, hot bacon, pasta, and abundant fresh-ground black pepper blended together in the plate at the last second to produce either a masterpiece or a mess. In truth, I've made more of the latter.

The subway ride home is relatively uneventful. Only one urine-soaked paranoid schizophrenic taking up three seats and muttering to himself about Spartacus, Fred Flintstone, and Veronica Lake plotting to start World War III.

At home I set the greens out on the counter, put the perishables in the fridge, and head for the answering machine in the bedroom. Two messages waiting.

"Beep, beep, whirr, click, click, beeeep."

"This is your father callin' from Bayport." *Ya fatha cawlin' from Baypott.* "Hiya, Son, howya doin'? Got somebody else here wants to say hi." Pause.

A new voice begins. "Hello, big brother." It is Jimmy. "How's the big shot in the big city? Making those big deals with all the other big shots down there? I moved a buncha your shit outta your old room and down to the basement today. I need the space to make myself an office. I hope you don't mind, big bro'. Got a few deals of my own I wanna work on up here. Unlike some people I know, I think Bayport's a pretty good town. I'm settling in pretty good with Dad here. So give us a call sometime when your busy schedule lets up. You know, have your secretary pencil us in or whatever it is you tycoons do. You know the number, Brother. Here, I'll give you back to the old man." The voice changes back. "That's right, Son. Give us a call. Let us know how you're makin' out."

"Click. Beeeep." Next message.

"Macallan, I've got a surprise for you." It's Wendy. "I think you'll find it very interesting. I'm meeting an old girlfriend for a quick drink. She's giving me the surprise. Marie says we're having pasta tonight. Yum. So, uh, expect me between, uh, seven and seven-thirty. Okay, honey? Bye."

I start setting the table. Oversized peasant dinner plates for the pasta, matching bowls for salad, the heavy hand-blown green wineglasses I like best. I'm thinking about my day in the office, my life in New York, and how different it is from anything my father and brother could ever imagine. They belong together, those two. The odd couple of Bayport. Although in truth, I have always been the odd one, the odd man out in the Macallan clan. I was the one who had no choice but to leave. I am the family exile, the prodigal son who can never return. They always made each other comfortable and made me uneasy. What's worse, the more I accomplished, the more I strived to achieve, the more I felt them secretly sneering and snickering at me. But that's okay. The ever increasing distance between us hurts me and heals me at the same time. Still, I crave the old man's approval, a nod that it is okay for me to be so different. That he is proud of the son he could never understand. So once again I dial the first telephone number I ever learned. The pickup at the other end is immediate.

"Hello." It is Dad.

"Hey, old man, how are you doing?"

"Hi, Son. You hear our message on the squawk box?"

"Yeah, you're getting to be a real pro with this advanced telecommunications technology."

"Well, I gotta. To keep in step with my fancy New Yorker son."

"Is Jimmy there?"

"No, he went out. Gone to see a fella over in Nashua. Maybe he's gotta deal of his own going. How's the big city treatin' ya?"

"Oh, so-so. I've had better days."

"That Harry Woodman givin' you trouble?"

"Trouble? No, he's giving me a lot of meetings to go to, raising my overhead by half a million dollars, planting an asshole MBA espionage agent in my office. But no, he's not giving me trouble. He's giving me, uh, challenges. And his name is Woodcock. Wood-*cock*."

"Son, I tried to tell you about those people. What kinda trouble is he makin'?"

"Temporary setbacks, Dad, just temporary."

"I tried to warn you. They're not our kinda people."

"Really, Dad, I'm just griping. Like in the army. The guys at American are assholes and sons of bitches, I know. But they're the assholes and sons of bitches I chose, and I can handle them. It's going to be okay. I'm working on a plan right now that should go a long way toward making up the half-million."

"Geez, half a million here, half a million there, you sure talk big down there. Sounds like all the money in the world to me."

"At this moment, it does to me, too, Dad. It does to me, too."

"So what's your plan?"

"I haven't got it all worked out yet. It occurred to me on the subway just now." My father has never really understood what I do. Yes, he can understand that I publish a magazine and that it makes money, but his attitude toward the so-called media remains suspicious and skeptical. For one thing, reading puts him off. His education stopped with high school, and as far as he's concerned, the world of the printed page begins and ends with the *Bayport Daily Telegraph*. What's more, he has a provincial New Englander's mistrust of all enterprises that don't deal in plain, tangible day-to-day necessities, as if they are not really work or wholly honest. Until I sold *Elixir* he never took any interest in my business dealings.

"Come on, Son, tell me whatcha got planned."

"You really want to know?"

"Sure, who else you gonna talk to about this?"

"Well, I figure the thing to do is a special issue. Next spring."

"What's a special issue?"

"You know, a thirteenth issue, above and beyond the regular ones."

"What good'll that do?"

"Extra money, that's what."

"Can you just go ahead and do a thing like that?"

"Why not? Publishers do it all the time. You get a big, important subject, write it up in a big, important way, find a few big, important advertisers who have reasons to care about the subject. Give 'em all big, important hard-ons and bingo! Big special issue filled with ads. Minimum expense. Maximum profit. If you do it right, it's as close as you can get to printing money—outside the U.S. Mint."

"Mmm. Just like that?"

"Well, not quite. You have to sweat to pull it all together, but with a lot of effort and a little bit of luck, it's very doable."

"Son, things come so easy to you."

Shit. He's going to start in again. "Dad, please don't say it."

"What?"

"Shit luck and ignorance."

"I wasn't gonna."

"Good. Thanks."

Pause.

"I was gonna say you got a way a finding these things. I don't know where you get it from. You sure as hell don't get it from me or your mother. I struggled like a sonofabitch all my life, and I, well, I wish some of it would rub off on your brother. Nothing but green lights. Green lights since you were a little kid."

Just then I hear Wendy's keys in the front door.

"Macallan!" she sings out. "O-o-o-h, Ro-o-bert!"

"Wendy's home, Dad. Gotta run. Wanna say hi to her?"

"Sure, put her on."

I yell to Wendy from the bedroom to pick up the phone and say hi to my father.

She picks up. "Hi, Clint," she says, her voice echoing over the line from the living room. I hang up, take my shoes off, toss them into my closet, and glance in the full-length mirror on the back of the closet door. Is that a hint of a jowl starting? A Macallan jowl? Will the master blueprint of heredity give me the same cheeks as my father? Since childhood I've had his nose and his blue eyes; why not, as middle age approaches, his jowls? What other traits of his, I wonder, will bubble up from the genetic stew and brand me as the years go by? I close the door and proceed to the living room, where Wendy is finishing the phone call.

"Uh-uh, I guess you can't help but have that kind of weather this time of year." She gives me a patronizing smile, a smile directed at Clint. Wendy says that the weather is the only topic she can get her laconic, stone-faced New England father-in-law to discuss with more words than "ayuh" and "nope."

"Uh-huh." She nods. "Uh-huh. Me, too. You take care now. Bye."

She hangs up.

"Your father's turning into quite a chatterbox. He would have gone on all night about the lawn and the unexpected shower."

"Maybe he's getting senile."

"Nah, maybe now that he's got a roommate again he's finally realizing that he's been lonely since your mother died."

"Maybe."

Wendy looks very crisp and professional in her blue silk business dress with matching jacket. But not for long. First, she steps out of the shoes. Then she plucks the earring from each ear and removes the string of pearls from her neck, depositing them on the end table by the sofa. She undoes the wide black belt and tosses it away, then reaches behind her back and unhooks her bra through her dress.

"Aaah," she sighs. "I hate clothes. Someday I'll have a job where I can wear a muumuu, with nothing on underneath." She has made it over to where I'm standing. A gentle hug, a soft kiss. "Hi, sweetie." We linger like this, not quite embracing.

"How was your day?"

"Fine. How was yours?"

"Fine. A few more surprises in the magazine wars."

"Oooh, that reminds me. Your surprise!" She takes my hand and walks me to the dining alcove and sits us down at the table.

"This is going to be incredibly interesting to you, and possibly incredibly valuable. Which means, of course, incredibly valuable to all of us, born and yet to be born."

"Just what kind of surprise is it?"

"A business surprise. A publishing business surprise. It's something no one at your office or anyone else in your business could do."

"Okay, you've got my attention. What is it?"

"Not so fast. I think we should make a deal for it."

"A deal?"

"I do something special for you, you do something special for me. Tonight."

"Done."

"Whatever I want."

"Whatever."

"Okay, it's a deal." She jumps up to fetch her purse in the living room. "You didn't have to make the deal, you know," she says over her shoulder. "I was going to give you the surprise anyway, you know."

"Yeah, I know."

She returns holding a stiff, smallish piece of paper.

"I ran into an old girlfriend today. A girl I went to Dalton with. I haven't seen her in years. Years! Debbie Bornstein. I think I've told you stories about her, haven't I? So we're catching up. Her husband is on Wall Street. How nice. My husband is a magazine publisher. No kidding, she says. She's a media director at McCann Erikson. What's your husband's book? *Elixir,* I say. Of course, she says. She knows all about it, all about the acquisition, what a great magazine. Congratulations, et cetera. But—there's something troubling her, I can tell. Come on, Debbie, we've gone through gym class together, our first cigarette, our first diaphragms, out with it. She starts in about the rumors she's heard and all that. Then, she says she got an invitation to a huge party at Elton Mackey's place where he's supposedly going to announce a magazine to compete directly with *Elixir.* It's supposed to be the event of the year, but she doesn't think she can go. A new business pitch she's working on. We talk a bit more, but it's lunch hour and we're standing on the corner of Fifty-seventh and Park. So we plan to meet for a drink later. We do, we talk, I make her a proposition, she says, Why not, and . . ." Proudly, she flashes the Mackey invitation in front of my face. "Ta-da!"

"Thanks a million, but I can't use that."

"Of course you can't. But I can. Undercover."

"Under what?"

"Undercover." She lowers her voice to pseudomale range and intones with mock seriousness, "Your mission, Mr. Phelps, is to discover what El

Mackito, the notorious strong-arm dictator and trade magazine publisher, has up his sleeve. Should you or any of your IM force be caught or killed, the secretary will disavow all knowledge. This tape will self-destruct in five seconds. Good luck, Jim."

"You're crazy."

"No, I'm not. I'm Debbie Bornstein. I've already called and reserved my seat on the chartered jet. I'm going to be picked up by a Mackey limo in front of Debbie's apartment building on the morning of the fifteenth. Debbie says the Mackey people know her by title, not by face. She just inherited the job from her recently departed boss, and her boss was the one they knew. Don't worry. They couldn't tell a Debbie Bornstein from a Wendy Wolfson, anyway. They're from Cleveland."

"I guess so. It just seems a little out of order."

"What order? Macallan, you need this information. *Elixir* needs this information. *We* need this information."

"Absolutely."

"So who better to get it than a complete outsider? Information is everything in marketing. Everything. I preach this to my clients all day. Did I ever tell you about the small, single-brand company that outflanked Procter and Gamble?"

"No."

"It's a famous case study. A classic of marketing."

I often forget that Wendy has an MBA. I used to tell myself that I fell in love with her in spite of her degree, not because of it. I may be beginning to change my mind.

"This company, call it Acme, had a liquid household cleaner, great on greasy countertops. Nothing else quite like it. P and G starts eyeing the category. Develops a product that's very similar. Decides to test market it in three cities. They want to be sure they're right before they roll out nationally. That's the way P and G operates."

Suddenly, she sits up very straight. "Robert?"

"Yes."

"Do you think I have multiple sclerosis?"

This time, I felt it coming. The abrupt change in our topic of conversation. I don't know how or why. I just did.

"Do you what?" I smile. Wendy knows just enough about medical diagnosis to give herself a good scare once every couple of weeks. She keeps a copy of *The Physicians' Desk Reference* on the bookshelf in our bedroom and refers to it too often. I learned to stop bringing home medical reading from the office about diseases and symptoms. It only fueled her imagination.

"Do you think I could have MS?"

"What on earth gives you that idea?"

"Well, this morning I woke up with a stiff neck and I thought my vision was starting to blur. That's how MS starts, you know."

"What about the book you were reading last night till all hours? When

I conked out, you were lying there, with your head propped up like that against the pillow. That'll give anyone a stiff neck. And as for blurred vision, do you *think* your vision was blurred or were you actually walking into walls and stuff?"

"It did seem to clear up by lunchtime."

"Another miraculous recovery."

"You don't think I have it, then."

"Sorry, not this time."

"Okay. Well, anyway, Acme managed to get wind of P and G's plan well in advance. They went into the P and G test cities and slashed prices, practically giving away product with big 'stock up now' specials. The housewives socked away Acme's cleaner in bulk. When P and G hits the shelves with big introductory discounts and a blitz of TV commercials, nobody bought it. Why? They already had too much cleaner at home. P and G looked at the test market results, shrugged, and walked away from the countertop cleaner business. It was no big deal to Procter; just another new product, one of dozens they test every year. But to Acme, it was everything. Everything. That's what I mean about information, Robert. Information."

"You sound like Atwood."

"Well, he's right. Maybe I'll get to meet him and see his amazing comb-over hairdo."

"I'm sure you will." Pause. "I don't know, honey, it seems like this is, I don't know, dangerous."

"What's the danger? This isn't like infiltrating Qaddafi's headquarters. It's a media party given by this weird guy who wants to be the Malcolm Forbes of the Rust Belt or something. It's a mild case of industrial snooping, that's all. You said yourself that Dudley was planted by Woodcock to spy on you."

"Right."

"And that Atwood must have had Leo or somebody feeding him inside dope about the negotiations with American."

"Yes."

"So?"

"It's settled, then, I'm going."

"My wife, the Mata Hari of magazine publishing."

"This is going to be fun. Now, about our deal."

"Oh, yes, our deal."

"In return for this vital information."

"I will do whatever you wish tonight."

"That's right. Whatever I desire."

"And what is it you desire?"

"Tonight, I desire a love slave."

"But I'm already your husband."

"It is not the same thing." She folds one leg up against her chest, which raises her dress seductively; she points the other leg into the air in my direction, bending the knee slightly and arching her foot. "Robert, you must do my bidding."

She smiles.

"I would like you to begin by removing these plates and glasses from this table of ours."

"But I was about to—"

"Ssshhh. I've got a better idea. Get this stuff off the table, this sturdy, solid table of ours. This sturdy, solid table whose limitless possibilities we've never really explored before." She has unhooked one stocking from her garter belt and is slowly peeling it off.

"On the dining room table?" I ask.

"Macallan, wouldn't you like to be able to shock our children someday? Just when they reach the stage where they're convinced they invented sex and they're so-o-o embarrassed by their dorky parents they can't stand it. Wouldn't that be just the moment to take Junior aside and say, 'Junior, you know the dining room table where you learned your table manners?' "

I begin clearing off the table at once.

"No, Leo, I wouldn't bring Dudley into this ordinarily," I say. "That is, if I thought I had any choice. It's just better for us to bring him in voluntarily now rather than have him snooping around, telling corporate there's something going on and we're holding out on him."

"It's fine with me, Bob. Besides, I've already told you I don't share your hesitations about the boy. Now why all the secrecy?"

Leo and I are sitting in my office with the door closed, waiting for Dudley to finish a phone call and come down the hall to join us.

"It's not secrecy. Just discretion. I've got an important idea I want to discuss. I think we should do it in private."

"You want to give me a little preview while we're waiting?"

If Dudley has Woodcock on the horn, he could be a while. Dudley has learned his corporate protocol from a master. He wouldn't dare to keep me waiting unless he's tied up with someone more important than me, in which case he will rub it in my face with excruciatingly polite arrogance. *"So-o-o-o sorry to hold you up, but you know how Mr. Woodcock is. Once he gets wound up about something, you just can't get him off the line."*

"Leo, I've got an idea for making up the profit shortfall we're currently looking at. Something we can do to help bring us in on target for the coming year."

Leo smiles at me. Slightly patronizing. "Let's call a spade a spade, Bob. We're talking about *your* targets for *your* earn-out."

That's the first time Leo's been so bold. So, it finally starts to come out. "That's not entirely true, Leo. Yes, my earn-out does depend on those profit levels. But so does your bonus and your next raise and the title American gives you if, and I repeat if, I decide to leave at some time in the future." So there, Leo. "When I say *our* profit goals, I mean *ours*. Can I count on you or not? Just tell me."

Leo backs down and turns on his charmometer to high. Big smile. "Of course, Bob, you can count on me. You know that. From the day I brought in your first big account to the day the sheriff comes to close the door, you can count on your trusty old Mr. Sales."

Thanks, Leo. Fuck you, too.

There's a knock on the door and Dudley lets himself in.

"Hi." He seats himself next to Leo. "Gee, I'm so-o-o sorry to keep you waiting, Bob. But when Walt Drummond calls"—very good, Dudley, the vice chairman himself—"you know Walt; once he gets wound up about something, you can't get him off the line."

"No, I don't know, Walt, but I can imagine." Lots of points for that one, Dudley.

"So what's up, guys?"

"Leo and I are discussing ideas for making up the projected shortfall in profits for the coming year."

Dudley shoots me his most earnest and concerned teacher's pet look, both of us tacitly recognizing that he and Woodcock are the principal reasons for the shortfall. "Good idea. We've been so focused on investment spending lately."

"We sure have. I've got a plan I'd like to go over with you and Leo." I hand them each a single Xeroxed sheet with the projected numbers for the special issue. "I'd like to do a special thirteenth issue before the end of the fiscal year."

"Geez, Leo," Dudley says admiringly, "that's great. Just great."

"With the extra revenues I've projected here, I think we can absorb all our new extra costs . . ."

"Please, Bob, investment spending," Dudley offers helpfully.

"Yeah, investment spending. We can pay for all that and still turn the profit we said we would."

"I think it's a great idea, Bob," Leo says. "But you're looking to get a substantially higher premium from this single advertiser—whoever it turns out to be—than we got from Steiner-Rochelle on our last special issue."

"Well, that was two and a half years ago. And I think we've got a bigger subject this time."

"What is it?" asks Leo.

"Hypertension. Jerry has three specialists locked up: a cardiovascular guy at Harvard, a neurologist at Hopkins, and a pharmacologist at Cornell. Plus, we gear the life-style articles toward helping the physician relax and avoid the perils of hypertension for himself. Real clinical information, real editorial service. That sound like a selling hook you can use, Leo?"

"Oh brother, can I ever. Right off the top of my head, I can think of product managers for two new tranquilizers who might be interested.

Maybe even a nonpharmaceutical advertiser or two, who knows? When can I see an outline of the material?"

"End of the month, Jerry promises."

"Just leave it to Mr. Sales."

"This really gets me thinking," Dudley says, always looking for brownie points. "Bob, I'd really like to contribute some ideas for this project."

"Much appreciated, Dudley. Why don't you share them directly with Leo? That okay with you, Leo?"

"Sure. Of course."

"I tell you, Dudley, the biggest favor you can do on this is to keep it very low-profile for the moment. I know you have to keep the channels open with Harry and corporate. But impress on Harry that this project is still in gestation. It's important that we keep the lid on it until we're ready to go public with it."

"Sure, Bob, I understand."

"So let's keep this plan limited only to those with a real need to know. Nobody else. Until we're really ready. Okay?"

"Okay," says Dudley.

"You bet." Leo winks. "You know you can count on me."

M A Y

CHAPTER FOURTEEN

I stare at the innocent pink message slip. It records a phone message from Laura Chasen at eleven-forty-eight this morning. It tells me the number where she will be in London next month. It also has her current number, a mess of foreign codes from somewhere else. "Call me tonight," the note says. "I'll be in bed."

The doorbell to our apartment rings. Again. And again. And again.

"Macallan! Open up!" It is Wendy. I stuff the pink message into my pocket. "Come on, honey, open up. I'm laden."

I march to the door and unsnap the top lock.

"You're what?" I ask from behind the closed door.

"I said I'm laden."

"You're not supposed to get laden with anybody but your husband."

"I'm sorry. Mackey showered me with gifts, and I couldn't resist. So I'm a fallen woman, okay? Now open up for Chrissakes. I'm lugging a ton of shit."

I open the door and Wendy drags herself in. She can barely manage the oversized leather golf bag (mercifully without clubs) slung over one shoulder. In her other hand she dangles a leather gym bag bearing the Mackey logo and filled to bursting; farther up she holds a thick press kit tight in her armpit. Any second now her purse strap will fall off her free shoulder and send all her burdens tumbling.

"Wheww," she sighs, dumping the whole mess onto the floor in front of me. "That was some party."

"Did you spend the day with Elton Mackey or Mark Cross?"

"Actually, Santa Claus is more like it. You publishing guys really like to lay on the gifts with advertiser types."

"Yeah, some of us do."

"A not so subtle form of persuasion."

"Called bribery."

"Look at this stuff, Macallan. I could have had more junk, but this was all I could carry. I mean, this was the minimum amount of free toys Mackey's people expected you to take home. They had Mackey fishing rods, Mackey golf jackets, Mackey caps, Mackey golf balls, sweaters, everything."

"Name recognition is very important in publishing, you know."

"The entire medical advertising community could be outfitted in Mackey regalia from head to toe for the rest of its life, if it wanted."

"Would it?"

"Well, I'm an old-fashioned girl when it comes to legible clothing. My labels stay strictly on the inside. Besides, I only brought this stuff back as part of my intelligence-gathering mission. Don't you want to debrief me?"

"Don't we usually kiss a little and take your dress off before I debrief you?"

"Come on, Macallan, you're not being a good spymaster. I've just come back from my first undercover espionage mission and you're making lounge lizard jokes."

"Sorry."

"What's the matter?"

"I dunno. Just trying to lighten things up."

She takes me by both arms and holds me at arm's length, inspecting my face and probably the soul behind it.

"I think you're nervous, that's what." She pats me on the shoulder and gives me a little peck on the cheek.

"Yeah, I guess so. How bad does the situation look, Agent Wolfson?"

"I'll file my report in here." She takes me by the hand, walks me into the living room, and stands me in front of the couch. "Make yourself comfortable," she says as she gives me a little push backward. I fall into the couch and lay back on the pillows. I watch her start to pace back and forth in front of me. Wendy paces whenever she's got a lot on her mind. "I should get more comfortable, too," she mutters to herself, reaching down in midstride to pluck off one shoe, then the other. Brows knitted, composing her thoughts, she unhooks her bra from outside her dress and gives her shoulders a relieving shake.

"So tell me," I ask, "did your cover get blown? Did anyone suspect you of not being Debbie Bornstein?"

"No. When I got to Debbie's apartment building this morning, she'd already told the doorman that a friend would be there to pick up a limo under her name. I gave him five dollars just to be sure there were no slip-ups. I only had to hang around the lobby for a few minutes before the driver showed."

"Was it Ricky?"

"No, this was definitely a rental. A big white stretch. There were already three other guests on board. This was the only tricky part, when I piled in with them. Debbie told me that the Mackey people don't know her, but there would be other people at the party who did. People she's worked with at other agencies, a client or two, like that. She gave me a list of who they might be, just in case, but I wouldn't recognize them anyway. So in close little group situations like the back of the limo where there are no Mackey people, I would say that I was Wendy Wilson from McCann, Debbie's new number two person. You know, Debbie couldn't make it, some last-minute thing, that's why I'm wearing her name tag. The thing we were counting on is that the party would be big enough to make Debbie *and* me inconspicuous."

"And was it?"

"More than big enough. When we got to Teterboro, you could have sworn you were at a national convention of limo drivers, or that you were witnessing the entire membership of the New York Stock Exchange trying to escape to Rio after being subpoenaed by the SEC. A sea of rented stretches flooding this fancy private airport. Mackey had a tent set up by the runway where the limos were dropping everyone off. In the tent, we were greeted by your old friend Atwood and given our seat assignments for the flight to Cleveland. He had two jets waiting to take off."

"Mackey's jet wasn't there?"

"Not that I could see. These were regular commercial passenger planes, must have chartered them for the day. You know, DC-somethings or Boeing whatchamacallits, you'd recognize them, lots of seats."

"So how did you like Atwood?"

"He's everything you said he'd be. And creepier. Twice during the course of the party he tried to cop a feel as he passed me through the crowd. Big smile, 'Ooops, excuse me, missy. A little close in here.' Can you believe that? 'Missy'?

"Anyway. There were hostesses herding people around. They must have recruited them at the Playboy Bunny Retirement Farm. My God, I didn't know they still made bimbos like that. There were enough of them to make you invest your life savings in peroxide futures. And all these hostesses are in white lab coats, just like in the hospital, with cute little embroidered logos on the pockets that say: 'Mackey Media Clinic,' and they've got clipboards and stethoscopes around their necks like they're making hospital rounds. Atwood was having a brilliant time with their stethoscopes. He'd make a big joke of asking one of them to check his heartbeat; then he'd grab the stethoscope and check her heartbeat. He'd go for big laughs with the guys. Ha, ha, ha. He's such a jerk. He's also left-handed, so he kept feeling under their *right* breasts for the heartbeat."

"Wendy, he wasn't really trying to check their—"

"I know; I know. Just makes him an even bigger jerk, as far as I'm concerned.

"So we all get on the planes and they've even got the stewards and stewardesses wearing those Mackey Media Clinic coats. Thank God they were the real plane crew.

"There's champagne flowing everywhere. It's now about ten in the morning. The flight to Cleveland takes an hour and change. The jets land

and park together at the private air terminal. Two other Mackey jets pull in, the one from Chicago and the one from the West Coast. Just like at Teterboro, there's the Mackey reception tent and a sea of limos behind it to cart us out to the party. We all get sorted and piled in. Then, the limos pull out in a line, an honest-to-God motorcade, must have been fifty limos long. Let's see, uh, yes, got to be more. Somebody said there were over three hundred guests. At somewhere between four to seven guests per car, sure, had to be at least that. So we parade out to the expressway in this endless motorcade. Like we were heads of state or something."

I say, "Now you know how Ferdinand Marcos felt when Imelda used to send him down to the Seven-Eleven."

"And how. Oh! I met the famous Imelda Mackey later in the day."

"Vera the Shopper. How is the old gal?"

"She didn't have time to show me her shoe collection, but I got the picture." Wendy resumes her story line. "So, we get to the mansion. The limos line up to drop us off at the front door, group by group. Mackey himself is standing there to greet us and usher us into the house."

"Was he wearing a lab coat, too?"

"No, a business suit. But he had a laminated ID on his lapel from the Mackey Media Clinic, identifying him as Dr. Elton Mackey, Chief of Staff. So the party spreads out all over the ground floor of the mansion and onto the lawn, where they've got another big tent set up, like a wedding. People milling, chatting, networking, the usual."

"Did you see the dining room?"

"Big white! Who could miss it? I had a chat with Vera Mackey about it. She says that it really kind of captures the, uh, quote, 'social character of Cleveland's elite,' unquote. She says that Cleveland is actually like old Virginia or maybe England. Even though the money is industrial, the connection to land is really what it's all about. She went on to brag about the counts and baronets and earls she hobnobs with in Gates Mills. Sounded mostly like broke Euro gold diggers marrying smokestack fortunes. Anyway, the big white dining room. Vera explained to me that the dining room started out inspired by the English aristocracy. But Cleveland isn't stuck in its traditions, it's able to adapt and be modern. And what, Vera asks, could be more modern than white? She tells me, 'Elton and I always wanted a pure white room. Something perfect and pure.' She says painting over the dark old wood was one of her best ideas. Her friends agree, too. Now, she tells me, the room combines priceless old-world craftsmanship with the clean, bright look of Formica. She says, 'I believe it makes everything we eat in here taste better. Wouldn't you agree?' How could I not agree?"

"Of course. So. You're milling around the party."

"Oh yeah. This is rich. Mixed in with the crowd of advertisers and agency types are people dressed like the greats of medical history. There's a bozo in a toga, beard, and sandals wandering around; he's supposed to be Hippocrates. There's Pierre and Marie Curie. Lister, Fleming, Dr. Livingstone, I presume—everybody. Authentic costumes, the works. From what

I could gather, some of them were actors hired for the day, but most of them were actual Mackey salespeople. When was the last time *you* made *your* salespeople dress up in beards and togas to go sell space, eh, Macallan?"

"It's been at least a couple of months. Not since that day when I made everyone go calling in the Groucho glasses with funny noses and mustaches."

"Anyway, all the people in costume are wearing buttons that refer to what their characters did—but in relation to Mackey's new magazine. Like Pierre and Marie's button says something like 'We may have invented radiology, but Mackey invented the *Panacea*.' Or the Fleming guy's button reads, 'I discovered penicillin, but it took Mackey to discover the *Panacea*.' They're all wandering around, mixing and being friendly, playing their roles, selling the new magazine.

"And the waiters. This was something to see. The waiters and waitresses are all wearing surgical gowns. Some with masks, some without. The team that's carving the roast beef behind the table? A surgical team, I swear. The guy who's spooning out the caviar serves you your heaping toast point in a petri dish, you know those little round glass dishes you grew cultures in in chemistry class. They had a team preparing pâté slices on oblong glass plates that looked like oversized microscope slides. Another team served punch in those tapered Pyrex lab beakers, with a straw. They had Bunsen burners under the chafing dishes. They ran the espresso through an elaborate glass pipe still that dripped out into your cup at the end. The medical theme was everywhere. And so was Mackey. He was glad-handing everyone in sight, working the crowd like a Presidential candidate."

"Did you get personally glad-handed?"

"Absolutely. I wouldn't have missed it for the world."

"What did you think?"

"To begin with, he's much more comfortable around men. He was in his element slapping backs and telling dirty jokes and doing all that male bonding stuff. I think he doesn't quite know what to do with women in positions of responsibility."

"Did he misbehave like Atwood?"

"Oh, God no. He was a perfect gentleman. Too perfect, really. You could tell he didn't feel free to be himself." Wendy puts her hands on her hips, Mackey-style, bends her knees outward as if she were suddenly carrying Mackey's big belly, and intones in a mock masculine voice, "You know, young lady, you are witness to one of the biggest f-f-f, one of the biggest moments in publishing. What you see here is the beginning of the classiest new magazine network ever. And I mean the fucking classiest. Pardon my French. You know our books from your trade accounts. Well, we're gonna do for hard-to-reach upscale professional men what we've already done for dry cleaners and car wash owners and tire dealers and stone crushers and foundry men. We're starting today with doctors; next'll come lawyers, then accountants, then on and on. Someday soon, you'll be able to buy 'em all with one upscale network. Mine. Remember, Mackey himself made you the promise. Now eat, drink, and be merry, young lady, for tomorrow we may be acquired.' "

"You do a pretty good Wacky Mackey."

"He makes a pretty vivid impression."

"That he does. That he does."

"Then, just as the party was beginning to run out of steam, the speeches began."

"At last, the sales pitch."

"Hot and heavy. Atwood was the opening act. A few minutes of low comedy to help the crowd settle down. Then they played a video on a half-dozen big screen projectors sprinkled around the tent. It opened like the old 'Dr. Kildare' show or 'General Hospital,' except that it was all about the 'Mackey Media Clinic,' where all your media problems receive the most professional therapy money can buy. From circulation blockages to reach and frequency failures to hardening of the ad budget, advertisers of all kinds bring their troubles to the Mackey Clinic. This is over shots of patients getting various treatments like surgical reduction of excess demographics, electroshock for the wrong psychographics, you name it. The video went over the existing Mackey books, *Car Wash Journal, Nuts and Bolts,* and the rest. Then—tum-ta-ta-tum—came the most important development ever from the Mackey Media Clinic. Announcing *Panacea!*"

Wendy goes back to the pile of Mackey offerings in the foyer and extracts a magazine. "This," she says, holding it up as she comes back to the couch area, "is the prototype issue they then handed out to everyone. It's an absolute rip-off of *Elixir.*" She hands it to me to flip through.

"See? The same heavy stock you use. Same glossy photos. There's a travel article written by a doctor. A medical business management article. A food and wine article. Art news and investing notes for collectors. Medicine in fact and fiction book reviews. There's the big scientific article, anchoring the book with professional interest and credibility, just like you do in *Elixir.* It's your magazine, honey. Your magazine exactly."

It *is* my magazine. To a tee. It's a little spooky and a little scary. Except that this isn't the real thing. This is the dummy. You make up titles for the kind of articles you plan to write and dummy in the text. This is not a first issue, it's a tool for selling the first issue. I know. That's how I sold the first issue of *Elixir.* Although my dummy didn't look anywhere near as good as this. Of course, Mackey has more than the few thousand dollars I had and he's got the benefit of five years of me developing *Elixir* into something that, when copied, makes a pretty impressive show. He has even included copies of advertising pages from *Elixir.* My ads tipped into his book, with little notes to the advertisers added by Mackey, like the message above the Trentex ad, directed at the product's divisional marketing director: "Max McGuinn, you can make medical history with *Panacea.*" Personalized headlines for all the heavy-hitter advertisers attending Mackey's shindig. An audacious touch, sure to be remembered with a smile when Mackey's salesman makes the first call for a real insertion order.

"We were expecting this," I say, musing through the pages.

"I know," says Wendy, "but what I don't understand is this—he hasn't bothered to add any improvements. At least not that I could see. If this is what he ends up delivering, he'll merely come up to parity with you. So what advantage will he offer? I mean, usually you try to offer—"

"If he can sell it harder or cheaper or whatever, he doesn't have to have a product that's substantially better. And if he's willing to lose money for a little longer than most companies would be, he can put a big squeeze on us. A big squeeze." I put the magazine down. "So what else went on?"

"Mackey got up to speak. He went on about the great-moment-in-publishing-history stuff he'd been practicing on me earlier in the day. He introduced some muckety-muck from the University of Cleveland Medical School who thanked him for his generous contribution. Mackey had the photographers rush in to take shots of him handing over the check. Apparently, *Panacea* will have an advisory committee chaired by this guy or one of his colleagues."

"University of Cleveland Medical School?"

"Everybody there made out like this was real credibility.

"Then Mackey went into this speech against *Elixir*. He used the same coy language that the invitation did. His references to the word *elixir* were strictly with a small *e*. But everyone got the message: 'Don't be fooled by false elixirs.' 'What you thought was an elixir really needs to be cured itself.' That kind of thing. Then, he started alluding to the same issues that came up in the rumors. He made out like he was this honest little guy with editorial integrity who would be strong enough not to have to sell out to some giant to keep from going under, how his magazine would never become a shill of big advertisers from the corporate parent's flagship books. He then referred kind of obliquely to special opportunities he would be offering to advertisers . . ."

"That means deals for free space."

"He also said there'd be even more special opportunities for advertisers who could focus clearly on the future of medical publishing without remaining tied to the past."

"That means even bigger deals if you promise to ditch *Elixir* when you advertise with him."

"That's what I figured."

"Nothing surprises me so far. Is that it?"

"No, there's one more thing. He made a special warning about special issues. He said that the first symptom of a dying publication is big special issues. He said that *Panacea* will never need to do special issues because its regular issues are going to be so special. Then he offered to outdo any deal offered to any advertiser, should any advertiser be foolhardy enough to think of backing anybody else's special issues over the next twelve months. Robert, he knows about your plans. How did he find out?"

"Somebody told him, that's how. My question is who."

JUNE

CHAPTER FIFTEEN

"So what exactly have you been up to at this executive conference?" Laura Chasen asks. "I want to hear all about it."

I cradle the phone between my neck and shoulder, kick off my other shoe, and lay back on the beige hotel bedspread. Everything in Grosvenor House, that grand dowdy dowager of a hotel overlooking Hyde Park, is beige, cream, or white. Walls, floors, fabrics, fixtures, everything. No, correction. The lobby is mostly dull gray.

"We've been shepherding a small herd of cardiologists around London in tandem with a small herd of drug company executives, trying to get them to mate."

"Ooh, sounds sexy."

"Only if old-fashioned male bonding excites you, like they used to practice when Ike was president."

"I remember reading about that in business school. I think it was in our History of Golf class."

"Well, no golf here, just us guys doing everything together. Everything. We eat together, we sit through presentations of medical papers together, we go to the theater together. If we happen to end up in adjacent stalls in the men's room, we even shit together. It's a full-court press selling effort for a new angina drug. Of course it's all under the lofty pretense of professional education. We just finished our last lunch together. Thank God. This afternoon is free time, the first I've had since I got here."

"Sounds absolutely fascinating," Laura says with no small hint of sarcasm. "What a wonderful experience."

"Actually, it's been kind of boring and tiring and, uh, stressful." Leo in particular has been a pain in the neck, walking around acting like the heir to the throne, making grandiose speeches on *Elixir*'s future, imply-ing clearly in his tone of voice that he will be running the show as soon as I disappear. I humor him because I need him right now and because it is not worth slapping him down. And because, for all I know, he may get the job. The whole thing leaves me with an unpleasant taste. Espe-cially all the toadying we have to do. Laughing at jokes that are not funny, pretending to be best buddies with men I consider assholes, all the phony, insincere things you do every day to make a sale. I never liked it much before. But I never minded it much, either. Now, sud-denly, I do mind it and very much. "Maybe," I add, talking as much to myself as to Laura, "this experience has even been a little, I don't know, degrading."

"Then why, dear one, do you bother to do it?"

"Because it's in my contract. Besides, if I don't do it, I stand a good chance of becoming poor again." Maybe that will happen anyway, I can't help thinking.

"In that case, you'd better grin and bear it until you're free to live the way I do."

"Well, I am bearing, if not grinning." I try to sound friendly and interested, but nothing more. "So, Laura, where have you been since Bangle Bay? When I last saw you, you were running to catch a yacht for St. Barth's."

"Yes, and I gave you a little memento of me. Do you still have it?"

"Why? Do you need it back?"

"No, there's plenty where that came from."

"Come on, where have you been? What wonders have you seen?"

"Actually, the months have been a little short on wonders. I've had some business to attend to."

"You? I'm shocked."

"I spent the better part of March and April in Milan, cleaning up the last of Mother's estate."

"I didn't realize you'd lost your mother, too?"

"Two years ago."

"I'm sorry."

"It's okay. Really. We had essentially stopped speaking years before."

"Oh."

"You didn't realize that I'm an orphan, did you? It's actually very liberating. You don't have people examining your every move and inter-preting it in terms of the power of their own DNA. It lets you be yourself more. Know what I mean?"

"Uh-huh," I say and wish I really did. "So your mother was Italian?"

"Isabella Destino, last of the seminoble, semirich Destinos of Milan and Como. A few knights way back there in history, a Renaissance cardinal complete with bastard sons, a silk factory that supported five generations in a certain style, one second-rate homosexual poet who died of syphilis in Morocco, and a little back street in Como that still bears the name Via Destino."

"Very impressive."

"That's what Father thought when he married into it. He ran in the other direction. But quick."

"It must be something to have all that, uh, heritage."

"Tell me about it. I just lived a bureaucratic nightmare. Lawyers, judges, magistrates, clerks. Seedy, smelly government offices day after day. And I ended up paying a two-hundred-thousand-lire tax bill. That closed the last of the Destinos' account with the Italian government and history. If I'd have known there'd be nothing left to inherit, I would never have left St. Barth's. Bangle Bay is lovely, but there's nothing quite like a *French* island."

"So I hear."

"I just *love* running around topless. Makes me feel like a little girl again."

"I'll bet it does."

"Really. You should see me." She laughs. Pause. "So when is your conference over?"

"Tonight, after dinner."

"Then we have all night and tomorrow and—"

"Uh, no, not exactly. I have to leave first thing tomorrow morning."

"Where to?"

"Uh . . . Geneva."

"Then I'll join you. I've got lots of money in Geneva. We can visit it together. That'll be fun."

"I'm, uh, afraid we can't do that. I'm uh, meeting some people there." Macallan, you are strictly an amateur at this.

"You mean," she asks testily, "as in W-I-F-E?"

I hold the phone in silence.

"Listen"—she sounds peeved but trying to hold it back—"I canceled my trip to Thailand to meet you here, and you're telling me that between your boring business conference and your wife you—"

I try to avoid admitting it to myself, but as much as I have tried to make it impossible to see her, in hopes of getting myself off the hook, I do want to see her. Suddenly, I wish I could dismantle all my plans. I blurt out, "Meet me at the Old Ferkin pub in Shepherd's Market. Soon as you can. Now."

"What?"

"The Old Ferkin, Shepherd's Market. You know, that little piazza or whatever you call it, off Curzon Street."

"I know where it is, silly. But why there? Why not the Ritz? Or Green's? Some place nice and a little, you know, romantic? Not a *pub.*"

"Because my doctor friends and my clients and my employees are out blowing their expense accounts in every fancy place in Mayfair."

"Green's is in St. James's."

"Whatever. I want to see you alone, without running into any of them."

"Okay. Sure."

"How soon can you meet me there?"

"Let's see, I'm coming from Ralston Street in Chelsea. Uh, I don't know. An hour?"

"It's not that far. It's the middle of the afternoon, for Chrissakes; the traffic's light."

"I'm a woman, Bob Macallan," she says coyly. "Or have you forgotten that?"

I take a deep breath. I can slow down now. In spite of everything I planned not to do, I have set events in motion. "No, Laura, I haven't forgotten."

I walk outside into a warm, sunny afternoon, the first sun I've seen all week. There's a thrill I always get here. There's something about Mayfair, especially the neighborhood around Grosvenor House, that brings out the snob and the adolescent dreamer in me.

First, it's those fat English limos. What a contrast to our tinny, machine-stamped Caddies and Lincolns. The heavy, hand-wrought fenders of the old Rolls-Royces and Daimlers are like armor. They are not just cars; they are mobile fortresses carrying privileged cargo safely past the dangers of a vulgar, distasteful world. They let me believe there really are rich people who breathe a different air from the rest of us.

The shops along Mount Street and South Audley Street seem to offer further proof. Unlike the glitzy establishments on Bond or Jermyn Streets that stoop to seduce shoppers with showy windows full of merchandise, these antique shops, art galleries, hunting outfitters, haberdashers, and whatnot are conspicuously empty of displays and people. We are so exclusive, so expensive, they seem to say, we do not need customers. The occasional vintage Bentley, seen whooshing away from the curb, makes you imagine that an expensive purchase has just been made. Silently, invisibly, with nothing so rude as cash or plastic cards ever being handled. Transacted with a handshake, a nod, or a trusted servant's signature in an old bound ledger.

I walk down South Audley Street and turn into the park behind Grosvenor Chapel. Towering old trees, the red brick walls of old townhouses and apartment buildings overlooking shaded green lawns. The space reminds me of quieter corners of Harvard Yard, except that the grass is thick and full and perfectly trimmed. The benches, the plaques say, have been donated by Americans grateful for the peace and resonance they felt in this park. The lure of the mother country is still powerful, even irresistible.

Past the gate and down the hill another silent residential street of expensive townhouses. Then the bustle and noise of Curzon Street explodes before me. Traffic everywhere, old mansions converted into tony offices, expensive restaurants with nothing but dark corners. I duck under the covered passage at Number 47 and into the quiet of Shepherd's Market, two centuries ago a market square, now a carless preserve of quaint pubs and cafés, all restored to perfection.

The Old Ferkin is one of the more historic spots in Shepherd's Market, but it is hardly unique. A blur of dark wood and polished brass. Standard-issue British pub atmosphere, straight from Central Propping. I sit at the bar and order a Scotch. A single malt—in honor of the ancestors—Laphroigh, smooth and full of peat smoke. I sit. And sip.

The pub is thinly populated. In a while it will be packed with office workers drinking off the day. I order another Laphroigh. I sit and sip some more. Two women in their early twenties, secretary types I imagine, sit a few stools down from me and chat. There's a blonde and a brunette, both plain and common but made pretty by the juicy blush of youth. A beam of late afternoon sun pours in through a stained-glass window and falls on the blonde's crossed legs. Like most of the clerical women I've noticed in the business districts of London, she is not wearing stockings. The sunlight caresses her legs and sets fire to a thousand tiny white-gold flecks of stubble. It looks like two, maybe three days' growth, no more. It is, at this moment, after my Scotches, sexy. Maybe sexier than perfectly smooth summer legs because it is just a tiny bit rough, a teasing little hint of our furry animal souls. She chatters. Her friend chatters. Her crossed leg sways like a pendulum in the light. Soon the sunbeam will vanish. I sit watching, sipping another Laphroigh. And another. Time passes.

A female hand gently encircles my right biceps. I do not move. Here goes, Macallan. Just be cool. Pretend you are a man of the world.

"Are you watching the blonde's legs in the pool of sunlight?" the woman asks, whispering in my ear.

"More her delicate golden stubble," I say, still looking at the girl. "It's kind of earthy, but not too."

She holds her head beside mine, our cheeks just touching. "A woman who hasn't seen a razor in a couple of days hasn't seen a bathtub either." Suddenly the girl looks cheap and ugly. "Remember, she's English." The woman turns her head and kisses me softly on the cheek. "Hello, Bob Macallan."

I turn my head and face her. "Hello, Laura Chasen."

Laura's hair is the same golden honey color I remember, but the contours of her face seem softer and she seems smaller now than before. Or maybe she just grew larger in my imagination over the months since Bangle Bay. She is dressed very simply but strikingly. A big white silk blouse with exaggerated shoulders and collar, very open at the neck, and trim black pants that show off the curve of her hips to great advantage.

She lifts her right hand and jingles a wristful of silver bangles. Her perfume fills my nostrils. Jasmine, I think.

"In honor of Bangle Bay," she says.

I raise my glass of Scotch. "In honor of the health care business." I slug back the contents.

"So?" Laura smirks. "It must be thrilling, spending all this time with a group of dedicated businessmen."

"Yeah, I guess it is." I smirk back.

"Tell me, do you guys really spend *all* your time devoting yourselves to excellence?"

"Every waking minute."

"And sleeping, too, I imagine."

"That's true. For businessmen, the pursuit of excellence is a biological imperative."

"What a lucky man. You must be saturated with professionalism after spending a whole week with salesmen and pharmaceutical executives."

"Absolutely dripping. You should see the dry-cleaning bill I'm running up at the hotel."

"Well," Laura says, sidling up to me and fondling the sleeve of my shirt, "considering the week of excellence and professionalism you've had, I don't suppose there's any way I could convince you to run away with me to the Comoros?"

"I think you may be surprised. First, just tell me where the Comoros are."

"Lovely islands, part African, part Arabian, part Indian, part French, about halfway between Madagascar and the Seychelles."

"But do they have businessmen there?"

"Kiwanis Club, Jaycees, you name it. They've even got an Expense Account Hall of Fame in the capital city."

"So that's where it is! I'll bet I know some of the honorees in the exhibits there."

The smiles Laura and I exchange are easy and natural. It feels like we are old friends. Then I remember why we are meeting. "So?" I say awkwardly in a tone that sounds too polite. I feel myself acting like I'm on a date, reverting to the last frame of reference I had when I was single. "Can I, uh, get you something to drink?" You jerk, Macallan.

"No." She takes my hand firmly in hers and stares directly into my eyes. "Not unless you think we have to waste a lot of time in here on preliminaries."

I feel my head recoil, shocked at her bluntness. Then relief that one of us has gone straight to the bottom line.

"No, not at all."

She takes my other hand. "Then let's get out of here and go back to your hotel room and make love. We can talk later."

We move without words, without effort.

I open the door with the computerized plastic key. Laura ducks in front of me into the room. I close the door behind me and stand. Laura slides up against me. We wrap our arms around each other, and our mouths join, open just enough to admit the other's tongue.

Every first kiss I remember has been awkward. Too timid, too ardent, too wet, too dry, too much or too little of something that made it somehow uncomfortable and unsure. But not this first kiss. This one is frank and grown-up and utterly purposeful, with no misunderstanding or uncertainty on either side.

I feel Laura's hands up and down my back, I feel my arms behind her shoulders holding her close. I feel hard bone and soft breasts against me, my hands caressing the back of her head, my fingers running through her hair, down her neck, brushing against her ears. I feel her fingers on the back of my neck, her tongue in my ear.

Our mouths open wider. Wetter. I feel the tiny blond hairs on her upper lip, smell her perfume, lightly jasmine, and the dank breath from her nostrils breathing into mine. Taste our tongues together, rough and eely. Mouths joining, liquids flowing, tongues swimming over hard teeth, drinking in the other.

I am in London in a ninth-floor room in Grosvenor House. I am in the Caribbean on a cliff. I am everywhere. I am dissolving into this other body. Tips of fingers touching, hot with eager sweat, fingertips on cheeks and eyes, her hands, my hands, squeezing breasts, squeezing something not quite bony but very stiff. My raging hard-on.

In a flash I see everything, smell it, taste it. Clothes tossed aside in a messy pile, adrenaline surging with the discovery of new, unfamiliar flesh. Wet mouths searching, sucking everywhere. Nipples pebble hard. Hands sculpting smooth contours, grabbing bones and blood, cupping and spreading expanse of ass. Soft tummy to nibble on between hard hips, tongue tasting belly button, wisp of hair trailing downward, growing thicker, growing darker. Sudden smell from secret folds, salty hairs tasting of ocean, thick smell of low tide, slippery lips of silken sea flesh bare and open, drenched and drenching. I am lost, unseeing. Then plunging, sliding, slapping. Violent thrusts exploding into creamy animal pudding and melting away. Heavy smell of cunt pierced with sharp smell of come. Blending, souring, filling nostrils. Sticky skin, slippery skin, curly hairs caked with milky glue. Sweat in cracks, sweat on curves. Tongues tasting slits and holes, armpits and toes, fingers probing, mouths sucking, licking, eating. A single beast feeding on itself.

Then there is rest. Limp arms, limp legs entwined. Then sleep. Then rise, with sweat dried rank and breath stale, to devour again but more ravenously than before. Now the smelly beast is truly free, joyful and unashamed. It has nothing left to hide. So it combines with itself and feeds on its own flesh. Again. And again. And again.

I see us rising from stained, soggy bed linens. We dress. We are having tea at the Ritz. Gilt and crystal, damask and silk, bone china whiter than white. We touch hands politely, we chat amusingly. We respect the stuffy, imperious room. And we smile at our nasty little secret. The secret between Laura's legs—our mingled juices dripping out of her into her panties, marking with pungent animal odor a glorious gooey wet spot. To show the beast where to begin again.

In the here and now, I withdraw my tongue to tease a little. Technique. A little deliberate kissing artifice remembered from freer, younger days.

Suddenly, my passion feels put on and alien.

Is this worth betraying Wendy for?

Come on, Macallan, this is fucking. Fucking! Stop thinking and follow your dick. You remember how.

Are you that desperate for novelty, to get laid with a new woman?

No.

Then why the Ritz?

I don't know. Why?

Is it worth risking the woman who knows you better and loves you better than you do yourself?

No, absolutely not.

Then why Laura's cunt in the Ritz?

How should I know?

You know, Macallan. You know.

I nuzzle my face against Laura's hair to escape the kissing for a moment. *Why Laura Chasen's cunt, dripping with my semen, in the haughty London Ritz?*

Because, Macallan, what you really want to fuck is *her* freedom and *your* fear.

I hear myself try to whisper, "No."

No, Macallan. Fucking Laura won't let you possess her freedom. Or give you the power to conquer your fears. No. No matter how many times you come inside her.

She kisses me hard and cups my balls.

"No," I repeat, "we can't."

"What'samatter?" she mutters, her tongue darting out of my mouth, tracing a wet line across the edge of my lower lip.

"I just can't." I stiffen my arms to force her away from me.

"What's wrong?"

"I can't do this, Laura."

She brushes her hair off her face. "It's so right. Can't you see it? Can't you *feel* it?"

"Maybe. I don't know. But I just can't. Not now."

"You're chickening out on me."

"I can't. I just can't. Laura, I think you'd better leave."

"That's not what you really want."

"I really can't. I just can't."

She steps back and looks me over. "You're still too new to it all." She

143

collects herself and gets ready to leave. "I understand and you will, too. You just need a little more time."

"Please?" I motion toward the door. "I'm sorry. Really I am."

"You don't have to be sorry." She goes to the door and opens it. "The least you can do is kiss me good-bye."

I walk over to her. We embrace in the doorway. She raises her mouth to mine. We kiss with lips alone, gently but firmly. She takes my hand and places it on her breast. I do not resist. The kiss ends. "It's okay," she whispers with our lips still almost touching. "I'm inside you now." We break apart.

"You'll always be inside me," she says from outside the doorway. "Till the next time. Remember, you are still my project. I have made you my job." She turns and walks toward the elevators. I hear a door close down the hall.

CHAPTER SIXTEEN

It is a gentle morning flooded with sweet air and soft light fractured through the treetops. The Château de Divonne sits alone in eighteenth-century splendor on the hill above Divonne-les-Bains, the busy casino town just over the French border, where the fun-starved international crowd from Geneva comes to escape. The road behind the Château's stone gates is framed by poplars planted long ago to shade horse-drawn aristocrats. Also planted nearby is a more recent nicety of the privileged class. A helicopter pad. The round concrete slab, once brightly painted with a giant bull's-eye, is faded, cracked, and weathered to the same degree of romantic decay as the rest of the property. From the look of things, one might conclude that the elite have been arriving at the Château by air as well as land since long before the French Revolution.

Wendy and I arrive in the maroon Peugeot 404 she rented earlier this week for her conference. "I'm so-o-o happy to get out of Geneva," she sighs as she downshifts through the gates. "That city goes way beyond clean."

"Beyond clean?" I ask.

"All the way to sterile. Sterile! It's so pretty, so perfect, so-o-o antiseptic. All of it—the lake, the mountains, the promenades, the—"

"The money," I add, as we varoom uphill toward the Château, poplars whizzing by on either side.

"Yeah, the money. I think that's the problem, Macallan. Geneva's designed to be the perfect home for money. People only go there to visit their money. They go someplace else to live and enjoy it. Like what's-her-name said, 'There's no there there.' "

144

"Gertrude Stein."

"Yeah, Gertie."

"Gertie?"

"Just another nice Jewish girl."

Wendy steers into the courtyard parking lot. We crunch to a stop on the gravel. The four-story building of white limestone is sprawling and impressive, but not overpowering. It has a mansard roof, floor-to-ceiling windows on the first floor, and elegant sculpted lintels—everything a well-proportioned French country palace of the pre-Versailles era ought to have.

"Now this is my idea of a hotel," Wendy says as I pull our suitcases from the backseat of the car. "After four days of speeches on Euro-marketing and five nights in the Hotel du Rhône, I tell you, I am psyched for this." She stops just before the front stairway and takes a deep breath, taking in the noble building before her. I stop alongside her. "When I was in Divonne," she muses, "on the summer school program, we all dreamed of meeting a rich, handsome man who'd sweep us off our feet and spirit us up here for a wild romantic affair. Doesn't this look like the perfect place for a *secret* assignation? A *passionate* tryst with a sophisticated and deliciously immoral stranger? Doesn't it, Robert?"

I set our suitcases down on the gravel for a moment and ponder the Château with mock intensity, hoping to hide my discomfort on the subject of secret assignations and passionate trysts. I say nothing.

"That's what we fantasized about when we saw this hotel."

I maintain my pose, frozen.

"Or at the very least," she giggles, "dinner." She pinches me on the left buttock and walks to the steps. "You know how teenage girls love to eat."

"And how," I say, picking up the suitcases and following her into the Château.

Our room on the third floor is square, tall, and airy. The walls are covered in elegant cloth with a big, open classical floral pattern. The look is neither masculine nor feminine. Just very French.

Wendy is jabbering on the phone in French, finalizing our lunch plans with her old friends in Vesancy, the little dairy village nearby. She sounds happy and excited. I sit in the chair by the window, looking down over Divonne's shopping center, "campings," tennis clubs, and condos. Beyond, I see the highway, farms, and, through the trees, a silvery slice of Lake Geneva. It looks like the last of the morning haze may soon burn off.

Wendy's rapid-fire French is indecipherable. I can sometimes pick out a word or two that I remember from high school classes. But that's it. There's no point in my trying to keep up. Wendy lived in France as a high school student and again in college; she has maintained her French friendships and contacts on both sides of the Atlantic and makes a point of tuning in the odd bits of TV from France that appear on obscure cable channels back in New York. Her accent does not sound like an American's, either. Even snotty Frenchmen comment on how good it is.

"*A bientot,*" she says and hangs up the phone. That one I understood. "Macallan, are you ready for a little *dejeuner sur l'herbe?*"

"You can't fool me, that's an impressionist painting. With two guys and a naked lady on a picnic."

"Well, are you still game?"

"Of course. But which one of you women is going naked?"

"Come along and find out," she replies, smiling. Wendy has been telling me about her friends in Vesancy for years. Their farmhouse and their wonderful, simple, beautiful life. "I warn you, Nadine and Pierre don't speak a word of English."

"Then we'll understand each other perfectly. I don't speak a word of French."

The valley of Lake Geneva is a flat-bottomed bowl about one hundred miles long. Rising up on the south side are the snow-covered Alps. On the north side are the Jura Mountains, older, lower, round, and green. Divonne marks the start of the hills that rise up into the Jura.

Leaving the Château, we drive for a few minutes across the hillside. We turn at an unmarked road by an empty green field. The road takes us up to a small wood at the base of a still bigger hill. Just behind the wood where the Juras begin sits the village of Vesancy, hidden from view and the twentieth century.

Vesancy is one lazy little road lined with stone farmhouses and stone cow barns. There is very little outward difference between the two types of structures. The town looks deserted except for an old woman carrying a basket full of laundry around to the back of her house and an old man in coveralls sitting on a wooden box, smoking a cigarette. In the center of town sits a small, squat medieval château with a single round turret, a happy little comic book castle.

"That's the Château de Vesancy," Wendy explains as we come to a stop, "once home of the local nobleman, now the seat of the municipal government."

"Municipal government? Where are the limos and squad cars? The union bosses? The graft and corruption?" We sit in the Peugeot, the sweetish odor of cow dung in the air, watching little birds chirp and geraniums bloom in the window boxes of the fat little tower.

"She says it's called *Life and the Little Death,*" Wendy explains to me about the book Nadine is reading. " 'Life and orgasm,' that's what it means. They call orgasm 'the little death.' "

"Hmm," I say, helping myself to another glass of fruity red wine.

Wendy leans closer to me to whisper something confidential. The wine must be getting to her. Our companions cannot understand. "They also call a woman's pussy 'the little wound.' " She giggles.

"The French have a word for everything," I say. But I don't think she was listening. She is back in the thick of the conversation with her two friends. Nadine and Pierre are about Wendy's age. Nadine is a sparrowy, angular brunette. Pierre is a hulking, fair-haired Gaul—Vercingetorix from the farm. The house they rent down the village's only side street belongs to Pierre's mother. They treat me with the amused courtesy usually reserved for senile old relatives.

I do not mind being left out of the chatter. I do not mind much of anything. The passage of time on planet Earth stopped shortly after we flopped into the reclining canvas chairs on the grass near the apple trees. Like magic, one bottle of wine after another has appeared and vanished. Without any visible effort, Nadine has brought forth fragrant homemade pâtés, juicy roast chickens, green salad fresh from the garden, loaf after loaf of warm, crusty bread, a medley of cheeses, and a just-baked strawberry tart that is nothing less than regal. A feast of simplicity in the lazy afternoon sun.

Just breathing the air is intoxicating. Even the bees seem to have gotten tipsy. The little yellow jackets are everywhere. They alight on the food, on the rims of our wineglasses, on our sleeves. *"Les gueppes."* But there is no threat or hostility in them. They simply want to join the party. They provide a continuous soothing buzz, background music of the peaceable kingdom.

Finally, as the afternoon light starts to turn yellow, Nadine begins gathering up the plates and silverware. Wendy and I make a gesture of offering to help, but our hosts turn us down flat. With a few spare motions, they make cleaning up look as easy as everything else.

"Come on, honey," Wendy says. "Let's not be rude by watching our hosts work." She stands up from her canvas chair and takes a big stretch, as if getting up after a nap. "Let's go for a little walk. I want to show you something."

She takes my hand and leads me up the grassy hill above the village. We climb past ramshackle fences and clumps of trees. Just ahead, at the top of the rise, is a little stone chapel, gray and plain with a little spike of a steeple.

"Keep your head down," she says. "Just watch the ground."

I study the long grass as we take our last steps before reaching the chapel.

"There now." Wendy takes me by the shoulders and turns me in the direction of the village. Standing in front of me, blocking my view, she gives me clear instructions. "I want you to look up slowly. Very slowly. Start at your feet and raise your head little by little. Okay?" She steps aside. "Now. Go ahead."

I see the grass below me. Then the slope of the hill we are standing on. Below, the rooftops of the village come into view. Then the fields we drove through on the way up from the Château. The vista opens up more. The valley of Lake Geneva spreads out—flat, flat, flat. A quilt of farms, roads, towns. Then the lake itself appears, silvery and blue, across the entire horizon. The city of Geneva is at the far right, huddled around the tip of the lake. The Jet d'Eau, Geneva's senseless towering column of water, spritzes upward into the sky, a symbol of bland Swiss might. Then blue sky. And more blue sky. Then, floating in thin air, golden white, the jagged peaks of the Alps. An endless ribbon of icy spikes suspended above the valley, defying all gravity and distance.

"That's what I wanted to show you," Wendy whispers as she hugs my arm.

Silence. I put my arm around her. She nestles.

"It's gorgeous, Wendy. It really is."

More silence.

"Robert?"

"Yes."

"Let's make a baby."

"Here?"

"Right here. There's no one around."

"What?"

"Shhhh." Wendy pulls me down to the ground. The grass is a thick carpet. "Just lay back and relax." I see the sky above me and feel Wendy unzipping my pants and taking me into her mouth, licking and sucking. I am limp. She licks and sucks more. I am still limp. She is working now. Working hard. I am still limp. I don't know why.

"What'samatter, honey? Is it the wine?"

I grunt. "Keep on, just give me a minute."

She applies herself. Diligently. No results. I can feel her about to get upset, about to panic. This has never happened before. Never.

"Come on, honey," she whispers before diving in again. "You can do it. Fantasize your sexiest fantasy."

For an instant my mind goes blank, then the image appears. I feel my cock surge and stiffen and swell. I hold before me the image of Laura Chasen.

"Oohh, that's it," Wendy says with a little shudder. "Come on, sweetie."

We roll over. She opens up to me.

I pierce the little wound.

I die the little death.

JULY

CHAPTER SEVENTEEN

It is a bright, steamy Tuesday morning. *Elixir's* ancient window air conditioners, for all the noise and stale chill they create, make the office a sanctuary from the clammy world outside.

So far, it has been a summer of trying to hang on. Trying to hang on to our low-cost real estate in the face of Harry's desire to move us uptown. Trying to hang on to advertisers who are being seduced by Mackey's new medical publication. Trying to hang on to control of *Elixir* while Harry's idiotic management seminars and bureaucratic bullshit monopolize my time. *Elixir* and I are hanging on. Just barely.

Later this morning, Leo and I have a meeting to close the big deal with Max McGuinn, the big deal for all of the ad pages in our upcoming special issue on hypertension. It is really Leo's meeting. I am going along to add the extra weight of the publisher's credibility, to show how much we care about Max's advertising dollars, how much we care about him, and to make sure that we do, in fact, close the sale.

These are the official, publicly stated reasons for my going along. No one could disagree with them. They are entirely appropriate. They are also entirely false. The reason I am going, the reason I would never admit to anyone, is that I am growing to distrust Leo. Strongly.

It's been building since I spotted Atwood's card on his blotter during my "secret" negotiations with American, since Mackey somehow knew about the special issue. Then, early in July, Leo borrowed *Elixir's* highly confidential circulation list to do some analysis for a presentation. A normal and harmless routine event. Except that at the end of July Mackey sent out teasers for his new magazine to every one of our subscribers. It is *possible* that it was just coincidence.

Then there's Leo's attitude. He's much nicer to me than he's ever been before. Gone is the thinly veiled condescension, the Dutch uncle patronizing. For the first time since I hired him, Leo actually treats me like a real boss. I can feel him "handling" me as if I were one of his clients, with respect and protocol and ready good humor. He's never done that before. Suddenly he's behaving with painstaking professionalism and making a visible, public point of it. It can't be because he suddenly respects me.

There's another new pattern. He's missing, unaccounted for, for blocks of time during which he leaves no number where he can be reached. Two hours on a Tuesday morning, the odd hour after a client lunch. Afterward, he'll check in and say that he was with such-and-such a client on such-and-such a call. Leo always left word of where he was going *before* he went there. That was how he set up the scorecard for his adoring fans back in the office: These are the prospects I am going out to conquer. Pay heed to the names of my victims. Upon returning, he would trumpet his victories to the secretaries, other salespeople, or anyone else who would listen. Even the cleaning ladies, if he happened to come back late.

Then there's the way he cultivates Dudley, soliciting his ideas with interest and respect, when I know goddamn well that he looks down on the "wet-behind-the-ears kids" who are taking over "his" industry. Yet Leo keeps Dudley in his office for long heart-to-hearts about God knows what, for long periods with the door closed, Marie tells me. And in our internal meetings, he punctuates important points with a conspicuous wink in Dudley's direction, as if they had worked out the script long before.

So, I've decided to stay close to Leo. Closer than I've ever been before. I have just reviewed his presentation materials for this morning's meeting with McGuinn. They are impeccable. Leo is still the thoroughly buttoned-up space salesman, no matter what his other schemes. All the statistical arguments about added reader frequency are lined up neatly, to provide more than enough justification for buying half the ad pages in our special issue. McGuinn will need that to cover his ass, should any higher authority question this use of marketing funds, although Leo insists that McGuinn has the last word on his ad budgets. But the real argument, as it is for any publication at any time, is judgment. Does it *feel* like the right thing to do? And in this case, with a new hypertension medication just launched by his company and an old standby medication to defend, McGuinn shouldn't need a lot of computer printouts to convince him that he ought to be in our issue, an issue that's going to be an "everything you've ever wanted to know about hypertension." An issue that tens of thousands of physicians are likely to keep on their shelves to refer to time and again.

But as powerful as the marketing presentation is, even more powerful is Leo's connection to this client. Which goes back to before I learned to read. Leo claims to have him in his back pocket. "I've got more than the negatives of McGuinn with the goat," he likes to joke. "It was my pet goat."

So we're off to close the deal with McGuinn. With my copy of our slick presentation package under my arm, I proceed down the hall to pick up Leo.

"Sure, we've got big plans," I can hear Leo saying to whoever he's got on the phone. I stop outside his doorway, just out of sight, to listen a bit. "We're talking about folding our research department into American's. . . . Uh-huh, any day now. . . . Sure, with all the added firepower, we'll do even better than before. . . . Uh-huh, that's right. . . . Well, sure there'd be a hiatus. That's inevitable. But it wouldn't be more than a couple of months, I guarantee. Then we'll give you more customized studies on what gastroenterologists think and what color their patients are shitting, more than you ever thought possible."

I listen with total attention. Everything Leo is saying is a lie. There are no plans to fold our research department into American's. No one has ever brought it up. It would make no sense. American is geared up to do mass-market surveys of its shifting, ever changing millions of general interest readers. *Elixir* specializes in a contained universe of 250,000 physicians, a universe we track and study with great precision. Our research needs would get lost inside American's huge machine. Besides, Harry would have to check with me first, long before making such a move.

"Of course I am," Leo says. "I'll stake my reputation on it. This merger is a great thing for you guys, uh, especially a company like yours. . . . Sure. I told it like it really was at Becker, didn't I? . . . I told it like it was at *Elixir*, before the acquisition, didn't I? . . . Well, I'm tellin' you like it is now. . . . Of course. . . . Uh-huh. . . . Uh-huh. And I was right about what was going on at Becker when I left, wasn't I? . . . You bet. Well, I'm telling it to you straight this time, too. . . . Yes. Sure. You know what I stand for. Believe me, if things should change, you'll be the first to know. The first. . . . No, none. . . . That's right. Now, how about that lunch? . . . Yeah, next Thursday's good. I'll have my girl call with the reservations. . . . Great, Phil. See ya." He hangs up.

Leo just pledged his undying loyalty to *Elixir* on the basis of a completely phony promise. Given the nature of this business, it could be an honest lie or an evil lie. Maybe he's building sand castles in the sky, like any imaginative salesman. Or maybe he's setting up an opening that will allow him to jump ship later, without sacrificing any personal credibility. "I was right about what was going on at Becker, wasn't I?" he said. There was nothing going on at Becker when I hired him, except for the extra $50,000 I was offering him. "If things should change, you'll be the first to know." I'll bet he used the same ploy with his Becker clients when he was negotiating with me. But who's he going to jump to? He's blatantly working the Dudley-Woodcock connection to feather his nest with American. That must be Plan A. Maybe this is Plan B. If American doesn't work out, go with someone else. But who? He's already worked for just about everyone else in the industry. With the exception of someone who would really appreciate getting all sorts of confidential information about *Elixir*. Elton Mackey.

I turn and enter Leo's office. His back is to the door; he is putting on his suit jacket and inspecting his reflection in the glass of one of his "Leo-and-celebrity" photos on the wall.

"You look pretty persuasive to me," I say in my best good-buddy voice.

"Huh?" I have caught him off guard. He spins around. "Hey, I didn't hear you come in. Just, uh, preparing myself a little."

"Leo, you get better-looking every year. Don't the ladies all tell you that?"

"It depends which ladies you're talking to."

"You know 'em all, I thought."

"Well, all the ones worth knowing."

"Like the ones at the Aviary?"

This is Leo's escort service of choice. On the business card he once showed me it read:

The Aviary
Rare and exquisite birds from all over the world.

The phone number was easy enough to remember. PLaza 4-BIRD.

"Yeah, the Aviary. Dependable vendor," Leo says with a little smile. "That Betty is one helluva smart businesswoman. You wouldn't believe some a the high rollers she's got for clients. I'm talking about the biggest names in real estate, CEOs from the Fortune 500, U.N. ambassadors, you name it. Strictly crème de la crème. Lotta guys really get off on the idea that they're puttin' it in the same snatch as big shots with a hundred million in the bank and a fleet of Gulfstream jets."

"Big shots like Elton Mackey?"

Leo is stopped cold by my suggestion. "Uh, I suppose so," he says, looking genuinely puzzled. "Why him?"

"I don't know; he just came to mind when you said a hundred million dollars and private jets." I can hear the edge in my voice, and I must get rid of it.

"Nah, he's not Betty's kinda client. Not that I ever met the guy." Leo sticks to the topic. "She handles Wall Street types. And international pooh-bahs, you know, Arabs and Japs. I don't know about Cleveland. Say, what's Mackey got to do with the price of tea in China, anyway?" Leo sounds confused, maybe even on the verge of being hurt.

"Nothing, nothing." I pat him on the shoulder. "Just nervous about the special issue, I guess. The presentation material for McGuinn looks good."

"Thanks. You gonna join us for lunch?"

"I can't. Got a command performance at American. Woodcock is hosting some securities analyst. He wants me to be in the room to nod and agree while he has Drummond tell him about American's new entrepreneurial spirit."

Leo whistles admiringly. "Vice Chairman Drummond. Not bad company."

"That's a matter of opinion."

"Well, *I'm* impressed." Leo buttons his suit jacket, brushes out the wrinkles, hitches his necktie tightly into place, and picks up his briefcase. "Hey, boss, let's go make a sale."

"Let's."

As we head out together, Marie wishes us luck. In the elevator, after a brief silence, I turn to him. "I couldn't help overhearing your conversation about folding *Elixir*'s research department into American's. There's no plan for anything like—"

"Oh, that?" Leo's smile snaps into place; his eyes turn to happy slits. "That was Phil Mead on the line. You know Phil; he's got a research fetish. I was trying a little something out on him. It's an idea I've been kicking around with Dudley for a while. I wanted to send up some trial balloons before submitting an actual report with a plan to you. I gotta tell you, though; clients seem to go for it."

Leo sounds plausible; he always does. But this is not the time to try to figure this one out.

"Okay, we can talk about it later."

The elevator doors open. Our heels echo through the musty Gothic cathedral lobby of General Insurance. Soon *Elixir* will be moved up to midtown, to American headquarters. Under Harry Woodcock's wing, or thumb, depending on how you look at it.

Out on the sidewalk, the air hits like a blast furnace. I head for the curb in a southerly direction to wave for a cab; Leo heads northerly for a waiting limo.

"This way, Bob!" He waves to me before reaching down to open the rear curbside door. "We're going in style."

I should have known.

I settle in next to him in the backseat. "Is this just for us, Leo?" I am grateful for the cool inside and the fact that this rented statusmobile has neither bar nor TV. Cost control, cost control.

"This is for the client. I'm taking Max downtown for lunch," Leo explains. "To that new Italian place all the artists supposedly hang out at. Stronzo. Too bad you can't make it. The waitresses wear black turtlenecks and black tights—with miniskirts up to here and legs to match."

"Very artistic."

"Yeah, very."

"How's the pasta?"

"Does it matter?"

"I suppose not."

As the car makes its way uptown, Leo and I go over the presentation materials one last time.

"Fellas, it's a great idea. It really is." Max McGuinn looks happy. Happy to be sitting behind his desk wielding the power he does, happy to be signing up for our special issue, and, most of all, happy to be jousting with his old buddy Leo.

Max is fifty-five-ish and paunchy. A big, fleshy, plain-featured Irish bruiser. His puffy cheeks are streaked with red—tiny spiderwebs of broken capillaries that make his bright blue eyes seem to shine all the more. His abundant wavy gray hair is held perfectly in place with some kind of shiny goop.

After almost two hours of our romancing him about his plans and our special issue, he is more than amenable; he's enthusiastic. Leo has primed him perfectly through preliminary meetings, scoping out which drugs Orem-Diedrich, Inc., wants to advertise, how they want to advertise them, and with how much budgetary support.

"I gotta hand it to you," Max says of our master plan to tie in ads for a slew of seemingly unrelated drugs. "This is brilliant. The subject is hypertension—everything you always wanted to know. Perfect for our big splash launch of Meldene and support for Trimafac before it goes off patent." The former is Orem-Diedrich's new high blood pressure medication, the latter its old standby. "But then, with this 'whole patient' reference guide, you also make it a great vehicle for Medacor, Pepcill, Prucardia, Zentec, and Clonoral."

"You bet," Leo says. "We give you high blood pressure and throw in peptic ulcers, duodenal ulcers, depression, and chronic arthritis pain as a bonus."

"Did I hear you say at no extra cost?" Max asks, kidding.

Leo gives it back to him. "The way you're gonna chisel us down, practically."

"If I could only live to see the day."

"You just might," Leo says with a grin, "if you stay away from Meldene, Trimafac, Medacor, Pepcill, Prucardia, Zentec, and Clinoral." They have been at this game for years. Max, the legendary "detail man" who rose from the streets of Hell's Kitchen to the top levels of pharmaceuticals marketing on his ability to massage medical egos and pummel more educated colleagues into submission. And Leo, the legendary pharmaceuticals space rep, who holds sway over clients with personality, outside favors, and the secrets of his little black book. They are mighty relics, dinosaurs from the Era of Salesmen. Right now they are having a good time sniffing around each other. Two brontosauruses engaged in an ancient, unrushable mating ritual.

Unfortunately, I have to make them move faster. I'm about to be late for my appointment at American. And we still have not closed the sale.

"Remember the gatefold we did for the launch of Practizene?" Leo is reminiscing about the big ulcer drug of the 1960s, the first launch he managed.

"Oh, yeah," says Leo, holding up an imaginary copy of a magazine.

"You poked your finger through the dotted line right here where the duodenum was."

" 'A breakthrough *you* can make in ulcer treatment!' " Max says, recalling the headline of the ad. The two of them share a laugh.

"Oh, yeah," says Max. "That was a great campaign. I guess we really started special effects in pharmaceutical advertising with that one. First of the reader involvement gimmicks."

"Remember when they came out with scratch and sniff panels?" Leo says. "We used to joke about using one for Daltex."

Daltex is the company's high-octane prescription laxative.

"Uh-huh," Max giggles, "the sweet smell of success."

Max and Leo laugh some more. Ha-ha-ha. I laugh, too. Ha-ha-ha. We're having a wonderful time, the three of us. This is not funny. Why the hell won't Leo close? What is with him? Come on, get with it, Leo. This is a sales call. We've been here all fucking morning. I shoot him an angry glance.

He looks right through me.

"Hey, Max," he says, still chuckling, "you ever talk to the guys over in Consumer Products?"

"Sure, sometimes."

"Well, I don't understand those *disposable* douches?"

"Whaddya mean?"

"Did they think women were *saving* it?"

Ha-ha-ha. We all laugh some more. What a grand old time we're having. I've got to get this meeting back on track. I need an answer before I leave. I need an answer now.

"You know, Max," I cut in, "our production people are really chomping at the bit. There's a ton of edit material we'd like to design around your ads. You know how they are about lead times. If we can lock up our agreement right now, I can give them the go-ahead. In fact, they'd be happy if I could phone them right now."

Max and Leo stop laughing and look at me as if I were the world's biggest spoilsport.

"I think we're pretty close," Max says.

"Yeah," Leo jumps in, trying to manage me and stand guard on behalf of his client. "We're doing fine, Bob. Just fine." Leo pats my arm reassuringly.

I am not reassured. I want my answer now.

"Max, I'm sure you understand," I say, barging past Leo. "We have so many things to prepare to pull this off. And I don't just mean in the issue. You know all those extra 'bennies' we were talking about." I'm referring to the free mailings and merchandising favors that normally accompany a big sponsorship like this one. "Designing that stuff is a big job. And we want to be sure it's all coordinated with a single look. Besides, Max, you know how much you like to get involved in the graphics." I try a little joke of my own. "I gotta get my art directors started now, so you'll have time to change everything." It gets no laugh. "I really do need to know now." Max looks disappointed; Leo looks angry. I don't care.

Max sighs. "Like I say, Bob, I think we're close. Real close. I just have to check with a couple of people upstairs."

Leo defends his client. "Yeah, Bob, I told you about the people Max has to check with." Bullshit, Leo! You told me that Max has already checked with everyone he has to check with. Which is no one. Max has final authority on this. We all know it.

"I don't anticipate any problems," Max says. "Like I say, the proposal looks great."

"But there's a lot of prep work," I say. "That's why we need the lead time." I will get my answer now.

Leo jumps in again. "Bob, the design boys'll jump through hoops for us; you know that. Max and I are doing fine. Really, we are. I think I can safely say that the sale is as good as closed." Leo looks at Max for confirmation. Max nods his assent. Leo looks back at me, ready for me to back down. "As good as closed."

That's not good enough. "I need to know now."

"Come on, Bob," Leo says with a wink. "We don't need to know this second. Max and I are looking forward to a nice leisurely lunch, with maybe, uh, a little preclosing celebration this evening." He must be talking about the Aviary. "We can afford to wait a little."

No, we can't, goddammit. It's my magazine. Fuck you, Leo. We're gonna close this before I leave.

"I'm sorry, Leo, but we can't wait. Max, I hate to do this, but I have to level with you. There is another advertiser who is extremely interested in sponsoring the special issue. I'm not at liberty to tell you who it is. Nobody else knows anything about this, not even Leo. I've been doing everything I can to keep him at bay. But he's really starting to put the heat on me. I hate to do this, Max. But as publisher and president of *Elixir,* I have to be fair about this opportunity. Now, please understand that I want Orem-Diedrich to have first crack at this. I'd love to see you get this one, Max. But I can't keep this other company on the hook any longer. Can we get your assurance that it's a yes?"

There's a long, silent pause.

"I'm sorry to do this, Leo." I return his reassuring pat on the arm. I offer Max a look of infinite sympathy. "Can we count on you, Max? We really need to know."

Max looks at Leo, confused. Leo looks at me, steaming.

"Well, uh . . . I guess so."

"Is that a yes, Max?"

"Uh . . . yeah. That's a yes."

"Max, that's wonderful." I reach across the desk to shake Max's hand.

"We are going to make you the happiest advertiser that ever walked the face of the earth."

"Leo," I say, offering him a mock punch to the shoulder, "you're the best. Absolutely the best."

Leo's cherubic smile betrays nothing. The red in his face betrays everything.

"Here, Max, let me call our production department." I have now taken full control of the meeting. I reach for Max's telephone and dial the office. "Hi, Jeannie, it's Bob. Put me through to Ted, will ya. . . . Ted? . . . Listen, those layouts we were working on for Orem-Diedrich. It's a go. Full steam ahead. I'm with Max and Leo right now. I expect us to be back here with the full presentation a week from today."

I look at Max, then Leo. They nod approval.

"Uh-huh, a week from today. And remember to make those designs good. But not so good that Max can't improve them. I don't have to remind you that he is still the most talented art director in the business." A laugh all around. "Okay, Ted. See you back at the office." I hang up.

"Max, congratulations. I'll let you and Leo work out the particulars. I'm sorry, but I have to run. I would have loved to join you for lunch. Leo tells me Stronzo has a lot of tasty dishes. And that the food's not bad, either."

Another round of laughter among us boys.

I get up to leave.

"Max, thanks again." Hearty handshake. "We'll be in touch soon. You're in the best of hands with Leo."

I confide to Leo in a loud whisper, "I know you're going to give this gentleman a most memorable afternoon."

"And evening," Leo adds with fake but convincing good cheer.

"See you back at the office. Good work."

I excuse myself and make my exit. As I close the door to Max's big corner office, I breathe a sigh of immense relief.

It worked.

Everything I said was a lie. There is no other advertiser. There never was. There are others who *could* be lured over time, but we have been going full blast against Orem-Diedrich. I've been so busy with Harry's corporate bullshit I haven't had time to make sales calls of my own. But Leo cannot be sure of that and neither can Max. After all, I do have advertiser relationships that go back before Leo came to work for me, so the bluff is plausible. It was a calculated risk. And it worked. Leo is certainly pissed off now. But I can't worry about that. What the hell was he up to, anyway? Why was he stalling? Why wouldn't he close the sale in front of me? He had to know that I wasn't about to walk out of Max's office without getting the order. He may think of Max as *his* client, but it's still *my* goddamn magazine. At least until I get the rest of my earn-out.

There must be other people riding down in the elevator with me. But I do not notice them. Or anything else. All I am aware of is my train of thought.

So it's a yes for the special issue. Yes for the profit targets. I feel great. Great. I did it. I'm going to pull it off. Harry Woodcock and his mole Dudley and the American bureaucracy and Leo Sayles notwithstanding, I'm going to pull it off. Harry will be mad at me for being late for his meeting. But so what? A few more months of bullshit. Then freedom. Independence. Choice.

The little cartoon man inside me is bursting his buttons with pride and self-satisfaction. Pop, pop, pop, pop! For the briefest of moments, I indulge myself in the happy little feeling that I am invulnerable.

CHAPTER EIGHTEEN

Outside the Orem-Diedrich building, I catch a cab headed west toward American. It slams to a halt seconds after we pull away from the curb. Maybe it's because the light at the corner of Fifty-third Street and Third Avenue is red. Or maybe there's a blockage of some kind. We're too far from the intersection to know. Crosstown traffic in midtown is always hell. Especially around lunch hour. Especially in the heat. Horns start blowing ahead of us. The cab sits motionless. We wait, the driver and I. And wait.

Sun pours in through the grimy rear window. The wheezing, farting taxi with the caved-in backseat is an oven on wheels. The air inside is dead still and unbearably thick. Stale, acrid odors rise off the floor. The sooty vinyl upholstery is hot and sticky. I pass the time reading and rereading the legal notices and instructions posted around the interior. I memorize the driver's name (Daziqi, Ahmet) and compare his ID photo with the slice of face reflected in the rearview mirror. I try to imagine the heartrending story of his immigrant struggles. I study a hangnail on my right thumb. The meter now reads $2.50. Still we have not budged. I jam three one-dollar bills through the Plexiglas partition and leap out of the cab.

I start walking west at a brisk but controlled pace, trying not to encourage any more sweat than necessary. Without breaking stride, I loosen my tie, unbutton my collar, and remove my suit jacket, keeping my arms away from my sides to avoid pitting out my shirt. What a ridiculous getup this business uniform is in New York's tropical heat and humidity.

As I cross Park Avenue, the crowds get thicker. I feel my heels sink into the tar. I break into a half-run now, jumping up and down between curbstone and gutter to maneuver around people, parked cars, and the occasional sidewalk vendor. I bob and weave like a prizefighter. I start to sweat like one, too. My forehead is dripping; my neck is drenched. I can feel my shoulders sticking to my shirt. A river runs down my spine, another down the center of my chest. My collar has wilted and soaked the noose of my necktie. I can feel sweat from my armpits dripping furiously into my sleeves.

Across one block, down another, across, down, across, down, across.

Soon American's tower looms across Sixth Avenue. Crowds of office workers mill listlessly around the plaza. A few sun-worshiping secretaries sit or recline around the fountain, necks craned upward in the direction of the gritty rays, blouses open by an extra button, shoes dangling by a toe.

My jacket still held at arm's length, I go through the revolving door into the sudden chill of American's lobby. As I proceed toward the forty-eighth-floor elevator bank, I try to collect myself. I stop to inspect my reflection in the glass of the building directory. I look ridiculous. My light blue shirt is now dark blue, except at the cuffs. The wetness turns the material transparent wherever it clings, making my nipples and patches of chest hair plainly visible. The suit jacket in my hand is still pristine, but so what? I can't put it on. My hope is that the air-conditioning will dry me off before I have to look presentable. I am now forty minutes late for Woodcock's appointment with Vice Chairman Drummond and the important securities analyst.

In the forty-eighth-floor reception area, I announce myself to Legs.

"Bob Macallan to see Harry Woodcock, please."

She gives me a look that mixes horror and disgust with her usual condescension.

"I'm sorry, Mr. Woodcock is in conference right now."

"I know that. I'm supposed to be in that conference with him."

She gives me the look again. "It's a closed-door meeting, sir."

"I know. I'm supposed to be on the other side of the closed door."

"They gave specific orders not to be disturbed."

"It's okay. Really. They'll be more angry if you don't let them know I'm here."

"Very well," she sighs and dials Woodcock's secretary. "Yes," she says into the phone, "he says he knows he's late. . . . I see. . . . I see. Very well." Legs looks at me again, this time communicating the added disapproval she just received from Miss Boardman.

"They're in with Mr. Drummond right now and really cannot be disturbed. Why don't you have a seat." She gestures toward the seating along the wall of windows.

The far end of the big couch is directly under an air-conditioning vent, an invisible river of cold air pouring down from it. I seat myself directly in the path of the flow. Maybe this will help to dry me off. Beside the pile of magazines on the end table is a telephone. I call for the morning message Wendy always leaves when she's away on a West Coast business trip.

"Number of messages received," the synthesized female voice says, "three." The first message comes on.

"Uhhmm. Hi, sweetie." Wendy yawns. "One, two, three. Now I'm up. Sort of. There, that's better. A few minutes ago, I thought I might be coming down with Guillain-Barré syndrome. I couldn't move my arm. I was real scared. Then the circulation started to come back. I guess I slept on it funny. I know, 'another miraculous recovery.' Well, it is. I should be out of the board meeting a little after lunch today. I'll be on the four o'clock plane this afternoon and back in our bed tonight. Mmm, I like that. Did you sleep okay? Miss you. I hope the sale went through. I just know you were brilliant. I gotta get up now. Love you."

The machine says that Wendy called at 9:08, 6:08 L.A. time. I can't imagine who might have left the next two messages. Our friends almost never call on weekday mornings. The machine beeps again.

"Hiya, Son, this is your father callin'. Got a favor I'd like to ask. Your brother's got a meeting in New York next week. Working on a new deal. The guy he's seeing is putting him up in a fancy hotel. Says he's gonna be real busy. But it'd be nice if you'd invite him over to see you. Maybe ask him to lunch, show him around the big city a little. Be friendly, you and him. Son, I'm getting older and for once I'd like to see my boys start acting civil to each other. Now I don't expect you to be best friends. Just stop acting like oil and water for once. Jimmy wasn't gonna call you, but I talked him into it. So be nice to him. Please. For your old man's sake. And, oh, don't tell him I called. He'd break my neck if he knew. Thanks, Son."

The machine beeps and says that message was at 11:05. It beeps again, and the third recording comes on. "Hey, Brother Bob. I got an appointment down in the big city next week. That's right. New York. Workin' on a deal with a guy in the muffler and tailpipe racket. He's putting me up at the Broadway Palace. You know it? I unnerstan' it's pretty posh. Hey, Brother, while I'm in the neighborhood, how about I come and visit your office. See where my big brother makes all those millions a his. Whaddya say? That's next Wednesday. I'll give you a call from my hotel. Be seeing ya, Bro'. In the Big Apple. That's what you sophisticated New Yorkers call it, isn't it?" The machine says that Billy's message came in at 11:15. It beeps the final message signal. I push the reset button and hang up as I hear the tape whirring back to start.

A visit from Jimmy? In New York? I guess the world is changing faster than I thought. Jimmy hates New York, detests it. Always has. He sneers at New York the same way he sneers at me. The muffler and tailpipe racket? That could be just the right place for him. Kind of tacky, rough-and-tumble, automotive. Maybe things are starting to work out for him, finally. It wouldn't be bad to turn down the tension between us. Initiate a little brotherly détente after all these years. It couldn't hurt. It might even feel good. Yes, I'd love to show Jimmy around a little. Love to. Good news on more immediate fronts, too. My shirt is drying off under the cascade of frigid air. I'm starting to look presentable again.

The phone rings at the reception desk.

"Yes, he's still here," Legs says, glancing back at me.

In a moment, the broad-shouldered, big-boned Miss Boardman appears, carrying the full weight of her Puritan disapproval. Her manner is just this side of civil.

"Mr. Woodcock was very concerned about your tardiness," she says with a frown. The last person I heard berate me for "tardiness" was another stern Saxon battle-ax. Miss Chatham, terror of the fourth grade.

"Mr. Woodcock waited and waited. Finally, he had to bring Mr. Briggs in to see Mr. Drummond without you. The schedule couldn't stand any more stretching. They're finishing up just now. I managed to catch him as they were leaving their meeting with Mr. Drummond. He asked me to have you wait in his office."

Just then, Woodcock, Drummond, and a third man, presumably the securities analyst, appear in the reception area. Miss Boardman moves her body in front of me. She might be trying to block my view of them, their view of me, or just be trying to be an obstructionist bitch.

I lean to one side slightly to get a glimpse of the scene. Drummond, another silver-maned Ivy League ex-marine, and Woodcock, a slightly younger version of the same American Communications, Fairfield County, Master Race prototype, are escorting the short, nerdy analyst to the elevators. They are doing a very slick job of making him feel tall, handsome, and powerful.

"I'm so glad you could spend this time with us, Mr. Briggs," Drummond says, pretending he is actually making contact with the eyes behind Briggs's Coke-bottle-bottom glasses.

"Please, it's Barton."

"Barton," says Drummond.

"Barton," Woodcock echoes with his most obliging smile.

Drummond resumes his sales pitch. "I hope you see what we mean about the changes going on here at American. The entrepreneurial spirit. I think you'll agree that it puts the *American Fitness* chapter in perspective. Seen over the long haul, that was a little hiccup in earnings." Sure, a fifty-million-dollar hiccup, paid for by hundreds of hapless staffers and thousands of unwitting stockholders. "What's important is the learning experience. We went out and took the risk. We shook up the corporation and learned from it. We're better for it, stronger for it." At least Drummond is, having risen to vice chairman as a result of it. "We're cultivating more of that risk-taking mentality here. Nurturing it. We really are."

He pauses and looks at Woodcock with a frown. "I wish Bob Macallan had been able to make it today. You'd see exactly what I mean by our laboratory for entrepreneurship. You know Bob built that medical book from nothing, with no outside investors, no big corporation behind him. Of course, we like to remind people that he got his training right here at American. In the Henderson Program. Isn't that right, Harry?"

"Absolutely." Woodcock looks upset at Drummond's displeasure. "He used to work for me back then. One of the best we ever had in the Program. I spotted him as a real comer, tried to give him the right kind of mentoring. I remember we used to have long discussions about publishing; I'd help him shape and discipline those wild young ideas of his. I like to tell people I taught him everything he knows. But that's only partly true." Woodcock tries to break the tension by laughing at his own little joke. Drummond forces just enough of a chuckle to be polite. Briggs is silent.

An elevator door opens across from the trio. Briggs starts disengaging himself from the huddle. "Thank you, gentlemen, I've learned a lot about American today. Really, I have. I appreciate it. Thank you." He backs into the waiting compartment.

"No. Thank *you*, Barton," Drummond says. "Remember, any questions, you call me. Direct. Any time."

As the doors close on Briggs, Harry mimics Drummond with a rather lame, "Thank *you*, Barton."

Drummond pauses in front of the elevator, collecting his thoughts. "That went pretty well," he says, as much to himself as to Woodcock. "As well as could be expected, under the circumstances. Besides everything else you taught him, I wish you'd taught your entrepreneurial wonder boy about keeping appointments. It would have made us *all* look better, Harry." With that little zinger, Drummond turns abruptly and walks back to his office, leaving Harry alone at the elevators.

Briggs and Drummond now gone, Miss Boardman stops her impersonation of the Great Wall of China. She turns and heads in the direction of a very upset Harry Woodcock, meeting him just beyond the desk where Legs sits practicing her snotty attitude. She whispers something to him, and he stops cold. He looks up, sees me sitting on the couch, and scowls.

"I'll see you in my office," he says in a loud stage whisper, *"Mister* Macallan," and storms off in that direction.

"I have tried with you, Macallan." Harry is letting me have it with both barrels. "I have really tried."

I am sitting. He is standing behind his desk, pacing and gesturing.

"I can't imagine how I could have been fairer to you. Nobody could have been fairer! And not just fairer, more gracious, more welcoming, more, more, more . . ." He's running out of adjectives. "Jesus Christ, Macallan, I sat here in this very office and did everything a man could possibly do to bury the hatchet. I ate a big helping of humble pie for you right, right . . ." He gestures toward the conversation area with the matching Barcelona chairs. "Right over there. I have done everything a man could be expected to do to put the past behind us and let you come in with a clean slate. And this is how you repay me."

"Harry, I wa—"

"Let me finish. Now you probably think I gave you this kind of treatment because you *deserve* it. But it's got nothing to do with you. It has to do with values that you can't understand, values you never could understand. Do you know what I'm talking about? Huh? Do you?"

I know he's not interested in a response, but I will try just the same.

"Harry, I've been trying to explain. I was in a sales call. An absolutely crucial sales call."

"See, that's what I mean. You have no idea what I'm talking about."

"Yes I do. We know what sales means to—"

"That's what I mean. How could I expect you to understand?"

"Understand what? I told you this sale is absolutely vital to—"

"To you." He says it like an accusation. "To *you*. To *your* earn-out. To getting the rest of *your* money. That's what I mean, Macallan. I'm talking about this company, this great company, and all you can talk about is you."

"But, Harry, *this is business.*"

"You're goddamn right. This is business. And this business, American Communications, now owns the business that used to—I repeat, used to—belong to you. Which means that your job is whatever I say it is."

"Harry, I was making money for the company. For American."

"Your responsibility to American was to be here. Don't you have sales-people you can trust?"

"Of course I do."

"Then why don't you let them do their job?"

"I had to be there to make sure tha—"

"Then you don't trust them, do you?"

"I trust them, it's just tha—"

"It doesn't surprise me. Not at all. I, I mean American, trusted you to be here to help make an impression on a very important securities analyst, and you didn't come through, either. So you probably expect the same flakiness from your subordinates. It's a good thing I've got Dudley in there to show your people how team players operate."

"Harry, that's not f—"

"Don't you realize that this company could soon be under siege? You've read the rumors in the paper. The stock price is soft and the quick-buck artists are sniffing around us." He glances out the window, downtown toward Wall Street. "It seems inconceivable, but American Communications could become a takeover target of one of those," he hesitates, "one of those Jewish raiders." He says it with a sneer. "Henderson would turn over in his grave. One of those garment district asset strippers taking over a great American institution like this. My father used to call it 'the tragedy of Ellis Island.' We should never have let them into this country." Harry shudders, the thought chills him so. "Fortunately, management is acting now, preventively, to manage perceptions in the investment community and, hopefully, to get that goddamn share price back up where it belongs. For better or worse, and it looks like worse, you are part of that effort."

"Harry, I'm not part of your big corporate strategy. I run a dinky little subsidiary that doesn't turn over enough money to pay the salesmen's bar bills at any other American book. It's small-time, American's little experiment with an entrepreneurial laboratory. I'm supposed to be left alone. That's the deal Levine sold me."

"Le-*v-e-e-e-n*," he sneers. "Saul Levine never made policy for American Communications."

"His name is Ted."

"Whatever. He's returning to Seligssohn Brothers, anyway."

"He is?"

"Oh, yes." Harry looks genuinely pleased. "I accepted his resignation this morning." He sits down, calmer. He pauses and takes on a cool, icy tone. "Take a good look at me, Macallan. I am your past. I am your present. And, most importantly, I am your future—for as long as you are under contract to this corporation. Of course, if you want to leave now, I won't stop you. Just leave the rest of your earn-out behind." He smirks at me, waiting.

Ever been tempted to bite off your nose for the sheer satisfaction of spiting your face? This is one of those moments. It takes all my willpower to keep from leaping out of the chair and telling Harry to go stuff it all. I feel a twitch in my left cheek. I hope he cannot see it.

"No, I didn't think so," he snickers. "Not when your big score is hanging in the balance. Macallan, I'm on to you. I want you to know that. I was on to you when you were a snotty trainee, and I'm on to you now. You've been laughing at us, haven't you? At me."

"Harry, I don't know what you're talking about. I'm not laughing at—"

"Oh yes, you are. I can feel it. You were just plain cocky back then. But now, now that you got lucky and took this company to the cleaners for ten mill', now you're really laughing. I hear all about it. Dudley is a good man; he picks up more than you think. And I see your behavior. Today isn't the first appointment you've missed. I heard about your no-show at the leadership seminar last week. Don't think I didn't. I was there when you came in late to the luncheon with the trainees. I heard all about the way you ducked out early of the off-site managers' meeting at Arrowhead. That, in my book, shows contempt. Pure contempt. And it is duly noted."

"Harry, you've got it all wrong. I've got a business to run. I don't have time for all these corporate—"

"How much does it take to buy your loyalty? Isn't ten million enough? No, never mind loyalty, that would be too much to ask in your case. I'm talking about your sense of responsibility. Your sense of decency. This company gave you your start. Do you have any idea of what a privilege it was to have been in the Henderson Program?" He turns off his righteous indignation for an instant to check a detail. "If I recall correctly, you're not even a Yale man."

"No, I went to Bal—"

"How did you manage that? Never mind." He turns his moral outrage back on like a light switch. "Not only did we give you your start; we made you rich. Rich beyond anything you deserve. Hasn't any sense of gratitude or responsibility sunk in? Is all this," he gestures around him, referring, I guess, to the corporation, "is all this here just for you to take?"

"Of course not, Harry. I—"

"You'd probably be very comfortable with those rag trade raiders. Who knows, maybe Grubman or the Belsky brothers are paying you to help undercut this company. I wouldn't put it past them. Or you. An egotistical, greedy short-term taker, that's what you are, Macallan. You're not a builder. You're a taker. You're what's wrong with American business, you and the rest of the quick-buck artists of your generation. Where do you get off thinking you're smarter than this entire company? That rules apply to everyone but you?"

He's not soliciting an answer. I offer none.

"The days of your taking advantage of this company are over."

"What do you mean by that? I've got a contract and a deal."

"I know that. And I've got a responsibility to do what's best for American Communications."

"You can't throw me out."

"I have no intention of doing that."

"Then what is your intention?"

"I'm going to make you toe the line. You want the rest of your money? You're going to give us full value for it. If we want to use you as window dressing to support the stock price, you're going to show up and stand in the window for as long as we say. Posed in your underwear, if we say so."

"All right. I hear you."

He looks down at his empty blotter and back up at me. There is fire in his eyes. "That's the last time you make me look bad in front of Drummond. The last time! You are going to understand that *you* work for *me*. And *I* work for the best interests of this company. Now maybe that will mean letting *Elixir* make those profit targets. Or maybe it won't. You'll have to wait and see. But I can tell you this much. When you move onto the fifth floor of this building in a few weeks, things are going to be different. I'm going to be very close to your little company. Very close indeed. I'm having Dudley look into folding all your operations into corporate. All of them. Promotion, research, printing, fulfillment, accounting, all of them. At the full corporate overhead allocation. That could well be the best thing for this company. That's a decision I'll make in time."

He pauses to let that sink in. That would definitely send my costs through the ceiling and my earn-out out the window. And there's nothing I can do—contractually, politically, or otherwise.

"You're right, Macallan." Harry tries to impersonate me and the plea I made earlier. *"This is business."* He leans forward on his blotter and toys with his expensive pen caddy. "Let me tell you something, young man. I've been at this game a lot longer than you have. And I'll be at it long after you're gone."

I sit in silence, trying to look impassive and unmoved, collecting my thoughts. My sweat-soaked shirt is almost completely dry, but I feel clammy and chilled from the inside out. The only sounds I hear are Harry tapping his gold pen on the marble base of the caddy and the whoosh of the air-conditioning. I feel a tickle in my nose. Suddenly I buckle over.

"Aaaachoooo!"

Shit. I've got a cold.

CHAPTER NINETEEN

I spot him about twenty feet ahead of me. I expected to meet Jimmy upstairs at *Elixir*. That's how I've been imagining it since I got the phone message last week. Instead I find him wandering around on the sidewalk in front of General Insurance, gawking at the tall buildings just like any tourist.

"Hey, Brother Jimmy!" I holler.

He turns, recognizes me, and gives me a big high sign.

"Hey, Brother Bob!" he hollers back.

This is the greeting Jimmy and I have exchanged since the days of fighting over toy trucks and plastic soldiers. The same four years and an even bigger world of differences separate us today.

We shake hands warmly, carefully checking each other out. It's been two years since I saw him last, and my fat little brother has gotten fatter, making him look even shorter than his five feet, four inches. Decked out in a loud plaid sport jacket, bright yellow tie, and bright blue slacks buckled under his substantial gut, he looks every bit the small-town car salesman he has been off and on since he dropped out of Bayport Community College ten years ago. His face—so pretty as a boy Mom's friends used to call him "Angel"—is now distorted with fat and bloat. The only features I recognize are the eyes of bright Macallan blue and the angry little mouth.

"Welcome to the big city, Brother." I had forgotten how much taller I am.

He fingers the lapel of my lightweight gabardine suit. "You look prosperous, Brother."

"Don't be fooled. It's pure Mel Ginsburg. Cheap and strictly off the rack." I sniffle.

"Geez, you sound terrible. What'sa matter? Gotta cold?"

As if on cue, a sneeze blasts through me.

"Uh-huh, for a week now," I say into my handkerchief. "Can't seem to shake it. It's the goddamn heat outside and the goddamn air-conditioning inside."

"Hmm. Tough break. Now tell me, big brother, what'sa story?" He points to the Gothic letters above the pointed arch of the building's main doorway. "How come it still says General Insurance Company up there, instead of Macallan Industries? I figured for ten mill' you get your name on the building or something."

"Your brother is strictly a little fish in this pond. In fact, I'm probably the smallest tenant here. You'll see. No views, no thick carpet, no mahogany paneling. Just nice low rent." I add under my breath, "At least for now."

"I get it. Keep the overhead low so when you clean up, you really clean up." He reaches his arm across an imaginary poker table, scrapes an invisible mountain of chips into his lap, and laughs.

"You look good," I lie to him.

"No, I don't. I'm a fat shit. And I figure at this point in life I'm gonna stay a fat shit. But you know something? I don't care. Anybody got a problem with that can go fuck himself. You know, Brother, out there in the real world," he gestures over the tall buildings and back toward the rest of America, "you don't have to be glamorous to get what you want. Now you gonna let me see your operation or what?"

"Come on up; I'll show you what glamorous isn't."

In the elevator, I ask him about his plans.

"Yeah," he says, "I'm looking at a franchise deal. You ever hearda 'Mister Muffler'?"

I shrug.

"No, I guess you wouldn'ta. Guy I know's got three a these locations out in Tucson, wants to unload 'em as a package. Great business, mufflers and tailpipes. Been watching it from the dealerships all these years. People are helpless; they don't know shit about what's going on under there. You get 'em in the door with a low-price offer and scare 'em up to a high-price installation. The help's cheap, margins are great. Kinda like magazines. Except people actually need mufflers and tailpipes."

I vow to ignore this and all future jibes.

"So you're here for a meeting with a potential backer?" I ask. Franchises require capital. Jimmy can't have much.

"Yeah, a backer." He smiles.

"Listen, if you want a lawyer to talk to about partnership agreements or a banker or anything, I've got some good connections here in town I could—"

"Naah, I got it all under control."

I know enough from previous rejections not even to think about offering financial support.

"One little thing I gotta do, and then I got myself a deal. 'Mister Muffler' is gonna be another way of saying 'Mister Money.' Just watch."

"That's great, Jimmy. Great. But if there's anything I can do to help, just let me know."

"Sure, Brother, no problem."

The elevator doors open at my floor. We step out onto the dingy linoleum of the dingy corridor. Jimmy looks at the fading sign that reads: CLAIMS INVESTIGATIONS, NORTHEAST REGION.

"Hey, where's the blond receptionist with big hooters who the boss is porkin' on the side?"

"Sorry, Brother. No blondes, no big hooters." I point to a little sign in the shape of an arrow that says: ELIXIR PUBLISHING CO., INC., SUITE 1810. I walk him down the rabbit warren corridor to the gray fire door with an identical ELIXIR sign, minus the arrow. I open the door and usher him inside. "Be it ever so humble, Jimmy."

Frumpy, dependable Jeannie is at the front-desk telephone console.

"Good morning, Jeannie."

"Good morning, Bob." She barely looks up.

"I'd like you to meet my brother Jimmy."

That gets her attention.

"Oh, hello there." She extends her hand. "Nice to meet you." Her eyes bounce back and forth between Jimmy and me, me and Jimmy. Something is not adding up. Jimmy picks it up, too.

"My brother got all the height," he says. "I got all the brains." He used to say that when we were teenagers, too.

Jeannie, finally satisfied with her genetic inspection after a few more seconds, announces, "You've got the same eyes. The same eyes."

Jimmy harumphs something under his breath.

"Any calls?" I ask.

"Nothing yet," she says. "Nice to meet you," she calls after Jimmy as I guide him back through the corridor toward my office. The next stop is Marie at her desk outside my office door.

"Marie, this is my bro—"

"I knew that," she says, jumping to her feet and offering Jimmy her hand. "I could tell right away. Hi, I'm Marie Padrone. Bob told us all about you."

"He did, huh? Did he tell you that he got the height, but I got the brains?"

Marie laughs politely at the brotherly jab. "Wiseguys, the two of you." She is trying not to be too obvious about her back-and-forth inspection.

"Will you testify for us?" I ask.

"Absolutely."

"I wouldn't be so sure," Jimmy says. "My mother used to take in all sortsa strays off the street. Aaoooooow," he howls like a dog. "You still bay at the moon like you used to, Brother?"

Marie smiles and sits down, looking for a way back to work and out of the line of fire.

"Can you hold my calls for a while, please?" I ask.

She nods and dives into a pile of correspondence.

I put my hand on Jimmy's shoulder and escort him toward my office. "Come on in, Brother."

Like the rest of *Elixir*'s premises, my office would never make it into the pages of *Executive Style*. Off-white walls, gray industrial carpeting, boring generic desk, secondhand couch, bookshelf, and cabinets. Jimmy inspects the bland, smallish room as if it holds some mighty secret. He stalks into every corner, peers through the bookshelf, flips through the magazines on the end table next to the couch as if he's gathering evidence of some kind. "Hmmm," he mutters. "I see, I see." He finishes the circuit standing behind my desk. He pulls my chair out.

"May I?" he asks.

"Sure, go ahead."

He settles himself in. I take the visitor's chair on the other side of the desk.

"So, Brother. This is where you make those million-dollar decisions."
He fondles my desktop paraphernalia—stapler, pencil cup, dictating machine, lamp, "in" and "out" boxes—leaving each object in a slightly new position. Just the way he did when we were kids back in Bayport. He never used to visit my room; he would invade it.

"You weren't kidding," he says. "This is pretty plain."

"I've got nobody to impress."

"You impressed American Communications pretty good."

I think for an instant of the looming shadow of Harry Woodcock and laugh. Because crying or raging won't do any good.

"I say something funny?"

"No, no. Just thinking."

"How did you talk 'em up to ten big ones?"

"I didn't. They said that was their best offer. It was a lot more than I thought I'd ever get. So I took it. Maybe I could have gotten more, I don't know."

He leans forward conspiratorially. "Tell me, how much is an operation like this *really* worth?"

"Hard to say. American blew thirty million trying to start a fitness magazine and they got nowhere. So if they can buy something like this that's already established for a third of that, it's a bargain, relatively speaking. But to a company in, say, the muffler and tailpipe business, an operation like this probably isn't worth ten cents."

He nods smugly.

I change the subject. "So how's Dad looking? I only see him on the phone these days."

"He's good. Still doesn't look anywhere near sixty-six. You know, it was his idea that I come see you." He looks around the office with the air of a prospective buyer. "But now that I've been here, I'm glad I came. This ain't such great shakes. He asked me not to tell you it was his idea, but I don't see any harm. Do you?"

"No, of course not."

"Didn't he talk to you and say please don't tell Jimmy?"

So much for father-son confidentiality.

"Uh-huh, he did."

"He's pretty smart, that old man a ours, don't you think?"

No, I don't think he's smart. More like sweet and ineffectual. To keep from telling a complete lie, I answer, "Sure, he was smart enough to bring us back together."

"No, I think he really *is* a smart guy. I don't think you do."

"Sure I do."

"No, Brother, I think you think he's kinda dumb."

"No, I don't."

"Yes, you do."

"No, I don't."

169

"Yes, you do. Like you think anyone who didn't graduate from a fancy ass school like Baldwin isn't worth your time a day."

"Come on, Jimmy; let's not start that."

"What Dad wasn't was lucky."

"I'll grant you that." I think of his plans and schemes collapsing one after the other like dominoes, his confidence growing fainter and fainter with each successive disaster, finally retiring after Mom's death, living mainly on her insurance death benefit and pension.

"No, Brother," Jimmy says, "you had all the luck. Hogged it, I'd say. Didn't leave enough over for the rest of us."

I knew there was a reason my brother and I never get together voluntarily.

"Listen, Jimmy, I'm sorry for the way things have worked out." I stop a moment to rethink that. "I don't mean I'm sorry, 'cause I'm not really *sorry*. I just mean that I'm sorry that things haven't worked out so well for Dad and you."

"And what about Mom?"

"What about her?"

"She worked herself into the grave paying for that Baldwin education a yours."

"She smoked and got lung cancer."

"Same difference."

Seeing Jimmy again, I can't help but think of the way Mom pleaded with me to be a better brother: "Support him, don't criticize him." "He looks up to you." "You've had so many more advantages than him." "Have some sympathy for him." But in my childhood confusion and lack of confidence I needed someone to beat up, and runty little Jimmy was right at hand. The more acclaim I won from teachers and school, the more I lorded it over him, the more Jimmy ran in the opposite direction from my kind of achievement. "Why can't you be nice to your brother and accept him?" Mom would ask, sometimes close to tears. It's true, I was an arrogant shit-heel to my little brother. Because beating on him gave me the illusion of having the confidence I didn't really possess. I spent years and years pounding on this person named Jimmy, trying, I realize now, to make him feel bad so that I could feel good. Maybe I've earned a lifetime of spleen being spit back at me. Or maybe I can reconcile the two of us. Let me try once again to make things all right. For Mom.

"Jimmy, you know since I started doing well, I've tried to offer to help in any way possible. And I always get refused."

" 'Since I started doing well'?" he quotes me. " 'Since I started doing well'? What kinda pretentious crap is that? You mean since you got rich. Since you got fucking rich."

"Okay. Since I got rich."

"What'sa matter? You afraid to say it in front of your poor relation? Your poor, unsophisticated brother who doesn't dress real good or hang out with your fancy friends or do whatever else you suave, sophisticated New Yorkers think is important. What'sa matter? You afraid to say it? Like it's gonna make me feel like some kinda second-class citizen?"

The terrible fact is yes. And we both know it.

"That's ridiculous, Jimmy. You're my brother." Images of Mom dance in front of me: "Why can't you be a real big brother to him?" "Maybe Jimmy wouldn't be such a problem if you'd be nicer to him." "Maybe he'd be more successful, if he had a brother who was on his side." The litany of her pleas for compassion would go on: "Look at the advantages you've got. You're taller. You're a good student. The teachers like you. School is easy for you. You make friends so easily. Everything you take for granted is a struggle for Jimmy. Can't you tell he looks up to you? You're always in the spotlight. Poor Jimmy has to struggle for every little thing. I poured my whole life into your success. Can't you see how much more you've gotten? Can't you help Jimmy?"

I sniff noisily, trying to breathe. I reach for my handkerchief; I feel a sneeze coming on. It arrives—a three-blaster, "Aachoo! Aachoo! Aachoo!" I bury my face in my handkerchief, honking and drizzling. I am a mess. I excuse myself and go to the men's room to clean myself up and to try to forget my feelings of guilt. When I return, Jimmy has his feet up on my desk. He looks smug.

"You sound like shit, Brother."

"Jimmy, I don't think of you as my poor relation or second-class or anything like that. I'd like to help in some way because I'm fortunate enough right now to be in a position where I—"

"I'd forgotten what you sound like blowing your nose."

"Huh?"

"You blow your nose the same way you always did."

"What?"

"You sound like a goddamn Canada goose."

"Jimmy. Let me give you some help. Jesus Christ, we're brothers. There's a lot of misunderstanding between us. But that's kid stuff. Look, I'm in a position to be of real use to you. Let me share the wealth a little. What do you say? You must need some capital for Mister Muffler? Let's talk. Come on, let's put the past behind us. For Dad's sake." Pause. "For Mom's sake."

Jimmy gives me his slyest shit-eating grin.

"Feelin' guilty, Bro'?"

"No," I lie. "I feel like I'm lucky enough to be able to help you and that you ought to take advantage of the opportunity, that's all."

He yanks his feet off the desk, sits up straight, and claps his hands happily. "Hah, hah! Gotcha!"

"What are you talking about?"

"Gotcha, big brother. Gotcha!"

"What are you?"

"Zapped you. Got your guilt up. Wrapped you around my little finger, didn't I? You were all set to give me the shirt off your back just so you could feel better."

"That's—"

"Don't try to cover. I really had you going there, big brother. You know; I can't understand how you made all this dough. You're not all that smart. And you sure as hell aren't that tough. You think I need your help? No way. You think I'd take your help? No way. I was just trying to see if you're still the same soft-headed dopey brother I remember. And you still are. I got my deal in Tucson all laid out. With real businessmen in a real fucking business, not in some candyass operation like a magazine. As far as which of us is gonna end up with a bigger score, well, the game is a long way from over. I'd say it's a good thing you're gonna get out early with your pile, 'cause I don't think you've got what it takes to make it really big. What you got is luck, Brother. Shit luck an' ignorance."

I'm too angry to express my confusion and too confused to express my anger. Who is this person sitting across my desk from me? And what is my relationship to him supposed to be, anyway?

"You know, Brother, there is one favor you can do for me while I'm here in the Big Apple." He gestures toward my phone.

I nod.

"Don't worry, it's a local call." He reaches into his side jacket pocket, pulls out a business card, picks up the phone, and dials. As it rings, he reclines again and puts his feet back up on the desk and cradles the phone against his shoulder. I would love to yank his cheap, ugly shoes off my desk and throw him the hell out. But I restrain myself.

"Hello? This is Jimmy Macallan. Just calling to confirm our meeting. . . . Uh-huh. . . . Uh-huh. . . . That's right. . . . No, no problem at all. Piece of cake. . . . Yeah, the top. That's right. Not left. . . . Uh-huh. I'll be leaving in a couple of minutes, so you can expect me . . . uh, yeah. How long you figure it'll take? . . . No, I know how to get a goddamn taxi. . . . Yeah, I'll be there in five minutes. . . . Oh? It'll take longer? . . . I see. . . . Uh-huh. . . . Okay. . . . Yeah. . . . No, no problem at all. . . . Right. . . . Right. . . . Okay. Bye." He hangs up. "Thank you, Brother Bob." He stands up, ready to leave. Hands on hips, he gives his back and shoulders a stretch, like someone just waking from a nap. "Well, off into the real world."

He looks at me.

"Aren't you glad the old man suggested we get together? I sure am. I'll be sure to give him your best when I see him tonight. And I'll be sure to tell him that you behaved like a real gentleman, as always, and that you and I are the best of friends. Come see me in Tucson any time you need a muffler."

He walks to the door and takes hold of the knob.

"Stay there, Bro'. I can find my way out. Lemme give you a piece of advice. Don't be so sensitive. You know, Brother, you're still a patsy. A wimp, a pussy—a wussy. You gotta get outta that dreamworld a yours. Wake up and smell the coffee."

He turns the knob but holds the door closed.

"You wanna know something about all those years we spent growing up in Mom and Dad's house?"

I hear Mom saying, "You got the best of us, Robert. You got all the best. Can't you help Jimmy just a little?" I say nothing.

He looks at me with a smug, superior grin and says, "I was the favorite. I always was."

He gives me a wink, steps outside, and closes the door behind himself.

I wait long enough for him to leave *Elixir,* get down the elevators and out of the building. Then I get up and leave, to take a walk around the block and clear my mind.

When I come back from my walk, I find the door to my office almost closed. Through the open slit I see Dudley bent over my desk, snooping in the drawers.

I clear my throat theatrically, "Ahem."

He looks up, guilty and scared, the intruder caught in the act.

I open the door fully and step inside. "What the hell are you doing, Dudley?"

"I, uh. I, uh . . ."

I move the door to an almost closed position behind my back. "Something I can help you with?"

"I, uh, I, uh . . ."

I have never before seen Dudley at a loss for words.

"What is it, Dudley? Is there something you need in here?"

He looks nervous, almost panicked. I walk over to join him behind my desk. He slams the drawer shut and stands squarely behind it, as if to defend it from me. The gesture stops me in my tracks.

"What the hell are you doing, Dudley? Get out from there this instant." I step forward to take back the turf that is mine.

"No, Bob." Dudley kicks away my desk chair and lays his hands on top of the desk, taking possession of it. "Bob, I'm going to have to ask you to sit over there." He points with his chin toward the visitor's chair and couch.

"What the hell are you doing?"

"I, I, I'm under orders from Mr. Woodcock." As the surprise of being caught in the act starts to wear off, he gathers composure and confidence. "I have specific instructions to be here."

"Dudley, get your ass out from behind my—" A sneeze is about to interrupt me; I reach for my handkerchief. "Aaaachooo!" I must pause a moment to mop myself up. "Now, Dudley, what is all this about?" I take another step forward. He holds his ground. He is not just collected, he is starting to get cocky.

173

"Bob, why don't you take it easy for a few minutes. Harry's on his way here from headquarters."

"What for?"

"With security."

"Security?"

"Corporate security."

"What the hell is corporate security?"

"Security guards. From headquarters." Dudley cracks a little smile. He reaches back for my chair and sits himself down, settling the territory he has conquered.

"Why is Woodcock coming here with security?"

"It's out of my hands, Bob. Harry will explain everything. In the meantime, I'm under orders to be sure you don't touch anything in this desk. Now, please, Bob, just sit down."

"Dudley, do you have any idea what an idiot you are making of yourself?"

"Bob, please."

"Is this the way they taught you to do a corporate reorganization in business school? Is this part of your postgraduate thesis work or are you just having a psychotic episode?"

Now I've offended him. In a grave, low voice, he replies, "This is very serious, Bob. I'm here with the full force and authority of corporate management. Certain evidence about your behavior has come to light. For your own good, I suggest you do as I say."

"Now what could this be about? Let's see. Oh, no! You found out about last Thursday—that expense report I put in for a five-dollar taxi to Orem-Diedrich. You suspect that I took the bus. It must be that twenty-four-hour tail you guys have on me. I thought I lost him. But he's good. He's very good."

"Bob," he says, his righteous tone unchanged, "I really don't think this is a laughing matter."

Dudley wouldn't be so brave or so stupidly sanctimonious if this weren't for real. I sit down in the visitor's chair, not to capitulate but to compose myself.

"Maybe I shouldn't say anything unless I have a lawyer here. Because it might incriminate me. Say, aren't you supposed to read me my Miranda rights or something?"

"Bob," he says as if to a child, "let's just wait quietly. Okay?"

"Dudley, just why the fucking Christ were you in my desk, anyway?"

No reply.

"Did you find what you were looking for?"

Nothing.

"Well, did you?"

Stoneface.

"Did you? Huh?"

Dudley lowers his eyes to the desk and mutters something I cannot make out.

"I can't hear you, Dudley. Did you find what you were looking for?"

"Yes. I did."

"Are you gonna tell me what it is?"

"It will all come out when Harry gets here."

"With security," I add.

"That's right."

"Come on; gimme a hint. What did you find?"

Stoneface again.

"Hmmm, let's play twenty questions. Is it animal, vegetable, or mineral?"

Dudley studies his watch with great interest.

"Is it bigger than an elephant, smaller than a breadbox?"

Silence.

"Oh, no! My Day-Glo-colored condoms! You found them! They're not regulation American Communications condoms, I know. But I can explain everything. I bought them before the acquisition, really I did. And I included them on the list of assets. They belong to American now. If you want to have them destroyed or sold off to reduce the company's debt, go ahead. The gray pinstripe ones corporate issues are fine with me. In fact, I like them a lot better. So does my wife. 'There's nothing like a good corporate fucking,' she tells me. And I agree. Wouldn't you, Dudley, there's nothing quite like a good corporate fucking?"

"Bob, your behavior is not very appropriate. Can't you pl—"

Suddenly something snaps inside me. "Listen, you little snotnose." I get up and bound over to the desk. "Just what the hell did you find in there, asshole?" I lunge for the top drawer. He jumps to his feet, holding it shut. We wrestle as I try to grab it open.

I hear a voice behind me say, "See, I told you he might get violent. Restrain him!"

Suddenly, four arms in shirts of police blue grab me and pull me away from Dudley. I shake myself loose and turn around.

It is Harry Woodcock and his two goons from corporate security.

"Harry, I don't know what this is all about. But you'd better have a goddamn good explanation."

"Explanation? I think you're the one who's going to need explanations." He looks past me to his boy Dudley. "Good work, Dudley. Did you keep him out of the desk?"

"Uh-huh." Dudley is still catching his breath. Woodcock puts his arm around him.

"And whoever said a career in publishing wouldn't be exciting? You can sure tell the trainees about this one." Fondly he pats the rumpled collar of Dudley's suit jacket and smooths it neatly back in place. "Did you find it?"

"Yeah, I'm pretty sure I did. But I haven't had a chance to listen to it."

"No, I didn't think you would. You've, uh, had your hands full, as I anticipated."

"Harry," I protest, taking back the center of attention, "just what exactly is going on here?" I look squarely at Harry. He is glowing. He looks like a guy who has won the lottery and met the girl of his dreams, all on the same day.

"What's going on here?" he asks, mimicking me. "What's going on here? You're finished. That's what."

CHAPTER TWENTY

We are all sitting around my office quietly, having regained our composure. Dudley is on the couch; I am back in the visitor's chair; Woodcock is seated behind my desk; the two goons from security are posted outside my closed office door, creating God knows what impression on the *Elixir* staff.

"Macallan, I always knew you were a fraud," Harry announces in triumph. "And now I have proof. It just fell into my hands this morning." He waves a white business envelope in the air. "Like manna from heaven." He opens the envelope and extracts a three-page document.

"This is a letter from the new owners of Magazine Fulfillment, Inc., of Harrisburg, Pennsylvania. Ever heard of MFI, Macallan?"

I nod. MFI is a smallish player in the big game of processing and storing magazine subscription correspondence and computer records.

"Yes, Harry, I've heard of MFI."

"I'll bet you have," he says, grinning. "Well, this letter concerns the records of a certain now defunct book called *MD Office*. Ever heard of that?"

I nod. Of course I have. *MD Office* went out of business three years ago. Just before it closed, its aging owner, Jack Parsons, offered me two pieces of avuncular advice. The first was to buy his subscriber list of 70,000 doctors for two bucks a name and fold them into *Elixir*'s readership. The second was to hire Leo Sayles at any price to make sure *Elixir* got the foundation of big-time pharmaceutical advertisers it would need to avoid the fate of *MD Office*. I took both pieces of advice, swallowed my terror of towering debt, and made my investments in the subscriber list and Leo pay off. Jack, I heard, died a few months ago on a golf course in Florida. In the end, I guess we both got what we wanted.

"Yes, Harry, I know *MD Office* and you know I know it."

"Well, it seems that the late Jack Parsons was not the world's greatest record keeper."

"That's true." Jack's office was knee-deep in papers, his organization was impressionistic at best, but he was a solid, honest guy. "So what?"

"It seems that MFI has no records to show that the subscribers to *MD Office* were ever paid subscribers."

"That's ridiculous, Harry. Of course they were paid subscribers, everyone knows that."

"Really? Well, MFI has no record of that. For all we know, those seventy thousand doctors got free subscriptions."

"Harry, that's impossible."

"We paid you that outrageous asking price of yours based on certified paid subscriptions of just over two hundred thousand doctors. *Paid*. That's what you represented to us. Yet you acquired one-third of those names from *MD Office*. And now we have reason to doubt the validity of those names."

"Harry, we're audited regularly and there's never been a problem. Never." I'm referring to the Audit Bureau of Circulation, ABC. It is *the* authority in magazine publishing, like the Supreme Court only more final, like the Vatican only more divine.

"An audit is a sampling," Harry says. "Sometimes anomalies get by. You've always been lucky."

"Now wait a minute, either—"

"Lucky until today. MFI's owners have notified the ABC of this problem with your circulation, and the ABC is about to take a very close look at exactly what you've got here at *Elixir*. A very close look, indeed. I'm afraid this will put this magazine under a cloud of suspicion for a few months."

Harry hands me the letter from MFI. It is just as he told it. They have recently bought the company, and in the course of reviewing their computer tapes these missing records have come to light. The letter goes on for two pages detailing the situation and apologizing to American for the inconveniences this will cause, but, they say, in the interest of maintaining the integrity of all magazines in the eyes of the advertising community, it is essential that this be reported to the ABC for further investigation. The third page is a Xerox of the ABC's letter to MFI acknowledging the claims and saying that it will notify American immediately that a new audit of *Elixir* is about to be carried out. If news of this got out on the street, it could cripple *Elixir*. Even a hint that ABC might be re-auditing can do irreparable damage to a magazine's reputation.

"You've not only been cheating American, Mr. Macallan, you've been cheating your advertisers. Holding us all up shamelessly. Fraudulently. No wonder you can make success look so easy. You cheat."

"Harry, this is beyond reason."

Harry looks past me to Dudley.

"Was it where I said it would be?"

"Uh-huh," Dudley replies. "I moved it to the front of the drawer. Initials 'JP' typewritten on it."

Harry reaches into the top right-hand drawer of my desk, fishes briefly, and pulls out a microcassette, just like the kind I use in the dictation machine on my desk.

"Voilà," Harry says, flourishing it about.

"Just what is that?" I ask.

"Icing on the cake. Icing on the cake." Harry leans forward, both elbows on the desk. "I received a telephone call this morning, Macallan. Right in the middle of all the excitement this letter of yours was causing. It was a phone call from someone I don't have to identify to you. Someone who says he knows you, this operation, *and* the late Jack Parsons. He says that Parsons told him, before he died, that you tape-recorded a telephone conversation you had with Parsons at the time he was closing *MD Office*. He says that Parsons told him you made the recording to keep Parsons from ever spilling the beans about a certain deal you two had made. Furthermore, this mutual friend told me I could probably find this cassette in the top right drawer of your desk. Which is exactly what Dudley seems to have done." He waves the cassette triumphantly. "Shall we have a listen?"

"Harry, this is completely ridiculous. I never made any such tape of any conversation with Jack Parsons. I—"

"Does this cassette fit your dictation recorder here?" Harry asks.

"Yes. It also fits five million other machines just like it."

"Are you set up to record phone conversations with it?"

"Of course, that's a standard configuration. Millions of business—"

"Then, let's have a listen."

"Harry, I want to call my lawyer."

"You'll have lots of time for that. Let's have a listen." He pops the cassette into the dictation machine, turns it on, and pushes the "play" button. We wait a few seconds for the voice to come on.

"What kind of a deal are you offering me?"

That is my voice; it's definitely my voice, tunneled over the telephone. But where this tape came from I have no idea.

"A dollar a name for each MD Office *subscriber. That'd make seventy thousand dollars in all."* That's definitely a deep Virginia drawl over a cheap dictating unit with a bad phone connection. It might be Jack. Then again it might not be. There are a lot of old Virginia gents who could sound like him, especially muffled and crudely recorded.

"A dollar per name," my voice says.

"That's right. But let me ask you something. Would you like it better if that were all paid circulation?"

"Of course, I'd rather have paid circulation."

"I could make them all paid MD Office *subscribers, if you wanted."*

"How are you going to arrange it?"

"With a dollar more per name."

"Two dollars per name."

"That's all it would take. I'll arrange it all at the fulfillment house. Don't worry. There'll be no records to contradict us. No evidence."

"I'm glad there'll be no evidence."

"So is it a deal?"

"I can't wait."

"Talk to you soon."

"Good-bye."

Harry snaps the machine off.

"That tape!" I shout. "Whatever it's supposed to be, it's bogus! It's a fake!"

"That sure sounds like you, Macallan," Harry says. "Doesn't it sound like him to you, Dudley?" Dudley nods. "Sounds like your voice to me. Isn't that your voice?"

"Yeah, it's my voice. But that's not my conversation. And that's not Jack Parsons. At least it's not me talking to Jack Parsons. That conversation never happened. I don't know who created it or how they did it, but it's a fake. I paid Jack Parsons two dollars a name for authentic paid subscribers. You hear me, paid subscribers to *MD Office* who have since become paid subscribers to *Elixir*. Not fake paid subscribers, real paid subscribers. I can prove it in a minute. Let me call my—" I get up and lunge for the telephone. Harry grabs it away out of reach.

"Macallan, do I have to call the security men back in here? Now sit down and let's get through this in a civilized manner."

Stunned and confused, I sit down again.

"From now on," Harry says, "we're letting ABC prove whatever needs to be proven."

"Harry, that's—"

"Let me finish. Do you want to hear what's going to happen to you and this little magazine or are you going to keep interrupting me?"

"Okay, go ahead."

"Thank you, *Mister* Macallan." Harry is having difficulty hiding the delight behind his mask of self-righteous anger. "I have spoken with Drummond and our attorneys, and we have a clear action plan. First of all, while ABC is performing its audit of the circulation, we will also be making inquiries of our own. We're going to go over everything you represented about this company. Everything. But in the meantime, we have to think of the advertisers. You obviously don't understand this, but integrity is all-important in our business. So, even before this thing is settled, we will offer all *Elixir* advertisers free space credits equal to the amount they have been overcharged as a result of your fraud since American acquired this company."

Harry pauses, leans back in my chair, and puts his feet up on my desk.

"Now we have to keep the ship afloat during this time of crisis. Fortunately, we had the foresight to have Dudley in place here, learning this operation. So we're all very comfortable with him taking over as president and publisher. I think it's precisely the kind of seasoning assignment that a fast-tracker like Dudley deserves."

There's no point in giving in to my desire to stand up and shriek. I might as well take it all in before reacting. Harry leans even farther back and studies the ceiling, assuming a professorial tone of voice.

"You always thought of yourself as a fast-tracker, didn't you, Macallan? But you were too eager, too pushy. You know, you can't cut corners in business; it always catches up with you. Now Dudley, on the other hand, understands what's important. And you see, by not being so impatient, he ends up getting further than you ever did and faster, too. Kind of a Zen concept, eh, Macallan? Go faster by going slower; lead by following. Maybe you can learn something from Dudley. For your next life."

Harry takes his feet off the desk and sits up straight, changing back from musing philosopher to crisp executive.

"As soon as ABC passes its verdict, we will adjust the rate base very, very publicly to reflect whatever the audit says. *Elixir,* I believe, can recover from this incident. But you, Macallan, I don't think you will."

I feel the adrenaline surging through me. I have to work hard to keep my breathing controlled. I speak through tightly gritted teeth. "Harry, this is all a lie. I can prove it."

"It has the ring of truth to me. I had you pegged from the start, boy. From this moment on, you are through here. Our contracts with you are on hold, pending the evidence that will render them null and void. I hope you haven't made plans to spend the second half of your earn-out, because I can assure you you will never see it. And I hope you didn't piss away any of the five million we already paid you. Because, young man, we are coming after you for that. With a vengeance. And after we get that back, there'll be punitive damages, as well. When we're done with you, you won't have the proverbial pot left."

I am breathing with exaggerated regularity. Deep, controlled breaths to hold my hysteria in check. In. Out. In. Out. I try to speak again, but my mouth is clamped shut. I continue my slow breathing. In and out. In and out. I realize I am breathing through my nose. For the first time in a week, I am breathing through my nose. My head feels clear now. I can feel the blood pumping through my temples. I breathe in through my nose, consciously this time, and ungrit my teeth ever so slightly. "Harry," I mumble, "this whole thing is a hoax. A setup."

He ignores me. "Furthermore, from this moment on you are enjoined from setting foot inside this company or from using any of its facilities, lists, equipment, bathrooms, you name it. You are not even to talk to anyone at *Elixir,* nor they to you."

I stand up slowly. I reach across the desk to the telephone and pick up the handset. I hold it against the side of my face and begin dialing the number that I think is my law firm's. Harry lets me finish dialing and waits another second for the phone to start to ring. Then, with a small snap of his index finger, he pushes down the switch hook on the phone to disconnect my call.

"You'll have to find a pay phone for that, I'm afraid. I told you; you are hereby enjoined from using any of this company's equipment or facilities. Any."

He grins up at me.

I stand with the handset against my face, breathing, breathing. Suddenly, I am aware of an odor invading my nostrils. I look to the handset, pulling it away from my face just a bit. I hold it up to my nose to make sure that

180

I am smelling what I am smelling. It is unmistakable. It is House of Lords cologne.

As if from a distant dream, I hear Harry talking to me.

"I think you'd better put that down and leave now. Come on, put the phone down and go about your business elsewhere, Macallan. We've got a lot of work to do here."

I stand frozen, holding the handset.

"Come on, let's go." Harry gets up, walks to the door, opens it, and calls in the two security guards. "Please escort Mr. Macallan out of the building now."

I feel the four arms take hold of me and usher me out the door. A blur of people is standing in the corridor outside my office. Marie, in front of the blur, is the only person I can make out.

"Bob," I hear her asking, "what's going on? What's going on?"

I feel the guards moving me past her. My feet freeze in place for an instant.

"What's going on, Bob?"

I hear her, but I ignore her question. "Was Leo in my office this morning?" I ask her.

She doesn't seem to hear me. "What are they doing?" she asks.

"Marie, was Leo in my office this morning? Answer me. Please."

"Uh, yes. Before he left for Max's. Bob, what is this all about?"

"Did he use the phone while he was there?"

"I don't know." She is not much interested in my questions; she wants an answer to her question.

"Did he use my phone?" I ask again, insistent.

She is not focusing on my question. "He said he was looking for some old correspondence."

"Marie, did he use my phone?"

"Yeah, I guess so. Max called and I put him through on your line."

"Did he make any other calls from there?"

"I don't know. What is all this about? What's going on?"

Harry steps between Marie and me. "Come on, Bob, let's go." He turns toward the assembled group of *Elixir* staffers. "Dudley and I will be back in just a minute to explain everything. Just take it easy, folks. You're all in good hands. Go back to your desks. Everything's going to be all right."

The guards and Harry move me down the corridor. I feel like I am sleepwalking. I make no effort to resist.

"Get him outside the building," Harry tells them as he closes the outer door.

"Come with me, sir," says the goon holding my left arm, as we board the elevator. I feel the car descending, then I hear the hollow of the grand lobby echoing around my head, then my skin feels the air of this blistering July morning. I am raging, I am fuming. But only inside. The arms let go of me. The goons disappear.

I am alone on the sidewalk. Suddenly, panic overtakes my fury. I have lost everything.

An empty feeling settles in. It is strangely calming. Familiar.

Then it hits me. *This is what I've been expecting all along.*

CHAPTER TWENTY-ONE

When I was sixteen, I got it in my head to run for president of the junior class. I remember hearing teachers and older kids from Bayport High saying that you had to demonstrate "leadership" if you wanted to get into a good college. Naturally, I wanted to prove that I had it, too. Whatever it was. I assumed that leadership meant being the center of attention, like the candidates giving their speeches at the big rally. That was leadership. They looked like the happiest people on earth. And the winners? It was clear that they had ascended to a higher level of existence. I desperately wanted to be like them. A leader. A winner.

My mother was interested and supportive.

"Of course you can do it, sweetheart," she said on the afternoon I told her of my plans. She was standing at the sink peeling potatoes. She put down the peeler, shook her hands dry, and walked over to give me a hug. "You can do anything you put your mind to. Anything at all."

When I brought up the subject at dinner later that afternoon (the evening meal at the Macallan house never started later than five-thirty or lasted longer than fifteen minutes), my father just grunted. "Oh," he said without emotion and went back to his meat loaf and mashed potatoes. I remember him giving my mother a look that I took to be disapproval.

"He can do it if he wants to, Clint," she said, looking first at him, then at me. "Robert is very popular. And very articulate. I'm sure," she added insistently, "he'll make a big success of it. A *big* success."

I didn't know it at the time, but Clint was on the verge of losing his job as manager of Ned Wiggins's factory.

"Uh-huh," he said, not looking up from his plate.

"Robert Macallan, junior class president," Mom said, proudly framing a big election banner in the air with her hands. "I like the sound of that." She let the banner evaporate and picked up her fork to continue eating. "He'd be the first Macallan at Bayport High who did more than just show up," she muttered, looking directly at Clint.

Just then, eleven-year-old Jimmy knocked over his glass of milk, making a big white splash on the floor.

"Jim-meee!" Mom cried as she went scurrying for the sponge. Mildly annoyed, she got down on the floor on hands and knees and began mopping it up. As she finished, her head was eye level with little Jimmy. He turned his face to her and gave her his most angelic, wide-eyed look. "Can I have some more meat loaf, Mom?" he cooed. "It's real good."

Her annoyance disappeared. "Of course, honey," she said, picking herself up off the floor. "Anybody else for seconds?"

"I'll take some," Clint said.

"How about you, Robert? Seconds?" she asked.

I never cared much for Mom's meat loaf. Or any of her cooking, for that matter. I didn't have much to compare it with; I just knew that what she served didn't make me look forward to eating. Everything tasted pretty much the same. The principal difference between dishes was in texture. It was either heavy and dried out or heavy and greasy. "No, Mom," I said, "not for me."

"No?" she asked, disappointed.

"Come on!" Jimmy piped up impatiently. "Gimme some more! It's yummy! More, Mommy, more!"

She went to the stovetop and brought back the remaining third of the meat loaf. It was sitting in the pan in a puddle of watery pink juice, all gray and pebbly, oozing yellow grease. She fixed her gaze lovingly on Jimmy as she served him and Dad and herself another helping.

The following day, I marched down to the principal's office to see Miss Brophy, the secretary with the famous bad breath, and sign myself up as a candidate. I began organizing my campaign with Matt Erwin, my best buddy, and Stevie Cramer. They were my "machine." Mimicking what we had seen older kids do in past years, we decided to meet in the cafeteria, in gym class, and in the hallways to corral groups of kids and tell anyone who would listen about Bob Macallan for class president. We had little in the way of issues to campaign on, but neither did the other candidates.

They included Donny Martin, a math nerd who was slightly outgoing but a math nerd just the same. Then there was Horace Bartlett III. "Hoddy," as he was known to all. In the era before malls, Bartlett's Department Store was not just the biggest store in the whole Bayport area, but the final arbiter of taste, style, and civilization, such as it was. Horace Bartlett I had started out selling army surplus right after World War I and built it up through the 1920s into the region's foremost retailer. Horace Bartlett, Jr., had inherited the reins and maintained its unchallenged dominance. Everyone knew that Horace III, "Hoddy," would inherit it all. His family sent him to the local public schools to give him roots in the community and then planned to ship him off to Dartmouth. Just like his father.

Hoddy was blond, round, and pasty—the Pillsbury Doughboy in a green cable-stitch sweater, chinos, and penny loafers. A less than mediocre student, he attracted attention with his easy, joking manner and good-natured put-downs. But his most visible social asset was his Pontiac GTO convertible, royal blue with white vinyl top. It had gleaming wire wheels and twin chrome exhaust pipes that snorted and rumbled, announcing his arrivals and departures. It was the ultimate teenage social vehicle, *the* dream machine for cruising, laying rubber, and Saturday night make-out sessions. Everybody wanted to be Hoddy's friend and he was happy to oblige—in the way that a cheerful, crafty boss keeps employees in line with slightly condescending warmth and personal attention.

The campaign was to last for two weeks. I decided that the key to winning was to have an issue, an idea that really meant something. After all, wasn't that what the newscasters said voters looked for in real candidates in adult politics? Wouldn't that impress the teachers? My idea was a proposal for "Junior Symposium," a big two-day college and career workshop designed to help our class learn more about their elective course choices for their junior and senior years and what their decisions might mean to admissions directors and employers. I talked it up earnestly and energetically. Kids would listen respectfully, knit their brows thoughtfully, and pause, then admit that the Junior Symposium was a good idea. I know that I got my message across. Kids I hadn't even gotten around to meeting would approach me in the halls and tell me that my idea was catching on.

Hoddy Bartlett, on the other hand, had an official campaign idea that was a very un-catchy "Bartlett for President." But it appeared everywhere. On banners, on caps, on buttons, on T-shirts. All professionally printed by the typesetting shop at Bartlett's Department Store. It was a most impressive and powerful display. But it was Hoddy's *un*official campaign that electrified the masses and united them behind him: "Hod wants your bod." It was on everyone's lips in every corner of the school. It became a greeting, a farewell, an exclamation, a password, a code that simply meant "I'm cool."

Faced with Hoddy's tidal wave of no-content popularity, I stuck even harder to my issue. With knitted brow and teacher's pet seriousness, I told my story over and over again. At home, when Mom asked me how things were going on the election front, I lied to her and myself and said, "Great. My idea is winning people over."

Clint was never the one to raise the question and always seemed to be doing something else during my answers. I hungered for his support, for his interest and approval. I was determined to make him show me openly that he wanted me to win. I wanted to know that he thought I stood a chance. I felt there must be some piece of advice that he was holding back, some secret of fatherly confidence that he might share with me, to help me win. But I knew I would have to pry it out of him.

One afternoon, about a week into the campaign, I decided to stop by the factory and pay him a visit after school. I was feeling particularly good. I had stopped by the football field and had cornered a group of cheerleaders with my campaign pitch. They responded with interest and even some girlish enthusiasm. Especially Ginny Conway, who, I later found out, had a minor crush on me. I left the field buoyed up by the prospect of becoming a big grown-up success. In fact, what I was feeling was the rush of teenage hormones.

I walked from Bayport High to the factory, a sooty two-story brick structure with a pitted gravel parking lot. At the front door I met Clarence Folwer, the crusty old Yankee maintenance man, taking his afternoon break.

"Hey, Clarence, my dad upstairs?"

He stared at me with sunken, beery eyes and shook his head.

"How 'bout those Red Sox?" I asked, oblivious to his mood. "My dad upstairs?"

"Ay-uh," he said. As I moved to pass him in the doorway, he put his leathery hand on my shoulder to stop me. "You're the spittin' image a your old man, son. You know that, don'tcha? I remember him when he was your age. I was his foreman in the shipyards when he first got outta high school." Clarence had fallen from the upper reaches of Bayport blue-collar life to his job sweeping the floors at Wiggins's factory. The reason was his fondness for Narragansett beer. "Nasty-gansetts," he called them.

"You'd be lucky to take after your father," he said. "He's the salta the earth. You remember that, ya hear?"

I could smell the Nasty-gansett on his breath. I ran past him up the stairs into the darkness of the main factory floor. It was quiet. Break time on the afternoon shift.

I saw my father at his dirty steel desk in the far corner. He was bent over the center drawer, putting papers into a small bag. I ran up to him.

"Son?" He looked up, surprised.

"Hey, Dad, I think I can win that election. Isn't that great? I really think I've got a chance. I just met a group of the cheerleaders, and they think my idea is terrific. Cheerleaders! You know how much influence the cheerleaders have, you know, around school and stuff."

"Yes, Son." Clint looked even more preoccupied than usual. It did not occur to me to ask why he was taking papers and pens out of his drawer and putting them into a paper bag.

Then I heard Ned Wiggins's voice bellowing down the length of the building.

"I stopped paying you ten minutes ago, Macallan!" he shouted. "You got no business being in that desk now. That desk is mine." He swaggered up to where we stood. I stared at Wiggins, a tall, fat, pasty man with cruel black eyes. My father stared down into his little bag, silent. "That's the problem with you, Macallan. You're ten minutes behind on everything you do."

Wiggins looked Clint and me up one side and down the other.

"That your old man?" he asked me accusingly.

I nodded, scared and confused.

"You look just like him," he sniffed. "Guess you must be ten minutes behind the rest a the world, too." He turned and walked back toward his office at the far end of the factory.

"Come on, Son," Clint said, rolling up his little brown bag. "Let's go."

We rode home in silence, Clint saying nothing and explaining less. I was stunned and frightened. Even worse, I began to ask myself if Ned Wiggins wasn't right. About Clint *and* about me. After all, he was a big man in Bayport, rich and respected, his reputation as a bastard notwithstanding. I tried not to take Clint's humiliation personally. But I did. Mom told me not to worry about going to a good college, that we would find a way to send me. Between her job at the insurance agency and whatever Dad did next. But I did worry. I worried a lot. I tried desperately not to show it to anyone at school. I studied in class and campaigned out of class with all the frantic naive sincerity I could muster, hoping to show Ned Wiggins he was wrong.

On the day of the big election rally, the whole junior class gathered in the auditorium to hear the candidates speak. Donny Martin was first. He commanded a small but fiercely loyal constituency of math nerds, fatties, skinnies, stutterers, acne sufferers, children of non-English-speaking parents, and other social misfits. He went to the podium, mumbled a half-minute speech about high school being anything but the best years of your life, and sat down. The applause he received was not widespread but very deeply felt. Then I got up and delivered an organized, impassioned, painstakingly rehearsed pitch for my Junior Symposium. I spoke for exactly the five minutes allotted the candidates about how my plan would make us the best prepared, most mature, most successful class ever to go through Bayport High. My style was part William Jennings Bryan, part Dale Carnegie, part television game-show host—a set of influences absorbed in the Bayport Public Library and my parents' living room. I got a big, sincere round of applause.

Then Hoddy Bartlett got up to speak. Before he reached the podium, the whole auditorium seemed to be chanting, "Hod wants your bod, Hod wants your bod," in a deafening whisper. What he delivered was not really a speech. He just joked in his offhand way for the first four minutes. He talked about wanting to make the most of his junior year. Maybe, he said, he'd be lucky enough to stay back next year just to make sure he hadn't missed anything. He kidded about the burning issues around us, like tires in the student parking lot and cigarettes in the bathrooms. The crowd ate it up. Then at the very end, with hardly any time left, he turned serious. He talked about being proud of Bayport High and how you didn't need a varsity letter to show your school spirit. How everyone helped make our school great just by being proud. He said it was the people that made our class special and he was proud of all of us. He admitted modestly that he would be proud to lead our class, because the people in it were such great guys and gals with so much to be proud of. And since he was proud of us and we were proud of him, it would make us all even prouder of everything we were proud of if he were elected president. None of it made any sense. But he spoke with endearing fake humility. The crowd went wild. He ran past his five-minute allotment; I counted four, maybe five, minutes past. None of the teachers on the podium made a move to cut short his speech. It made me furious.

We cast our ballots in the back of the auditorium, and a few minutes later Hoddy Bartlett was pronounced the winner. The moment had more the feeling of a coronation. That afternoon Hoddy could have been elected pope or emperor for life. After cheers and a chorus of the Bayport fight song led by the football coach, the crowd began to break up into cliques and then disperse. It was past three, and school had officially been out since two-ten.

I was devastated. Not so much because I had lost, but because I had not understood what the game was really about. That's what hurt and humiliated me. I thanked Matt and Stevie and sent them home, promising to meet them that night at Deering Burgers. A few people stopped to compliment me as they filed out of the auditorium. Good job, great idea, nice speech. I was too preoccupied to hear them. How could I have been so stupid? So innocent, so gullible, so completely . . . unprepared. The contest was not fair, the playing field was not level, the game was rigged, and even the referees lied about it. It was a bigger serving of humble pie than I could digest at one sitting.

I was brooding alone in a corner of the empty auditorium when I heard Hoddy call me. "Hey, Bob," he said, extending his right hand, "put 'er there." He was as friendly as if he were soliciting my vote.

We shook.

"You did a real good job. Poor Donny Martin never had a chance against us. But I guess he knew that all along."

"I guess so," I replied with forced cordiality, not sure what he meant. He and I had hardly run as a team against the hapless math whiz. I stood looking awkwardly around the empty auditorium, trying to avoid eye contact with him.

Finally, Hoddy cracked one of his famous grins. "Shit, man," he said, landing a mock punch on my shoulder, "let's blow this candy store. Can I give you a lift home?"

"Uh, sure." Curiosity about seeing Bartlett's GTO from the inside crushed the few remaining shards of my angry pride. He spent the walk to the parking lot complimenting me on how well I had campaigned. He had observed everything I did and remembered it respectfully and in detail. "You did a real good job," he concluded as we reached the blue convertible. "Maybe we should do that 'Junior Symposium' of yours. Maybe you'd like to be chairman of the thing?" I nodded and shrugged.

I sat down in the right front bucket seat, the prized "shotgun" position only Hoddy's best friends got. As he fired up the big engine, I looked around in wonder at the car's interior. Less than a year old and it was beat up and messy, with scuff marks on the dash and upholstery, overflowing ashtrays, gum wrappers, and half-used napkins from McDonald's littering the floor. Hoddy possessed the most desirable, most beautiful, most expensive teenage icon on earth. And he treated it like an old sneaker. Lying across the backseat was a dirty yellow sweater, all stretched out of shape and fraying. Something that looked like dried leaves was ground into one sleeve. I remembered seeing that sweater in the window at Bartlett's the previous fall. It had been too expensive for me even to fantasize about owning.

I told Hoddy where I lived. It was far from the big house on Congress Hill he came from.

"My old man woulda killed me if I hadn'ta won," he confided. He kept his eyes straight ahead. I listened. "Really. He laid it right on the line. No presidency, no mountain-climbing camp in Colorado this summer. He said I'd have to work in the store in some dumb job. That'd really suck."

I nodded, as if I could identify with his plight.

"You ever been climbing in the Rockies?"

I shook my head no. I had never been anywhere outside of Bayport to do anything.

"It's one of the few things my old man wants me to do that I want to do, too. 'Son,' " Hoddy said, imitating an authoritative, formal voice, " 'I've got a plan for you. I want you to learn leadership. And responsibility. That's what I've been teaching you on the boat since you were a little boy. Sailing, Son. It builds self-confidence and character.' " It was common knowledge that Horace Bartlett's sloop was the biggest boat at the Bayport Yacht Club. I remembered having it pointed out to me once when I was on the Plum Island public ferry.

Hoddy switched back to his normal voice. "But mountain-climbing camp, now that's gonna be fun." He revved the engine as we turned onto the big straightaway of Cumberland Street, the rush of engine power pushing us backward into our seats. "So you see, I had to win. Or else. I had too much riding on it."

"Sure," I mumbled. I saw my chances for getting a scholarship at a good college evaporating. "Not a leader," I could hear the admissions officer saying, as he condemned me to a second-class life. Hoddy reached forward and snapped on the radio. Loud. The racket blotted out the need for a response. I was grateful. We let the local rock station do the talking for the rest of the drive.

When we pulled up to my house, Clint was home. It was the middle of the afternoon. Every other father on the street, and in the rest of the world for all I knew, was out at his job. But my dad was in the driveway, lying under our rusty old Chevy, tying up the drooping tailpipe with a coat hanger. He had already replaced the missing taillight with a sheet of red cellophane and secured it with wads of gummy black electrician's tape. The car looked ridiculous, like some hillbilly's wreck held together with chewing gum and baling wire.

I opened the GTO's passenger door and got out. "Thanks for the lift," I shouted over the music, "and, uh, congratulations." Pause. Swallow hard. "Mr. President."

"Hey, Macallan," Hoddy said, turning down the radio for an instant, "that symposium thing is a good idea. Let's talk about it, okay?"

I nodded and closed the door. The GTO roared away, its sculpted body gleaming brilliant blue, its perfect taillights edged in glorious chrome.

Clint pottered away under the Chevy as I scuffed my way along the tar.

"That you, Son?" he asked from beneath.

"I lost, Dad," I said to the feet sticking out from under the rusted fender.

"Hand me the big wrench outta my tool kit, wouldya. I think I got this sucker just about fixed." I found the wrench in the greasy metal box and handed it to his outstretched hand. Through the gaping hole in the rusted fender, I could see his shoulder on a dirty old blanket. He made one more adjustment and said, "Yup, that'll do 'er." He pulled himself out from under the car, stood up, and dusted off the back of his pants legs.

"Pretty clever, your old man," he said, admiring the new taillight of red cellophane and black tape. It looked like a cancerous mechanical growth. "The *bahstudd* at the dealers wanted five dollars for a new one. Five dollars! That's if he could get one on back order. Says they stopped makin' parts for this model eight years ago. Guess I showed him, eh?"

I looked at the car with genuine teenage horror. "Yeah, I guess so," I said. Clint began replacing his wrenches and screwdrivers in the toolbox.

"I lost, Dad," I said again.

He closed the lid and picked up the toolbox.

"I'm sorry, Son." He had heard me the first time. Something in his voice told me that he was not surprised.

"Hoddy Bartlett trounced me," I said, letting myself begin to feel bad. "He walked all over me."

"Why don't you give me a hand with the rest a this stuff." He indicated the ratty blanket poking out from under the car and beside it the pile of greasy rags. As I bent down to pick them up, I thought of joyrides in gaudy GTOs and expensive yellow sweaters. I tried to imagine mountain-climbing camps in Colorado and the confidence you'd gain learning to command a magnificent sloop. I tried to imagine a father who had a plan for his son, a plan for building him into a man who would take being a leader for granted. I tried to imagine a father with powers he wanted to pass on to his heir.

"Dad, he expected to win." I felt a wave of anger and sadness crashing down over me. "He didn't just hope to win or try to win. He *expected* it. And he got it."

"Of course he did," Clint said. "He's Horace Bartlett's son." He sounded almost pleased at what he was saying. I could not imagine why.

"What about me?" I gasped. "What am I supposed to expect?"

"Well, you're Clint Macallan's boy," he said. "Come on into the house, Son." Then he turned and walked away.

I stood alone in the driveway, my legs too heavy to move.

CHAPTER TWENTY-TWO

"Robert! Robert!" **Wendy's** hurried, excited voice says on the answering machine. "I can't possibly leave this message on a machine. I'm flying home in the nearest cab. I love you. Bye." The tape clicks to a stop. "Five-ten P.M.," the friendly computerized female voice says, noting the time of Wendy's call. "No more messages."

I have been surprisingly functional since my life was ruined earlier today.

I have accomplished a lot. I walked home fifty blocks. I talked with Josh Rieder, a very smart lawyer, and let loose the litigious dogs of war. He acted appropriately outraged and combative, making plans and suggesting actions, but underneath I thought I picked up a sense that there was not a hell of a lot he could actually accomplish.

In fact, my behavior has been exemplary. I have not had a drink. I have not thrown a tantrum. I have not bought a handgun or an automatic rifle to injure myself or anyone else. I have not done any of the things that normal, red-blooded American males are expected to do when they lose everything they have ever worked for.

Instead, I have sat for uncounted hours in the reading chair in our bedroom, keeping a close watch on a four-inch crack in the plaster high above our bed, right where the ceiling meets the wall. So far, my vigilance has paid off. The crack hasn't moved, gotten bigger, or tried anything funny. The trouble is, if I leave my post, there's no telling what it might do. So I sit, silent and peaceful—watching, watching, watching. I guess this must be what it's like to be a spy or a cop or a private eye on a stakeout. People think it is endlessly fascinating; in fact, it is endlessly boring. But once you accept the boredom, it becomes very soothing. Yes, like meditating. Maybe that's what people really envy about spies and cops and private eyes.

I can't help feeling that I am back where I started, back where I was meant to be all along. Back to nothing. In a way, it is comforting. I am finally off the hook. My worst fears about being Clint Macallan's son have finally been realized. And now, as I confront them after fleeing them with such desperation for so long, I see that they're not really so bad, after all. Look, I am still alive. I am still breathing. I am just . . . diminished. No, not diminished. That's not what Clint would say. I am humanized. Cut back down to size. Who the hell did I think I was, anyway? Finally, everything starts to come clear. All those years I thought Clint was looking at me with the simple man's awe of a superior creature. How stupid and egotistical of me.

With that puzzled look of his, he was really only asking who the hell I thought I was. Because he knew. He made me. He was further along in the genetic program and knew what was coming. He had only to wait and *I* would see. I am part of him; he is part of me. Welcome back to the family, Son.

So this is how Macallan men feel when they come into their legacy. I take a deep breath and look around. The sun still shines through my window. It is the same sun as before. And if I lose this particular window, I will look out on another one in a less expensive neighborhood. See? It's easy.

A part of me says no, I will not let it happen. Another part of me says it is inevitable. I think of Clint losing in one business venture after another. I remember the firm set of his jaw and the clenched lower lip and how, over the years of disasters, it changed from a look of resolve into a look of anger, then resignation, and, finally, calm. Calm. Yes, like meditating.

The fathers of the other boys I grew up with taught their sons the aggressive male arts. I could never figure out where or when the fathers taught them, but the other boys knew these things and practiced them with a confidence they had inhaled from a strong man. They knew how to win at games, how to bully and boast, how to bluff, how to grab, how to lie and cheat, how to use others, how to demand without deserving. And never show a trace of guilt.

Clint, on the other hand, had only one proud, silent lesson to offer. He showed how a man could lose and lose and lose again, and still not lose his dignity. Clint held onto his dignity through it all. It was dignity with resignation in the face of defeat, but dignity all the same. That was his grim peasant gift, the only legacy he could offer.

For me, strength and confidence were an act I put on for the outside world. The problem was never getting others to believe. The problem was getting *me* to believe. No matter how well I had made the charade work in the past, I had always felt that my richly deserved disaster was imminent. Just because defeat had not yet come did not mean it would not come soon. Maybe it was just overdue. Maybe it was waiting for the stakes to get good and high, in order to make defeat that much more appalling, that much more final.

And now, it has finally happened.

This must be the heritage Macallan men pass on from generation to generation. So what if the genetic imprint is a stamp that reads "failure"? At least it is a clear identity. A recognizable one. And, it seems, an inescapable one. All I can think is, Please, God, don't let me pass it on any further.

I hear Wendy's keys in the door and the slam behind her.

"Ro-bert!" she sings out. "Ro-bert!"

I hear footsteps running through the apartment. Into the bedroom.

I see Wendy in the doorway, out of breath.

"Ro-bert! Sweetie. You know, don't you? You figured it out! I can see it in that shell-shocked look of yours. I telegraphed it in my voice, didn't I? Oh, I am no good at secrets, no good at all."

Wendy is walking up to me, beaming with love, bursting with happiness, touching me softly on the arm. "You're bowled over, aren't you? You're overwhelmed. I am, too. I know you're uneasy, but it's all going to be wonderful. This is the beginning of our real lives, this is where it all starts. Oh, Robert, I love you so much. This is the day I want us to remember forever. This moment."

I feel myself looking at Wendy. I see Wendy smiling, taking my left hand in both of hers.

"Robert," she says, "I'm pregnant."

★   ★   ★

Wendy looks like someone picked her up and threw her against the head-board. Her arms hang limp, her legs are splayed open like a Raggedy Ann doll. She has been frozen in this position, mouth open and silent, for somewhere between five seconds and five minutes. I am no one to judge the passage of time.

Finally she speaks. "Those bastards! Those crummy bastards!"

"Which ones?" I ask vacantly.

"All of them. Woodcock, Dudley, Leo, Mackey." She pauses. "And Parsons."

"Parsons is dead," I say matter-of-factly.

"I don't care. Him, too. They're all crummy bastards. Oh, Robert, how can they do this to you?" She sits up straight. "To us?" She holds her tummy with both hands. "Us!"

"I don't know. I guess they just did." I know I need to say *something* about her pregnancy—our pregnancy. I just don't know what. I decide to remain silent and let my wife lead the conversation. After all, isn't that what all Macallan men do?

Just then, a kindly stranger appears and takes my place in the room. He looks just like me.

Wendy asks, "Is it really possible we could lose everything?"

The kindly stranger answers for me. "It is possible," he says in a soothing voice. How uncanny. He even sounds like me. "I don't think we will. But it is possible." No panic in his voice, no fear. He is perfectly calm, utterly serene.

"That's not fair!" Wendy cries, shaking her fist in the air. "Somebody's framing you, setting you up. It's all lies. Dirty rotten lies! Oh, I hate those bastards. Those crummy bastards."

"Sometimes that happens." He is the most peaceful man on earth.

"I could kill them," she steams. "I could just kill them!"

The stranger nods, unaffected but sympathetic.

Wendy stands up and throws an angry punch at the cosmos. The force spins her around. "Grrrrrrrrrr!" she cries. She flops back onto the bed and takes one very deep, very slow breath. Then another. And another. And another. She and the calm stranger sit in silence for what must be a long time.

Finally, Wendy peers down at the floor, then raises her head. She is lucid again; the shock and anger have raged through her and are gone. She sighs and gives her shoulders a shake. "Okay, Wolfson, okay, let's think." Her voice brightens. "Come on; let's figure out Plan A." She jumps to her feet and bounds over to the placid stranger. "Come on!" She punches the stranger's shoulder. "Plan A!" The stranger looks intently at the floor. "Come on," she insists. "Let's figure out Plan A."

The stranger does not respond.

"Robert, what's wrong?" She grabs the stranger by the shoulder.

Nothing, the stranger seems to indicate with his calm shrug, absolutely nothing.

"*Ro*-bert! Come on, we've got work to do."

No response.

"Robert, you've got to pull yourself together. For the three of us. I know you're freaked out; I know the timing of all this has gotten screwy. But whether you like it or not, you're going to be a father. Now. Not sometime in the indefinite future." The stranger shakes his head at the floor. "Don't you think I know why you've been running from it, avoiding it? Breathing a sigh of relief every month my test comes back negative? Because you're afraid you're going to turn out like *your* father. Afraid of the damage you might do to your baby—our baby. The way Clint did to you. I know that, honey. But don't you see? You can be any kind of father you choose. Any kind at all. The only way you could end up like your father would be if you *chose* to be that way." She gets down on her knees and holds the stranger gently around the shoulders. "Just be the man you really are, the man I fell in love with. You can slay all the dragons. The ones out there." She motions at the window. "And the ones in here." She taps the stranger's forehead.

I look up. The stranger has left the room and left me sitting in the chair again. The aura of resignation and stillness he brought with him is also gone.

"I'm scared of having a baby," I hear myself say. I sound sort of groggy. "And now with all this—"

"Don't you think I'm scared, too? I'm the one who's pregnant!"

Slowly I am coming back to life. "I just figured that once we had a lot of money, if we could be really secure, then I'd feel, we'd feel, you know—"

"Yeah, I know. But it doesn't work that way. Robert, money isn't the thing that can fix any of this. It never was. Money wasn't the thing your father deprived yóu of. It was confidence. And you don't *need* a lot of money to pass that on. You just need to act with confidence yourself."

I touch Wendy's hand. I feel my strength coming back. "But it wouldn't be bad to have a lot of money just the same." I smile.

Wendy smiles back. "I agree."

We hold hands for several long, satisfying minutes of silence. Finally she stands up and brushes her skirt to get out the wrinkles. "So let's get to work. What do you say to a change of scene?"

Slowly and clumsily I pull myself up out of the reading chair, as if I were a man who has not moved in five hours. "I hear the living room is beautiful this time of year."

"Josh says it doesn't matter who's behind it," I say insistently.

"What do you mean, it doesn't matter?" Wendy puts her yellow legal pad down on the carpet beside her and looks up at me. "Someone is planting lies about you, destroying your company, defiling your character, ruining our future. Isn't that a—"

"Whoever it is, we can nail him later, if we still need revenge and want to spend a lot of money on lawsuits. But that's not the main event. Right

193

now, we've got to find a way to prove that the *MD Office* subscribers I bought from Parsons were real paid subscribers."

"But everyone knows they were paid subscribers."

"Not everyone. There are upwards of eleven thousand magazines out there." Oh, facts, lovely facts. Nothing combats depression and hopelessness like remembering facts.

"But in your industry—"

"Ultimately, ABC will vindicate me, have no fear." I feel myself getting stronger. You idiot, Macallan. It's not the facts. It's Wendy. "Nobody, but nobody, can fuck with an ABC audit. Not Woodcock, not Leo, not Mackey, not God in heaven. The problem is that ABC will probably take too long to clear my name. It could be a few months. And there's no telling how much damage Woodcock will do to the balance sheet in that time. He's already restructuring, putting Dudley into my job, probably promoting Leo to help cover Dudley, maybe bringing in more good old boys from corporate, certainly going ahead with moving *Elixir* into headquarters."

Wendy mumbles under her breath, "That bastard."

"If we sit back and wait for ABC to clear up the charges," I say, explaining things as much to myself as to Wendy, "Woodcock may still be able to screw me out of the earn-out. If he plays it right, he may even be able to claw back the money we've already got."

"But how? If you've been vindicated?"

"Josh says it's possible. Possible. That's worst case. But the longer Woodcock can keep my contract in limbo, the longer he can keep me away from *Elixir,* the greater his ability to screw me."

"That means we've got to clear your name now," she says, her dark eyes shining. "We can't afford to wait for ABC. We've got to fight this on our own."

"Precisely."

She gets up and sits beside me on the couch.

"Oh, sweetie, how did you handle this all day by yourself?" She strokes the side of my face. "I would have gone crazy if I'd had to wait all day to see you. Ugh, that stupid conference. How did you manage? What did you do?"

"I did what I always do when Harry Woodcock throws me out of American Communications. I took a long lonely walk through midtown, thinking, sulking, talking to myself, getting pissed off, pondering the injustice of the universe, having revenge fantasies, arguing the merits of different action plans. I'm sure I looked like I just got out of the loony bin, flailing my arms at no one, having discussions with the air. Believe me, if you'd seen me coming toward you on the sidewalk, you'd have crossed to the other side of the street."

"I love you," she says, giving me a kiss.

"I love you, too."

Pause.

"We're gonna pull this one out of the fire," she whispers.

"Right," I say, hoping to conceal my uncertainty about the eventual outcome. One of the things that still amazes me about Wendy is this feeling she has, a feeling so deep inside her, so much a part of her she is not even aware of it. It is a certainty that whether things work out this way or that way, they will be okay. A feeling that tomorrow will bring something good, if not better than today. She has a feeling of safety about her own life, a fundamental unshakable confidence that the world will not cave in and crush her. It is a feeling I have never known. A feeling I cannot imagine.

Wendy picks up my hesitation. "I said, 'Right, Macallan.' Right? Junior is listening to hear confidence from his dad."

I reply with more conviction. "Right."

"Good. That pad of paper you've been scratching on while I've been making lists. That your four-point Macallan action plan?"

"Yeah. Patented. Circle-R."

"Let me hear it. Come on. Item one."

"Item one. Produce hard evidence that *MD Office* subscribers paid for their subscriptions."

"Item two?"

"Do it immediately."

"Item three?"

"Stuff the evidence in Harry Woodcock's face, so he'll be forced to reinstate me at *Elixir* and put my contract back in force."

"Next."

"Item three-A."

"Three-A?"

"Take delicious pleasure in firing Leo Sayles."

"You're sure he planted the tape?"

"Nobody else wears that awful House of Lords crap. Besides, he had to be the one leaking stuff to Atwood during the negotiations. He had to be the one who fed the list of chiefs of staff to Mackey, too. Maybe he knows the new owners of MFI. And I know he's got some kind of weird arrangement with McGuinn, I can just feel it. Leo has been feathering his nest in every possible direction, with everyone who could possibly help him. Mackey, Dudley, everybody. I always knew that Leo had an ax to grind. I just never figured he was getting ready to use it on me. No, first thing I do when I get back is nail that two-faced SOB."

"Weren't you just counseling against wasting energy on revenge?"

"That's why I list it as item three-A. Subpoint."

"Okay. Item four?"

"Publish the special issue, generate whatever extra revenues are needed to cover Harry's expense increases, and make my numbers as stated in the contract. Collect the rest of the money, escape from American Communications, and you and I begin a new life together." Wendy frowns at me. I add, "With the baby."

"That's better," she says. "May I see?"

"Sure." I hand her the sheet of yellow legal pad paper.

"I see item one. Then all this stuff that's crossed out. Then the other items way down here. What's all this crossed-out stuff? It practically covers the page."

"Trying to figure out exactly how to accomplish item one."

"Let's talk it through, partner. Systematically." Wendy enters her consultant's mode. "Now, who out there can prove your case?" she asks.

"The only people who really can are the *MD Office* subscribers themselves."

"Okay, how can you reach them?"

"They're all on the *Elixir* subscriber list. But I can't get at the list. Not at *Elixir*, at least. I can't so much as talk to anyone there. Woodcock made that clear."

"What about the tapes at MFI?" Wendy asks.

"Are they really missing? I don't know. Jack Parson was a slob, it's true. So, yes, it's possible, even though the computer records he sold me were in apple pie order. But after publicly blowing the whistle the way it did, MFI is not about to open its doors to me so I can prove them wrong. Which brings me back to the lists at *Elixir*. The simplest thing would be to rent the list. Companies do it all the time. The problem is that I can't rent the list."

"What if we set up a dummy corporation to front for you?"

"Plausible but problematic. If *Elixir* does any checking, we're dead. Besides, it'd take a long time just to set up the right kind of cover. Then there's the time it'll take to poll the subscribers. And there's a complication in that, too. Because, you've got to figure out how to—"

"Hey, hey, slow down, honey. Let's take it one step at a time."

"Okay."

"Now the names are all there on the *Elixir* subscription list. All we have to do is get the list. Right?"

"That's right."

"And the easiest way to get it short of breaking in and stealing it is to rent it."

"Uh-huh. Just call Steve in the circulation department and he'll bill you. It's one of the ways we publishers make money the easy way."

"The problem is they can't know it's us."

"Right. You can bet that Woodcock has read Steve the riot act about who gets near that list."

Wendy is thinking.

"Can just anybody who's for real rent the list?"

"No," I answer. "You've got to be a legitimate marketer with an up-and-up use for the names. After all, publishers don't want the wrong kind of junk mail going to their valued subscribers."

"But what if a legitimate marketer with a real business reason rented the list and gave it to us? Does the magazine have any way of checking how the names are used?"

"Not right away. The unspoken threat is that if you do something with the names that you didn't contract for, the owner of the list will tell the world. And no one will ever do business with you again."

"Then all we need is someone completely legitimate who will rent those names and secretly give them to us for our own use."

"Yes. That's the ideal. The problem I was having was—"

Wendy has stopped listening to me. She gets up from the ottoman, walks back into the front hall foyer where her purse is sitting. I hear her riffling through her purse. She reappears in the bedroom with her address book and starts riffling it.

"I've got an idea," she says over her shoulder.

"Really?"

"Tell me about the next step," she says, concentrating on her address index but still listening to me.

"The coding," I explain, "tells us exactly who the former *MD Office* subscribers are."

Wendy looks up from her datebook. "That's the universe we have to sample."

"Right," I say.

"Then what we have here is a classic market research assignment."

"I suppose."

"I can help, Robert. I really can. In case you forgot, of all the pregnant marketing consultants in New York, I am perhaps the sharpest and best connected."

"Oh yeah." I smile. "I almost forgot."

Satisfied with her search, she puts the book down. She switches into high-gear thinking mode, pacing back and forth, up and down the length of our ersatz Oriental carpet.

"We have to poll those readers. Right, Robert?"

"Right."

"And get responses from a sample big enough to be projectable against the whole seventy thousand."

"Exactly. But we need tangible proof from them."

"Fine," she says. "We build that into the survey design. Very doable." She's almost treating me like one of her clients now, and I'm impressed. Thinking intensely, pacing faster, she says, "So speed is the issue."

"Right. And nontraceability to us."

She stops in midstep and says, "Got it. Processing." She pauses. A light bulb seems to have switched on over her head. "Okay. Direct mail is out. Too slow. Too traceable. This calls for telemarketing. Instant contact. Almost instant response."

"That'd be ideal."

"Now you need proof from these doctors, not just their word."

"Uh-huh."

"We can build that into our survey. What we need is a random sample that is statistically projectable against the whole universe. With some kind of written proof from the subscribers that they actually paid for *MD Office*. That's all very doable. Very doable."

"In a few days' time?"

"How does the end of next week sound?"

"Like a miracle."

"We can deliver."

"And how are we going to pay for all this market research?"

She looks up from her datebook with a sly grin. "Don't worry," she says, doing a hoarse-voiced impersonation of Marlon Brando as the Godfather: "I take care a everything. I know who to call. I make 'em an offer they can't refuse."

I smile at her. She puts down her datebook and walks over to me. I reach up to put my arm around her waist and pull her down on the couch beside me. We kiss softly and slowly. "I love your strength," I whisper.

"And I love—I mean *we* love—yours." She takes my right hand and places it on her perfectly flat tummy. "It's all going to work out. The baby, the magazine. All of it. I just know it is."

"I hope so."

"No, it is. It really is. You know how long I've known it?"

"No. Since when?"

"Since that moment we made love on the hill in Vesancy. I haven't felt you come like that since . . . since . . . ever. I could feel it in you, in me. Something special. Something powerful. That was the special beginning I was hoping for. And look, it's starting to come true." She puts my hand back on her tummy. "You remember the way you came up there?"

"Uh-huh," I say, wishing I did not remember that I was thinking of Laura that day. Unwillingly thinking of her, stupidly thinking of her. I tell myself that the incident was a fluke of male mechanics, the same harmless combination of hormones and curiosity that makes girlie magazines an unfailing source of hard-ons. Harmless, guiltless.

"You were so wonderful that day. So strong, so passionate," Wendy says, stroking my crotch. "I checked the calendar when I got the test results. It's like ninety-nine point nine-nine-nine percent certain. That's when we conceived."

Harmless and guiltless, I repeat. Harmless and guiltless. I feel something going terribly wrong. I vow silently to do whatever it takes to make it right again.

"Isn't that just perfect?" Wendy asks with a dreamy smile.

I nod, dying a little inside.

Whatever it takes.

CHAPTER TWENTY-THREE

They say that watching a woman get dressed is sexier than watching her undress. Watching Wendy get ready for the office this morning, I agree. It is a turn-on to observe her walking around unself-consciously, singing to herself, covering up gradually with bra, panties, black thigh-high stockings, slip, clingy silk dress, and jewelry. But the lightly erotic mood is shattered at the end when she gets up from her bent-over position on the edge of the bed wearing athletic socks and sneakers.

"Let's go, Macallan," she says, grabbing her purse and briefcase.

"Should I or shouldn't I?" I ask, holding a necktie in hand.

"Bag it. You're not a corporate soldier anymore. Starting today, you join the guerrillas in the hills."

"Done," I say, letting it drop to the floor of my closet, then fishing out a sweater in place of my suit jacket.

Outside it is cool and sunny. We stroll across the avenues and down a bit to the brownstone on West Sixty-eighth Street, just off Central Park West, where the firm of Truedale and Wolfson resides. The office occupies the first floor of the old brownstone. It used to be the garden apartment that Liz and Wendy shared right after graduate school. When Liz and Wendy decided to become freelance consultants after a few years as marketing bureaucrats in a big, dumb, prestigious company, the space became their office as well. Liz sewed a large needlepoint sampler stating the firm's motto; it still hangs in the foyer by the coatrack. TRUEDALE AND WOLFSON, it reads. "We give small companies the guts to act like big ones. And big companies the smarts to act like small ones."

Wendy's office is in the front facing the street, Liz's office is the former bedroom in the rear (she took an apartment around the corner shortly after Wendy moved in with me). Iris is their cocoa-colored twenty-seven-year-old secretary, office manager, and night school MBA student. Her desk is in the former living room, by the glass doors facing the garden view of brick walls, old trees, bird feeders, and wrought-iron patio furniture. The rooms are all painted in pastels, with shades that run from lilac in Wendy's office to rose in Liz's to peach in the living room. There are potted plants everywhere, including the bathtub, where many have been brought in for protection against the coming cold weather. Across from the sink is a small wicker cabinet jammed full with rolls of toilet paper and three different brands of sanitary pads.

Liz is out this morning visiting a client downtown, Iris says. She is surprised to see me.

"Taking the day off, Bob?" she asks.

"Not exactly. A little enforced exile from American Communications."

"We're here," Wendy chimes in, "to wage guerrilla warfare. To recapture our homeland from the evil domination of the powers of the Dark Side."

"Huh?" Iris asks.

"I got nailed in some sleazy corporate politics," I say. "Somebody trumped up phony charges against me, and my contract was put in limbo until I can clear my name."

"Eeek," says Iris. "Anything I can do to help?"

"Nah," says Wendy, guiding me into her office. "Just tell anybody who calls for me that I'm out. We'll be on the phone most of the morning."

"May the Force be with you," Iris says.

"Thanks," Wendy says, closing her office door behind us.

Wendy takes me by the shoulders. "Now sit right there," she says and plants me in the padded white chair facing her pale wood desk. She sits at her desk, bends down to remove her sneakers and socks, and extracts a pair of pumps from out of the desk's file cabinet drawer.

"First"—she clicks her heels on the floor and turns to face front—"we call Carlos Wildenstein." She flips through her Rolodex and stops at his card. "You listen in on your extension," she says, indicating the phone on the little table next to me. "Push the 'mute' button, so we don't hear you breathing in the background." Wendy dials and, as the call rings, holds her left index finger in the air, then cues me to pick up.

"CW Holdings," I hear the operator answer.

"Carlos Wildenstein, please," Wendy says.

"One moment, please."

It rings twice.

"Mr. Wildenstein's office."

"Is he in this morning?" Wendy asks.

"Who shall I say is calling?"

"Tell him it's Wendy Wolfson."

"May I ask what this is in reference to."

"Just tell him it's Wendy Wolfson; he'll know."

"One moment, please." We're put on hold. Wendy smiles at me. The secretary comes back on. "He says he'll be right with you. He just has to finish this call to London. He said please don't hang up. He'll be right with you."

"Thanks." We go back on hold.

Carlos Wildenstein, the golden boys' golden boy, was a business school classmate of Wendy's. Phi Beta Kappa from Princeton, he was captain of the squash team, associate editor of *The Daily Princetonian,* and a very accomplished ladies' man. Although not unusually handsome, Carlos managed to woo one campus beauty after another with his dazzling intelligence and killer charm. An Argentinean of obviously mixed blood, Carlos had been sent to boarding school in England. As a result, he speaks English with an accent that can be part Spanish, part German, or part British—depending upon his moods and what he wants from his audience. Carlos grew up Latin American rich. But the seed money for his miniconglomerate he earned himself, in his dorm room on the telephone, trading heating oil futures with a computer program of his own invention. By the time he got his MBA, he had socked away nearly three hundred thousand dollars. Although Carlos spent the two years of business school chasing Wendy unsuccessfully around study carrels, they remain friends. Married now with three babies, he still likes to flirt with her, half-seriously.

"Wendita?" he asks, clicking in. "Is that really you?"

"Yes, Carlos, it's me."

"Wendita, when will you come to your senses and run away with me?"

"How are Suzanne and the babies?"

"Ach, they are beautiful. Glowing. Wendita, I long for a son. A son. I remember your hips; my instinct tells me they were made to bear boys. Sons."

"X,Y chromosomes are male-determined, *amor.* Ask Suzanne nicely; I'm sure she'll give you another turn at bat. If at first you don't succeed."

"Ach, you are still impossible. How can I console myself?"

"Buy another company."

"I just did. In England." The Latin accent suddenly disappears; his voice becomes animated. "A small maker of bicycle chains. The finest in the world. A homely, invisible, low-tech company with the kind of cash flow that'd bring tears to a CFO's eyes. Beautiful, just beautiful."

"Carlos, I'd like to make a deal with you."

"A deal?"

"That's right. Remember your food importing company?"

"How can I forget it? It's a thorn in my side, a continuous source of irritation and disappointment."

"I can fix it for you."

"You want to buy it?"

"No, I can fix it. Whip it into shape, your packaging, distribution, pricing, the works."

"That's a big assignment."

"I figure it's an eight-, maybe a ten-week assignment."

"You want to come work for me?"

"As a consultant, yes. I'd like to offer my services for two months, working specifically on that project. By the time I'm done, CW Imports will be ready to make money or sell off, whichever you choose."

"That's a very interesting and very expensive proposition. That's a lot of consulting time."

"I figure it'd bill in the neighborhood of twenty thousand dollars. But, like any good consulting job, its ultimate value to the company's owner would be worth much, much more than that."

"Naturally."

"And the best part is, you can pay for the job in barter."

"You want my body, don't you, Wendita? You know you can have it for free. Anytime."

"It's not your body I want to trade for, Carlos."

"I am disappointed."

"Don't be. In return for my services, I want CW Imports to rent the subscriber list of a certain magazine for a mailing."

"But they don't do mailings."

"That's okay, I want them to start."

"Is that part of my new marketing plan?"

"No, it's part of *my* marketing plan. I want you to rent those names and give them to me. Just turn the computer tapes over to me and let me worry about what to do with them."

"How much will that cost?"

"About twenty thousand dollars."

"Why don't you just go ahead and rent them?"

"I can't."

"Is it the money that's a problem? Maybe I can help."

"No, it's not the money. Not exactly."

"Then what exactly is the problem? Wendita, which magazine do the names come from?"

"A medical magazine."

"Which one?"

"It's called *Elixir.*"

"Isn't that, if my memory serves me right, the magazine your husband publishes?"

Pause.

"Yes."

"Wendy, are you having a problem of some kind? Come on; I'm your old friend. You're not scrounging up consulting assignments, and your husband isn't looking for extra circulation income. What's the story, *querida*? You can tell Carlos."

"Carlos, we need that subscription list for a few days. On a confidential basis."

"Why doesn't he just bring it home from the office?"

"He can't."

"Isn't he still the publisher? Didn't he sell out to McGraw-Hill?"

"American Communications."

"Same thing."

"He got caught in some very nasty politics. They're trying to screw him out of everything."

"*Ach,* those big corporations. You mustn't ever get involved with them. If there's a wrong here, tell me how I can make it right."

"Carlos, just rent the list, turn it over to us for a few days, and I will be in your debt forever. Or at least until I can turn around CW Imports. Can you do this for us? And keep it strictly hush-hush?"

"Absolutely. And you're really serious about the consulting?"

"Yes, totally."

"That means I'll see you in my offices regularly."

"For a couple of months."

"You'll let me take you to lunch?"

"Sure. When we reach key decision points in the plan. But only in well-lit restaurants."

"How soon can you begin?"

"As soon as we get *Elixir* back on track."

"Then hurry. Tell me how to rent this list of yours."

"Thanks, Carlos. I'll call you later this morning with the details."

"*Hasta luego,* Wendita."

"Bye."

Wendy hangs up and looks at me with a smile.

"He's harmless," she says. "You don't have to worry."

"I know."

"Okay. One down. One to go." She flips through her Rolodex, stops, and dials a second number. She cues me to pick up again.

"Research One. Good morning."

"Beth Pilson, please."

"One moment, please."

"Ms. Pilson's office."

"Is Beth in this morning?"

"Who shall I say is calling?"

"Wendy Wolfson."

"I'll see if she's in."

We go on hold.

"Hi, Wendy."

"Hi, Beth. How's business?"

"Couldn't be better."

"Really. What's going on?"

"Well, we've got focus group projects for a deodorant, a toothpaste, and a breakfast cereal. We're doing major studies in hair care, home power tools, and big concept tests for a new toilet paper and a floor wax."

"That's not a combination product, I hope."

"No, but in marketing you can never be sure. Some of the most unlikely things get tested. So what's new at Truedale and Wolfson?"

"Not much. Say, Beth, remember the T and M detergent assignment I recommended you for?"

"Remember? We'd just left the agency; we had no business, no clients, no prospects. It was our first job. It paid the rent; it bought our first business cards."

"And remember the Freshettes relaunch project?"

"Of course, that put Research One on the map in package goods. We used that credential to get the assignments with Procter, Colgate, and AHP. Why? What's up?"

"Beth, I need a favor from you. A big favor."

"How big?"

"Big."

"Big like what?"

203

"Big like a major telemarketing survey. Pronto quick. Very pronto quick."

"How pronto?"

"I need the results next week. This morning would be better."

"You and everybody else. What's the product?"

"I need a randomly sampled questionnaire from a list of seventy thousand doctors. I'll provide the list."

"What do you want to find out? Doctors are very hard to get ahold of, especially for a telephone survey."

"All I want to ask them is one simple yes-or-no question."

"They're still damn near impossible to get on the phone."

"Wait, it gets harder. I need to get them to sign a piece of paper saying that their answer has been yes."

"Now you're talking extreme difficulty."

"If they answer yes, I want to tell them I'm sending them a written form, attesting to their answer, and I want to ask them to sign it and send it back in the mail."

"This is getting harder all the time. What do you want to prove?"

"I want to receive enough return written responses to prove something to an outside third party."

"About what?"

"I want to prove from this sample that all seventy thousand doctors were paid subscribers to a now defunct medical magazine."

"Who's your client?"

"Never mind. How many responses do I need to prove that?"

"To a third party?"

"A very hostile third party."

"Let's see here. I'm looking at my handy chart of confidence levels. If you ended up with three hundred eighty-four signed replies, that'd give you a ninety-five percent confidence level, plus or minus five percent. If you had six hundred sixty-three signed replies, that'd put you at a ninety-nine percent confidence level, plus or minus five percent. Against a universe as small as seventy thousand, the ninety-five percent confidence level would probably stand up in court. But if this party is so hostile, the ninety-nine percent confidence level would be unarguable. The only thing better would be seventy thousand replies. And that'd never happen."

"So how many doctors would we have to sample to end up with the six hundred sixty?"

"Six hundred and sixty-three."

"Yeah, six hundred and sixty-three."

"Well, like I said, doctors don't sit home all afternoon watching the soaps. They're busy and hard to reach. Suppose we started with a random selection of three thousand. Half of them prove to be unreachable. They won't talk to us, they've moved, they're dead, et cetera. So we get through to fifteen hundred. How many of them are likely to answer yes?"

"Every single one of them."

"Great. We tell all fifteen hundred we're sending them a simple form with a stamped, preaddressed envelope to sign and put back in the mail to us. Of those fifteen hundred who say they will sign and return the envelope, a certain percentage will not receive it, and another percentage will ignore it when they get it or forget to mail it in. Another percentage will steam the stamp off and throw the rest away. So if we do well, out of fifteen hundred affirmatives over the phone, we should expect just under fifty percent return rate. Which should put us at around six hundred responses. Somewhere between ninety-five percent and ninety-nine percent confidence level, give or take five percent."

"So we need to poll three thousand?"

"Uh-huh. And when do you need it done? Real world."

"Yesterday."

"That's an expensive study."

"How expensive?"

"Twenty-five, maybe thirty thousand dollars. Gotta go for the best telemarketing resources for a target like doctors."

"That's the retail price, right?"

"That's all we do here, Wendy."

"I know, but what's your cost on a project like that?"

"Wendy!"

"Come on, Beth, what's your cost on a project like that?"

"Who's your client? You working for one of those chiseler types?"

"Beth, this is Wendy talking. Wendy who got you your big breaks when you really needed them. Now what is your cost on a thirty-thousand-dollar research project like that?"

"Twelve, maybe fifteen thousand."

"Fine. I'll give you twelve, maybe fifteen thousand to do it for me."

"What's this about, Wendy? Who's the client?"

"Me."

"You?"

"My husband and me. It's his magazine. The company that acquired it is now saying he cheated on the subscription list of a magazine he bought three years ago. It's politics of the most sleazy variety. And none of it's true. None of it. Beth, can I get your help in this?"

A long pause.

"Sure," Beth answers, finally.

"And?" Wendy asks.

Another pause.

"And?" Wendy asks again. "You'll do it for cost?"

"We'll do it for cost."

"Beth, I knew you'd do the right thing."

"How soon can you get the names and phone numbers to us?"

Wendy looks at me questioningly. I mouth the word "Friday" in response.

"Friday," Wendy says into the phone.

"Okay," Beth says, "if there's no postal strike or breakdown of the long-distance telephone system, we should have six hundred sixty-three response cards in your hand no later than two weeks from Friday. With luck, a little sooner."

"That's perfect, Beth. Thanks a million. I'll call you back this afternoon. Bye."

Wendy hangs up and gives the floor a little ra-ta-ta-tat with her heels.

"We're gonna do it, Robert! We're gonna pull it off. We're gonna show those crummy bastards. We're gonna show 'em."

I reach for the phone and begin dialing a number.

"Who are you calling?" Wendy asks.

"All your wheeling and dealing has given me an inspiration of my own. I'm going to give our old friend Gene Merritt a call and see if we can put the old-boy network to work. In a way that's sure to get Harry Woodcock's attention."

AUGUST

CHAPTER TWENTY-FOUR

The message on our answering machine sounded very human and sincere: "Hey, Bob Macallan. Elton Mackey here. That's right, your friend and his." He bellowed with laughter at his own little joke, "Ha-ha-ha. Hey, but seriously. Listen, guy; I'm uh, uh, I just wanted to tell you that I'm sorry. Sorry to hear about all your troubles. An ace of a guy like you doesn't deserve that kind a shit. Listen, buddy; I wanna, uh—hey, if this gizmo cuts me off I'll call back and finish, okay? Okay. I, uh, want us to sit down and have a talk, you and me. No bullshit. Man to man. I think there's business we can do together that'll be good for both of us. You know, I mean, pardon my French, but *fuck* those guys at American. Anyway, I'm gettin' ahead a myself. I'm gonna be in your neck a the woods next Wednesday. I figure we could meet for lunch. I gotta quiet table at a place called Abelard's. You know, the fancy fish place on Fifty-third Street. How about twelve-thirty? So it's a date. I know it sounds crazy, me asking you to lunch like this after everything that's happened. But hey, that's why they call me Wacky Mackey. Seriously, guy, I'm lookin' forward to seein' you."

So here I am at Abelard's, the most fashionable fish restaurant in midtown, only a little suspicious that filet of Macallan might be the catch of the day. Despite the crowds of expense account lunchers, Abelard's is hushed—a chill, dark womb, decorated with trellises on the walls and sculpted clouds on the ceilings, worlds away from the gooey summer heat.

As the maître d' ushers me toward the back of the restaurant, I see Mackey stand up at his corner table and give me a big wave, the kind that looks like it will be followed by a big two-fingers-in-the-mouth whistle. But Mackey does not whistle. He is dressed in a quietly expensive gray suit, with white shirt and muted maroon tie. His gut, however, sticks out beyond the carefully tailored tropicweight jacket. The suit fits all right; it is just not adequate to contain the man. As I step up to his table, he extends his big, open mitt of a hand.

"Hey, buddy, I'm glad you could make it. Real glad."

I present him with my hand and say quite formally, "Mr. Mackey."

He looks hurt. He withdraws his hand temporarily and shrugs as if to ask what he has done to be treated so badly.

"All right." I let my facade crumble. "El."

"Atta boy." We shake, but there is no crusher grip this time. "Let's sit down and have a drink." The waiter wants to hand us menus, but Mackey waves them away. "Another Absolut on the rocks for me." He slugs back the last of the drink before him and hands the waiter the empty glass. "How 'bout you, Bob?"

"Sure. Same." I have no intention of getting to the bottom of my glass. I will nurse my one drink and watch Mackey inhale his three or four more.

"Bob, I told you on the phone that I'm sorry about your troubles. And I really mean it. I want you to believe me." He is giving me the big, soulful puppy eyes. "Do you believe me?"

"Yes, I believe you." Very convincing, even to me. Almost.

"Great. Now tell me, how are you doing? I mean what are you doing? Do you have any new plans, had any new offers or anything?"

"Not really. I—"

"That's good." The waiter brings our drinks. "Great. I mean I want us to be able to talk about the future without having you distracted by other, uh, distractions." He lifts his glass. "Here's to you."

I raise my glass and nod. He takes a big swallow, I take a little sip. "Bob, if I could sit here and give you advice, you know, like a father, this is what it would be," he says, waving his glass in the air for emphasis. "Kiss off those bastards at American. Cut your losses. Leave all that behind you and move *forward.*" He slugs down the rest of the drink. "Keep moving ahead. That's what you gotta do right now. Don't dwell on the past. Just keep moving." He motions to the waiter to refresh his glass and points toward my nearly full glass to indicate another for me. He gestures for me to drink up, another piece of fatherly advice.

"That's why I brought you here. To talk about your future. *Our* future."

Obediently, I glug down my vodka. He nods with approval, then leans forward as if to prevent anyone around us from hearing. "Just tell me straight," he whispers. "Did you really try to strangle him?"

"Strangle who?"

"The big asshole from American. Woodman."

"You mean Woodcock?"

"Yeah, him. That's the story that's all over the street. That you hauled off and belted him, jumped on top of him, and started strangling him. They had to call security to peel you off him. They say the sucker was half-dead."

"No, that's not how it happened at all. He had the security guys with him when he came. It was all prearranged."

"Well, did you land one, at least?"

"I did sort of take a swing at his little friend Dudley, but that's as far as it went." Let me test him while we are on the subject. "You know how rumors get blown up once they get started." I study his face for some kind of reaction. Nothing.

"Geez, Macallan, I'm disappointed. Next time, you make sure to get off at least one good punch, you hear?"

"Yeah, I hear."

He waves to the waiter for another drink, just for himself this time.

"Bob, before I make you my proposition, will you give an old man the chance to shoot his mouth off a little?" Another rhetorical question. "Thanks." A new vodka arrives. He fortifies himself with half of it. "Bob, do you know what the business world is?"

I give him a look of rapt attention to indicate my keen interest in the answer. He smiles in return, then continues the lecture.

"Business is ten percent tough shit. And ninety percent bullshit. Now the tough shit—that I know you understand. The problem you're running into is the bullshit. Not that you don't understand bullshit. Nobody, but nobody, could build up a successful magazine without having more bullshit than oughtta be allowed by law. It's the flow of the bullshit that's tripping you up. The business world, you see, it's like this huge river of bullshit. Hundreds of millions of tons of steamin', runny, smelly, wet bull turds rushing downstream. Sloggin', splashin', roarin'. Kurrroooosh!" He makes a motion with his hands to indicate a mighty current, like the rapids of the Colorado. "See what I mean?"

I get his mental image all too clearly. I nod.

"The problem, Bob, is that you're trying to swim *upstream*. You can't buck the current. The trick is, you gotta get the flow *behind* you, you gotta get the bullshit working *for* you." He waves his hand gently in the air to show a lucky rafter riding happily down the stinking river. "Take your friend Woodman."

"Woodcock."

"Yeah, him. Now that guy has the bullshit working for him. Everybody in the big, wide world thinks he's a hot shit publishing talent. And why shouldn't they? He's a senior executive hoo-hah of American-fucking-Communications. I mean if they were gonna organize a White House commission or something on running magazines, they'd put him on it. Or a guy just like him. Now you and I know that the only thing he knows about running a magazine is how to run it into the ground." He adds parenthetically, "Which is exactly what he's gonna do to your book." Pause for effect. I absorb it. "But the bullshit says he knows magazines. And that's all that counts. So guys like him get asked on the panel and guys like me who really do know what for—"

The waiter appears at the table, holding menus again and looking eager to recite his litany of specials. Mackey preempts him.

"Listen, why don't you bring us the tuna steaks." He turns to me. "Take my word for it, it's the only thing worth ordering. Believe me, you'll like it."

"Sure, El." Resisting him would not be worth the effort. Besides, I don't mind tuna steak.

"Make mine rare, real rare," he instructs the waiter. "You, Bob?"

"Medium rare, thanks."

"With the works," Mackey adds.

"Can I get you something to start?" the waiter asks.

Mackey holds up his now empty vodka glass and wags it. "We've already started." The waiter vanishes to fetch another drink. "Tuna's as close I can get to real steaks these days." He sounds apologetic, patting his chest just over his heart. "Goddamn doctor." He taps his forehead to regain his train of thought. "Now as I was saying?"

"White House panels."

"Oh yeah. You do understand why I'm telling you all this."

"No, not really."

"But you know where it's all heading."

"You want me to come run *Panacea* for you and beat *Elixir* into the ground. And the other stuff we talked about before—the upscale network and all that."

"Exactly. And I'm gonna sweeten my last offer, believe me I am. I'm gonna let you write your own ticket. I'm gonna see to it that you make up every cent you lost in this American deal and a lot more to boot. Remember what I told you about zeros?"

I nod to keep Mackey's stream of conversation moving.

"Then you know the kinda money I'm talkin' about." I nod again. He smiles. I smile back. We understand each other at last. "But before we get into that, I figure you're entitled to know why I'm so hot to do this thing. What's in it for me."

"The question had crossed my mind."

"You don't think it's more money, do you?"

"No, El, what you're talking about is too much trouble and expense. There are at least a dozen easier ways for a guy like you to make another twenty million."

"That's right. Then what am I after?"

"Beats me."

He leans back in his chair and slaps his thighs. "Some a the bullshit. That's what. Some a the action that the guys like Woodcock take for granted and don't deserve."

"You want to be on a presidential commission?" I ask. "You don't need me for that. Besides, that kind of thing is for sale. Why don't you just make some big political contributions, buy yourself a senator or a couple of congressmen?"

"I contribute plenty already. Believe me, those Washington fucks could teach the Mafia fucks a thing or two about extortion. No, it's more—more, uh"—he rubs a delicate imaginary substance in his fingertips—"it's more subtle than that. Now what do guys like Woodcock have that I don't?" Another rhetorical question. "The bullshit! He's got the bullshit carryin' him off to glory. The Woodcocks a this world end up heaped with honors because they get the bullshit behind 'em. They become fucking ambassador to somewhere and once a year get to piss on a tree with Henry Kissinger and Ronald Reagan in the woods at Bohemian Grove. Why? Because the bullshit says they're builders and doers. And bullshit honors bullshit."

He leans forward, about to share a secret with me. "Now, what do they *really* do inside those big companies? Huh?" I, too, lean forward. "When they're not kissing ass they're kicking it. What does a Fortune 500 executive really do? He steals the credit for good things he *didn't* do. He blames other people for bad things he *did* do. And he feeds like a goddamn parasite off the money machine that guys like old man Henderson built." He leans back into a normal posture. "All those guys in the big companies are like that. Fucking bureaucrats playing the organizational chart like a goddamn chessboard. They don't work. *They work the system.* They don't manage the business. They manage *impressions.* Buncha phony baloney smoke and mirror artists. All of 'em. You know it as well as I do. No, better than me. Shit, look what they just did to you. Any guy that makes it at a big, dumb place like American has only one real talent—makin' himself look good, no matter who else pays or how much it costs the company." Mackey has worked himself into a moral outrage that appears quite genuine. He is flushed and breathing hard.

The waiter arrives with our tuna steaks. Mackey uses the interruption to descend from his soapbox. He looks at his plate with lusty interest. "Let's eat, guy," he says and digs in. He attacks his food with eager concentration, cutting, stabbing, poking pieces into his mouth, chewing, tasting. He executes each action with great precision and delight. There's something slightly animal in the way he feasts. It is not slobby or primitive, it is primal, the enjoyment he takes in devouring the oily tuna flesh. Civilized men do not demonstrate this much pleasure at the table. But Mackey does.

We clean our plates without further conversation.

"I need the right kinda ornament," he says, breaking the silence as he finishes his last bite, "the right kinda credential." He inspects his plate to see if he has missed anything. It is completely bare except for a puddle of juice from the tuna and a streak of herb sauce from the vegetables. He mops them up with the final piece of crust from his bread plate. "I got all the money I need to get invited where I wanna go. But face it. I'm not special, I'm just another industrial-strength multimillionaire. I gotta have something that gives me a classier calling card. Something to give me a little more, uh, *cachet.*" He spits out the word with more than a hint of scorn: "ca-*shay.*" "That's how you say it, right? The guy who works in the lobby a my apartment building taught me that word. I gave him ten bucks for it. Brilliant guy. Speaks seven fuckin' languages. Looks great in a uniform, too. Whaddya call him? The con-see-*urge?*" Mackey smiles at his deliberate mangling of the French.

"Yeah." I smile back. "The con-see-urge."

"That's what I thought. You know that apartment would be part a your deal. Anything belongs to the company is yours. Nice place, couple a blocks from here. Thirty-eighth floor, wraparound terraces. I only use it once or twice a year. Great place to bring broads. Master bathroom's gotta tub like a swimming pool and floor-to-ceiling mirrors. Yeah, great place for broads." He smiles at some recollection. "Ever had three women at once, Macallan?"

I shake my head no. "Sounds like it'd be confusing."

"That's the whole idea." He laughs. "Let's see, there's the apartment here, the jet, the limo, condos in Boca and Hilton Head. All at your disposal. You got first call on all the toys. After me, that is. Think about it, Macallan. Four hundred thousand a year base." He spots a tall, leggy woman in a very short skirt and locks his eyes on her as she crosses the restaurant. "Four hundred thou' base and all the tuna you can eat." She disappears into the ladies' room; he looks back at me, satisfied that he has devoured her, too. He pauses, taking a deep breath, to let himself digest her properly.

"So," I ask, "you're looking for an ornament? Something with a little more ca-*shay*?"

"Yup. You know, the way guys in my position'll buy a football team or an art gallery or a vineyard. Something special that gets you the right kind of attention." Again he turns on the puppy-eyed sincerity. "Bob, I want this upscale magazine network. But like I told you before, I'm not really the guy to make it happen. Sure, I've launched this *Panacea* deal pretty decently, but all I did was copy what you did. I can't keep it up forever. I don't know the guts of it like you do. I figure it's my good luck that the guy who created the original is suddenly available."

Funny how that happened, I think.

"Frankly," he confides, "I don't have the energy or the interest to really see it through. And when it comes to building the rest a the books, well, shit, I'm getting close to sixty. That's no job for me. I want to *have* these books, but I don't want to have to do the work to have 'em. Know what I mean?"

I nod.

"I'm being pretty honest with you," he says, fidgeting with his diamond-encrusted Rolex, "for a man in my position."

"I know that," I say and wonder exactly what he means. "But why do you suddenly want to start hobnobbing around at the White House and partying with, I don't know, Brooke Astor and Queen Elizabeth?"

"That's *my* problem. A man reaches a certain point in his life, he wants to have, uh . . . that's *my* problem, Macallan. Here's what I want from you. You build me this network, and I'll get you more dough than you ever dreamed of. Let's not go into the particulars now; we can work out bonus formulas and stock and bennies and deferred comp, all that, with the lawyers. You just build me that classy group a books and along the way I'll do something better than make you rich." He stops to let me wonder what could possibly be better than making a lot of money.

Time's up. He gives me his answer. "I'll let you be your own man. That's what. Think about it. You'll run your own show. I mean that. Absolute autonomy. I don't know shit from Shinola about what you do, and I don't wanna know. You just go and do it. Every now and then, just let me make a speech somewhere or go to a party and pretend like I had something to do with it. That's all. I want you to be your own man. 'Cause that's what'll make you strong for me and my purposes. I can't say that to anybody else who works for me, but I can say it to you. Because you and I understand what it means to be your own man. Guys like you and me know that nothing else in life matters as much as being your own man. Nothing."

I remember that phrase from my father. He was always saying that being your own man was the most important thing of all. I think the way he finally achieved it was by retreating from the world into his own little cocoon of comfortable silence and self-denial.

"Your own man," Mackey says, waving his right index finger, "not answering to anyone else. Not being beholden to nobody nohow for *nothin'*. Makin' it on your own, your own way. That's worth even more than the dough. Think about it. Macallan, I'm here to do more than just save your bacon. I'm here to save your self-respect."

Suddenly, a sharp female voice invades our table. "You boys seem like you're having a cozy little chat." It is Vera Mackey, overdressed to kill and loaded down with shopping bags from establishments like Chanel, Hermès, Bendel's, and Bergdorf's. Beside her is a young man, pretty and foppish, in a pink polo shirt, blue blazer, and chinos, laden with still more shopping bags. I stand up to greet her; Mackey remains seated.

"Had a good haul?" he asks, a note of resignation in his voice.

"Not bad for a Wednesday." She reaches in front of her husband's face and takes my hand. "Mr. Macallan, how lovely to see you again." Just like the last time, her grasp lingers a little too long. "Has Elton been filling you full of promises?"

"Vera," he says, getting annoyed, "why don't you and your little friend go buy some more stuff. We have business to discuss."

"Ooh, I haven't introduced you, have I?" She yanks her companion to center stage. I wasn't sure at first, but now it's clear that Vera is a little tanked. "Peter Piper, I'd like you to meet my husband, Elton Mackey, and Mr. John Macallan."

"His name's not John," Mackey says, staring impatiently at the table-cloth.

"Well," Vera snaps back, shaking her escort by the arm, "*his* name's not Peter. It's something with an *R*, Richie or Rodney. But I can't resist calling him Peter. Peter Piper. Isn't he just the loveliest young man? Tell me, El, can you guess how many peckers Peter Piper picked? Oops, did I say peckers instead of peppers?"

"Vera," Mackey says, still looking down, "can you leave us to finish lunch in peace. Please." Even Piper, who looks like he's used to baby-sitting tipsy rich dowagers, is starting to look embarrassed.

213

"Has he offered you the big job yet, Mr. Macallan?" she asks. I smile politely to avoid answering. "Has he given you the speech about being your own man?" She turns on a not bad impersonation of her gruff husband. "About gettin' it all on your own, bein' beholden to nobody nohow for *nothin'*. Making it on your own, your own way." She smiles and turns off the act. "He always lays that on at the end to sucker them in. But let me tell you something. He was once a poor kid in a stupid, nothing job in a little printing company. He was going nowhere. He was nothing! Then he started going out with the boss's daughter. Told her he loved her, told her he loved her forever. To prove it he knocked her up. In those days, you had to get married. But it was okay with her; she thought it was true love, just like he said. When they had the baby, the father-in-law gave him a big promotion so they could support his grandchild. Well, to make a long story short, he drove the father-in-law out of the business and into an early grave. Then, once he took over the company, he started sticking his pecker into every two-legged woman in Cayahoga County. At first, I was upset. Then in time I learned what it was. Elton, you see, loves to fuck people. All kinds of people. That's all there is to it. Fucking people is what he does best, and he never seems to tire of it. I just thought I'd share that with you. You seem like such a nice young man. Come, Peter."

With that, Vera turns and starts walking away. Stunned for an instant, Peter Piper spins around and dashes after her. Mackey sits studying the tablecloth.

I resist the urge to tell him that only one person could ever save my bacon or my self-respect and it's not him.

CHAPTER TWENTY-FIVE

How much does a bag filled with 700 response cards weigh? On this unusually cool, cloudy summer morning, as I get out of the taxi and cross the plaza to the revolving doors of the American Communications tower, the answer is "nothing." It is no burden at all.

Research One delivered them yesterday afternoon in a heavy canvas Postal Service sack. Having had my fill of encounters with American Communications security staff, I decided that the sack would attract attention and make me look like a deliveryman who forgot to use the service elevators. So I transferred the cards to a large Saks Fifth Avenue shopping bag. Now, as I enter the building in my gray suit, black Saks bag in hand, I look like any executive who might have gone shopping.

There's an empty elevator car with open doors waiting to whoosh me up to forty-eight. I get a solo, nonstop ride, like the old-time chief executives in their private elevators. American Communications doesn't know it yet, but it is giving me a most auspicious welcome back into its arms.

As the doors open, I see Legs, lost in private concentration, picking with the long red fingernails of her right hand at a hangnail on her left thumb. I pad across the carpet and arrive in front of her desk unnoticed. I stand silent and motionless for an instant.

"Ahem," I say, clearing my throat for effect.

"Uuuuh?" She looks up, startled and embarrassed, her nasty little grooming chore exposed and unfinished, her condescending cool utterly blown. "Uh, may I, uh, help you?" She raises the injured thumb to her mouth and gives it a little suck. She smiles nervously at being caught unawares.

"I'm here to see Harry Woodcock. Tell him it's Robert Macallan."

"Oh yes," she replies with a nod of recognition. Legs doesn't actually remember me, she just remembers that she remembers that Robert Macallan has been among the names passed through her more than once in the recent past. "Just a moment, please." Another uncharacteristic little smile. She calls Miss Boardman. "Robert Macallan is here to see Mr. Woodcock." There's a long pause. "Oh." Her voice drops. "I see, I see." She hangs up the phone and looks at me. She is quite unfriendly now, having regained her snotty confidence after talking to Miss Boardman. "Mr. Woodcock cannot see you under any circumstances. He's tied up in meetings all week. If you have a message of some kind, you can leave it with me."

"No. I'm here to see Harry Woodcock."

"I'm sorry. Mr. Woodcock cannot see you."

"You mean Mr. Woodcock won't see me."

"That's right."

"No, that's wrong. Mr. Woodcock *will* see me."

She reaches for the telephone again.

"If you're thinking of calling security, don't."

She stops cold. It amazes me how conditioned we are to following instructions delivered in a voice of parental authority; I guess we never fully outgrow childhood conditioning.

"Mr. Woodcock and I have important business to conduct."

"I'm sorry. *I* have been told otherwise."

"Mr. Woodcock just doesn't know it yet, that's all. Listen, let me talk to his secretary for two seconds. Really. If I can't get her to change his mind, I'll leave quietly, okay?"

Legs looks skeptical.

"Believe me, it'll be the easiest way to get rid of me, a lot easier than calling security. Come on, give his secretary a call and tell her I insist on speaking to her. Make me the villain. You be the victim. It's okay. Nobody will blame you. Come on, call her."

"Very well." She dials. "Hello, Miss Boardman, it's Fiona at reception. Sorry to bother you again. Uh, I know this is highly irregular, but this gentleman insists on speaking to you before he leaves. He's very insistent, I'm afraid. Very." Pause. "Yes, I know. But I thought we might avoid making a scene with security this way. . . . Yes. . . . Yes. Thank you. Thank you very much."

Legs gives me a dirty look and passes the handset.

"Hello, Miss Boardman?" I say into the phone.

"Mr. Macallan," Boardman snaps in her sternest, most disapproving schoolmarm voice, "Mr. Woodcock is absolutely indisposed and cannot under any circumstances see you. Do you understand? If you have any matters to take up with him, I suggest you address them to this office in writing. Now, will you please—"

"Miss Boardman, you're doing a splendid job of shielding your boss. I congratulate you. But there's a brief message I want you to give Mr. Woodcock right now."

"Mr. Macallan, I've already—"

"Miss Boardman, hear me out. Please. Believe me; this is in your best interests. If you don't give this message to Mr. Woodcock now and he finds out later—and I assure you he will—he will be mad. I mean *really* mad. So take your pick. Shield him now and I guarantee he'll be furious later. Or give him my message and this whole incident will pass."

I can almost hear her thinking.

"Very well, Mr. Macallan, what is your message?"

"Tell him that I have in my hand evidence that clears my name. Tell him that if he won't see me right now, my lawyers will go directly to Walt Drummond. Tell him he can see me now or wait to see what happens when Drummond hears the lawyers talk about slander, defamation, and damages. Tell him that. Please, Miss Boardman. Verbatim. Right now."

"Very well, Mr. Macallan. I will call you back." Boardman hangs up.

"Thank you, Fiona," I say, ceremoniously handing the phone back to Legs. "Fiona. My, what a lovely name."

She wrinkles her nose and goes back to picking at her hangnail, making a big show of ignoring me. I stand by the desk watching the view from the forty-eighth floor and the progress of Fiona's cuticle surgery for what seems like two or three minutes. Then Miss Boardman appears in the reception area.

"Mr. Macallan," she sneers accusingly and gestures for me to follow her down the corridor to the big offices with mahogany doors.

Harry is seated with his right arm resting on the desk, chin in hand. "Thank you," he says, looking through me to Miss Boardman. "You can close the door." She does. We are alone.

The fingers under his chin reach up and cover his lips as if to silence any potential greeting. He takes a deep breath from behind his hand and stares at me icily. He is not about to speak.

"Thanks, I'd love to," I say and walk to the visitor's chair directly across from him. I sit down and place my bulging shopping bag on the floor beside me.

Harry does not move or change expression. I take a fistful of reply cards from the shopping bag and hold them up in the air.

"These, Harry, are signed statements from doctors attesting to the fact—

the fact—that they were paid subscribers to *MD Office* at the time its subscriber list was acquired by Elixir Publishing. Paid subscribers, Harry. Paid. This isn't me saying it. It's them. I have a little over seven hundred of these signed reply cards. Seven twenty-four, to be exact. That's better than one percent of the total seventy thousand in question. This is a random sampling, tested by Research One, a highly reputable market research firm. I have their objective report and all its documentation right here."

I reach into the bag with my free hand and extract a thick ringed binder. I drop it on the desk in front of Harry. It lands with a little thud. "In the world of statistics, this amounts to what they call a 'confidence level' of ninety-nine percent. We can be ninety-nine percent confident that the other sixty-nine thousand three hundred doctors were also paid subscribers. I might add that this confidence level is accepted not just in marketing, but in a court of law. Here, why don't you look at a few of the replies." I drop the dozen or so in my hand beside the Research One binder. Without moving his head, Harry lowers his eyes to look at the cards in front of him.

"Maybe you'd like to look at them all," I say. "All seven hundred twenty-four of them." I stand, pick up the Saks bag, and drop it on top of the desk, just to the left of Harry, so that it does not hide him from my view. The bulging, crinkled paper bag looks ridiculous here on the desk adorned with sleek executive knickknacks. "What do you say?"

Harry sits silent and unmoving. I turn and begin pacing around the office, the better to invade Harry's turf and release my own tension. "This conclusion is identical to the one ABC will reach. Identical. We've just reached it sooner; that's all. Now we don't have to wait for ABC to call this matter closed, don't you agree?"

Not a sound from Harry.

"I knew you'd agree."

I walk along the wall of windows, talking half to the air. "A lesser man than me might be screaming for revenge now that he's been vindicated. He might try to rout out the parties who framed him and caused him all this heartache and trouble. He might have armies of attorneys preparing nasty, vitriolic lawsuits designed to create a lot of ugly publicity. But that's not how I'm reacting. No sir, not me. No, Harry, this is business. You and I are locked together in this deal for *Elixir*. I want to help you understand that we have interests in common. I want you to see that we should both want the same things. I want to help you see that."

I stride back to the visitor's chair and sit down. "Harry, while I was, uh, on vacation these past couple of weeks, I got involved in a little financial analysis project with Blaine Consulting. You know Blaine, the famous management consultants? Corporate strategy? The corporation as portfolio manager? All those computer models with cash wells and black holes? Of course, you're familiar with Blaine. R. Bingham Addison, the retired president of Blaine, is *also* chairman of the finance committee of American's board of directors. Small world, isn't it? Good old Binkie Addison. I had lunch with him at the Union Club last week. Everyone knows he swears by the principles he helped formulate at Blaine. Well, this analysis I did with the Blaine people happens to take a look at the payout from a hypothetical acquisition that closely resembles *Elixir*. Very closely. Based on detailed information I just happened to have at hand. We looked at what happens to American's, uh, rather, the acquiring company's, ten-million-dollar investment under two different scenarios. In the first scenario, we integrated the acquisition totally into corporate's infrastructure. We moved the offices into headquarters, canceled all its contracts with its suppliers, and started purchasing everything from headquarters at full corporate allocation. In the second scenario, we kept the book independent from corporate, we kept its very favorable supplier contracts in force, we left it alone to operate as it always had. We were looking to see how much cash the magazine would throw back to corporate under each scenario, to see which scenario would pay back corporate's investment sooner and result in a bigger contribution to American's, I mean the acquirer's, bottom line over time."

I reach into the inside breast pocket of my suit jacket and extract a business envelope. I remove the letter within and hold it up. "Harry, you'll never guess what the Blaine study concluded. It's right here under the letterhead. I'll let you read it in just a second. They found that under scenario one, the acquirer would be likely never to recoup its original investment. Never. Not at least as far into the future as the Blaine computer models could see. The little magazine became, as Blaine calls them, a 'black hole' *into which* corporate can pump cash fruitlessly into infinity. But under scenario two, where they left the book alone, it paid back its purchase price in four years and turned into one of those 'cash wells' *out of which* corporate can pump money on and on into the future. 'A very interesting finding,' you might well say, 'but a hypothetical one. So what?' Indeed. But bear with me. It gets more interesting.

"You see, I have copies of this little study on ever-so-credible Blaine letterhead waiting to be sent to three carefully selected parties. First, there's Addison. As chairman of the board's finance committee, ex-president of Blaine, and a friend of mine, he's going to read it very carefully indeed. But he'll be even more interested when he finds out who else will be reading it. Remember those raiders who are sniffing at the door? Mel Grubman and the Belsky brothers. You know how they keep claiming in the press that American's current management and board are not maximizing value for the shareholders, that they're squandering the corporation's profit potential. I don't have to remind you of the trouble they're trying to make. Well, a study like this in their hands, along with certain other information I possess, could be just the ammunition they've been looking for. Just the stuff for starting an ugly shareholder suit against American's board and management. And the funny thing is, it doesn't matter whether they win or lose. It's the embarrassment that hurts. Imagine the embarrassment Addison will feel as chairman of the board's finance committee, the embarrassment Dillon Edwards will feel as chairman of the board itself. Imagine the heat they will put on Vice Chairman Drummond, all because of a tiny division that happens to fall under the purview of a certain executive they thought they could trust to make American look good."

I hand the Blaine letter across the desk and drop it in front of Harry. He picks it up and scans the first page silently. "There are copies with cover letters just waiting to be messengered simultaneously to R. Bingham Addison, Mel Grubman, and Peter and Mort Belsky. But I don't see why any of them should ever have to see it. Do you? I think it's all completely unnecessary. Don't you?"

Harry puts the letter down and clasps his hands in front of himself, waiting for me to finish. He takes a deep breath and says nothing.

"Thanks, I'm glad you asked. Harry, what I want is really very simple. I want back into my company to fulfill my original contract. I want *Elixir* left alone. Alone. It's not too late to stop the move into this building. I want *Elixir* to stay put in the General Insurance building at our nice cheap rent. And I want all the other plans you and Dudley made canceled. Immediately. What's more, I want Dudley out. Out. We will continue to buy our own printing, our own fulfillment, our own computer services, our own staplers, our own paper clips, the works. *Elixir* stays independent, with me in charge, making the decisions—until my contract runs out in May and I collect the other half of my earn-out. Fair and square, as planned. That's not unreasonable. That's nothing more than what I negotiated originally with American—in good faith."

Harry emits a little sigh. But no words.

"You can make all that happen, Harry. You know you can. The same way you were about to make your first set of plans for *Elixir* happen."

I pause for a moment to see if he is ready to respond. He is not.

"Harry, I don't want you to feel that I'm forcing you into anything. Not at all. I want this to be a good deal. There should be something in it for *both* of us. I want you to be happy about it. In fact, I want you to come out of it looking good, looking like a hero. And I've got an idea of how you can do it. Do you want to hear it?"

He says nothing. But he stares right into me, eyes narrowed as if to focus deadly laser beam looks into my head.

"Harry, I can help you become a hero. Really, I can. I can help you become the hero—the champion—of profitability at American. Honest."

I hope my irony isn't showing. I can't help but think of Harry's willingness—eagerness—to squander millions in the cause of corporate politics. "See all that analysis in the Blaine study? No one but you and I know what it really means, which company it was meant to apply to. Go ahead and use it. It's yours. I give it to you. Pretend it's your own thinking. You'll sound like a genius as you justify one brilliant management decision after another concerning *Elixir*. Honest. You'll be doing the right thing, and you'll look great doing it. Guaranteed."

Harry's expression is getting less hostile by the moment.

"Come on. Let's put aside our own petty, selfish motives and think about serving the best interests of this great institution. Isn't that what you always tried to teach me? Let's focus on stewarding the wealth of the shareholders. After all, that's what they pay us for. Let's concentrate, you and me, on keeping this company in the hands of the management team that is rightful heir to Andrew Henderson and the values he stood for. Let's work together to keep American from falling victim to those, what did you call them? Ah, yes, 'pushy rag trade interlopers.' Come on. We can accomplish great things together, Harry. Great things. The sad part is that we'll only be working together for a few more months. Then I'll go my way and you'll go yours. But I look forward to these months being happy, productive, and mutually rewarding—based on the understanding we've reached here this morning. So what do you think? Do we have a deal?"

Harry looks first at the shopping bag, then at the Research One report, then at the Blaine letter. He picks up the Blaine letter, fondles the paper between thumb and forefinger, and puts it down again. He nods thoughtfully, then looks up at me and slowly begins to crack a smile. "Of course we have a deal," he says, starting to turn the unctuous Woodcock charm back on. The grin gets bigger and in an instant the old Harry is back and ready to play ball—this time with me instead of against me. He stands up and extends his hand, my oldest and dearest friend. "Bob, let me be the first to say, 'Welcome home.'"

CHAPTER TWENTY-SIX

I have to revise some of my assumptions about Harry. He is not the stick-in-the-mud bureaucrat I thought he was—at least not when he's been properly motivated. For once, Harry made the wheels of the big corporation fly. We shook hands just before lunch on Thursday. By four o'clock that afternoon, he had cleared his new plans with American and notified *Elixir* of the changes in command. I have no idea what he might have said to Drummond. The memo he sent to the staff of *Elixir* read:

> At American Communications, trust is everything. Trust between American and its readers, trust between American and its advertisers, trust between American and its people. We must be prepared to go to great lengths to preserve that trust and, sometimes, to even greater lengths to be sure we are seen to be preserving it.
>
> It can be an uncomfortable burden. In recent days, it certainly has been.
>
> However, we would never wait for outsiders to tell us when justice has been done. From the very instant the challenge against *Elixir* was registered at ABC, we began conducting investigations of our own.
>
> I am happy to report that those results are in. Our hopes have

been vindicated. As far as this corporation is concerned, there are no questions about the validity of *Elixir*'s circulation.

Naturally, we will make sure our advertisers are aware of the ABC findings as soon as they come in. But we are confident that ABC will only corroborate what we have already concluded on our own.

Therefore, I am delighted to make the following announcement:

Starting Tuesday, September 3, Robert Macallan will return to *Elixir* as president and publisher.

Special thanks to each and every one of you for your excellent work during the difficulties of the past few weeks. Dudley Townsend will come back to headquarters as part of corporate staff. I hope the contributions he was able to make can begin to measure up to the lessons I know he learned from you.

American has great hopes and plans for you and your leader, Bob Macallan. Keep up the good work!

Yesterday morning, Friday, Harry sent me new keys to the office (the bastard had the locks changed the day after he threw me out) and had movers pick up my boxes of personal files and office paraphernalia, the ones that had been so rudely shipped out two and a half weeks before. By Friday evening, everything was set for my triumphant return on Tuesday.

But I am returning first, in private and unannounced, on this steamy Saturday morning of Labor Day weekend. Wendy and I are making the trip downtown to General Insurance, wearing shorts and T-shirts and sneakers, to set up my office.

By the time we arrive around ten, the list of workers who have signed in at the security desk is already a page long. The quiet of big office buildings on Saturday is special. What you hear is the low hum of a select group of people getting more work done in a few undisturbed hours than the fully populated building gets done all week. Wendy and I sign in on the last two lines of page one. The guard wishes us good morning and peels open a new page on his clipboard.

The *Elixir* offices are empty and dead quiet. Nothing seems to have changed, except for the boxes of my things, now piled up in the corner of my office. The two other mover's boxes, sealed, addressed to American headquarters, and parked in the hall by my door, must be the remnants of Dudley's tenure in my job. My desk, couch, tables, bookcases, lamps, and chairs are all exactly where I left them. A tribute to either Dudley's consideration and precise memory or his lack of imagination.

Wendy and I are unpacking. She is filling up the bookcase, I the desk. "Is there any special order you want for these books?" she asks. "Nah."

I am replacing stray odds and ends into my "junk" drawer. I find myself reliving memories as I handle the matchbooks from restaurants I haven't visited in years, dog-eared postcards from an old friend, half-filled boxes of Tic-Tacs, a "Los Angeles" palm tree paperweight from the magazine publishers' convention three years ago, a sales videocassette titled *The New MD Psychographics*, a worn art gum eraser, a box of three golf balls imprinted with the *Elixir* logo (the centerpiece of Leo's first promotional campaign), and other scraps of time. I feel as though I am putting these memories away one by one. I may be replacing them into the same drawer they came from two weeks ago, but they are going to a different place inside me.

"You sure you don't have a special order for these?" Wendy asks, hefting a pair of blue publishing directories.

"Really, no. A little randomness is good. I don't want this place to feel too settled or too permanent."

"But you gotta be able to find things."

"I know where everything I really need is." During my exile, I was surprised by how much I missed coming to the office. Now that I'm back, I'm surprised by how detached I feel. This is definitely a new chapter for me.

We unpack in silence for a few minutes more.

"There now," Wendy says, emptying the last of the boxes on her side of the room. "Robert Macallan is reinstalled and reinstated."

"Make yourself comfortable. I'm almost done," I say, looking up from my desk.

"Thanks, boss." Wendy puts both hands on the left arm of the couch and vaults herself over sideways, landing with a crunch in a fully reclined position. "Ugh," she says, feeling the creaky, uneven springs against her back, "at least I know this has never been your casting couch." She crosses her legs in midair and tries to get as comfortable as she can. "Robert," she muses, "where do you think we'll be a year from now?"

"I don't know, but it sure as hell won't be in here."

"Oh, Robert, let's talk about what it'll be like when we're a family."

"Aren't we a family now?"

"No, silly, we're just a couple."

"Oh, I see."

"Are you worried that you'll feel neglected? Because of the baby, I mean?"

"I don't know. We know we'll always have memories of all the good times we had when it was just the two of us."

"Ro-bert, you make it sound like we're going off to a labor camp in Siberia."

Suddenly, we hear keys opening the outside front door of the office suite. I raise my hand in a gesture of silence. Wendy and I stare at each other as we hear the door being opened, then closed, then locked again. We hear footsteps click along the linoleum and a male voice humming a little tune. The footsteps go down the hall from us and into another office.

With finger held to my lips, I get up and walk silently to my doorway. I peer around the doorjamb and down the hall. Fluorescent light spills out of Leo's office. I hear footsteps in the room, file cabinet drawers being opened, his happy humming. Yes, it is definitely Leo. It sounds like he's humming the old Glenn Miller tune "String of Pearls." He gives out an emphatic little "da-da-da-da-*da*-dum" on the chorus.

Wendy looks like she might be about to speak. I pull myself back inside the doorway and give her a traffic cop signal to stop. I cup one ear and lean in the direction of the office down the hall.

Leo is opening and closing the steel drawers of his file cabinet. He stops humming. I hear the casters of his chair slide across the floor. A pause. He begins talking. It must be over the phone. I strain to hear.

"Hello, it's me. . . . Yeah, I've got them. They're in my briefcase now, safe and sound. . . . No, I didn't leave any behind. . . . Uh-huh. . . . Uh-huh. I told you I would. . . . That's right. No one will ever know, except you and me. . . . Fine. Now I'm gettin' outta here. Talk to you next week." Click. The chair slides back again. The footsteps move across the floor. I press myself against my wall, in hopes that he will not come down this way. He doesn't. The footsteps go out to reception. The door is unbolted from the inside, opened, closed again, then relocked from the outside. No more sounds.

Wendy and I remain silent, looking at each other. I give Leo more than enough time to summon the elevator and descend before I speak.

I look directly at Wendy but say to myself, "That settles it."

SEPTEMBER

CHAPTER TWENTY-SEVEN

Tuesday morning, I decide to arrive at the office at my regular old time of nine-thirty, just as if the past few weeks had never happened. I spent the better part of the long Labor Day weekend wrestling with other possible scenarios and found them all unsatisfactory: too forced, too casual, too sticky, too something. There is one thing I learned growing up in stolid, tight-lipped New England. If anything is about to force you to admit to other people how complicated human relationships are, ignore it. Pretend it never happened.

And so, precisely at half past nine, I open the door to Suite 1810. Jeannie is at her post, ever reliable and ready to answer the telephone. "There you are," she says, standing up. "We were trying to guess when you'd show up. I said nine-thirty. Marie said eight-fifteen. I shoulda bet that dollar with her. Welcome back, Bob." She buzzes someone twice. "We missed you."

I am delighted to see her, really delighted. I had not expected to feel that way. "Thanks, Jeannie. I missed you, too." Without even thinking, I lean across her desk to give and receive a little hug. It seems like the most natural thing in the world, which also surprises me.

"It's nice to have you back," she says, "even if it's just for a few more months."

Suddenly, the reception area fills up with people. My people. Ted and Roni, Wayne and Steve, Joe Bartolo, the writers, production people, secretaries—the same crowd that was a blur of confusion when the security guards rushed me out is a blur of confusion again. This time it is a happy blur. "Hey, Bob." "Welcome back!" "You're back!" I feel hugs, handshakes, back pats, cheek kisses. I just scored the winning touchdown in overtime, the home run in the bottom of the ninth.

Joe Bartolo has his arm through mine. "This is better than a birthday party," he says over the noise and chatter. "This is Christmas. Tell me, how did you get Dudley and the boys to back down on the move to headquarters? I don't have to tell you what that does for my numbers. How did you do it, Bob? Come on, how?"

"I asked him nicely, that's all. Real nicely."

"Come on, what did you tell him?"

"I said, 'Please, pretty please, don't fuck up Joe's expense-to-revenue ratio.' "

Joe frowns.

"Actually, I said, 'He'll tell his brother-in-law Vinnie in the cement business.' That's when they said, 'Sure, anything you want. Anything at all.' "

"Wiseass," Joe says, throwing a mock punch to my stomach, "always a wiseass."

"We've got a lot of stuff to go over," I say.

"Yeah, a lot." Joe turns away for an instant, then looks at me with a more serious expression. "So now, you can, uh, make those numbers pretty sure, get your money, and get outta here."

"Who knows?" I reply, smiling uncomfortably.

"You, uh, considering maybe signing up for another year here in the salt mines with your old sidekicks?"

"Gee, Joe, I don't, uh—"

"Never mind. It's none a my goddamn business, anyway. Just figured I'd see what was on the horizon. This place has been like a goddamn roller coaster lately, that's all."

"Joe, I'm back now. I'm here one hundred percent. The old team. Corporate isn't going to fuck with us anymore, believe me."

Joe's manner says he isn't buying it. He seems stiff, formal, distant. "Sure, boss. How's about we get together around ten-thirty? Go over some numbers."

"You're on," I say enthusiastically. Joe turns to melt back into the crowd. Before he goes, I put a hand on his shoulder. "Joe," I say, "it's good to see you again. Really, it is."

"Same here," he says, but it sounds unconvincing.

Jerry, the managing editor, is at my side now. As usual, his tie is askew and his shirtsleeves are rolled up; his thick horn-rimmed glasses are spotted with fingerprints. Jerry must have seen *The Front Page* as a teenager and never quite recovered.

"Mr. Greenstein," I say, shaking his hand vigorously, "keeper of the flame. You look good. Have you been okay? All our plans still intact?"

"Sure, fine."

"Did they keep your editorial product sacrosanct while I was in exile?"

"More or less."

"They didn't send the Syntax Police to homogenize your style?"

"No, but they threatened to. You got back just in time." He fishes the notepad he always carries out of his back pocket and gives it a once-over. "Bob, I've got quite a list to go over."

"You bet. Why don't we have lunch today?"

"Gee, Bob, I'd love to, but, I can't today."

"Okay, well how about tomorrow?"

"Uh, let me see, I, uh—"

"Come on, we'll go to the back room of Patterson's and dream up some new conference ideas, whaddya say? Remember when we cooked up the laser medicine theme? It'll be just like old times."

"Gee, I can't really do it then." He's starting to look uncomfortable.

"Then let's grab some beers at six tonight. We always did our best brainstorming then. Come on, pardner."

"Geez, Bob," he says, fumbling and avoiding my glance, "I gotta ton of stuff to do around the house tonight. Lisa's been off her feet with that twisted ankle. Maybe we could sit down together later this morning."

"Sure, Jerry, you say when. I'm at your disposal. I want to hear everything. Everything. Here, give me a little taste from your idea list."

"Well, I've been in touch with Slowik, the research hematologist from Mass General, remember him?"

"Of course. Synthetic anticoagulants. Is he ready to go public?"

"He's telling me it'll be four or five months now. I see a feature on how his life changed after his big breakthrough, a real inside look at the medical star system. So, if we want to follow right after his big announcement, that'd mean, I guess, a publication date of, I suppose, August or maybe September next year."

"Great, just great, Jerry. Celebrity medicine. *People* magazine for doctors. What a coup that'll be."

"Of course, you'll be gone by then, won't you?"

"Well I, uh, don't really know if I, uh . . ." I want to kick myself for being so awkward.

"Listen," Jerry says, using my fumphering as a chance to go back into the crowd, "I'll sit down with you later today and go over everything. Welcome back, Bob."

I spot Ted Willis, the head art director, and take him by the arm.

"How's the special issue coming?" I ask him, noticing for the first time how much gray is creeping into his long hair, which today is carefully pulled back in a ponytail.

"Everything's on schedule so far," he says.

"McGuinn being a pain in the ass about the graphics?" I ask.

"No, not really. He likes to make a little change here and there in the layouts. Just to feel like he's doing something. But mostly he says okay and leaves us alone."

"How much farther along are you?"

"We've got the look pretty much all blocked out. We're refining the two gatefolds; we're still waiting for the neurological slides from Hopkins. Can't really lay out those pages until we get them. Then, we've got a couple of possible looks to choose from for the 'Hypertension' logo." Ted stops in midthought and changes direction. "Say, we were all set to start buying printing and production from corporate; it was a done deal. Then, all of a sudden, it's not. We can stick with Campion for type and Alpha for separations and engraving after all. How'd that happen? So suddenly?"

"Corporate finally realized we can do it better and cheaper ourselves."

"That's what I kept trying to tell that dominatrix they sent over from manufacturing. But she wouldn't hear of it. I swear that bitch must wear black leather panties under her gray tweed suit."

"Long as she didn't get you into a doggie collar."

"No, you stopped her just in the nick of time."

"Glad to be of service," I say.

"Just one question, Bob."

"Shoot."

"What's going to happen when you leave?"

"Gee, I don't know just yet. Things have been happening so quickly lately. But I'm going to do my damnedest to see that they keep their mitts off you. Believe me."

"Sure, Bob," he says, looking down at the floor. "Welcome back." He turns and walks away.

Steve, the circulation manager, takes me by the elbow. "Hi, Bob."

"Steve, how've you been?" Lanky, thoughtful, thirtyish Steve in his horn-rimmed spectacles reminds me of a junior Ward Cleaver in training.

"On pins and needles. Are we waiting for ABC or aren't we?"

"Officially, we and the rest of the world still are. But unofficially, American says everything is kosher. It'll be fine. How's business otherwise?"

"Fine. Quiet, as you might imagine under the circumstances. No, wait! Got a real strange one, right after you left. An import/export company. Gourmet foods. Calls up and wants to do a mailing to our doctors. Got some kinda low-cholesterol pâté or something. In a big hurry. Never done direct mail before, he says. Wants to rent the whole list. I quote him the price; he doesn't bat an eyelash. Messengers me a certified check almost before I hang up the phone. Don't even get a chance to bill him. What a character. Low-cholesterol pâté, imagine that."

"Yeah." I smile. "It's some crazy business we're in."

"And how. Welcome back," he says, "for a while at least."

Marie is beside me now.

"And how was King Dudley during his brief reign?" I ask her.

"On the phone to corporate most of the time. And in meetings with Leo."

"Really?"

"You'd think they were joined at the hip, the two of them."

I see Leo standing in the corner away from the crowd, in a huddle with Roni, Wayne, and Mike, the other salespeople. Their greetings have been conspicuously absent.

"Really?" I say, now half-listening to Marie, half-watching Leo.

"Oh yeah, long meetings with the door closed, long lunches with God knows who. Leo used to brag about showing Dudley the ropes."

"How developmental of him." Leo and I finally make eye contact, if getting recognition from Leo's smiling, inscrutable eye slits across a room qualifies as eye contact. Leo nods at me, flashes a little wink, and makes an "okay" sign with his right hand. I nod solemnly in return. I wonder if he knows what is coming. How can he not know? How? Easy. Maybe he really does take me for as big a fool as I think he does. I'll know soon enough.

"I've got a list of phone messages for you long as your arm," Marie says. "Why don't you get this workday under way?"

"You're right, Marie. As usual." I raise my arm to get the group's attention. "People," I say in a voice just short of shouting. "People!" That gets some quiet. "Marie just reminded me that we're in the publishing business, and if we all don't get back to work soon, we won't have anything to publish. So before we go back into the salt mines, let me say thanks for this lovely welcome home. I really missed you all, and I'm glad to be back. I want to catch up with each and every one of you individually. I just want to say that I think you are a terrific group. Now what, you're probably asking, was the past few weeks all about anyway? It's a fair question. I'm kind of asking it myself. It was about a misunderstanding. But that's all cleared up and, most important of all, it means full steam ahead for *Elixir*. This process of becoming part of a bigger company has its bumps, I guess, and we've just been over one of them. American is a great company with terrific resources that we can really take advantage of. And we will. But one of the reasons American was so interested in us is our independence and entrepreneurial spirit. And what we've done is clarify with American the independence we at *Elixir* need in order to do what we do. Which is put out the best medical life-style book in the business. I want you to know that I'm proud of everyone in this room. You guys are great. The best. Now let's get back to work."

Applause. I think my words were appreciated. I think I really meant them. No, I'm sure I did. I certainly meant to mean them. They were not just automatic management bullshit, I tell myself. Then why did that thought cross your mind, I ask. The message from Joe and Jerry and Ted and others is clear: You're abandoning us. Are you the guy we connect to or should we be looking elsewhere?

Just then a voice from across the room tries to speak above the clapping and chatter.

"Just let me say . . ." It is Leo. "Just let me say . . ." The clapping subsides. "Just let me say on behalf of all of us, and I think I can speak for everyone, Bob, we want you to know that nothing, but nothing, could shake our confidence in you and your vision. We missed you. And we couldn't be happier now that we've got you back. So, welcome home, Bob, welcome home."

More applause, but softer this time. The crowd begins to disperse, people heading for their desks. Jeannie resumes her post at the reception desk. Leo lingers in his corner after the others have gone. I stand in my spot on the other side of the room, making no motion to go see Leo. There is an awkward silence between us.

I stand. Leo stands. More awkward silence. Then Leo gives in.

"Welcome back, Bob," he says and starts to cross the room toward me, right hand extended in preparation for one of those big, sincere Leo Sayles handshakes. I raise one hand to signal him to stop. My voice is not welcoming.

"Leo, let's go to your office."

He halts in midstep, the charm still on full blast. "Good idea. Just what I was going to suggest."

As he turns, I walk past him briskly and head down the corridor toward his office. I enter first and go to the center of the room. He walks in after me and stands in the doorway.

"Close the door," I say coldly.

"Sure, Bob. Good idea. We've got a lotta stuff to go over."

He closes the door and stands facing me. There are two visitor's chairs in front of his desk. I am standing between them, blocking his route to the big executive chair behind his desk. With a small gesture, I offer him the visitor's chair on the left.

"Have a seat," I say.

He hesitates for an instant, shifting back and forth on his feet, as if looking for a way to run around me to the Seat of Power behind the desk.

"Sit down, Leo."

"I, uh, I've got my notes in the desk. We gotta lotta stuff to go over, Bob. I gotta bring you back up to speed. You know how fast this world keeps goin' round and round."

"Just sit down." I sit myself in the right-hand chair and gesture for Leo to take the one beside it.

"My notes, Bob. My notes." He takes a halting step forward.

I shake my head and motion toward the chair next to me.

"Just sit down."

Leo hesitates, thinking for an instant, and finally obeys. He looks a little confused and hurt.

"Say, Bob, what's up? What's the matter?"

I stare at him in silence. I want the moment to hang in the air with maximum discomfort. It does. Leo responds with a nervous attempt to charm me.

"You know, Bob, there's a lotta good feeling out there." He points toward the reception area. "A lotta good feeling. You're a lucky man, Bob, a very lucky man. I mean you've, uh, made yourself lucky. You know we all missed you. You know that, don't you? That was a bitch of a misunderstanding, wasn't it, a bitch of one. I knew it'd get cleared up quickly, I knew it. And any day now, the ABC report'll come in. Then it'll be smooth sailing all the way. Yes sir, *smooth* sailing. That's what I been tellin' all our accounts. And believe me, they're hangin' in there with us. All the way."

He pauses to think again, then emits a forced little chuckle. "But you know, isn't it just like Jack Parsons to lose those records. Great old guy, that Jack, but no businessman. Old Jack, still screwing the rest of us up, even after he's gone."

I keep my deadpan stare locked on Leo, letting him ramble on.

"Now I gotta tell you, the ABC challenge did do some damage. It did. But it's nothing we can't fix. And I've already got some ideas I been workin' up. But with that rebate program of Woodcock's, well, we kinda rubbed the problem in everybody's faces. It may even be the smart thing to let 'em keep the space credits even after ABC clears us. You know, at this point, they kinda figure they got it comin'. Now, I got a summary status report, client by client." Leo half-stands, holding himself by the arms of the chair. "It's in my desk. Take me just a second to get it." He starts to raise himself fully, asking permission with a questioning look. I nod solemnly for him to sit back down. He does.

"Geez, Bob, don't you want to go over my status report?"

"What were you doing having meetings with Howie Marcus?"

"I haven't had any meetings with Howie Marcus."

"Yes, you did."

"Well, sure, when he was trying to get you to sell way back when. But not since then. Not since you told him to fuck off. Marcus is your old buddy, not mine. I told you then he was bad news. It took you a while to listen to me. What's this about?"

"You ran out of here to have lunch with him just a few weeks ago. Marie saw you."

"Marie's got it wrong. I haven't seen him in at least seven, eight months."

"Yeah? Well, do you know Ken Atwood?"

"Huh?"

"Do you know Ken Atwood?"

"What are you talkin' about, Bob?"

Emphatically, almost phonetically, I repeat, *"Do-you-know-Ken-Atwood?"*

"Ken Atwood?"

"That's right," I snap. "Ken Atwood. Group Vice President, Mackey Magazine Group."

"Yeah, sure. Of course I know him. Everybody who's been in trade publishing for more than ten minutes knows Ken. What's he got to do with the price a eggs in China?"

"Do you know Elton Mackey?"

"Mackey? His boss?"

"Yes, Mackey his boss. Do you know him?"

"What's this third degree all about?"

"Just answer me. Do you know him?"

"Sure. I mean I met him a couple a times. You know, at a dinner, convention, industry bullshit, like that. I don't remember exactly when.

Sometimes he shows up at those things to press the flesh, see how the peons live or somethin'."

"What did Mackey promise you if I sold *Elixir* to him instead of American?"

Leo is dumbstruck by my question. He sits motionless and drained of expression. He looks down at his lap, cups his chin in one hand, then looks back at me, his face a vacant question mark. "Huh?" he asks.

"A finder's fee? A bigger title? A bigger expense account? What?"

"I don't know what you're talking about."

"You told Atwood my every move. What was in it for you?"

"Bob, what are you talkin' about?"

"You were disappointed when the deal went to American. But you recovered. You're flexible. You became asshole buddies with Dudley to get yourself a direct pipeline to Woodcock."

"Bob, this is business, I try to get along with people, but what's that got to do with Atwood and those crazy—?"

"During my vacation, I did a little research. You know what I found out?" I do not wait for a reply. "You know who the new owners of MFI are? The guys who somehow couldn't find the computer tapes from *MD Office*? Well, MFI was bought by Cuyahoga Information Systems, Inc. Ever hear of them?"

"I don't think so."

"They're eighty percent owned by a Netherlands Antilles corporation called EM Investco, which you discover, if you bother to trace it, is a tax-dodge shell corporation owned by none other than EMC, which is, of course, Elton Mackey of Cleveland. And on the new board of MFI is none other than your friend and Mackey's VP, Ken Atwood."

"Bob, I don't know what all this has got to do with—"

"Wait; it gets better. You introduced me to Jack Parsons. You two were buddies from way back. You knew Jack and his operation inside out. Maybe you did get your finder's fee in the end—by leading Mackey to MFI."

"Bob," Leo pleads, "what are you—?"

I barge ahead. "Now if anybody was in a position to have Jack's voice on tape it was you. Maybe a convention speech, party tape, phone conversation, I don't know. But there are just too many goddamn coincidences here. And there's a nice crossover of interests when it comes to getting me out of the picture. And all the different currents cross at one common point. Because whether it's Mackey who wants me out or Woodcock, there's one person who stands to benefit. One guy who's in a position to help either or both of them make it happen. And that guy is you, Leo. You."

"Bob, what the—?"

"You just happened to be prowling around my office earlier that morning when Woodcock came charging over. And you just happened to be out of the office when all the shit hit the fan. Only somebody close to Parsons and Mackey *and* me could help make the phony cassette happen. Only somebody close to Mackey, Woodcock, and me could get in here to plant the tape and then get through to Woodcock to tip him off. But, Leo, when you called that morning, you left the smell of your goddamn cologne all over my phone. Leo, you've been trying to fuck me left and right. But it's over now. Over."

"Jesus, Bob. Jesus."

"Go ahead. Deny it. Go ahead. And while we're at it, what were you doing here on Saturday, taking files out of the office?" I reach across his desk and grab his phone and put the handset to my ear. I hunch my back conspiratorially and re-enact a hushed mock conversation with the dial tone. "Yeah, I got the stuff. All of it. Yeah, it's in my briefcase. That's right. No one'll know but us." As I pull the phone away from my face, my nostrils get a final whiff of House of Lords.

Leo looks genuinely alarmed for an instant but quickly recovers. "Oh, that?" he asks, smiling broadly, inscrutably.

"Yeah, that." I sneer.

"*You* were here on Saturday?"

"You bet your ass I was. Right down the hall."

He pauses, keeping the smile up. "Oh, Bob, Bob, I can explain . . ."

"No, you can't. You can't explain anything. Leo, since the day I hired you, you've had it in for me. I'm just this kid that you made into somebody. And when you didn't get what you figured you had coming to you—which is everything—you went to get some outside assistance."

"Bob, I don't know what you're talking about. All this stuff with Mackey and Atwood and tapes, I don't—"

"I'm just about finished, which means you are, too. It almost worked. Almost. But you're just a space rep, Leo, a salesman. And an old-fashioned one at that. If you were meant to be a publisher or an owner or anything more than what you are, it would have happened a long time ago. You're right about one thing, though. The world *is* spinning faster and faster. And you've done about all the damage you're gonna do." I pause. If he is reacting, he is not showing it. He is holding onto his client-ready smile. "Leo, you are fired. Fired. I want you out of here this instant. I'll send you your last check and all your personal effects—after we go through them to make sure there's nothing confidential among them. Just get out of here and don't ever let me see you again. Ever."

Leo stiffens in the chair, his back perfectly upright. The charm has drained from his round face; his beady little eyes are now wide open.

"Bob, you've got this all wrong. I don't know what you're talking about with this crazy conspiracy thing. It's craziness. I don't know what you're talking about; I really don't. Believe me."

"Leo, you're good, I'll grant you that. But you're not that good. I'll never believe you. I've given you my final word. Just pick yourself up out of that chair and get out of here, and I'll thank you not to talk to anyone on your way out. Unless you want me to help you physically out the door." I feel three years of accumulated mistrust bursting out of me all at once.

"Size it up for yourself. You've got twenty pounds on me. But I've got twenty *years* on you. And I'm in better shape than you ever dreamt of being, what with all the oceans of expense-account booze you've poured through that body of yours."

Leo stands up, carefully buttons his suit jacket, and slowly brushes away the wrinkles. Fastidiously, he pulls at one shirt cuff, then the other, to get just the right amount of white showing. He takes a deep breath.

"Young man, you are making a mistake. A big mistake."

I shake my head no.

"Oh yes, you are. I *made* you. I made this magazine. Without me, *Elixir* would have folded like a hundred other shoestring start-ups. I brought this magazine my credibility. My contacts. My experience. My years in the business. My word. Do you think those important advertisers were buying *your magazine*? Hah! They were buying *my* credibility. Do you think they believed in *Elixir* when it was struggling to get a foothold? They believed in me! In me! They bought because *I* told them to. Because *I* serviced the relationship, because *I* built the trust, because they're *my* goddamn clients. You think you can throw me out, just like that? You think so? You don't even own this company anymore."

"I know, but I've got Woodcock right where I want him. I am in control of this company, acquisition or no. Nobody, but nobody, at American will back you up. I guarantee it. You are history. Maybe Mackey will have you. At last."

"You can't do this to me, Macallan."

"I just did. Now beat it."

"I warn you, you'll regret it."

"The only regret I have is ever hiring you in the first place."

"I warn you, I made this book. I can break it, too."

"Why don't you give your pal Atwood a call. Tell him you're available for full-time space sales in addition to your freelance espionage work."

Leo's face is flushed, his mouth contorted, trying to hold back the explosion.

"If *Inside Print* or *The Doughtery Report* calls," I say, regaining a more professional tone, "I'll say you resigned to pursue other interests, the usual face-saving bullshit, okay? Now leave. Just leave."

He sniffs deeply through his nostrils, pauses, and turns to go. He stops before taking the first step and looks back at me. "You will regret this," he says in an angry whisper. He turns and walks to the door, his posture stiff and erect. He opens the door and exits. I listen to his footsteps going down the hall and out of *Elixir*.

"Here's to taking charge," I say, raising my glass of house Chardonnay. "I'll drink to that," Wendy says, returning my toast with her glass of seltzer and lime. Click.

This impromptu splurge dinner is to celebrate my first day back at the office. Le Mec is the hottest and priciest new restaurant of the year. Normally, there's a two-week wait for reservations, especially for this prime dinner hour of eight o'clock. But it is the Tuesday night after Labor Day and there happened to have been a cancellation when Marie called late this afternoon. So here we are in this room of walls and ceilings covered in dazzling faceted shards of mirrors. The effect is like walking into a kaleidoscope. The rich and powerful occupy the private banquettes around the perimeter. Wendy and I have a table in the center.

"Can Leo really do any damage?" Wendy asks above the racket.

"I suppose he could try," I reply, feeling expansive after my day of triumphant return. "And maybe twenty years ago a guy like him could make good on threats like that. But I have to believe that the business has become more professional than that. There are too many people going over these marketing decisions with objective criteria. And besides, *Elixir* is established. We've got real numbers, even with this ABC challenge. Maybe in Leo's good old days it was strictly a personal sell. But not anymore. Publishing's a numbers sell. For the decision makers, it's a professional call."

"Do you think he'll go with Mackey's new magazine?"

"I assume that's how Mackey will reward him for planting that faked cassette. But I can't imagine Mackey making Leo publisher of *Panacea*. He's already got that heavyweight he stole from McGraw-Hill. He could make him sales manager. Yeah, that's probably the best he'd be willing to do."

"That's all?"

"That's all he's good for. He could never actually run anything."

"Why not?"

"He's a salesman. Period. He's got no ideas of his own; he's all show and personality. Mr. Expense Account. He hasn't a clue what substance is."

"So everybody just used him and then threw him away." Wendy takes a bite of her chicken poached in foie gras. "Including you."

"I suppose so." I take another sip of wine and a bite of my skatefish in black butter and caper sauce.

A little silence; we chat briefly about the rattle our bedroom air conditioner makes and eat some more in silence.

"I'm not saying that accusingly," Wendy says through a mouthful, jumping to another subject in her usual fashion, that is, without so much as a hint.

"Huh?" I ask, momentarily confused. I strain for an instant, thinking, then catch up to her train of thought. She is back on the topic of Leo.

"That guy's a dirty bastard, planting that tape and all. But in the end, he sounds like such a loser," she says, moving some chicken bones around on her plate. "All I'm saying is . . . now that everything's okay and we're safe . . . we can afford to show a little, uh . . ."

"A little what?"

"A little generosity of spirit."

"You're kidding."

"I am not."

I look directly into Wendy's eyes. "You really mean it, don't you?"

She nods.

"Okay, Wendy. I don't wish the bastard any harm—now that he's out of my way. Are you worried about his career plans or something?"

"No, he tried to screw us."

"You know, you're really funny."

"Why do you say that?"

"You *are* worried about Leo."

"No, I just don't like to see people get hurt. Even crummy bastards."

"Believe me, Leo will be fine. There'll always be work for a guy like Leo. Always."

"Okay." She raises her glass of sparkling water. "Here's to his next job being far, far away from us."

"I'll drink to that," I reply, taking another sip of my wine.

Wendy puts down her glass and pushes her chair out to get up from the table. "Ladies' room again," she says with a smile as she pats her tummy; her condition is not yet visible to the outside world. "I'll be right back."

As she walks away through the maze of tables, I think of Leo and pick at my food. I always seem to find something a little disappointing in finally getting to what people consider the top. Like this restaurant. The dishes are prepared to perfection and presented like works of art. People wait weeks to be charged a fortune for it and brag about it for weeks afterward. And yes, it is good. Very good, really. The whole experience is lovely. Still, when it's over, all you've had is just a piece of chicken.

When Wendy returns, she is wide-eyed. "You'll never guess who I spotted on my way to the john."

"Who?"

She makes a gesture of pulling a great hunk of imaginary hair from one ear across her head and over to the other ear. "Atwood, the guy with the comb-over who tried to grope me at Mackey's party. Sitting with none other than Howie Marcus and some other guy. They didn't see me, thank God."

"Who were they with?"

"I don't know. Some prep. Investment banker type. Not exactly three fellas you'd expect at the same table."

235

"Where are they?"

"Over there." She gestures with her head. "Corner banquette way to the left."

"I gotta check this out."

"The prep is sitting facing the wall next to Atwood. You can see his face in the mirror."

I get up from my chair.

Yes, I think, as I walk through the tables toward the corner. It had to be Leo. It had to be. He was the one point where all those people intersect. From the leaks to Atwood during my negotiations with American to the cassette in my desk, he is the common point. I remember vividly Atwood's card on Leo's blotter.

I walk with my head down, trying to look invisible and not to bump into anything. I spy the banquette out of the corner of my eye. Yes, there is the back of Atwood's Grecian Formula comb-over. I can see his face reflected in the faceted slivers of mirror on the wall. Across the table facing outward is Howie Marcus, too wrapped up in conversation to notice me.

Then I look closer. Their companion is the only other outsider who knew about my American deal before it was consummated. The man who made the deal happen. The Hale Hadley investment banker. Tim Conover.

"You can't let it make you paranoid," Wendy says in a loud, happy voice from the bathroom. I am sitting on the bed, thinking, half-undressed after Le Mec.

"You brooded all through dessert," she says, talking over the sound of water running in the sink and through the soap covering her face. "Good thing I'm pregnant or that raspberry tart of yours would have gone to waste. You know, I could get used to having two desserts." I hear her splashing the soap off.

The phone rings. In my tense, wound-up condition, I lunge across to Wendy's side of the bed and grab it before it can ring a second time. Who could be calling now? It is past eleven.

"Hello?"

Click. The line goes dead. I replace the phone, get off the bed, and go to my open closet door to hang up my suit and tie.

"Who was that?" Wendy asks. I look back over my shoulder. She is scrubbed and dry and standing naked, except for panties, in the bedroom doorway. There is now just the slightest swell to her belly, visible only when she's undressed like this.

"Wrong number, I guess. They just hung up." I go back to hanging up my pants.

"Oh," she says, "at least you didn't get any heavy breathing."

I hear her walk up behind me and slip off her panties. Her hand reaches over my shoulder; she tosses the balled-up panties into the laundry bag on my closet hook. As she withdraws her hand, she squeezes my arm and deposits a little kiss on my shoulder. Behind me, I hear the springs creak, the sheet being pulled back, and the rustle of a magazine as she climbs into bed. I stand, in boxer shorts and socks, staring at the row of business suits lined up like soldiers in my closet. My mother would have been proud. Respectability. The cleanliness and dignity of office work. I snicker to myself.

The phone rings again.

"Hello," Wendy says, picking it up. A pause. "Yes," she says with unusual coldness. Whoever it is, it is not a friend. I turn around to look at her. She is sitting up in bed, the sheet covering her from the waist down. I shoot her an inquiring look to find out who it might be, but she is listening with complete attention, staring down into her lap. I shrug to myself, slip off my socks and shorts, and drop them into the laundry bag. Naked now, I turn and face Wendy. She is still staring downward, listening, listening.

I have to walk around the bed to get to my side. I make a wide arc and stop at Wendy's dresser in the far corner to turn off the lamp. As I click off the light, Wendy sighs very deeply and hangs up the phone.

"Who was it?" I ask.

The only light in the room now comes from Wendy's bedside lamp. It rakes across her, picking up the ripples in the sheets and leaving half of her face and one naked breast in shadow. Her mouth is open, but no sound comes out. She reaches for the sheet and pulls it up to her neck, covering her body in a protective motion.

"Friend of yours?" I ask, standing motionless on the other side of the room. I take a step toward the bed, and she finally speaks.

"Don't."

I take another step forward.

"Don't!" she repeats, this time more urgently.

"Don't what, honey? Who was that?" I take two more steps ahead. She pulls one hand out from under the sheet and thrusts it at me, palm out, like a traffic cop. I stop where I am, naked in the middle of the room.

"Robert." Her voice is trembling, almost cracking. I cannot remember her ever sounding so upset. "Robert, I want you to answer a question. And I want you to tell me the truth. The absolute God's honest truth. Promise me."

"Who was that just now?"

She ignores my query. "Promise me," she says in a low, quiet voice. "I want you to promise me."

"Sure, I promise. Wendy, what's all this about?" I take another step forward. The traffic cop's hand goes back up. With the other hand, she pulls the sheet tighter against herself. I stop. "Who *was* that?"

"Just answer me." She takes a deep, frightened breath. "Did you have an affair when you were in London?"

The bottom of my stomach falls out from under me and plummets forty stories down. "Did I what?"

"Did you have an affair when you were in London?"

My head is filled with noise. Static. Panic. "No, of course not. Who was that on the phone?"

"Just answer me." Her voice is cracking; she is on the verge of crying. "Did you have a blonde in your hotel room? As she was leaving, did she press your hand against her breast? Did you kiss her with your mouth open? Did she say, 'You'll always be inside me. I can't wait till the next time'? Did that happen? *Did it?*"

At first, I cannot find my voice. I reach deep inside for it, but the nerve networks and the muscles don't seem to work. Nothing is connecting.

"Is it true?"

"Yes, but . . ." It sounds like someone else talking for me inside my body.

"But what?"

"It's not what you think. I didn't have an affair. Really, I kicked her out of the room."

"I asked you if anything happened in London while we were in Divonne. Three or four times I asked. You said nothing. Nothing!"

"It was nothing. It *is* nothing. Believe me. Who was that on the phone?"

"You lied to me, Robert."

"I didn't make love to her. Honest. I kissed her once. Then I sent her away. She kissed me like that in the doorway after I told her to leave. But nothing happened. Absolutely nothing."

"Who was she? Tell me, Robert. Who was she?"

I take another step toward the bed. "Who was that on the phone?" I ask. "Who was telling you this?"

Wendy pulls the sheet tighter around herself. She pulls up her legs and hugs them. "Tell me," she says again in the low, still voice. "Who was she?"

I realize I cannot make things any worse. "Laura Chasen," I sigh.

"Je-sus! I knew it!"

"Wendy, you don't understand. Who was that?"

"Oh, I understand perfectly well."

"Please, who was that?"

"That was Leo. He says he was standing in the hall in Grosvenor House about to close the door of his room when he saw the two of you. He heard it all."

"I can explain, Wendy. Honest I can. I can explain everything." I listen to my stupid, pathetic words with horror and revulsion. I cannot believe I just said that. But I cannot think of anything else to say. I cannot think of anything. Period.

Wendy lets go of her legs. Still clutching the sheet to her neck with one hand, she reaches underneath with the other hand and touches her tummy. She looks down where her hand is and winces as if she feels a pain there. Her glance rises slowly up to me. I am frozen where I stand. Naked.

"Robert," she says in a voice that is deafeningly quiet, "I think you'd better go. Leave this apartment," she whispers between clenched teeth. *"Now."*

OCTOBER

CHAPTER TWENTY-NINE

"Happy birthday, Son."

"Thanks, Dad," I reply with unconvincing cheer. Outside my office window, the city is endless gray and drizzle. I cradle the phone against my shoulder as I gather up papers for the big meetings that await me later this morning.

"Geez, thirty-six years old," Clint says, sounding bright and jocular. His tone is most out of character. Maybe he is looking out at one of those brilliant New England fall days, the kind I miss on days like this—with limitless blue sky, blinding ochre sunshine, and fiery gold and red leaves. "You're really gettin' on there, Son," he jokes. "Good thing I'm gettin' younger every year." He pronounces it "yunngah." "Might catch up with you one a these years."

"Maybe," I offer limply.

"You still sound kinda down."

Who? Me? I can't imagine why. My pregnant wife has thrown me out. She will not return my phone calls. I am living alone in a goddamn hotel. No, wait. That is the good news. The hotel is just a few blocks from the office. So I can be right nearby and not miss a moment of the collapse of everything I thought I had built at *Elixir*.

"You and Wendy still . . . uh?" Since Clint has never quite understood Wendy and her urban ways and probably never quite approved of her, he had only a congratulatory grunt when he heard she was pregnant. And since our blowup, he tries to stay away from the touchy subject.

"Yeah, still." I force a chipper tone. "Listen, Dad, thanks for calling with birthday greetings. I've been so busy I forgot what day it was." Not true. I just wish I could.

"How're you comin' with gettin' those advertisers back on board?"

"I'm giving it everything I've got. Believe me I am."

"That's good. You always had that gift a gab. Helluva talker my boy is."

239

By now, I get the feeling that Clint fancies himself something of an expert on the magazine business.

"Yeah, Dad, I'm going to have to do a lot of talking this time."

"I figure you're up to it. That's what you New Yorkers do best. You're all big talkers." God, I hope he's right. Talk is the only weapon I have to get myself out of this hole.

The day after I fired Leo, he started meeting with my clients. Suddenly, Steiner-Rochelle and PharmCo canceled their advertising. The polite brush-off letters cited budget cuts as the reason. A few days later, Leo was appointed national sales director of *Panacea* and started poaching my people—Mike Carmody, his favorite *Elixir* sales rep, plus assistants from my production and circulation departments. The continuous stream of phone messages the defectors leave at *Elixir* shows the hand of Leo and Mackey at war. They continue to unsettle further the already unsettled environment at the office. My old *Elixir* is coming undone. Just like the rest of my life. Even to my most loyal staff I have become a partial stranger, someone on the way out. Just as it was when I was starting out, I feel I must carry it all myself.

"So who are you seein' today?" he asks.

"Some of my former advertisers. You know, more big companies you've never heard of."

"Go ahead; give your old man a try. I been talkin' to you and lookin' at those *Wall Street Journals* your brother leaves around the house. Come on; who're you seein'?"

"The marketing muckety-mucks at Steiner-Rochelle and PharmCo."

"Steiner what?"

"Rochelle. Big Swiss-owned operation. You know, French Swiss, German Swiss. Herr Steiner and Monsieur Rochelle, two chemical barons from the late nineteenth century, turned the Rhine into a toxic sewer."

"Uh-huh," he says, sounding a bit lost. "Now PharmCo I heard of. They make that cough medicine that helps you sleep."

"Yup, that's PharmCo." I add under my breath, "The lousy fuckers."

"What'sat?"

"Nothing, Dad."

"Is that the one who was doin' your special issue?"

"No."

"Isn't that the one you said you were seein'? The special issue guy?"

"That's Max McGuinn of Orem-Diedrich. He's my special issue guy." I laugh a little from nervousness. "My special issue savior. I'm taking him out on the town tonight."

"Oh yeah, him. The big guy Max."

"Yeah, the big guy Max."

Pause. Silence. I shuffle more papers and drop them into my briefcase.

"You know where your brother is right now?" he asks, sounding more excited than I've ever heard him.

"Isn't he in Bayport with you?"

"No sirree. He's in Tucson, Arizona. Takin' title to three Mister Muffler shops. That franchise deal a his is closin' tomorrow. He's movin' out there for good."

"Hey, that's great." I've been in such a fog with my own problems I had forgotten about his plans.

"Your brother's gonna make a lot of money. Just like you. Maybe even outdo you. You never know." Is that a little hint of needling in his voice or is it just his clumsy way of expressing enthusiasm? "He's even gonna let me invest a little in his partnership."

"Gee, that's great, Dad."

"Helluva business, mufflers and tailpipes. You get 'em in the door with a low-price offer; then you scare the shit out of 'em and get 'em up to a high-price installation. Your brother's gonna be a big success. Watch out, he's gonna catch up to you pretty quick."

"Tell him I wish him all the best."

"I will. I'm callin' him next. Gotta make sure those lawyers aren't taking all his money. You know 'bout closings."

"Yeah, Dad. I know." I do not mean to let out an exasperated sigh.

"Hey, Son?"

"What?" I feel tired. More tired than I ever thought I could feel.

"You're gonna get through this fine. You're just not used to troubles. Things have always been so smooth for you." There is no point in reopening this old argument with him. I am too busy, and nothing will ever change his mind. "Besides," he says, still kidding, "you made so much money they can't touch you. Nobody can touch you. Isn't that right?" He laughs a laugh I am meant to share with him. He is not looking for an answer.

"Yeah," I reply with a fake smile in my voice. "That's right."

"Well . . . happy birthday, Son. You'll be fine, ya hear."

"Thanks for calling, Dad. Bye."

The whole lineup of Steiner-Rochelle marketing managers is sitting before me. Finally. This is my one and only opportunity to undo the damage Leo has done and set the record straight. Leo convened this group with a few hours' notice. I have been pleading for a chance to come here for nearly a month. So far, Hoffman and his crew have been listening politely, but I do not think they have heard a thing.

"Now look at this one here," I say, waving another expense report. "Two hundred and fifty dollars for a business lunch with you, Ron Hoffman, Steiner-Rochelle director of marketing. On a Saturday. At Ponti's in Mamaroneck." I pause and look at Hoffman. "You say you don't remember that lunch with Leo?"

"We've had so many meals together, Leo and I," he replies, scratching the wavy gray hair along the side of his fat head. "I could probably remember if I tried hard, but what's the point?"

"What's the point?" I ask.

"Yeah, what's the point?" He is completely deadpan. "Two hundred and fifty dollars for a business lunch with Leo in Mamaroneck on a Saturday. Done it dozens a times. So what?"

"So what?" I repeat, hearing an edge come into my voice. I must control myself better. "The point, Ron," I am waving Leo's expense report again, "is that Ponti's in Mamaroneck is not a restaurant. It's a shoe store. Leo was buying shoes for himself, and he used *your* name to cheat *my* company."

"Oh, that," he replies, still deadpan. "I remember those shoes. He wore them to a lunch we had later. Yeah, they were nice. Kinda cordovan with tassels. I remember now. One day, I told him he oughtta get some new shoes 'cause the ones he had on looked like hell. Maybe you weren't paying him enough; I dunno."

I am getting nowhere. Hoffman and his men have been drinking from Leo's bounteous trough since the day they joined the Steiner-Rochelle marketing department. And Ron, the oldest and most senior, has been drinking the longest and the deepest. They were accustomed to Leo's infinite largess. And I took it away from them.

My earn-out can survive losing this account and maybe PharmCo. But Orem-Diedrich, sponsor of the special issue, has also decided "to review" its ad commitments. That loss would be devastating. I have an appointment to see PharmCo later this morning. That meeting will be important. But my big showdown will be the meeting and private dinner with Max McGuinn at the end of the day. Just to make life more stressful, in between I have been summoned to see Harry Woodcock. He is "very concerned" about, of all things, the diminishing profit outlook at *Elixir*. For the moment, I have my hands full trying out a new show called "The Documented Misdeeds of Leo Sayles," and it is laying a giant egg.

"Bob, Bob," Hoffman says, "let's be adult about this. We all live in the real world. I'll bet that your company, our company, or any other company could be a lot more profitable if we didn't allow any of these—what should we call 'em?—gray areas of accounting to come up. But let's face it. Accounting is just a way of measuring life. And life isn't black-and-white. It's gray. So accounting, like life, is gonna be gray, too." He pauses to let the room appreciate his little moment of philosophy. Perfectly on cue, the five marketing managers smile admiringly at their boss.

"It's gray," he repeats in case anyone missed it. "I'll bet I could boost the profits of this company by, I dunno, one percent if I took a real sharp pencil to every penny our executives spend on T and E. What do you think, fellas?" Hoffman shoots an amused look around the table, like a father who pretends to be angry with his mischievous boys but is actually proud of them for tearing up the neighbor's flower patch. "How much could we save if I made you guys toe the line? Huh? How much?"

The group answers with a nervous laugh.

"But, you know something, Bob," he continues. "The more I think about it, the more I think maybe there might not be so much profit there in the first place, if we didn't keep things, well, lubricated." He telegraphs to the table that he is ready to philosophize again. The brave young men in crisp white shirts and striped ties prepare for another burst of spontaneous admiration. "You see, in life if things aren't lubricated, they don't move. They get stuck. Business is no different, Bob. I'm sure you know that. Lubrication. It's a necessary condition of action, know what I mean?" He makes a poking gesture with his middle finger, clearly pretending to be inserting it into an imaginary vagina. He swirls the finger around a little. His boys laugh obediently.

"Okay, let's forget about the expense account abuses," I say, trying earnestly to pick up my cause again. "As I told you before, there were breaches of trust and security that could have serious implications for companies like yours, where confidentiality is so vital. I even caught him smuggling confidential files out of the office one weekend. In addition, I know for a fact that he—"

"Bob," Hoffman interrupts, "we hear you. And maybe it's all true. But it's academic. We think you've got a fine publication there, really fine. But we just had our budgets cut to the bone. I'm talking to the marrow, young man. The dollars just aren't there for the next six months. Come back after six months and we'll talk. You know the door at Steiner-Rochelle is always open to *Elixir*. We wish you all the best, Bob. All the best."

With that, Hoffman gets up from the table. His five marketing managers arise almost simultaneously, and in a moment the conference room is empty. I sit staring at my pile of painstakingly documented, completely useless evidence against Leo.

Outside it is still gray; mercifully, the drizzle has let up. The PharmCo tower is a two-block walk up Third Avenue from Steiner-Rochelle. I pass a pay phone on the corner. I cannot resist the temptation.

"Good morning, Truedale and Wolfson."

"Iris, before you—"

"Bob?"

"Is she there, Iris? Please, just tell me whether she's really in or not. I can't take any more stonewalling."

"You know what I'm supposed to tell you."

"Yeah, but come on. Give a guy a break."

"She's out of the office, really she is. Not supposed to be back until after lunch."

"Is she with Liz?"

"No, Liz is outta town today and tomorrow."

"Did she say where she'd be this morning?"

"Bob, you're putting me in the middle between you two guys. It's not fair."

"Don't tell me about fair."

"Listen, call here tomorrow morning. I promise I'll put you through by accident. Okay?"

"Just tell me, has she been feeling okay? Any morning sickness or stuff like that?"

"She's been fine. So far she only stayed home one morning this week."

"Has she—"

"Please, Bob. I got two other lines ringing and I'm here all alone. Call tomorrow morning like I said, okay?"

"Thanks, Iri—"

Click.

Lately, I have begun to notice just how many pay phones there are on the streets of New York. Since I now make a point to keep a pocketful of quarters at all times, I decide to make another call.

"Hi," says the scratchy female voice, "you've reached the answering machine at 581-9058. You can reach Robert Macallan at his office, 408-3232. Please wait for the—"

I slam the pay phone down. Yet again.

PharmCo headquarters is a grim, gray upended shoe box of steel and glass from the 1950s. A pass is waiting for me at the guard's desk in the grim, gray lobby. I am to go to the marketing department conference room, a place I have been to in the past with Leo.

On the eleventh floor, the receptionist tells me that Mr. Detweiler is on the phone but will join me shortly, so won't I please go in and make myself comfortable. As with Hoffman, it took much pleading on my part to get Detweiler to bring his product managers to this meeting. Now, as I'm about to face a group almost identical in outlook and composition to the Steiner-Rochelle crew, I try to reorganize my presentation mentally. What have I learned? First of all, I can't be so frontal in my attack against Leo. I've got to find an area where we can all start by agreeing. That's right; get them nodding their heads. Stuff no corporate citizen could disagree with in front of a group of fellow citizens.

I'll invoke the integrity of a publication, the integrity of a business. That's it! I'll pretend I'm Harry Woodcock, the hypocrite's hypocrite. I take a piece of paper from my briefcase and, grateful for the delay, start to make a new outline. I dig into the job, arranging and rearranging the sequence of accusations. This time the expense account abuses are just frosting on the cake, little afterthoughts. Anyone will plainly see that I *had* to do what I did. To preserve the integrity of the publication. To keep God knows what other information and confidential data, especially proprietary research we do for advertisers, from being leaked to God knows who. From the sound of this, it could be that I have rescued the entire pharmaceuticals industry from the forces of evil. This will go over well, I'm sure.

A peroxide blond secretary pokes her head into the conference room. "Mr. Detweiler says he'll be a few more minutes. Can you wait?"

"Sure," I say, now confident and happy about the meeting to come. "No problem." I go back to the outline and give it a good once-over. I'm proud. No one could disagree with any of the charges I'm making and still appear to have any integrity.

I breathe a sigh of relief and look at my watch. The meeting was scheduled to start fifteen minutes ago. I was grateful for the time alone, but now that I've got my ducks in a row, I'm eager to get the troops in here and get things started. Another fifteen minutes go by. It's eleven-thirty. I get up from the conference room table and go back down the hall to the plump, dark-haired receptionist.

"Mr. Detweiler and the marketing managers on their way?" I ask.

She looks up from her magazine. "Haven't they come in yet? Here, let me check with his secretary." She dials. "Hi, Peggy, it's Terri at reception. . . . The meeting with Mr. Detweiler and the marketing managers in the conference room? . . . Yeah. The gentleman who's here. . . . Uh-huh. . . . Okay, I'll tell him." She hangs up. "Just a few minutes more. Mr. Detweiler got an emergency call from our French office. They're, uh, five hours ahead of us, you know, so it must be the end of the day there."

"Six."

"Huh?"

"France is six hours ahead of us." I get a flash of a memory. Calling my office from the chair by our window in the Château de Divonne. The sound of Wendy singing and splashing in the bathtub, the bathroom door open, her scratchy voice echoing off the marble floors and walls.

"Yeah, of course," Terri says, "just a few more minutes. Okay?"

I go back to the conference room to wait for the emergency call to end. What am I going to tell Woodcock? If all three advertisers hold with their cancellation decisions, *Elixir*'s annual profit picture could be bleak and my earn-out could be in the soup. We'll have to scramble to find new advertisers outside the clubby world of pharmaceuticals. Certainly not impossible, but very time-consuming and, with the lead times required in publishing, potentially dangerous. But if I can pull things out in this meeting with PharmCo and then persuade old Max, things will be fine. The question is, How exactly can I get Max McGuinn to reinstate his sponsorship of the special issue? Do I bowl him over with the professional reasons why the buy makes sense for Orem-Diedrich? I've got my numbers presentation all lined up, but he knows the numbers inside out. Do I try to become his crony like Leo? Will that move the inscrutable old man my way? Maybe a combination. That's right. I'll give him both. Professional media reasoning *and* professional glad-handing. I can do that; I know I can. Whatever the old guy wants tonight I'll get him. Just like Leo.

Another fifteen minutes have gone by. I get up to revisit the receptionist.

"Terri," I say as I walk down the hall, "any word from Mr. Detweiler and the marketing group?"

She turns around. "Nothing yet." She holds up a rumpled copy of the *Daily News*. "You wanna read the paper? Do the puzzle or something? Sports section?"

"No thanks, Terri. I'll just hang out."

"I'm sure they won't be too much longer."

"Thanks."

I go back to the empty conference room and pace.

When I look at my watch again, it is two minutes past noon. I've been here a solid hour.

I poke my head out the conference room and look down toward the reception area. "Oh, Terri!" I half-shout. "Any word yet?"

The dark-haired woman who turns around to answer my call is not Terri. I walk down the hall in order to see her better and figure out what is going on.

"Oh, hi," she says. "Terri went to lunch. I'm Roz. Can I help you?"

"There's supposed to be a meeting in the conference room with Mr. Detweiler and his marketing managers. About an hour ago. Can you check with his secretary to see if he'll be here soon?"

She shrugs vacantly.

"Can you please check? This meeting is very important."

She looks at me with mild disgust. I am just another one of the idiots she is forced to put up with. "I'm tellin' ya, his secretary's not there. I saw her leave."

"Can you please check for me? Please."

"I can, but it won't—"

"Just check for me. Please, just do it."

"Okay, okay." She picks up the phone and starts to dial. "But it won't do any good."

"Why not?"

"I just saw Mr. Detweiler go down in the elevator with two other men. They had their coats on and said they were going to lunch. Said they wouldn't be back till three or so. You still want me to call?"

"No thanks."

"Oh," she says, suddenly remembering something, "one of the gentlemen with Mr. Detweiler asked me to give you this." She hands me a business card. The name printed on it does not surprise me: *Leo Sayles, Vice President, National Sales Manager, PANACEA, A Mackey Publication.*

I walk back to the marketing conference room, gather up my papers once again, and hit the street, vowing to keep all pay phones out of my field of vision.

"Mr. Macallan, welcome, welcome." Woodcock ushers me into his office with his most convincing mock friendliness. "Have a seat, Bob, make yourself comfortable."

"Thanks, Harry." I settle in across from his desk, in the same chair I sat in last time.

"How are things going?" he asks.

"Not bad."

"Really? That's not what I'm hearing." A big smile.

"Well, things aren't great, that's for sure. But I think we've got them under control." The report from ABC came in last month, authenticating for all the world that all our paid subscribers are, have been, and always were bona fide paid subscribers. It never did the damage it might have since

American, through dear Harry, decided to take such a strong public stand behind us. With that kind of public commitment, it would have been hard for competitors, even Mackey, to make too much hay out of what turned out to be a very temporary question.

"Bob, I'm very concerned about these advertisers dropping out."

"So am I." Brace yourself, Macallan, here it comes. Just be cool.

"Are these losses related to your firing of Leo Sayles?"

"I can't say."

"I told you I didn't think that was a good move. Dudley, for one, said that Leo was quite a good salesman, a veteran pro, a fine resource."

"We've been over this, Harry. Leo was a very good sales rep and a very bad man. He had to go."

"And he took that kid with him to *Panacea,* what's his name."

"Mike Carmody."

"Yes. Dudley says he was all right, too. And some more staff have followed, I understand."

"We can do fine without them. Excess head count."

"That's not the point. Defections like that are terrible for an organization. Especially a small one like yours."

He is right. But I would never admit it. The underlying feeling of trust, sharing, and confidence I worked so hard to build at *Elixir* is gone. In its place is a mild undercurrent of paranoia.

"So what are you doing about these account losses?" Harry asks.

"Well, I'm having meetings and making presentations. That's what you do. You meet with people and get them back on board."

"How many have you gotten back on board?"

"Well, uh, none yet. But a couple of them are very, very close. Another meeting or two and we'll have them back."

"Really?"

"Yes, I think so."

"Really?"

"That's what I said. That's my best judgment."

"Like which ones? Orem-Diedrich? Steiner-Rochelle? PharmCo?"

"Yeah. They're all in process right now. I'm confident."

"I heard you were going to see all three of them today. Two morning meetings and dinner with the third."

"You did?"

"That's right."

"How did you hear that?"

"I have my sources. Remember, your staff are American employees now. Loyal American employees."

"I see."

"How are your meetings going?"

"Like I said, they're in process."

"Are you going to save those accounts?"

"I'm going to do my damnedest."

247

Woodcock drops the mask of cordiality. "I didn't ask you how hard you were going to try. I asked you if you're going to save the accounts. You remember, the monies? The profits you owe to American in exchange for becoming a rich man."

Dramatic pause. No, make that melodramatic.

"You know," Woodcock says, "if there's one thing I care about, it's profits. *Profits.* I think that's the only fair measure of what we do. Don't you agree?" He lays the irony on very thick. "Everything hinges on profits. If there are no profits, there are no employees, no community contributions, no taxes paid, no earn-outs, no nothing. Especially now, in this embattled environment American is in, we are all on the hot seat to produce profits." He picks up a binder and fondles it. It is the Blaine Consulting report I gave him. "All of us, Bob, are on the hot seat." He smiles devilishly. "Now I went to bat for you and got you the independence you wanted. But I can only justify that kind of independence to management as long as you can produce that stream of dollars." He gives the Blaine Consulting report a fond little tap. "But it looks to me that your stream is about to run dry." He sets the report down. "Now as the executive directly responsible for your profit performance, as the executive who went out on a limb to get you the independence you said you needed, that tells me that I owe it to this corporation to do something before it's too late."

"What do you mean, 'do something'?"

"Take charge of the situation. Bring you back into the corporate fold. If you can't deliver on your own what you said you could deliver on your own, I'm going to have to *help* you—in order to make the numbers we both want you to make."

"What exactly does that mean?"

"It means that your continued independence depends on the income stream that seems to be drying up. You either produce results your way or you produce results my way. If your way doesn't work, you leave me no responsible alternative except to step in and do it my way. I ran some computer numbers myself based on this very thorough Blaine study, and, given your impending shortfall, no one would disagree with me for taking back control." He smiles. "Not Drummond, not your friend R. Bingham Addison or anyone else on the board." The smile gets bigger still. "Not even Grubman and the Belsky brothers."

"Harry, you've got to let me fix this situation myself."

"I don't know, Bob. How much rope, I mean, how much time do you need?"

"Another month."

"Another month? Do you realize the damage that could occur in that time?"

I have no master plan ready to combat him. I don't know what I should say next. I am listening to hear what my counterattack is as it comes out of my mouth. I cannot imagine what I will say. I hope I will be convincing.

"Harry," I say, faking maximum confidence, "if you step in the middle of my valiant turnaround, I can make a lot of noise. Given all the press releases American has issued about its new entrepreneurial spirit, it's a story American's competitors would love to cover. And I'll give it to them. Can't you see it in *Forbes* or *Business Week*? 'Magazine monolith stifles spunky start-up.' Harry, the jury is still out on this. I demand more time."

That's a good threat, Macallan. One that Harry can understand. Well done.

"How much time are you asking for?" Harry snaps.

"A month. Give me another month. No, make it six weeks. Six weeks. Middle of November. I'll have the revenues back, I'll finish out my contract, then I'll be out of here and out of your life. And you can do whatever the hell you want to to *Elixir*."

Harry looks at his datebook, flips ahead a few pages, and makes a note in the future. "If this thing isn't back on track by then, I'm taking over. Then we'll see how much you end up with. And no one will blame me."

I nod assent.

"Results, Macallan. Or else."

"Yes, results." I pause. "Say, who is your source at *Elixir* now that Dudley is gone?"

"Macallan, it's not your company anymore. Those people work for me, for American. *I* am their future. *You* are their past. You have six weeks. I'm watching you."

"Anything else?"

"Not for the moment."

"Am I free to go?"

Pause. A little smile. "You are always free to go."

A knock sounds at the door.

"Come in," Woodcock says.

The door opens. It is Miss Boardman. She pretends I am not there.

"Mr. Drummond would like to see you for a minute," she says.

"Why, sure," Harry says, resuming his most jocular good-guy voice. "Bob and I are all finished, anyway. Aren't we, Bob?"

"You bet," I say, forcing a smile.

"Here, Bob, let me walk you out," Harry says, now the gracious host. We stand up and walk toward the door. Miss Boardman disappears down the corridor.

"Bob," Harry says a little louder than necessary, clearly performing for anyone who might be within earshot, "Bob, I want you to know you have my full confidence. I want you to go out there and slay those dragons. You have all my best wishes; you know that." What a manager, what a leader, what a motivator that Harry Woodcock is. He pats me on the shoulder, shakes my hand good-bye, and walks away toward Drummond's office suite. I proceed to the reception area and stop in front of the desk.

"Are you new or are you just sitting in for Fiona?" I ask the substitute Legs.

"Sorry?" she says, very proper, very clipped, very British.

"Are you sitting in for Fiona?"

"Who is Fiona?"

"Never mind," I say. I take the elevator down to the lobby. On the way back to my office I stop in the bank. I withdraw four thousand dollars in fifties and hundreds for tonight's festivities with Max McGuinn. I am preparing to use all the sleazy skills Leo taught me. Except for one. The money I will spend is from my personal account, not the company's.

"There's someone waiting for you," Jeannie tells me the second I open the door to Suite 1810.

"Who is he?" I ask.

"She." Jeannie looks at me disapprovingly. "She's been back there for over half an hour."

I am exhausted and beat up. I would love the chance to hide. I was looking forward to a little closed-door solitude before heading off for this evening's session with Max. This is just what I do not need. Another . . . thing. Maybe she is an official from the Audit Bureau of Circulation telling me that the post office never really delivered any issues of *Elixir*. Ever. Surprise! The past five years of my life and all this present turmoil have been nothing but a big practical joke, rigged by a perverse old classmate. As I turn the corner toward my office, I brace myself for another pummeling.

There is a woman sitting on the corner of Marie's desk, just outside my door. She and Marie are laughing together like old friends. Marie's eyes are wide with excitement, as if the woman she is giggling with were a celebrity or movie star. The woman is no famous actress, but she is a creature from a rarefied and glamorous world. She is Laura Chasen.

They are oblivious to my presence. Laura is leaning forward to share another delicious tidbit of girl talk with Marie. "No, my dear," Laura says, putting on a fake French accent, "zees we could do anywhere. But not on my yacht. Zees I cannot haff."

Apparently this remark is the punch line to the story. Laura and Marie rock backward with laughter. I clear my throat noisily. They look up in my direction, still giggling. Marie sits up straight, trying to regain her executive secretary composure. Very casually, Laura slides off the corner of the desk, walks over to me, and takes my hand, very social and la-di-da.

"Why, Bob Macallan! Marie and I were having such a good time I almost forgot I came here to see you. I've been regaling her with tales of the odd characters one meets at Bangle Bay. She's a wonderful audience. Makes me feel so charming. I'm afraid Marie is much more au courant about fun places around the world than you are."

I look past Laura to Marie. She gives me a sheepish grin and a shrug. "I told you, Bob. *Vanity Fair.* It's fun to read."

"So, Robert," Laura says, putting a hand up to my cheek and pointing my face back in her direction, "show me your executive suite. Marie and

I will finish our chat later. I understand you've only got a few minutes in between appointments."

Laura escorts me into my office, ushering me toward my desk. As she closes the door behind us, she says to Marie, "He wants you to hold his calls, please."

Marie smiles at her new friend as the door closes. Laura paces around the office, taking it in. "This is not at all what I had imagined," she says. "You know how people think. Publishing—style, fashion, the media, and all that. But the more I thought about it—and I've had quite a bit of time to think about it—the more I realized, this is very you. Unassuming, unpretentious, practical, and shrewdly inexpensive. There's really quite a lot of you to absorb in this seemingly plain room." She completes her circuit of the room and stands right in front of me. "Now tell me, Bob Macallan, have I truly and deeply surprised you?"

"Yes."

"Then be polite and kiss me hello." She puts a hand on each of my shoulders and presents her closed mouth to me. I lean forward and peck her waiting lips. Her hands drop, and one arm goes through mine as she escorts me the rest of the distance to my desk.

"I have made the ultimate sacrifice for you; I just want you to know that," she says. "I have actually come to this awful city. I had vowed never to do that again. See how you've turned my life upside down?"

"Laura," I mumble, smiling awkwardly. She is dressed in an expensive silk dress of bright cerulean blue, pink and white silk scarf, pearls, gold jewelry, dressy pumps, and matching handbag. With her hair blow-dried and coiffed, she looks like one of the Park Avenue ladies who lunch, the women with a talent for spending money as prodigious as their husbands' talent for making it.

"I'm in disguise. What do you think?" She pirouettes around for me to appreciate her outfit better. "Say it isn't me. Please."

"No." I smile. "It isn't you." Thanks to heredity, trust funds, and Sonia Rykiel, her disguise is perfect. "But it could be, if you gave it half a chance."

"Yes, I know. Another reason I avoid New York. Getting mugged isn't the only thing I'm afraid might happen." She sits down in the visitor's chair and gestures for me to sit behind my desk. I do. "Now, Bob Macallan. Something tells me that my timing is impeccable and that you are very happy to see me."

"Really?"

"Uh-huh." She can barely hide the smugness. "I called your home number and heard the message your wife left on the machine. Marie filled me in on the rest."

Salt in the wound. I exhale with a troubled puff.

"Poor baby. It's hard. Believe me, I know. But these things have a way of working out for the best." She holds her hands open at her sides as if she were a Christmas present waiting to be unwrapped. "Really they do."

"So, Laura," I stammer, trying small talk. "What on earth brought you to New York?"

"Come on," she snaps. She gives me that stare of hers, the one I saw in London, the one that says let's cut the crap and get right to it. "What brought me to New York? A Singapore Airlines jet, that's what." Pause. "What do you think?" Another pause, longer. *"You* did."

I look down at the blotter on my desk.

"I was in Thailand. In Phuket, on the northwest coast. You know it?"

"No," I answer, still avoiding eye contact. Suddenly, thoughts of a tropical paradise on the other side of the planet seem comforting and seductive. Worlds away from conference rooms and offices, corporations and clients.

"It's glorious," Laura rambles on. "Phuket itself is kind of touristy, you know, resorty. But most of the area around it is still untouched. Tropical forests, beaches, deserted lagoons. Anyway, there are these people you occasionally see around there, the Mokens. Their kids dive for coins that the tourists toss into the water. They're like the Gypsies used to be in Europe. The Thais hate them, naturally. But I did a little investigating. They're really a nation of true nomads. Maybe the last in the world. They are literally citizens of nowhere. They spend their entire lives on their boats, cruising the waters of the Mergui Archipelago. You know, along the coast between Burma and Thailand? In the Andaman Sea?"

I shake my head no.

"The only time they go onto dry land is to gather materials to build another boat. I managed to find an interpreter, and I went and spent a few days with them. I lived on one of their boats. It's called a *kabang*. Long and narrow with a bamboo roof. Pretty comfortable, considering there's no plumbing and no privacy. All they do is wander. Sometimes in groups of boats, sometimes individual boats all by themselves. They take everything they need from the waters of the lagoons. They don't store food or grow crops or make plans or anything. They just take what they need for each day and never think about the next day. They come together once in a while for festivals and ceremonies, like weddings." She leans forward, sitting on the edge of the chair, excitedly retelling and reliving her adventure. "It's wonderful. When two people decide to become a couple, the tribe builds them their own boat. And they just wander off together for the rest of their lives. The word that means 'to marry' is the same word that means 'to live.' In their language, there's no distinction between the two words. Isn't that beautiful?"

I nod, happy to let my mind drift momentarily away with Laura, choosing to ignore the direction in which she is trying to lead me.

"There I was, watching these people living this wonderful life in this magical place. The Mokens are completely open. They keep no secrets from each other. Ever. They say it keeps the heart from becoming heavy. They are happy people. Truly, they are. They made me think of you. You and me. And how we could live like them. That is, once you've got this boring business thing behind you." She wags a finger at me, emphasizing the point of her lesson. "We could do it, you know. So when I got back to Bangkok, I made up my mind. I caught the first plane to New York. And here I am."

"But, Laura, I'm a lousy fisherman."

"No, silly, I mean we could do it at our level of civilization. The Mokens prove that we could wander and be nomads and be perfectly happy."

Perfect happiness, eh? Visions of my troubles cut short my visit to Laura's dreamworld. "Sure, it's easy," I snicker, "long as you've got fifteen million dollars behind you."

She frowns at me, disappointed. "I thought you were just about finished with this business thing of yours. What's wrong?"

"What's wrong?" Suddenly, the events of today and the past few weeks hit me. I feel the floodgates opening. Leo and Hoffman and Detweiler and Woodcock and Carmody and Wendy. Yes, Wendy. Especially Wendy. And Laura, who has already caused more than her share of trouble. My stoic front shatters. "What's wrong? Well, for starters, I—" My breath is short, I cannot find the air. "I am . . . my life is . . . I am strugg . . . I am—" I cannot find the words. I see my hands grabbing the air, I hear my voice sputtering. I cannot explain, I can only explode. "You couldn't begin to imagine what I am going through. I am in hell right now. And I don't know if I'll ever get out. It's easy to be adventurous and free and la-di-da all over the fucking globe when you're rich. It's all just a game. You've already won. Rich people have this thing—"

"Who's calling who rich? Isn't that the pot—"

"*I am not rich!* When I met you I was only renting a small fortune. Turned out to be a pretty goddamn short lease, too. Right now, I can barely count on having a salary. My whole life and everything I've ever worked for is about to go down the toilet." Her eyes open wide. "Laura, you have no idea what struggle is. How could you? Right now, that 'boring business thing,' as you call it, is life or death for me. The poetic beauty of a tribe of Asiatic nomads is completely lost on a guy like me. I got my hands full worrying about all the shit I have to eat just to make a living." I lean back and sigh, letting off more angry steam.

Laura says nothing. Very deliberately, she sets her purse on the floor, gets up, and walks over to my chair. She stands behind me, hugs me with one arm across my chest, cups my chin with her other hand, and holds my head between her breasts. The motion feels real and unaffected, not quite like a lover, not quite maternal. Just tender.

"After all the distance I've come," she says, stroking my cheek, "you owe me the chance to show you, Robert Macallan."

I do not mind taking advantage of the free affection. No one has touched me in weeks. I rest my head back between the warmth of her breasts and feel myself simmering down. "To show you what?" I ask.

"That you're wrong. And that *we're* right."

"That'll never work, Laura. There's just too much—"

"You're a bigot, you know."

"I am not."

"Oh, yes, you are. You think that a certain bank balance automatically determines a person's character—their sincerity, their empathy, their depth as a human being. That's like saying all Poles are stupid, all Jews are cheap, and all blacks got rhythm. You're bigoted against rich people. I ought to be insulted."

"Laura, I'm married."

"Sounds to me like you're separated."

"It's just a—"

"Have you seen the last act of this play?"

"No."

"Then how do you know what will or won't happen?"

"Laura, I—"

"Why don't you try taking things as they come?"

"*Lau-ra,* I—"

She silences me with circular caresses that start at my forehead and rotate down over my eyelids. "Right now, you could do with some support and affection, right?"

"Hmmm." It does feel good.

"Then let's just see how things turn out."

I try to pull my head away for a second. "But Lau—"

She pulls me closer into her breasts. "Shhh." Her embrace is tighter, more enveloping. She intends to smother all argument. I decide to submit, at least for the moment. Silence follows. And warmth. Her breasts are pillows to get lost in. I hear her breathing and her heartbeat echoing inside her rib cage. Her fingertips dance over my face.

"So?" she coos. "Where are we going to have dinner tonight?"

That question shatters the spell. I pull myself away, spinning my chair around to face her. "I have a client to wine and dine tonight. A gluttonous, horny old pig who has my fate in his hands. I buy him food and drink and whores, and if he likes them, he will buy ad space in my magazine and everything will be okay. If he doesn't, I am dead meat."

She cups my face in both hands and rivets her eyes into mine. "No wonder you're so worried. It's all riding on this one client?"

"Everything."

"Then you've got to be in top form for him."

I nod.

"I can be there when you're done."

I mean to protest, but before I can speak, she seals my lips with her index finger. "No, I *will* be there when you're done. I am going to be there, I don't care how late it is. You can't put in a night like that and go home to an empty room. I won't let you go through this alone, Bob. Are you living in a hotel?"

I nod.

"Then give me the key to your room."

CHAPTER THIRTY

Max and I are heading for dinner, sitting in the back of the limo I have rented. Actually, Max is not sitting. He is stretched out, luxuriating like a pasha in a blue serge suit.

"Yes," he says, "this is the life." He flicks the gooseneck reading light behind us on and off a couple of times.

I smile at him. So far, the Oscar-winning performance I had planned for Max is coming off beautifully. In his office, he listened admiringly to my sales presentation, complimented me on the customized leave-behind report, called me a consummate publishing professional, then, at five-thirty, hustled us off to the Oak Bar at the Plaza, where he inhaled two double Manhattans.

"You ever been to Jake Johnson's?" he asks, glancing out the window at the passing blur of streets at dusk.

"Of course," I reply enthusiastically, "whenever I need a real, honest-to-goodness steak." Perhaps that was a little too enthusiastic. I make a mental note not to overdo the hale, hardy regular-guy bit.

"Same here," he says, "same here. You know, I wonder how it is that in the old days people used to eat all the red meat they wanted and still live so long."

"Good question. My grandfather lived to be ninety-five," I lie, knowing that he's very proud of his grandfathers, who lived almost forever.

"Both a mine did, too. And they drank and smoked and ate double helpings of corned beef right to the end. They didn't know that stuff was supposed to kill them, so it didn't. You know, I've got this idea. I call it the 'inverse placebo effect.' "

"I didn't know you were a scientist, Max."

"I'm not, I'm not. I've just been hanging around the lab boys too long. I gotta tell you, they know how to cover every angle in their research, except one."

"Which one's that?"

"Common sense."

He leads us together in a big laugh.

"So tell me your theory," I say, keeping the ball rolling.

"It's simple. We all know the placebo effect: You give a patient a sugar pill that he thinks is medicine. His mind convinces his body that he oughtta be getting better, and so he does. Well, the inverse placebo effect is just the opposite. You tell people that steak and butter and booze are gonna kill them, and what happens? Their mind convinces them that they're gonna die, and they do. The more we know about what's supposed to kill us, the more we convince ourselves we're gonna die."

We laugh some more.

"Max," I say, "that's brilliant. But you gotta keep it under your hat. You could put companies like Orem-Diedrich out of business with ideas like that."

"Shit, you could never put drug companies outta business. Ne-ver. It's the only business in the world that's recession-proof, depression-proof, you name it. People are always gonna get sick. In fact, when things go bad, they're gonna get sicker. I figured that out when I came back from the service in 'fifty-four."

The limo pulls up to Jake Johnson's Steak House, a wedge-shaped two-story granite relic of the Robber Baron era, a few blocks from Wall Street. Max and I enter. The place is roaring, jam-packed. The maître-d's (one for the back room downstairs, one for the side room downstairs, one for the upstairs room) are screaming names above the din. The crowd waiting at the bar is so thick that drinks are passed fire-brigade style from the bartender through other hands to the eventual customers. The men loosen their ties as soon as they enter; there is not a woman in sight. The light is harsh, the noise level impossible. The current owners, a Dutch-British consortium, work hard to preserve the aura of the place where Diamond Jim Brady and J. P. Morgan used to go to escape rich formality and be at home with the boys. The patterned tin ceilings have been painstakingly restored and distressed to look slightly in need of repair. Carefully sterilized sawdust is tossed about the dark hardwood floors in studied little piles, for effect, not for sweeping.

Max and I squeeze through the mob toward the desk that the maître d's share. I've been here before with Leo and clients at prime time, so I know what to do. On the way inside, I have already taken a fresh twenty-dollar bill and folded it into a rectangle small enough to fit in the palm of my right hand.

"Reservation for Macallan!" I shout at the maître d' as I try to squeeze past two enormous lugs in open silk shirts and gold chains. They are talking about construction.

"Whaaah?" the maître d' shouts back.

"Macallan! Party of two. Gotta reservation."

He points me to the bar. "I'll call ya!"

I push a little more to get past the cement kingpins and up to the desk. "Nice to see you again," I say as I reach across his desk. He reaches up and takes my hand for an instant. "Why don't you check the book," I say. He does not acknowledge the bill that has passed to him. Presumably the palm of his hand is sensitive enough to "read" the ridges of ink on the corner that say "$20." He slides his right hand into his jacket pocket, pulls it out empty, and says, "I gotta table upstairs."

Max and I are shown to our table. Upstairs is more prestigious than the downstairs side room, but far less prestigious than the downstairs back room. That room is reserved for the inner circle of the inner circle—has-been professional athletes, local sportscasters, Mafia chieftains, and their respective groupies. Our table is in the center of the upstairs room, not in a corner. That would have required a fifty-dollar incentive. The crowd noise is not quite so bad up here away from the bar, although the racket of dishes and silverware being tossed up and down in the dumbwaiter is continuous. Everything in this place is "manhandled"—the cutlery, the food, the customers.

"Don'tcha love it here?" Max asks as we settle in.

"There's no place else like it," I say, grinning.

"Yeah, it's the original," says Max.

A short, fat waiter in a full-length apron comes to our table. He looks like a homicidal version of the advertising character Beefsteak Charlie, but without the handlebar mustache.

"Whaddyoogentswanna drink?"

"Double Manhattan," Max says.

"Scotch and soda," I say, sticking with what I had at the Oak Bar.

"How do yoo gents wannit done?" There are no menus in Jake Johnson's. You have your choice of steak. Huge sizzling hunks of steak. Period.

"Medium rare for me," I say. "How about you, Max?"

"Same."

"You wannit pink but not too bloody?" the waiter asks impatiently.

"That's right," Max says, "pink but not too bloody."

"Putaytuhs fried or baked?"

"Fried," Max chimes in, relishing the thought of the grease. "I'm gonna enjoy. My wife's outta town."

I almost tell him that mine is, too. Then I reconsider and just say, "Fried."

"You gents wanna tumaytuh salad?"

"Sure."

"Yeah."

"Blue cheese?"

"Fine."

"Sure."

Having written nothing on his notepad, Beefsteak Charlie grunts and leaves.

Max picks up the conversation from the car. "I was a great detail man. A great detail man. It was easy for me. I got the gift of gab, and they're not bad guys, doctors. At least they weren't in my day, before everybody became a goddamn hotsy-totsy specialist. So I'm looking at these doctors; I was just a kid, but I was smart. They're people, too, I said to myself. Somebody's gotta be their friend, their buddy. Why not me? You only gotta know two things about doctors. One, they're tired. They're always tired. You gotta sympathize with that. Two, they got egos, big fuckin' egos, but they'd never admit it. So you gotta kiss their ass without lettin' 'em know that you know you're kissin' their ass. Simple. You sympathize, you kiss a little ass, you give 'em presents, you make 'em remember you fondly, and, by the way, you remind 'em which drugs they oughtta prescribe, and bingo! Sales in your territory start going up. Of course, the great thing about being a detail man is you never have to ask for the order. Know what I mean?"

"Uh-huh." I am listening with rapt attention, hanging on to every word, pretending that this is not the third or fourth time I have heard Max tell the saga of his success.

"For the kids today, being a detail man is just a rotation on their way to executive row. They're just technicians. They think they can find the answer to everything in their computers. So that's what I use 'em for. Technical answers to technical questions. I got this whole staff of MBAs with computers. They can give me all the technical information I could ever use. But there isn't an ounce of common sense, horse sense, or salesmanship in the whole damn group. I like to fire one of them once a year, doesn't matter which one or why. It keeps the whole group on their toes." He looks around the restaurant for a moment. "You got an MBA, Macallan?"

"Absolutely not," I say.

"Good man. You don't need it."

The drinks arrive. Max downs his in two gulps. He points to his empty glass as a waiter passes by, and another double Manhattan appears in no time. Beefsteak Charlie brings us our salads—round slices of tomato the size of softballs and white rings of raw onion, all smothered in gooey blue cheese dressing.

"Oh, am I gonna pay for this tomorrow," Max says and digs in.

I move my dressing around to expose the tomato, which is not really ripe, ignore the onion, and with a few strategic bites make the plate look like I am finished. Max orders another Manhattan. His capacity is truly amazing.

The busboy cleans the table and Beefsteak Charlie appears bearing a platter with a slab of charred flesh the size of first base. It is cut into thick slices, the red juices oozing out, the singed layer of thick yellow fat around the outside still crackling from the fire.

"Heeeyago, men," Charlie sneers, "pink but not too bloody." He drops the platter between us, produces two steak knives from inside his apron, and flings them onto our dinner plates. Another waiter appears with an equally large platter of steak fries, also crackling and dripping with grease.

"Putaytuhs, fried," Charlie announces as the potato platter gets dropped in place. "You gents want sumpthin' elssadrink? Beeyah? Glassawine? Same?"

"Same," Max says, pointing to his empty cocktail glass.

"I'm fine," I say, pointing to my half-consumed Scotch and soda.

Max goes at the steak like a man who hasn't eaten in days. He cuts off a huge chunk, chews it for a while, then, before swallowing, stuffs his mouth full of greasy potatoes and chews some more. He washes the whole mess down with a swig of his Manhattan and starts the cycle over again.

"The wife doesn't let me near red meat anymore," he explains during a break between bites. He is extracting a piece of gristle from the back of his mouth with his fingers. "Fish and salad, chicken and pasta," he says, mimicking what must be her refrain. "Jeez, this is good. Leo and I come here all the time." He stops himself, a little embarrassed, the booze finally getting to his self-control. "Oops, I forgot."

"That's okay," I say and charge ahead. "Leo is the reason you and I are sitting here enjoying this meal." After the failure of my attack against Leo this morning, I'm prepared to risk something completely different. "I want you to know that I know that I owe Leo Sayles a lot. A lot."

Max looks up from his plate of bloody meat with surprise.

"Leo is a great salesman," I continue, "but I had to do what I did. He was compromising the security of my entire operation and putting in jeopardy information that was held in confidence for our advertisers. I don't know why he was doing it. I may never know. But he was doing it. I've got the evidence to prove it. We can go over it some other time, any time you want. I just want you to know that Leo did all right by *Elixir*. We paid him very well, much better than Becker ever did. I gave him a tremendous bonus when we sold out to American, and he had no equity in the company. He just wasn't satisfied."

"I like your directness," Max says, "but you know that Leo tells a very different story."

"Yes, I know that."

"Leo's got relationships in this business that go back a long, long way."

"I know that, too."

"Word on the street is he's done some real damage. Accounts pulled out, that kind of stuff."

"Nothing we're not going to recover from quickly," I say confidently. "We're going to end up even farther ahead, believe me."

"Leo wouldn't approve of me saying this. But I like you, Macallan. You're a scrapper. You remind me of myself when I was your age."

"Thanks, Max, that's a real compliment." I muster all my physical willpower to keep a straight face while saying that.

"Now, as you know, we've had some deep budget cuts in these last couple of weeks. And I've got some tough choices to make about how to allocate the dollars I've got left. Now, I like that special issue of yours, I like it a lot. We've gone over your numbers, and they look fine to me. But there are other people up the ladder I gotta take into consideration."

That's a lie.

"Max," I say, "there isn't a vehicle out there that's going to give you the exposure for this many products for so many months. Remember, this is no throwaway monthly. This volume is going to be a reference. Something doctors will keep on their shelves and refer to time and again. And if you remember the design format we've—"

"Bob, I remember everything. It's a first-class opportunity, I want you to know that I know it. Regardless of how the decision goes. But, hey, let's not ruin this great meal by pulling out the rate card. I think this is the first time you and I have had the chance to spend some time together. Alone."

"That's right, Max, it is."

"Well, I'm having a fine time. I think you're really okay."

"Thanks, Max."

The busboys, seeing that we are done with the steak, come to clear the table. Beefsteak Charlie appears seconds later to tell us about desserts.

"We got apple cobbluh, strawberry shortcake, and chocolate cream pie."

I look at Max, he looks at me.

"You want any dessert?" Max asks me.

"Nah, I don't think so," I say. "I'm pretty full. But if you want some, please be my guest."

"Well, I don't think I want any dessert here. But I wouldn't mind tasting a sweet little delicacy, uh, back uptown."

I get the hint.

"Yooguyswannacoffee?" Beefsteak Charlie asks.

"No thanks," I say, "just the check."

This suite in the Parc Madison Hotel goes for $1,200 per night. I always wondered why Leo raved about the suites in this place. Now I know; they meet his needs for absurd grandeur. The living room is a gilt and mirrored salon from the palace of Versailles equipped with wet bar and VCR. Max walked in and went right for the biggest couch, lay down, and kicked his feet up. He knows this place well and the drill he is about to put me through.

"You don't mind me talking about Leo?" he asks from across the room.

"No, not at all. Anything Leo can do, I can do better."

"You're succeeding."

"Glad to hear it."

"Anything Leo can do, you can do better."

"That's the name of this tune."

"I see." Max scratches his chin in thought. "Hmm."

"What's on your mind?"

"You really mean it?"

"Absolutely."

"Well, I've had a lot of nieces come visit me up here."

"Nieces?" I ask, shocked at his choice of words. He is oblivious to me.

"Yes, thanks to Leo. Many lovely nieces."

"What kind of niece would you like tonight, Max? Tell me."

"I'd like a blond niece, Bob. A *real* blonde, know what I mean?"

"I know what you mean, Max. We can arrange it. Was that what you were thinking about just now?"

"Not exactly."

"Well, what was it, Max? Tell me."

"You really want to know?"

"Of course, I want to know. Tell me."

"You sure?"

"Max, tell me."

"I was thinking about a *couple* of nieces, a couple of real blond nieces."
His coyness surprises me.

"Max, why don't you take your shoes off and watch some TV." I toss
him the remote and walk over to the fake Louis XIV armoire to open the
doors that conceal the television. "Just give me a few minutes and we'll get
you two lovely blond nieces." Max leans back on the couch and starts
flipping idly around the dial.

The memory of Leo's card from the Aviary is burned into my memory,
along with its PLaza 4-BIRD telephone number. Betty was the name of
Leo's madam friend, I'm sure. I dial.

"Hello, the Aviary," says a polite, professional older female voice.

"Is Betty there?"

"May I ask who's calling?"

"I'm a friend of Leo Sayles. Betty knows him."

"But who are *you*?"

"I'm, uh, I'm, uh, Mr. Macallan."

"And how may we help you, Mr. Macallan?"

"I'm interested in some, uh, some, uh . . ."

"Birds?"

"Yes, that's right. Some birds. Is Betty there? Really, I'm a friend of a
friend of hers."

"Well, Mr. Macallan, first we're going to have to confirm who you are
and where you are before we can proceed any farther. Can you please give
me the number and expiration date of a major credit card of yours and the
telephone number and address where you are right now. I'll call you back
in a few moments."

I give her the information and hang up. Max has turned to the pay movie
channel and is watching, of course, the racy "adult" selection. It looks like
one of those "R"-rated Swedish nudie flicks from the midseventies, the
kind with flapping boobs and out-of-sync dubbing. It seems sufficiently
prurient, however, to capture Max's complete attention.

In a few minutes, the telephone rings again.

"Hello, Mr. Macallan, Mr. Robert Macallan?"

"Yes, that's me. Is this Betty?"

"No, I'm afraid Betty's not here tonight. But why don't you tell me how
I can help you? My name is Leilah."

"Well, Leilah, I'm interested in a pair of blondes."

"Two girls?"

"Yes, that's right."

"I see from our computer that you haven't used our service before. Are
you familiar with our rates and policies?"

"Well, no, not personally. But friends of mine—"

"Then you know that will be six hundred dollars for the first hour times two, or twelve hundred dollars. And an additional twelve hundred dollars for each hour after that. How will you be paying us tonight?"

"In cash."

"Do you have any special requests? B and D? Fetishes? Golden showers? Greek? I'm afraid we charge extra for those and not all our girls are available for them."

"No," I say, looking at Max stretched out on the couch, his jacket off, tie undone, and shoes off, watching soft-core porn with a look of pure bliss. "No, I think it'll be just the regular."

"You mean French and straight."

"Yeah, French and straight."

"A condom is a must, you know."

"Sure. Of course."

"Well, our blondes here tonight include Sheila, who's five-four and busty. There's Serena, who's five-seven with long, lovely legs, and Paula, who's five-five and with a real model's features."

"Well, what's really important is that the girls be real blondes, through and through. You know what I mean."

"Yes, of course. Could you hold just a minute, please." The line goes quiet for a minute.

"I'm afraid that Sheila is our only blond blonde. But we have Candy here tonight and she's an honest-to-goodness redhead, through and through, petite and very cute. Candy is very popular."

"Just a minute." I cup my hand over the phone mouthpiece. "Say, Max, they only have one real blonde. But they can give you an honest-to-goodness redhead to go with her. How's that sound?"

Max looks up from the movie just long enough to flash me an "okay" sign.

"That'll be fine," I tell Leilah.

"Okay," she says, "now you should tell the front desk of the hotel that you are expecting guests. We look forward to serving you, Mr. Macallan. Thank you for calling."

I hang up. Max has raided the wet bar and made himself a cocktail of some kind. Now he's eating pretzels, drinking, and watching naked Swedes, all with complete rapture. I call down to the desk to alert them that I am expecting guests momentarily.

The desk clerk's voice gives nothing away. "Yes, sir. Thank you, sir," he says.

In a few minutes, the doorbell rings. Max doesn't budge. I get up and open the door and there they are, Candy and Sheila, just as described over the phone. Candy is very redheaded indeed, petite, maybe just five feet. She is also very cute, with a round freckled face, small, pointed nose, and a dimple in the middle of her chin. Sheila, as promised, is about average height and quite busty. She makes up for her plain features with a glamorous, blow-dried-to-death hairstyle. The girls are in their midtwenties and,

262

except for the wary eyes and heavy-handed perfume, could pass for any respectable young women out to go dancing in the clubs. Candy wears an expensive black raincoat, a black lycra miniskirt and top, with black stockings and black pumps. Sheila wears a classic Burberry trench coat and an emerald green disco minidress peeking through underneath. They do not look like hookers to me.

"Come on in," I say, closing the door behind them.

Max is sitting up now, putting his shoes back on. He has shut off the TV.

"You must be Candy," I say to the shorter one.

"And I'm Sheila," the other one says. "We have to call the office to check in."

"Please, go ahead."

Sheila walks to the end table and picks up the phone. She doesn't have to look at the information card next to the phone to know that you dial "8" to get a local outside line in the Parc Madison.

"Yeah," she says into the phone. "We're here okay at the Parc Madison. Suite twenty-one twenty-two. . . . Yeah, there are two of 'em."

I shake my finger no-no at her and mouth the words, "Not me. My friend." I point at Max.

"No," she says, seeing me, "I guess it's just one. Must be a birthday present or something. But there are two guys here, just so you know. . . . Uh-huh, uh-huh, uh-huh. We'll see. . . . Yeah, call you then." She hangs up and walks over to me.

"You're Robert Macallan?"

"That's right."

"You wanna take care a business first before we see your friend?"

"Max," I say.

"Max?"

"My friend Max." I point to Max standing in front of the couch, so eager he hardly seems able to speak. The ravenous look he gave the steak at Jake Johnson's is nothing compared to the way he is ogling Candy and Sheila. "Say hi to the girls, Max."

"Hi, girls," he says, trying to act calm.

"We should get the business done," Sheila reminds me.

"Yes, of course." I reach into my pants pocket for the big roll of bills. I peel off twelve hundreds and hand them to Sheila. She counts them carefully, rolls them up like a cigar, and puts them into her purse. Without saying another word, Sheila and Candy walk deliberately to the bedroom door, open it, go inside, and close it behind them. A calculated few seconds go by, then the door opens again. Candy sticks her head out and in a teasing voice says, "Oh, Ma-a-x, can you give us a hand in here?"

Max looks like the happiest man on earth; he seems to float all the way to the bedroom. He enters and the door closes behind him.

I sit myself down on the couch where Max was. Noises start to filter out from behind the bedroom door. The faucet running. A giggle. Low voices. Bedsprings. The toilet flushing. I reach for the remote control and flick on the TV. It's tuned to Max's dumb Swedish nudie film, so I flip around the stations, looking for something bearable but noisy to watch while I wait.

I can remember watching "Starsky and Hutch" once, maybe twice before in my life. So tonight, of course, the only loud show on the dial is one of the two episodes I've already seen. But I'm grateful for the car chases, bad dialogue, and no-surprise ending, because it almost keeps me from hearing the bouncing, slopping, slurping, and foul-mouthed chatter leaking from the bedroom.

Starsky and Hutch wrap up their caper in about the same amount of time as Candy and Sheila. As the credits roll and the theme music plays, I hear the bedroom go quiet. The faucet runs, the hair dryer blows, the toilet flushes a couple of times, then the bedroom door opens. Sheila is the first to emerge, fully dressed and made-up, ready for the next customer. Candy follows close behind, also camera-ready.

"Everything okay?" I ask, getting up from the couch, because two ladies have entered the room.

Sheila strides over to me.

"I thought you said there were no extras, just French and straight."

"Yeah, isn't that right?"

"Your buddy Max is a major Greek, a *major* Greek," Sheila explains. "First of all, we're supposed to know if they want Greek in advance and it's two hundred extra besides." Sheila is not peeved or put out. Her tone is flat, completely businesslike. She holds her hand out for the money.

I reach into my pocket and peel off two hundreds.

"That's two hundred extra for each of us," she says, trying to sound patient.

"Oh, yeah. Of course." I peel off two more C-notes.

"It's lucky for you we don't do golden showers," Candy volunteers.

"That'd be another four hundred," Sheila explains.

I look up at the bedroom door and see Max standing there fully dressed but for his suit jacket, buttoning the cuffs of his shirt. He makes a whoosh motion with one hand as if to tell me to shoo the girls out.

Sheila extracts a business card from her purse and sets it down on the coffee table between us.

"Our card, gentlemen," Sheila says. "Call us anytime. *Ciao.*"

"*Ciao,*" Candy echoes, and they leave.

There is a moment of silence while Max finishes hitching his necktie into place. The look of boozy, horny bliss from before is gone. This is Max as crisp and professional as if he were at a midmorning meeting.

"Thank you, Bob. That was first-rate. You throw one fine party, young man."

"Glad you enjoyed it, Max."

He looks at his watch with the officious air of an executive who must hurry to the next big meeting. It is just past midnight.

"I've got to get back to Pound Ridge. Will you have your driver take me?"

"Sure, no problem."

He reaches for his suit jacket, which is slung over a chair, then goes to the closet for his overcoat. "Come on," he says, preparing to leave. "Walk me down to the car. We should talk."

I sweep up my suit jacket and room key, and together we head for the elevator.

"You know, I'm glad we've had this chance to get to know each other better," Max says on the ride down. "What with all the changes that have been going on at *Elixir.*" We are alone on the elevator.

"Max," I say, "whatever we can do to express our commitment to you and to our relationship with Orem-Diedrich. What we don't want is for that continuity to be interrupted." He is not going to cancel, I can feel it. Finally, I have beaten Leo at his own disgusting game.

"That's a good way to put it," he says, patting my shoulder. "That continuity has not been broken, not as far as I'm concerned."

The elevator doors open on the lobby. We head for the carport where the rented limo driver has been cooling his heels.

"Bob, I like you. And I'm gonna like doing business with you."

"That's great to hear, Max. Great to hear. Orem-Diedrich is an advertiser we value more than, uh, well, I can't begin to express what Orem-Diedrich means to our publication. With an advertiser like Orem—"

Max interrupts me. "I think Leo's giving you a bad rap. But I don't want to get in the middle of this thing between you two. I leave it to you guys to work it out."

"Absolutely, Max. It's over as far as I'm concerned. As I see it, it's all strictly the future. Onward and onward."

We pass through the revolving doors into the cool night air. The limo is waiting. The driver hops out of the front to get the door for Max and me. Max gets there first and opens the back door for himself.

"We're going to Pound Ridge," Max tells the driver in a stiff, formal voice, "up in Westchester. I'll direct you." He then turns to me and whispers like a father giving his son advice on prom night, "I think you'd better take care of the driver with something extra. Pound Ridge is way off his route."

"Oh, sure." I peel off a fifty and head for the driver. I hear Max behind me.

"You should probably do better than that, Bob," he says. "It's a long drive back."

Dutifully I peel off another fifty and stuff them into the driver's waiting hand. I walk back to the open passenger door where Max is about to climb in. It is time for my best salesman's farewell to Max—my new comrade, my new ally, my continuing advertiser, savior of my earn-out and possibly the rest of my life.

"Max"—I stick my hand out for a big shake—"it's been a pleasure."

"All mine. All mine." He shakes and gives me a little wink; I answer with a between-us-guys nod. "I want you to know you can count on us in the future. But on this special issue thing, I gotta go with Leo."

I am not sure I heard him correctly. "Sorry?"

"Leo and I had a long talk about tonight's dinner. And, well, you know how many years Leo and I go back."

It takes me a few seconds to come to.

"You had a talk about tonight?"

Max dismisses my question with a wave of the hand. "Yeah, this afternoon. He asked me where you were planning to take me." Then he knew all about it, I think but don't say. "Bob, he called all his old favors in at once on this one." Who told him, I wonder. "All of 'em, Bob, and the truth is I owe him so goddamn much over all these years. I'm sure you know what I mean." He pauses and looks at me earnestly. "You understand loyalty, Bob, I know you do. Without loyalty, this business of ours would be . . . uh . . . our business . . . wouldn't be . . . uh . . ." He looks away as he gropes for words. "Uh . . . we'd all be just a buncha . . . uh . . . without loyalty, we just wouldn't be able to do business." Again, he looks at me with the soulful cow eyes. "Leo asked for my loyalty on this one, and I have to honor it, Bob. You know I do and you understand why." Deep breath. He has done his duty as a man. Now he offers me the consolation prize. "But I can guarantee you this, young man. As soon as that special issue of yours is out and over with, you can count us back in as an advertiser. And I mean as a regular. With lots of pages."

I am speechless.

Max climbs into the backseat, closes the door, and quickly opens the electric window to continue his conversation with me. I stare down at him.

"You know, a lot of this business of ours is longevity. Being around. Hanging in there. Paying your dues. Showing you've got the commitment. And I think you've got it, Bob, I really do. Just remember, you've got my vote in the future. And, hey, thanks for a great evening. I owe you one, buddy." With that, he leans forward and tells the driver he's ready to leave. As the limo pulls away, he rolls up the window and gives me a salute like a politician in a passing motorcade.

I stand frozen in the carport. I cannot move. Scenes from this evening pass through my mind, scenes from this morning, from this afternoon, and the scene that has just transpired. The night air is chill, but I feel sweat dripping down into my eyes.

"Can I get you a cab, sir?" It is the doorman.

"Yes," I think I hear myself say.

"Where to?"

"Pierpont Hotel. Thirty-fifth and Madison."

The next thing I hear is his whistle out in the street.

There is a giant snake in my belly; I can feel it stirring. A thick, scaly python. It is trying to uncoil.

"Your cab, sir." It is the doorman. I feel him take me by the shoulders and point me gently into the open back door of the yellow taxi. I follow his touch. He settles me into the seat.

"It's okay, sir," the doorman assures me. "I told the driver. The Pierpont. Thirty-fifth and Madison."

"Thank you," I hear myself say.

He shuts the door for me.

"Wait a minute," I hear myself say as I open the door again.

"Something the matter, sir?" the doorman asks.

I reach into my pocket and pull out a bill. I cannot see what it is.

"Here," I say, offering it to him. "Thank you."

"Jeeez!" he says, admiring it. "Jeeez, thanks. Thank you, sir. *Thank you.*"

I hear the door close and feel the cab pull away.

The taxi driver wants to talk. I do not. I cannot make out what he is saying. I make no response. The arrangement seems to suit him fine. He keeps talking. I keep ignoring him, until at Fifth and Fifty-third a car runs the red light and barely misses our cab.

"Jesus fucking Christ, ja see that asshole!" the cabby shrieks. "Ja see that asshole! Must be a fuckin' Jersey driver, I tell ya, fuckin' Jersey drivers."

As he moves us extra slowly through the rest of the intersection, a strange calm comes over me. I feel the snake quieting down; maybe it wants to go to sleep now.

"This is a dangerous time of night," I say, my first words to the cabby. The fright and shock of the near-accident has awakened me, sort of.

"Huh?" He is surprised to hear me talking. "Y'say somethin'?"

"I said this is a dangerous time of night."

"Whaddya mean, it's only twelve-thirty." He, too, has calmed down.

"It's dangerous driving now, isn't it?" I ask. "Guys are drunk, think they own the road."

"Naaah," he says, "ya know when the most dangerous time a night is? I mean *the* most dangerous. Know when that is?"

"Isn't it about now?" I venture.

"Naah, most dangerous time's just before dawn. You know, just before it gets light. Hour before sunup, know when I mean?"

"I guess people forget to use their headlights."

"Naaah! Got nothin' to do with headlights!"

"No?"

"Nah! It's the guys been out gettin' nooky on the side. They're in a big fuckin' hurry to get home 'fore the wife wakes up. They go barreling down the avenues 'cause they think there's nobody else on the road. Seen 'em piled up all over at that hour. Watch out for those horny bastards tryin' to get home 'fore the wife wakes up. They're fuckin' killers."

I feel the snake stirring again. It is angry.

"This it?" he asks as he rounds the corner and heads up Madison and stops in front of the Pierpont Hotel. After returning to this canopy every night for three weeks, this strange place feels vaguely like home. The snake calms down. Maybe it is asleep; maybe it is just resting for a bit.

"Uh-huh." I hand the cabbie a five from my wallet, a dollar over the meter.

"Remember, watch it just before dawn!" he shouts as I get up and close the door. He pulls away, leaving me standing on the curb.

The Pierpont's late-night doorman rushes up to greet me. My arrival has caught him unready. He says my name and mutters something that sounds like an apology; apparently he recognizes me from my habitual late arrivals from the office. I walk past him in silence. I do not have the energy or the focus to chat with him. In this fashionable but moderately priced new hotel, the midnight-to-six sentry must be used to being snubbed by guests in all kinds of stupors, media trendies high on controlled substances, uncontrolled egos, or both.

I proceed through the lobby, newly renovated to look old, to the elevators. The elevator takes me to my floor. I walk automatically down the corridor to the left. Without looking up, I know when I have reached Room 1021. I knock on the door. In a moment it opens. I look up. There is Laura with bare legs and bare feet—wearing one of my white dress shirts, the French cuffs rolled halfway up her arms, the shirttails covering her to midthigh. The formal coif she wore this afternoon is combed out of her honey-blond hair. In one hand she holds a glass of white wine. She grins and raises the glass in greeting.

"He returns in triumph," she announces.

Suddenly, the snake in my belly recoils. It wants to get out.

Laura looks at me and goes pale. "What's wrong?"

I buckle over in hopes of containing the snake. It thrashes in the other direction. I stand up straight again. The snake wants to get out. It presses downward against my bowels and upward against my lungs. It coils one end around my throat. I cannot breathe.

"Get in here," Laura says urgently. I feel her grab my arm and pull me into the room. I think I hear the door close. Suddenly, the carpet slams against my forehead. Then the snake lashes out in all directions at once, uncoiling with a violent thrust. Then another. Then another. Then another. It lifts me up and drops me down. I cough and gag and gasp for breath. The snake is smaller now and tired. It lashes out inside me once more. I cough and gag and spit. Finally, it is gone. I am on my knees now, drooling and panting over the stinking mess I have made.

CHAPTER THIRTY-ONE

"Poor baby," **Laura** whispers, patting my forehead with the cold, damp washcloth. She smooths the blanket around me.

"You took care of the maid?" I ask, still a little woozy.

"She can make the down payment on a new condo with the tip I gave her. Believe me, that woman is going to pray to the blessed Virgin to make you sick every night."

"And you're still here?"

"What do you mean? Just because a man takes one look at me and throws up? Hey, at least it's an honest reaction. In today's market for relationships, that kind of directness is rare."

"Yeah." I laugh weakly. "I guess so."

Laura sits down beside me on top of the blanket. She has exchanged my dress shirt, which ended up helping to clean my mess, for a long flannel nightshirt she found in my closet. She pulled me up off the floor, steered me into the shower, ordered hot herbal tea from room service, and has now tucked me in like a championship mom.

"Feeling better?" she asks, setting the washcloth aside on the night table.

"Yes, much more like a human being. Thanks."

"No need for thanks. It's what I came here to do." I give her a questioning look. "Be here with you. Be here *for* you." Before I can protest, she takes my hand and holds it, resting it on her lap. The gesture is not sexual, but caring and warm. She looks at me with concern. "Just how bad is it? You can tell me."

"Couldn't be much worse," I sigh. "Max is canceling his advertising just like all the rest. His order was going to save my ass, but I guess it won't."

"So what are you going to do?"

"Try and figure out another way to save my ass." Pause. "But not tonight. In the morning when my sores have had a chance to heal a little."

"I'm sure you'll find a way."

"I'm not."

"You're not? But you built up this company, you sold it for all this money. I thought that, well, you know, my husband alwa—" She stops herself short.

"Did he now?"

"Sorry."

"No, go on. Your husband always said?"

"Well, you know." She is squirming with discomfort. She is not unattractive like this. "All that gung-ho business world stuff about confidence and the can-do spirit."

"Laura, you are sitting on the bed of a mildly depressive character. All that gung-ho stuff is something other people have. I am used to disaster. It's in my blood. God knows I struggle against it, but the way things seem to turn out, I can't help thinking it's also in my stars. Failure has a way of finding me."

"But don't you feel that no matter what—"

"No. That runs counter to the facts. Fact: things look bad. Fact: they have for some time. Fact: I keep fighting like a son of a bitch and things just keep getting worse. Fact: I have no idea how this is going to turn out."

"But don't you feel like a winner?"

"No. Laura, in all seriousness, I don't know whether I'm going to end up clipping coupons on the French Riviera or standing in the unemployment line. Really, I don't."

"You're exaggerating for effect."

"No, I'm not. It's not only possible that I could fail. It's probably more—"

"Don't be ridiculous. Look at yourself; you're—"

"You ever been poor, Laura?"

"Sure, I've been down and out more times and in more places than I can count."

"I didn't say broke, I said poor. No money anywhere and no idea if there's any way to get any—ever. That's how I grew up. I can't imagine how you could identify with it. I think there's just no way."

She pauses, searching for another tack. "My father always told me you had to see business as a game."

"Laura, I don't mean any disrespect, but . . ." I withdraw my hand from hers. "Of course it's all a game when you know you've already won." I hold one hand up and rub my thumb against my fingertips. Money. "For a guy like me, this is no game. A game is something you play on a sunny afternoon. You sweat a little; you get a score. Maybe you win; maybe you lose. When it's over, everyone relaxes over a few beers. That's my idea of a game. This, you pour you life's blood away, you get fucked over by a lot of really shitty people, you try desperately to claw a little something away for yourself, and then you die. Doesn't sound like a game to me."

"No, silly, I mean *treat* it like a game."

Suddenly, the gang of villains I have met today is standing around the bed. I feel vulnerable. No, I feel helpless. I have no plan. I am exhausted. Physically and emotionally. I arch my neck backward against the pillow and close my eyes. "Angghh." I wince.

"Want me to massage your forehead?" Laura asks.

"Thanks, but no thanks." I open my eyes. Laura is wide awake and studying me.

"I want to help you."

"Laura," I sigh, "I'm spent."

"Can I sleep with you?" I squint at her through my pain and fatigue. "No, no," she clarifies nervously, "I don't mean sleep with you. I mean *sleep* with you. You know, lie here beside you. A little human contact to help heal?"

My eyelids are turning to lead. The irresistible weight of gravity closes them for me. "Okay," I mutter, "turn off the light, please." The room goes dark; I hear the click of the switch; the room goes darker. Finally.

I feel Laura, still on top of the blanket, pull the bedspread over herself and snuggle beside me. She puts one arm around my waist. I turn on my side to sleep, my back to her. She turns likewise, nestling against me, spoon-style. The warmth of her through the sheet and blanket is comforting.

"Maybe I'll surprise you," she whispers as she gives my earlobe a good-night kiss. "Maybe I'll surprise myself." She stirs slightly, then settles in again.

A few minutes go by in the darkness. As exhausted as I am, I cannot find my way to sleep. I know what the problem is. I sit up in bed, upsetting Laura's snuggle. "Hey? What's the matter?" she asks. I reach over her and snap on the bedside lamp.

"Laura, we can't do this. We just can't."

"Of course, we can," she says, sitting herself up against the headboard. After lying down in the dark, she must have slipped off the flannel night-shirt. She now sits naked beside me. I can't help staring at her breasts. They are just as I had imagined them through her bathing suit at Bangle Bay. Round like pomegranates. Her nipples are small and round, like teenage girls' whose breasts are just beginning to bud.

"No, we can't," I insist. With that, she covers her breasts with one arm and reaches behind to retrieve the flannel nightshirt. "Yeah, get dressed, Laura. Please. I'm gonna." I climb out of bed on the side away from Laura and head for my closet. Pulling out underwear, socks, chino pants, and a polo shirt, I stand with my back to her and hurriedly get dressed.

When I turn around, she is dressed in slacks and a half-buttoned silk blouse. She is buckling her black patent leather belt and stepping into her shoes.

"Laura, I'm sorry."

She squints at me, more quizzical than angry.

"I'm married."

"I know that."

"No, I mean I'm *married*. I really can't be with another woman. You know, really *be* with anyone but her."

"Doesn't look like she's around here anywhere."

"Oh yes, she is." I point to my head. "And she's not going away. She's everywhere inside me and all around me. This fuck-up between us will get fixed. Sooner or later. My God, she's pregnant with our baby."

Laura's face goes ashen. "Oh, I had no idea."

"I can afford to screw up this business stuff. And you know something? I probably will. But I can't lose what I've got with Wendy. I refuse to. Can you please leave?" I walk over to her and, touching her shoulder, start guiding her toward the door. "Jesus, Laura, I don't want you to feel that I'm rejecting you. I find you attractive. It scares me how much I'm drawn to you and this crazy fantasy life you lead. But that'll never be me, not if

I make fifty zillion dollars. I just haven't got a clue what you could want with me."

"You haven't given yourself the chance to find out. I want to save you from the traps of that conventional life you think you have to lead. Nobody with spirit is ever happy with that, they just kid themselves."

Suddenly, the telephone rings.

"What?" asks Laura with surprise.

"Just a minute." I leave her standing by the door and grab the phone. "Hello?" I cannot imagine who it might be; it is almost two in the morning.

"This is the front desk, sir," a deep male voice says. "Your wife is on her way up."

"Holy shit," I say as the line goes silent.

"What's the matter?"

"Wendy's on her way up." I speak as much to the room as to Laura.

"This should be very interesting," Laura says with a little grin.

I grab her by the shoulders, not violently, but not politely or fondly either.

"Listen to me. This is for real. Nothing happened between us. If you do anything to jeopardize thi—"

The doorbell rings. I let her go, still glaring at her as I approach the door. I open it partway and stand in the open crack, keeping Laura out of view, I hope.

Wendy is in the hallway wearing baggy slacks and baggy sweater. Not exactly maternity clothes but getting ready for them. I know Wendy.

"Happy birthday," she says with a hint of a smile, "you bastard. I guess I should say 'belatedly'; it's past midnight." She holds up a small container of yogurt and a plastic spoon and offers it to me. "This was all I could find at this hour. It's your second favorite flavor. The deli was out of boysenberry." She steps up to the door. "Aren't you going to let me in?"

Instead of letting her in, I let myself out into the hallway and bring the door to an almost shut position behind me. Wendy looks puzzled. Before she can speak, I start spilling. "Wendy, my life is a mess, but there's one thing I know. I can't live without you. You've got to take me back. I mean if you'll have me. I mean you've got to. You've just got to. You're the only woman I want, the only woman. You've got to believe me. You've got to."

"I believe you, I believe you."

"Wendy, nothing happened in London. Nothing. I swear to you. Nothing. Do you believe me?"

"I've thought about it. Yes, I believe you."

"Now." I pause and gulp. "When I open this door, there's a chance you might get mad all over again. But believe me, this is the same as London. Nothing happened."

"Robert, what the hell are you talking about? Why won't you open the door?"

"Okay, okay. I'll open the door." Holding my breath and praying for

I'm not sure what, I lean back and push the door open, backing my way into the room. "Wendy, meet Laura Chasen." I look behind me; Laura is standing about where I left her. "Laura, my wife, Wendy Wolfson."

Wendy looks back and forth between Laura and me. Her mouth is open. She makes no sound, but she might as well be screaming at the top of her lungs. "What the hell is this?" she finally says in a hoarse, angry whisper.

"Your husband was in the process of throwing me out," Laura says matter-of-factly.

Wendy takes a step toward the door. I jump in front of her and slam the door shut with my whole body. "Wendy, you are not leaving. You are going to understand what did and did not go on in this room. You are not leaving, at least not without me. I mean it; I really do."

"You, buster, are in no position to lay down any rules." To Laura, "What the hell are you doing here? At this hour? Your hair is a mess. Looks like you've been sleeping on it."

"I haven't. I might have liked to. But Bob never let it happen. Believe him. It's true."

"Well, just what did happen?" Wendy asks, still visibly controlling her rage.

"Nothing," I say frantically.

"Sure is a lot of tension in here just to explain nothing."

"Can we sit down?" Laura asks.

"I don't think so," Wendy says coldly. "Why are you in my husband's room at this hour of the night?"

"It's my understanding that you threw him out. Doesn't that make him a free agent? Look, let's be adult about this."

"If you want this guy," Wendy snaps, making a gesture in my direction, "take him. If not—"

"He doesn't want me. He only wants you. He's made that perfectly clear."

"The same way he did in London?"

"I'm afraid so. I guess I just didn't believe him the first time."

Wendy turns to me. "Robert, I thought you prided yourself on your ability to communicate your point of view clearly and persuasively." Her sarcasm reassures me. She is getting back to normal.

"Wendy," I say, "nothing is more important to me than our marriage. Nothing in the world."

Ignoring me, Wendy says to Laura, "Aren't you the one who goes jet-setting all over the place? The trust fund vagabond who sent us to that party in Southpoint."

"I heard you had a nice time," Laura says. "And I also understand that Gene Merritt was very helpful with a certain board member of American Communications."

"What the hell do you want? You're not trying to be our friend, you know, like a friend to us the couple. But that's sort of how you're acting. And at the same time you're trying to seduce my man away from me, which a friend of *us* would never do. Why don't you just leave us alone?" To me, "I'm sorry I ever thought of going to Bangle Bay. It was stupid. It's not us. Next year, we'll go back to Antigua like we always did. At least the people there didn't—"

"Look," Laura cuts her off in midsentence. "I don't belong here. I didn't mean to interrupt your, uh, marriage, although it looks to me like you don't need me for that. I'm sorry that this happened while you're pregnant. I had no idea, even though I personally don't think that changes things all that much. I'm leaving now, but I've got a feeling I'll run into you at Bangle Bay one of these days. And who knows, we can all be friends then." She heads past Wendy, past me, and opens the door.

"Go fuck yourself," Wendy snaps.

"Looks like that's what I'll have to do tonight," Laura says and closes the door behind herself.

"And you!" Wendy spits from between clenched teeth. She runs over to me and starts hitting me, pounding me furiously on the chest and shoulders.

Dawn light is turning the hotel room pale gray. Wendy and I are lying on the bed. I am half-sitting up against the headboard, she is stretched out with her head nestled against my chest. We drift in and out of conversations that drift in and out of sleep.

She stirs faintly. It wakes me. I lean forward and kiss her on the top of her head.

"Gotta go pee again," she whispers and draws herself out of bed. "Unh," she says as she stands up straight.

"You okay?" I ask.

"I don't know, a little . . . ungh . . . I don't know." She walks into the bathroom, holding her tummy with one hand. She turns on the bathroom light and closes the door about two-thirds of the way shut. I close my eyes to block out the fluorescent light. There is the sound of her unzipping her slacks and sliding them down, then the tinkling sound of her peeing, then a distressing cry.

"Ro-bert! Robert!" she moans. "I'm bleeding!"

NOVEMBER

CHAPTER THIRTY-TWO

Wendy downs her milk and puts the empty glass in front of me for a refill. A lone shaft of Sunday morning sunlight shoots through the window of our tiny kitchen. It will shine for exactly fifteen minutes, then disappear as the sun passes over the building's courtyard. Leaning back from our postage-stamp-sized kitchen table, I reach into the refrigerator for the milk carton.

"Half a glass more," she says, patting the flannel nightshirt over her tummy, "for us." She is not pregnant. That would be impossible so soon after the miscarriage. The doctor described the incident as routine and probably inevitable; first pregnancies often spontaneously abort in the first three months. Most of the ones that do were never meant to be, he assured us. No, this talk of the three of us is part of the agreement we made as I was taking her home from the hospital. We are to talk about ourselves as if we were a family already. To get me used to the idea, more comfortable with the feeling of fatherhood. Lately she's been doing it about three times a day: at breakfast, before turning off the lights at night, and once when I do not expect it, when talk of babies seems completely inappropriate and apropos of nothing.

She finishes her milk and watches the lonely little arrow of Manhattan sunshine creeping across the linoleum floor. The wound in our marriage is healing well. To me, at least, we feel closer than before, even if we do share more silent, pensive moments than we once did. These moments, often ending in a touch or an exchange of looks, feel not like pain but like relief . . . and release. Looking up from her thoughts, she asks, "How's your headache?"

The throbbing in my forehead has been more or less constant for the last two weeks. This pain between my eyes is not us. It is definitely business-induced. *Elixir* has managed to recapture a few of its lost advertisers. But I am batting zero on finding a new sponsor for the special issue. "The pain may be starting to fade," I say, "or maybe I'm just getting used to it."

"You know," Wendy muses, "whatever your next business turns out to be, promise me you'll make it one where the people are better than pond scum."

"Name me one."

"There's, uh . . ." With index finger raised, she is about to start a list. She pauses and lowers the list-making finger. "I'll get back to you."

After getting a big no at Synfab late Friday afternoon, I have no more drug companies to solicit for the special issue. Not one. All weekend, Wendy and I have been discussing where to turn next. "You want me to get a yellow pad to start that list of potential new industries?" she asks.

I smile. Wendy and her lists. "We might as well start with the yellow pages," I snicker. She wrinkles her nose at my admission of frustration. "It's so weird," I say, thinking aloud. "I can't trust anyone at the office anymore. I don't know who's feeding stuff back to Woodcock, who might be tipping off Leo about what I'm trying next. I don't know who's been compromised. And I can't afford to risk finding out. You build up a company and then you can't even . . ." I let that sentence drift away. "It's strictly you and me now. Are you up to it?"

Wendy leans over and pecks my cheek. "We pulled it off getting all those doctors' responses, didn't we? Besides, baby's gonna need shoes."

"And private school like Dalton," I add, referring to her prestigious, ultra-snooty high school alma mater.

"What about the idea you keep coming back to?" she asks, ignoring my remark. " 'The big, undiscovered virgin of doctor advertising'?" She is quoting me. "I think you may have had the answer all along."

I sit up straight. We look directly at each other.

"Do you really think so?" I ask.

"Uh-huh. No other category we've come up with fits so well."

"I keep trying to shoot holes in the reasoning behind it."

"I don't think you can. Why don't you just go with it?"

"Okay. Let's." I shrug, accepting the decision to proceed, then smile tentatively. "Fin-an-cial ser-vic-es," we chime in unison.

"It's true," I say, reiterating what I have said before. "It's completely obvious, and it's been completely overlooked in my category."

"So that makes it an opportunity. Maybe the one of a lifetime."

"I find it hard to believe it's just sitting there waiting. It's like an elephant at a party all alone in the corner and completely unnoticed."

"Then we can't afford to wait for someone else to discover it."

"It just seems like this is the kind of find that happens to somebody else."

"If you don't jump on it, Macallan, somebody else will."

I look across the room for the sunbeam. It is still there. Does it look brighter than before? Maybe. Is it lasting longer than usual? Perhaps. Is it a sign? Who knows? I have been so adrift in the past few months, it is hard to know what is real and what is imagined. Go ahead, Macallan; believe. Believe that the sunlight is a sign. Believe that Wendy is a sign, a gift. Believe in anything and everything that's positive, whatever moves you forward. There are more than enough forces out there to pull you back. I jump to my feet and reach into the drawer for the yellow pages. "Let's look under 'I' for investments." I flip through the flimsy pages impatiently. This is starting to be fun again.

"Go for it," Wendy says with a grin. "Grab the virgin elephant by the hindquarters. And let her have it. You have my blessing."

"Y-y-y-yes!" I find the stock brokerage houses. My prospect list, my targets, my quarry. It is more than three pages long. "Somewhere in these pages is"—I run my finger down the listings—"is our new client." So many wonderful entries. From Argo to Morgan to Zalansky. Their lofty-sounding company names are more hopeful than descriptive, with words like "trust," "security," "asset," and "management," which serve as respectable covers for the thieving Wall Street houses and the gamblers and chiselers who run them. And to think that people accuse the media of hype and bullshit.

"Financial services!" I chant.

"Financial services!" Wendy sings in counterpoint. She has her pen poised, ready to jot down the first entry. I look at her and shake my head no. Pulling carefully, ever so carefully, I start to tear the priceless yellow pages out of the phone book. "Don't you worry none, little woman," I tell her in my dumbest movie cowboy accent. "When we're done with them Wall Street Jaspers, I'll buy you all the phone books yer little heart desires."

"Ahh," she sighs, the smitten cowgirl. "Elixir Kid, you'll always be my hero."

Just as I finish extracting the pages, the phone rings. I grab it.

"Hello, Son!" the voice on the phone says. Once again, Clint sounds chipper and upbeat. For once, our moods match.

"Hey, Dad!" I feel expansive. "Guess what?"

"What?"

"We're gonna pull this off. That pretty wife a mine," I say, using his phrase, "and me. We're gonna pull this off." Since our patch-up, Clint has gone back to his old way of referring to Wendy. He behaves as if nothing happened. He received the news of our reconciliation with a simple "That's good," and the news of her miscarriage with "I'm awful sorry." The ability to discuss delicate personal matters still eludes him.

"What're you talkin' about?" he asks.

"You know the special issue?"

"Sure do. You finally got a taker?"

"Not yet. But we will. And we know where it'll come from. We know where we're gonna go hunting. We know where we can spear us a virgin," I say, happily mixing metaphors.

"What'ya mean, Son?" He sounds confused.

"We know which industry our mystery sponsor will be in. It's virgin territory for medical magazines. And *Elixir* is going to get there first. With its big special issue on hypertension. Can you guess? Can you?" I am so relieved to be optimistic again I am giddy. After the couple of months we've been through, I tell myself what the hell. Act silly. Let off a little tension. "Come on now, take a crack. Try Special Issues for a hundred dollars. The question is . . ."

"Geez, Son, I, uh . . ."

This is not fair. "Dad, it's financial services. Investments. It's hard to imagine, but they've been overlooked as an advertiser in my neck of the woods. It's a natural. Doctors are famous for having all this money that they don't know what to do with. Wall Street is there to help them lose it. And *Elixir* will be there to help speed the process along. By disseminating, through lots of advertising pages, valuable information about an as-yet-to-be-named brokerage house. It's the First Amendment and Free Enterprise and the Greater Fool Principle all at once. There it is! Proof that America still works."

"What're you sayin'?"

I have lost him again. I must remember to keep things simple for his benefit. "Dad, we've figured out that we won't have any competition selling the special issue to a stockbroker, because no magazine has ever approached them before to advertise specifically to doctors."

"Oh, I see. Which one you gonna get?"

"Don't know. I'll start cold calling tomorrow. But I'm confident. Very confident. That's how I got started the first time. I feel good, Dad, I really do. For the first time in a long time. We both do." I look over at Wendy. She smiles at me in agreement.

"That's great, Son. Glad to hear it." Pause. "Stockbroker, eh. Let me know when you land 'em, ya hear." Another pause. "You know, I got some big news, too."

"Do you now? What is it?"

"I'm on my way to Tucson!" It is a proud, excited announcement.

"To visit Jimmy?"

"To work with Jimmy. We're gonna be partners. We're gonna whip those muffler shops into shape. He needs an experienced man he can trust. Sent me my ticket yesterday. Even got an extra room in his apartment for me. Yessir, Jimmy and I are gonna show that muffler business what for."

"That's great, Dad. Great place to spend the winter. A lot less snow. How long you going to be out there?"

"Son, I'm not goin' for a visit. I'm goin' out there with your brother to stay. I'm puttin' the house up for sale. Realtor tells me I oughtta be able to get sixty-five, maybe seventy thousand for it, even in this crummy market."

At the thought of him selling our house, my euphoria vanishes. All at once, a wave of disquiet washes over me. It surprises me because, I tell myself, I don't care about the old house on Monroe Street. It's ancient history. If someone were to ask me, I would say that I have little affection for the place. But suddenly the idea of him selling it gives me a feeling of being abandoned, orphaned. Suddenly, the memory of my mother feels deader, colder, more distant than before. It was her house, after all, where her life and her dreams collided, did battle, and died. I feel a dull distant ache. It annoys me now that he sounds so happy.

"Well, of course you can sell the house if you want to," I say, giving him permission he has not asked for. "It's your house."

"It's your house, too, Son. Got a lotta your stuff still here."

"Yeah, I guess I do." I think of the personal items still scattered around my room and the boxes of memorabilia from my first twenty-odd years stacked away in the attic.

"Here's what I figure we can do. I'm shippin' outta here second week in December. How's about we all get together for one last Thanksgivin' here at the house? Your brother'll be back for a few days to help me with some a the arrangements. And you can get the stuff a yours you want and take it down to New York." *Noo Yawk.* "What d'ya say? All us Macallan men up here at the old homestead one last time."

Clint's suggestion of family camaraderie is as out of character as his jocular mood. But with the house now about to evaporate into memory and my life remaking itself every three weeks, change must be the order of the day.

"Sure," I say. "I guess so." I look over at Wendy and raise my voice. "Thanksgiving in Bayport?" She looks up at me. "Last hurrah of the men of the Macallan clan on Monroe Street before the house gets sold." Wendy looks surprised and thoughtful at the news I am broadcasting.

"So you gonna be there, Son?" the happy voice on the telephone asks.

"Sure?" I announce in Wendy's direction. She shrugs a why-not. "Okay, then. We'll be there for Thanksgiving, you and Jimmy, me and Wendy."

"Just like old times," Clint says, a smile beaming in his voice.

"Sure, Dad. Just like old times."

"Now you give that pretty wife a yours a kiss for me, you hear."

"Okay, Dad."

"Bye, Son. See you in Bayport."

"Bye, Dad."

Click.

"What's this?" Wendy asks.

"He's moving to Tucson." I put the phone back in its wall mount and sit down slowly, my shock still evident. "To help Jimmy with the muffler shops. He's selling the house. Moving everything."

"Wow, that's big stuff."

"I've never heard him so happy. Like a different guy. Bouncy, cheerful."

"You look upset, Robert."

"I do not."

"You do, too. What's wrong?"

"Unnh!" With one hand, I brush away my concern in the air. "It's stupid."

"No, it's not, tell me."

"I don't know, it just got me upset to think of him selling the house."

"Of course it's upsetting, you grew up there."

"But I had such a lousy time. I never go back."

"It's still your house."

"Then, guess what. This is even funnier. I had a flash of jealousy. This is ridiculous. I'm a grown man."

"No, it's not, sweetie. Tell me about it."

"The way he was so happy for Jimmy. I mean I'm not unhappy that Jimmy has good news. I'm glad about it, too. It's just that I never heard him talk that way about anything I ever did. This is idiotic, looking for my father's approval. At my age, for Pete's sake."

"It's not so dumb. It's perfectly natural. But he's been proud of you before. I've seen him myself."

"Yeah, but not like this. This was different. And then—this is stupid, too—he talked about how Jimmy had sent him a ticket. I've tried to send him stuff time and again, and he never accepts a thing from me. Never. Too proud and independent, he always told me. He's even investing in Jimmy's company. How about that one?"

"You don't care about *that,* do you?"

"No, but he's never even been curious about what I do."

"That used to be true, but you guys talk about publishing now. You've said yourself that he's started taking an interest in what you do."

"It's not the same. With Jimmy, it's always been, uh . . . ."

Wendy comes over and puts her arm around me. "Naturally. He identifies with Jimmy. He can't possibly identify with you."

"I was just thinking of something Jimmy said to me when he was here."

"What?"

"In the middle of all his usual hostility, he said, 'You know, Brother, *I* was always the favorite.' At first, I said to myself that's ridiculous. Mom always made me feel guilty about beating up on Jimmy, and I accepted the guilt because I figured I was the favorite. I mean I got the grades, the accolades, all the right stuff. I had to be the favorite, right? I felt guilty because I was looking down on Jimmy. And all along he was the one looking down on me. The more I think about it, he *was* the favorite. *Is* the favorite. He was laughing at me when he left. Laughing."

"Oh, Robert, your family never knew what to do with you. You're so different from them. Can't you see? Jimmy is more like them. They can understand him and what he does. They can't relate to you, they can't understand where you've gone and what you've done. They never will."

"I guess so."

"Of course. And there's something else you've overlooked."

"What's that?"

"Jimmy needs them. You never did. They couldn't have helped you, even if they'd wanted to. You just took off on your own and eclipsed their world."

"Yeah, just now he said, 'Jimmy needs me. I'm on my way to Tucson.' "

"Of course, honey. Come on, it's expected. Who do you love more? Someone who needs you? Or someone who's going to be perfectly fine even if you fall off the end of the earth?"

"Yeah, I guess so."

"Let him go to Tucson. They'll be happy together, the two of them. It's perfect for them, mufflers, tailpipes, and all."

"Yeah, he was even quoting Jimmy about how you swindle the customers into higher-priced mufflers."

Wendy gives me a hug. "Let it go, honey. You belong to me, we belong to each other, and we live in a different world. I don't know if it's any better, our world here, it's just different. You can never go back to Bayport. Jimmy and your father will never really leave it."

"I wouldn't want to go back."

"I got news for you. You couldn't. Even if your life depended on it."

"I guess not."

"Come on, let's get back to our list."

CHAPTER THIRTY-THREE

"You want the Simmons data first and *then* the MRI?" Wendy shouts from the living room.

"No, MRI first, Simmons afterward!" I holler back from our little second bedroom. Lately, my real workdays have begun in here around seven-thirty in the evening. After a full day of going through the motions at *Elixir*.

"This investment profile of doctors, where does it go?" Wendy is now standing in the bedroom doorway facing me, holding a stack of papers against her chest.

"That's the big opener," I say. "Let's put it over there." I point to the wall opposite the window, along which we are collating ten sets of presentation leave-behinds for the final meeting with Greenthal/Peck, America's number one second-tier stock brokerage firm. The meeting is scheduled for the day after tomorrow. Greenthal/Peck is just a breath away from sponsoring *Elixir*'s special issue on hypertension, just a breath away from contributing the revenues that will ensure the profit targets stated in my contract. Greenthal/Peck is just a breath away from rescuing not just the rest of my earn-out, but possibly the rest of my life. I cannot begin to describe how I love this company and its senior vice president of marketing, Al Tully.

Barefoot Wendy, in her green plaid flannel nightshirt, bends over to lay out the ten copies of my opening mini-essay, "Smart Doctors, Dumb Investors," along the baseboard. For the past three weeks Wendy and I have been preparing presentations. Ten companies listened to me and said no. Greenthal/Peck listened, thought about it, and said hmmm, then maybe, then possibly interested, and in forty-eight hours, I hope, yes.

Secrecy has been essential. No one at *Elixir* can learn what I am up to, because it might leak to Leo or Harry. And I cannot risk having Leo or any of Mackey's people butting in on my seduction. There's no telling what a phone call or a strategically dropped innuendo or, worse still, a competing pitch from *Panacea* could do. As for Woodcock, he is just waiting for the special issue to fall through. That will be the excuse he needs to swallow up the magazine. God knows what he might try to help disaster along. No, until I have a signed insertion order in hand, I am not safe.

My salespeople, Roni, Wayne, and George Reicher, the replacement for Mike Carmody, have been pounding the pavement trying to win the bonus I promised for landing a special issue sponsor. Their lack of success has served me in two ways. One, in the process of pushing so hard, they've signed up extra ad pages from other clients and helped to recoup some of the dollars Leo took from us. And two, they've been so busy they have stayed out of my hair.

"I think you've got to integrate these extra bennies more into the main pitch," Wendy is saying, holding ten sets of the first part of the appendix. "Like when you're offering to give them a free booth at the three most attended medical conferences of the coming year. That's a humongous selling opportunity for these guys. All those greedy doctors wandering around under one roof, unprotected by nurses and secretaries. For aggressive brokers like the ones at Greenthal/Peck, that's like shooting fish in a barrel. Don't save that stuff for the end."

"You're right." I watch Wendy deposit another ten sets of papers along the wall. "You know something?" I ask.

"What?" Her back is to me.

"I was just thinking how much fun this has been, you and I working together like this."

"Uh-huh," she answers distractedly, not looking up.

"No, really. I mean it."

"Me, too." She finishes at pile number ten and turns around. "Yeah, we're a great team. And you're about to hit a home run." She swings an imaginary bat. "Thwack!" And watches the ball go over the fence.

"I'm serious," I say. "How about when this is over we go into business together, you and me?"

"You have anything particular in mind?"

"No, but we'd run it together."

She faces me, arms out, hands on her hips. "Could you take us being together like that twenty-four hours a day?"

"We're like that on weekends and vacations, aren't we? We always have fun."

"Yeah, but that's weekends and vacations. It's not the same as sharing an office. Decisions, tensions, conflicts, money, employees. All that work stuff is very different. Look at the shit Liz and I put each other through. And we have our own separate clients most of the time."

"True. But if any two people could get through it together, we could."

"The question is, Would we want to?"

"I don't know, would we? I'm asking."

Wendy surveys the piles of papers, brushes off her hands, and sits down cross-legged on the floor. "I guess we're taking a little chat break," she says. I sit down beside her. She goes on. "I've only seen two couples who did that, and they were both crazy. Now there's a good chance they started out that way. They were also in their seventies and it was ten years ago, so they're like our grandparents' generation."

"The Schoenwalds and the Engels," I say.

"Uh-huh. It's scary to think of them as role models." This was Wendy's youthful foray into the uptown New York art world. The Schoenwalds owned the art bookstore where Wendy worked summers during college. The Engels owned the ultra-prestigious gallery where Wendy interned after college. The experience cured her forever of all admiration for the bitchy, Byzantine world of high-priced culture. She went running to business school. By comparison, the corporate world seemed refreshingly direct and straightforward, even honest.

"They got really weird, those couples," Wendy says, "really weird. They were like this two-headed beast that kept trying to cut itself in half but couldn't. Mr. and Mrs. Schoenwald would feud for months. Months. Sometimes, they'd draw a chalk line down the middle of the store. Mr. Schoenwald wouldn't cross over into Mrs. Schoenwald's territory, and vice versa. They would speak to each other only through the employees. *'Tell Mr. Schoenwald he needs to call Harry Abrams,'* " she says, impersonating a soft-spoken old woman. " *'Tell Mrs. Schoenwald she has to move za Rodin section,'* " she snaps, imitating an angry old German. She switches back and forth: " *'Tell Mr. Schoenwald he's being very foolish.'* *'Tell Mrs. Schoenwald she's being very inefficient.'* But then they went home together at night and you knew damn well they talked to each other. They were like prisoners handcuffed together. They did crazy things just to show they were still separate people."

Wendy leans back on her hands, stretches her legs out, and wiggles her toes. "Now the Engels, they had it down to a science." She does an angry Mrs. Engel: " *'Go move the Miró drawing to the third floor and don't tell Mr. Engel I told you to do it.'* Then Mr. Engel would discover that the Miró had been moved." She does an infuriated Mr. Engel: " *'Vhy on earth did you move ze Miró?'* 'Uh, uh, Mrs. Engel told me to.' *'Did she tell you not to tell me?'* 'Uh, uh, yes, Mr. Engel.' *'Zen vhy did you tell me?'* "

We laugh together.

"You don't want us to become like that, do you?" Wendy asks. "They used to bicker with each other so much, both couples."

"Maybe they would have bickered anyway. A lot of couples, especially from that era, used to bicker. It's what kept them together."

"Maybe so. But there was also this weird competitiveness between them. Mr. Schoenwald and Mr. Engel were clearly the bosses. In their day, the man was always in charge officially. But Mrs. Schoenwald and Mrs. Engel were never completely comfortable with that arrangement, you could tell. So they were always doing little things to dig at their husbands' authority. They'd help with something; then they'd undercut them. Help and undercut, help and undercut. There was always this tension in the air between them. It looked yucky from where I stood. I'd hate to see any of that happen to us."

"Are you saying you wouldn't want us to be in business together?"

"I'm saying I want our next joint venture to be a baby. Then we'll see what feels right."

"Okay," I say, "we'll see."

We stand up and go back to collating and compiling the presentation materials, in silence now. We ferry papers back and forth between living room and bedroom, piling, stacking, rearranging. I try out different orders for the flow of ideas. Wendy either nods or wrinkles her nose as commentary. A grunt or a gesture between us serves as instructions for moving the growing stacks of papers. The work progresses with neither of us paying attention to the time. It could be half an hour that passes. It could be more or less. Finally, we agree that the job is finished. Silent nods and a handshake. I bring in ten covers, and we start to clip the binders together, one by one.

After another ten minutes, I stand up and survey the piles. "I don't think there's anything more we can do tonight," I say. "I think we're done."

"No," she says, standing up and stretching after crouching over the papers. "There's one more thing I think you should take into the presentation with you."

"What's that?" She is leading me somewhere, I can tell.

"A little something you can smile about during your brilliant performance at Greenthal/Peck. So you can bring it to mind in that room full of deadly awful Wall Street stiffs and think, *You guys'd never guess what happened to me the other night.*"

In a single gesture, she raises the flannel nightshirt over her head and drops it on the floor. Standing there naked, she asks, "What do you say? Just for fun?"

I look her up and down for an instant. Her beauty is in her imperfections, the peculiarities that make her Wendy and that make her mine. Her face, always animated, especially the big dark eyes; her breasts, not quite round, not quite pointed, and not quite matching; her knees, a little knobby; her curves around the hips and waist, like a cello, framing her soft, vulnerable tummy; the dark animal mat of her pubic hair; her funny toes. She is everywoman. She is my woman. Stepping quickly but carefully over the neat little mountains of demographic data, I reach Wendy, scoop her up under her legs, and carry her into our bedroom.

I am at my desk, office door closed, studying my presentation, flipping through my copy of the leave-behind, reviewing the logic, second-guessing my persuasion. I can find no holes. I have research and data to prove just about everything. The ideas flow inexorably one after the other: Doctors are uncertain, ineffective money managers. They need professional financial help in both their practice and personal finances. Doctors represent a growth market for Greenthal/Peck if the company can reach them en masse. But doctors are very difficult to reach through the conventional general media. The advertiser is forced to pay for too many extra nondoctor readers. What's worse, he cannot be sure that he will have the doctors' undivided attention in books aimed at the general public. Even more discouraging, general publications for "upscale" readers are already cluttered with competing financial services advertising. Enter *Elixir*. A magazine that "delivers" the cream of the medical profession at a reasonable cost per thousand, with no waste whatsoever. *Elixir* is a publication in which doctors believe and to which they pay attention because it is uniquely "theirs." Finally, there is no competing financial advertising to distract from Greenthal/Peck's message. And, best of all, doctors will save the special issue on hypertension, referring to it time and again, thus ensuring repeated impressions of Greenthal/Peck's message as the financial adviser uniquely suited to serve the needs of doctors. Ergo: Greenthal/Peck would be missing a great opportunity by not sponsoring *Elixir*'s special issue.

Al Tully has been enthusiastic about the special issue and has been lobbying vigorously for it. He says he cannot promise a yes, but he clearly hints that my proposal will eventually get the nod. He says he will need yeses from his national sales manager and the head of the portfolio management group and a final blessing from the new president of the firm, a son of a bitch by reputation, recently recruited from Shearson.

I have been forced to use subterfuge with my own people to keep this confidential. I hate doing it. It is bad faith with them. And I keep thinking they can read my thoughts, that they know every time I lie.

Tully and I have been talking back and forth a lot lately, meaning that Marie and Jeannie must field our calls. Mr. Tully, I told them, is my new broker. He is pursuing some important new investments for me. He must be put through at once. And since his calls with me are strictly personal and confidential, he will rarely leave a message. Presumably, Mr. Tully is the lucky guy with whom I finally decided to invest, since I've been talking regularly to other brokers at other companies for the past three weeks. Those, of course, were the companies that said no to sponsoring the special issue. It has been a good lie. But it does have one big drawback. The fictional process of screening all these brokers created too much interest in this secret new investment of mine. Buzz, buzz, buzz around the office. I can feel its presence, even if I can't overhear its content. I can imagine what they are buzzing about. What do you think Bob is going to do with all that money? One of those secret offshore limited partnerships? One of those 300 percent annual return thingies only rich people get to invest in?

"It must be fun," Marie said this morning, sticking her head in my office just after I got off the phone with Tully. She finally broke down and opened up the subject.

"What?"

"Figuring out how to invest all your money."

"It's turning out to be more of a worry than I thought it would be." I hope that sounds believable, satisfies her, and sends her back to her desk. It doesn't.

"You must get all these real super investments to choose from. The kind you read about with the oil wells and the computer companies and venture capital and all that." Oh no. Marie wants to talk investments with me. Seriously. What do I say?

"Uh, well, I used to think there were all these magic bonanzas out there that the Bass brothers knew about, but I didn't."

"Yeah, that's what I mean," she says eagerly, expecting the secret of El Dorado to drop from my lips any moment now. "That kind of thing." She invites herself into my office, sits down facing my desk, and spills it all out at once. "I'm still looking for a place to invest my big bonus. Do you think he could talk to me? Your broker, I mean. If he's the guy you chose after talking to all those different firms, he must be really good. I talked it over with my mother, and she said I should trust your advice, too. I really am a dummy about this kind of thing. I stuck the bonus in our money market fund, 'cause it's FDIC insured, but that's because I don't know what else to do with it. That must be what suckers do. But I've never had a lump of cash like this before. Can you do that favor for me, Bob? I'd really appreciate it. Next time he calls, can I say you gave me permission to ask him?"

This really threw me for a loop. "Uh, geez, Marie, you know your money is a big responsibility. Uh, I, uh, think you should do the most prudent thing that's right for you and your, uh, needs. I'm not sure that the guy I'm dealing with would be, uh, right, for, uh . . ." What an idiot, Macallan.

Suddenly, Marie backed off. "I'm sorry, Bob," she said, sheepishly getting up to leave. "I didn't mean to embarrass you. I forgot. You're not supposed to talk to rich people about their money." She backs out of the room like a rejected penitent. "I'm sorry," she mumbles.

Shit, Macallan, now you've gone and done it. I started kicking myself for three reasons. First, I made Marie feel, not just bad, but inferior. Second, I didn't help her with her problem. Third, until a moment ago, she was the only *Elixir* employee who I felt was still completely behind me. I want to help, but I certainly don't want to be responsible for the investment results of her bonus. But I must respond on some level to her request for help. That's the only way I can acknowledge her as a person, continue to make her feel that she's special in my eyes, and, I hope, salvage our trust.

So I called Geoff Hayes, my account officer at Manhattan Trust, the fancy private bank for what are euphemistically called "high net worth individuals." After receiving my first payment from American and paying the employee bonuses and all the taxes, the $2.7 million I entrusted to Manhattan Trust was just enough to qualify me for their services. Just barely. They prefer a minimum base of $3 million. Geoff is looking forward to the second half of my earn-out almost as much as I am. It is the only reason he gives me the time of day. They are not the rocket scientists of investing at Manhattan Trust, but they have a splendid reputation for preserving capital and making it grow slowly and surely. Which is a goal both Marie and I should have in common.

"Geoff, I need a favor for this small but growing private client. Me," I said.

"Always happy to oblige," Geoff said, putting on his best Jeeves the private banker routine.

"My most loyal employee needs a safe, solid place to park her once-in-a-lifetime bonus."

"Treasuries," Geoff says succinctly.

"Just what I was thinking," I say.

"She can go downtown anytime and register. Tell her there's an auction next Monday."

"Geoff, she can't do it on her own. Now she's nowhere near material for Manhattan Trust, but she's near and dear to me."

"We would love to help, Bob, but we do have our two point five million minimum."

"I know, I know. I'd like to give her your name just the same. And I'd like for you to get her started in T-bills. Hold her hand. Show her how she can roll them over. Preferably get her into longer bills, like a year. Give her the red carpet treatment, and bill all the transaction charges to me. But don't let her know."

"That's highly unusual, Bob."

"No, it's not. She's a key person in helping me get the other half of the dough I'm planning to park with Manhattan Trust. Now if you think I should look for another private banker when the rest of my ship comes in . . ."

"Bob, let's not be precipitous about this." It's the money he thinks I'll make from my *next* venture that Geoff is really after. He once showed me an elaborate presentation about the financial life cycle of the entrepreneur. It sounded like the brand of dog food that's timed for a canine's different ages.

"I'd love to help her in any way I can," Geoff says. "What's her name?"

"Marie Padrone. And remember, any costs bill to me."

"I'll send you a written confirmation to that effect for you to sign."

"What a gentleman," I say. "Bye-bye." I put down the phone and turn the Greenthal/Peck document open, face down, on my desk. I go out to Marie's desk in the hallway.

"Got a minute?" I ask her.

"Sure, Bob, you want me in there?" She avoids my glance. She is still embarrassed by our last conversation. I sit on the edge of her desk, right beside her.

"Listen, Marie," I say in a confidential tone. "I've been thinking about what you asked about."

"You have?" She looks up. "I'm sorry I brought it up. It's okay, really."

"Listen to me. This is as much as I know about investing. And it isn't much. Believe me, you don't want to deal with Greenthal/Peck or any other kind of stockbroker. Not with your bonus money. Remember those commercials on TV? We make money the old-fashioned way? Well, they don't earn it, they *churn* it. Here's the number of my private banker at Manhattan Trust." I scribble Geoff's name and number on her notepad. "He and I agree that the safest thing you can do is to buy U.S. Treasury bills. That's what I'm doing. They do it as a free service for their clients. And he'll be happy to make you a special client of his. So call him, he's expecting your call. Ask him to explain about treasuries. And if you decide you want to buy some, he'll arrange it for you. Free. He'll do it for you the first time, and then you'll be all set to renew later on your own, if you want to. It's easy. It's the safest thing you can do. So call him. He's a real nice guy."

Marie's jaw hangs open, speechless.

"Really," I say. "It's all arranged. It's the safest, smartest thing you can do."

"Wow," I hear behind me as I return to my office. "Thanks, Bob. Thanks."

I go back to my desk and open the booklet to go over my presentation one last time.

Soon after, I hear a knock. It is Wayne Crosby. "Got a minute?" he asks from the doorway.

"Sure, come on in." I close the Greenthal/Peck binder and lay it, cover down, on my desk. Cool, handsome Wayne looks agitated. "I've got a big idea for this special issue," he says, pacing around the office, nervously running his hands through his thinning, graying blond hair. "But I think this idea is even bigger than the special issue." This is a good salesman who can smell an extra bonus and then some. "I think the potential is huge, really huge." Wayne always drops the "h" in that word. "Yooge, really yooge" is what he says.

"Great," I reply. "Let's hear it."

Wayne's pacing leads him to the corner window, where he spots a full shopping bag. It stops his excited train of thought. "Hey, what's this?" he asks. It is my bag of medical promotional items. For Greenthal/Peck, to show how many gimmicks we can use to put their name into the hands of doctors.

"Promotional items," I say neutrally, "our all-time greatest hits."

"Gee, I don't think I've seen all these. Do they go all the way back to the beginning of the book?"

"Uh-huh."

"Who they for?"

"Oh, nobody. Just my collection."

"Can I borrow it? I'll return it tomorrow morning, I promise."

"Uh, sure."

"Gee, thanks." He fishes inside the bag and pulls out a calculator with a drug logo on it. "Hmm, good idea. When did you do this?"

"Three years ago."

"Excellent," he says and takes possession of the bag.

Shit. Now I have to hope that Tully has not misplaced the bag of promotional items I gave him at our first meeting. Otherwise, I will be missing some important props.

Wayne takes the shopping bag out of the corner and carries it to the chair in front of my desk. He sets it on the floor beside himself as he sits down. "Here's my idea, Bob."

I lean forward, pretending interest and enthusiasm. This is the first time I have ever *not* been eager to hear a new idea from an *Elixir* person. A part of me cannot believe it has come to this.

"I think we ought to take a run at a brokerage company." Wayne regains his excitement. He continues rapid-fire, full of enthusiasm. "Investment advice for doctors. A financial services advertiser. That's my idea. They're virgins in the medical category. We could own them if we get there first. And we could promise whoever the taker is that he could own our audience. At least until we signed up more of them for other issues." He pauses to let it sink in. "What do you think, Bob? Is that a great idea or is that a great idea?"

"That's a great idea, Wayne. I agree."

I am not quite sure where Wayne stands on the Leo issue. He put up with Leo cordially and respectfully and probably even liked him a bit. But there was no way Leo could get him to join him the way he did with Carmody. Crosby is very much his own man. But what seeds Leo and Carmody planted with Wayne, and how he received them, I cannot even guess. I do know that Wayne and Carmody keep in touch regularly. I have developed the sneaky, reprehensible habit of checking all the message boxes when people are out to lunch. Leo has seen to it that Carmody and Linda Baleine, the production assistant he took with him to *Panacea,* are in regular touch with their old friends at *Elixir.* Furthermore, I cannot take the chance that Wayne might talk to someone at American about his impending stroke of genius; it might somehow get back to Woodcock. Dudley still checks in, on a friendly basis, with annoying regularity. It's too late in the game for any risks at all. I must play this ultra-cautiously.

"I like it," I say. "I like it a lot."

Wayne looks pleased. I hope I do, too. He reaches into the inside breast pocket of his suit jacket and pulls out a sheet of paper. "Here's a preliminary list of potential brokerage advertisers. This is based on what I've researched about their product lines, the type of customers they deal with, and the geographical coverage of their offices. I come up with seven potentially good prospects."

He hands me the list. On it are four of the companies who turned me down and, at number three, Greenthal/Peck.

"Good job, Wayne." I hope my alarm and horror do not show. "You've really done your homework."

"I'd like to start making some calls, get this ball rolling."

Under each company is the name and phone number of the key contact person. At the companies I have already called on, he has all the names of the people I spoke to, including Al Tully. If Wayne starts calling these people, everything will get blown. But I cannot tell him what I am up to. At least not yet.

"I think you and I ought to put our heads together a little more before you make your first approaches," I say, making up my excuses as I go along. "Since they are virgins in our category, let's be sure our opening line is a real zinger." Knowing that Wayne is proud of his reputation with the ladies, I add a wink with that little thought.

He accepts the comparison of ad sales with sexual conquest and returns the wink. "Sure, a real zinger. When do you want to meet?"

"How about right after Thanksgiving?" I hand him back his hit list. "The rest of this week is pretty well shot. And next week, well, a short week with the holiday and all. The world is pretty much at a stand-still . . ." By the time we come back from Thanksgiving, I will have reached closure with Greenthal/Peck. And whether I got a yes or a no, I'll then be able to level with him. I will either call him off the case or enlist him to help me go after yet another investment firm. "You okay with that? Normally, I'd say let's get started yesterday. But I just don't see any percentage in going off half-cocked. I think we're better off waiting a bit and making sure we're totally prepared."

"Yeah, okay," Wayne says with more than a hint of disappointment.

"Hey, I've got an idea. Let's you and I spend a little time on it tonight. After the Pierce dinner." Yes, the Pierce dinner. The whole *Elixir* staff will be there, the biggest publishing industry bash of the year, black tie, of course. For me, it will be an evening of total masquerading. "I'll buy you a drink at the Plaza afterward. How's that sound?"

"Sure thing. Great. See ya there." His enthusiasm is halfhearted. Just as he stands up to leave, Marie comes in. "It's Al Tully from Greenthal/Peck on the line," she announces, happier than ever to see me and serve me.

"Hey, they're on my list, right here!" Wayne says excitedly. He checks the list again. "Hey, that's the same guy I've got here."

"Thanks, Marie," I say, trying to rush her out of my office. Wayne looks at me with innocent puzzlement. I reach to pick up my phone, stalling for a moment to think of an answer. "Yeah, he's my broker. Wants to take all my money."

It does not play convincingly, I can tell.

"He's their national marketing director," Wayne says. "He's on my list."

Okay, Macallan, get yourself out of that one. "Uh, he's also a broker, strictly for high-ticket jerks like me who want to lose it all in a couple of rolls. You know brokers, they don't want to give up those commissions, even when they get into management. That's the culture at Greenthal/

Peck. Everybody sells. Even the brass." I pick up the phone and punch the button to connect the line. I cover the mouthpiece to give Wayne a final shot, one that I hope will satisfy him. "Don't worry," I tell him conspiratorially. "I won't tip your hand."

Wayne nods and picks up the bag of items I was hoping to bring to my meeting.

"Remember what I said about tonight," I say, my hand still over the mouthpiece.

"That's okay," Wayne says. "We can start on it tomorrow. It'll be a late one."

As he turns to leave, I mouth the words "the door, please" at him. He gets the message and closes the door as he goes. I shudder for an instant as I think what a sleaze I have become. Only because the world has forced you to, I tell myself. Unless you were just kidding yourself before, another internal voice counters.

"Al," I say nervously into the phone. "Everything okay?"

"A-okay," he says. "Just checking in."

"A-okay here, too. Say Al, have you still got that bag of promotional items I left with you last week? Remember? With all the notepads and the calendars and prescription pads and whatnot."

"Gee, I don't know. I thought you were going to bring a new selection."

"Could you take a look and see if it's still there? We're running a little short of stuff around the office. Could you take a look? Please?"

"You mind holding on?"

"No, not at all."

"Okay," he says, "hang on." The phone goes silent.

I wait and wait. And wait and wait. This must look bad, but not nearly as bad as tipping off the wrong person that I'm about to make this presentation.

Finally Al comes back on the line. "I've got it," he says. "But the bag seems to be missing that nice calculator with the drug logo on it. The elves have a way of finding things around here."

"No problem," I say. "I'll bring another."

"Fine, fine," he says. "See you tomorrow."

"Right," I say and hang up. I rummage through my drawers angrily, looking for one of our old giveaway calculators. I have none. Shit, I say. Then I tell myself, Hold on.

I get up and walk out to Marie's desk.

"Marie, you got one of those old Zentane calculators we made up?"

"Let me look." She fumbles around in her desk for what seems like an eternity. Then she extracts the calculator in its little beige plastic carrying case.

"Ta-ta!" she says, handing it to me.

"Oh, thank you, Marie." I breathe a sigh of relief that is totally out of proportion to the simple request she has fulfilled.

"No problem," she says, looking at me quizzically. "No problem at all."

The Grand Ballroom of the New York Regent Hotel is, as usual, beyond grand. Its impossibly high ceiling, sculpted to look like a roof of sheltering palm leaves, ablaze with gold leaf, evokes a kingdom richer than heaven and far more exotic. The walls of deep jade green set off the extravagant chandeliers that hang in the air like frozen waterfalls of diamonds. The waiters scurry about in snappy maroon jackets with gold braid epaulets. They look far more important and official than the seated men in their black-tie uniforms. It looks like the men in tuxedos should be carrying the trays for the waiters and not the other way around.

With a little nostalgia, I look around the *Elixir* table at my old-timers: Marie Padrone, Jerry Greenstein, Joe Bartolo, Jeannie Polski, Roni Kessler, and Wayne Crosby. The way the company is changing, George Reicher might almost qualify, too, having now been with *Elixir* for almost three months. The familiar sight of them is comforting. And off-putting. I want to trust them and rely on them, but I know I cannot. At least not yet.

The Pierce Foundation Annual Awards Dinner always draws a stellar publishing crowd. Everyone turns out: The gentleman publishers who made their millions in real estate or fast food and use publishing as their ticket to a more glamorous and public life. The oddball magazine tycoons who preside over private empires, some built up from nothing, some inherited. The foreign moguls—French, Germans, Brits, Italians—who have been buying and selling American titles, seated with their hired-gun American managers. And, of course, the armies of foot soldiers: publishers, editors, sales managers, reps, writers, designers, circulation managers, and on and on. It is everyone's night to see and be seen, the once-a-year get-together for the entire publishing industry.

Elixir's tax-deductible $3,000 table is off to the side of the ballroom, far from the headline makers being photographed for tomorrow's gossip pages. *Elixir* is in the boondocks, among tables of regional publishers, controlled circulation technical journals, and a couple of very scuzzy rock 'n' roll books. Next year, the *Elixir* table will likely be part of the big cluster of American Communications tables, there in the prestigious center of the ballroom with staffers from *American Week, American Sports, American Enterprise, American Faces,* and the rest.

Joe Bartolo is fidgeting with his rented, pre-tied black tie and stiff collar, chatting with Jerry Greenstein. Roni and Wayne are swapping names of people around the room, people they will go to cultivate later tonight in the course of corporate and personal networking. I, for all the interest I provoke, might as well be a piece of furniture, which is as it should be. The buzz at this table is about the future and the crowd around us. I represent the past. I push my chair away from the table to get up.

"Don't go too far," Marie says, touching my arm.

"No, I'm just gonna wander around a little before the awards ceremony begins."

"We'll keep it warm," she says, patting the seat of my now empty chair. Marie is sweet to the end.

I walk in no real direction, looking at everything in general and nothing in particular. I see the elite of publishing everywhere, faces I recognize from articles in magazines. I watch the clusters of people around their bosses, making impressions, scoring points, playing the game.

I feel a tap on my shoulder.

"Hey, Bobby baby."

It is Ken Atwood. My first reaction is to clutch. Then I force myself to relax. "Ken baby," I say, getting into the spirit, "how's tricks?"

"Good. Hey, you on your way someplace special?"

"Not really."

"Well, come with me. Come on over and say hi. For old time's sake."

"Sure, lead the way."

He walks me through the maze of tables to the Mackey Magazine Group table. Wacky Mackey and his big bruisers are there, obviously the representatives of his rough-and-tumble industrial books. On one side of Mackey is Leo and on the other Brad Mills, the slick McGraw-Hill veteran Mackey stole to head up *Panacea* and the new upscale network. Leo and Brad clearly look a cut above Mackey's other soldiers in class and polish.

"Hey, boss, look what the cat dragged in," Atwood announces as we arrive at the table. The faces look up. Only Leo and Mackey recognize me. The other men go back to their conversations. Leo says nothing. His eyes burn through me. Mackey looks interested; he waves me over with a big, friendly gesture.

"Hiya, Macallan, come visit."

I stand beside him just behind Brad. Mackey grabs my hand with his bone-crushing paw. Leo makes a big show of turning his back to me to talk to the man next to him.

"You know everybody at the table?" Mackey asks. He points around the table. "That's Mel Klein of *Akron Business Booster* and *Ohio Commerce,* Ed Slotski of *Cement Age,* Sam Kostiuk of *Plastic Age* and *Rubber Age,* Stan Farricker of *Dry Cleaning Journal* and *Laundry Times,* and Eddie De Petro of *Car Wash Journal* and *Tire Times.* I'm sure you've heard of Brad Mills. Brad heads up my new upscale group, and, uh, I think you've met Leo Sayles before."

"Hello," I say to the table.

Some of the men nod; most are oblivious.

"Brad," Mackey asks, "can you take Leo on a little tour of the ballroom? I'd like to talk to Macallan here a little, in private."

"Sure," Brad says, getting up from his chair.

Mackey gives Leo a whack on the shoulder. "Leo, go show Brad how you get clients laid. Gimme a few minutes with the kid, will ya."

Leo gets up and stares at me for a moment. As he passes, he gives me a shove to push me aside. I catch a whiff of his House of Lords, strong as ever.

With two empty seats beside him, Mackey motions for me to sit down. "So, Macallan," he says, "it's been a long time."

"Uh-huh." I cannot believe I am sitting here with the man who has put me through hell. I am silent. I will let him carry the ball.

"So," he says, trying for a normal conversational tone, "pretty good party, eh?"

I nod.

"People in this room wait all year for this shindig. Think it's the most special goddamn event on earth. Think *they're* the most special goddamn people on earth 'cause they're in . . ." He stops to do his impression of an overeducated wimp, swishy and affected. "Because they're in *the media. The fucking media*," he snorts. "It's a racket just like any other, but you'd never convince half the jerks here tonight. They're suckers for the window dressing. Stupid, isn't it?"

I am sitting there, impassive, looking out over the crowd. He wants a reaction. He sticks his face in front of mine. "Stupid, isn't it?"

I nod grudgingly.

"But lucky for guys like you and me. We can pay 'em next to nothing. And they still end up grateful for the chance to be in this wonderful room once a year. And I tell 'em that's right, you *are* lucky to be *in the media*. It's stupid, but I make it work for me. It's like the way you feel about women when you're young. You think, Jesus H. Christ, have I gotta get that broad there. Whatta set on her. Or look at those legs. You got the biggest hard-on in the world for that particular broad there, 'cause she's got this and she's got that like no other broad. But once you get her into bed, turn off the lights, and stick your face in her snatch—you know what? You can't tell 'em apart, one from another. Same with businesses. You get down to the books and countin' up the shekels at the end of the day. How much did I give out, how much am I getting back? Does it matter how you get there? No. Does it matter who you fuck to get it? No. Does it matter whether you built it up or broke it up or just left well enough alone? Abso-fucking-lutely not." He pauses after his speech and rewards himself with a big gulp of bourbon and two handfuls of peanuts.

"So," he says through a mouthful of nuts, "you're not all choked up about leaving the wonderful, glamorous business of publishing?"

"I never said I was leaving."

"You'll leave. Soon as you get the rest a your little pot of money." He washes down the nuts with another slug of bourbon. "Then I guess I won't have to worry about *Elixir* anymore."

"What do you mean?"

"With you outta there, I can take it easy. American'll fuck it up without any help from me."

"Oh, I don't know about that." I do have some loyalty left for my baby.

"Of course they will. You know goddamn well they will."

He is right, but I won't admit it to his face.

"So? No hard feelings." He extends the hand again.

294

I play dumb.

"About what?"

"About what all I put you through."

"I don't know what you're talking about."

"Come on, are we gonna have a talk or are we gonna play games? Buddy, I've been fucking you over good and plenty. I just want you to understand that it was just business. Nothing personal. I think you're an okay kid. But you see, if *Panacea* was gonna get a foothold, I had to throw you off your game. I didn't knock you out the way I wanted to, but it was enough to get my book started. Remember what I said about competition? You break 'em or buy 'em. Well, sometimes when you can't do either, then you gotta at least throw 'em for a loop long enough to get yourself a foothold. But with you gone, my job'll be easy. All I gotta do is sit back and watch American run that book a yours right straight into the ground." Pause. Glug, glug. Sigh of satisfaction. "But I'm gonna miss you. You really gave me some fun."

"Some fun? Some fun?" This pisses me off. Visibly. I get up to leave.

"Hey, hey, take it easy, kid." He holds me down in my chair.

"Some fun? My goddamn life was on the line, everything I've worked for . . ."

I start to get up again. Maybe to hit him, maybe just to leave, I don't know. This time, he holds me down by both arms. He is very strong. "Jesus, kid, calm down. Take it easy. Yeah, some fun." He inspects me to see if I have regained my composure. "There? You okay?" Hear him out, I tell myself. Calm down. I nod at him to signal that I am okay. Fun? You scumbag, Mackey. I shudder to think how he has almost ruined everything. I really should slug him, I should get up and leave. But he has information I want. He pats my shoulder soothingly.

"All right," I say, calming down, "talk to me."

He leans back in his chair. He is about to pontificate. He studies his tumbler of bourbon, wipes some condensation from the glass, and begins, "Macallan, what does a hungry man with no money do?"

"I don't know. What?"

"Whatever he has to do to get his next meal." Pause for a fistful of peanuts. "Now, what does a man with a good job, two kids, and a mortgage do?"

"I don't know. What?"

"Whatever his boss tells him to do." Mackey stops for another sip and more peanuts. "Now a man who sold his magazine and has, uh, almost six million in the bank, what does he do?"

I smirk at him.

"He walks away from American Communications to figure out what he can and can't do next. That's you," he adds parenthetically, "in case you were having trouble following me."

I nod impatiently. Yeah, I got it, Mackey.

"Last question: what does a man with a hundred and six million do?"

"What?" This game is getting old.

"Whatever the fuck he wants." Triumphantly he glugs down the last of his drink. "He does whatever the fuck he wants to keep himself amused. Don't you get it yet? Do you think I start a new magazine 'cause I need the money? Or the glory? Jesus, I got all the money and all the glory I need. Do you think I need another win? Fuck no. I start a new magazine 'cause it's what I want to do now. I may change my mind next week. And so what? I'll do what I want to do next. Do you think life is like some kinda MBA business plan? With strategies and guidelines and measurable goals mapped out and an automatic bonus if you deliver what the plan calls for? No way. Life's a shitty mess. You make it up as you go along."

He grabs a passing waiter by the arm and points to his empty glass. "Double bourbon, rocks," he tells him. "Peanuts, too," he says, indicating his diminishing supply. Then he looks back at me and smiles.

"It's all about time, Macallan. Time. Tick-tock-tick-tock. We all end up the same. The more you see that it's all about amusing yourself, the more you realize you might as well go do whatever amuses you. I'm grateful to you, Macallan. Because not only did you serve a good business purpose, you gave me a lot of fun. You coulda made a lot more money if you'd stuck with me, but then I wouldn't have had so much fun." His fresh drink and new supply of peanuts arrive. He takes a fistful and another big gulp.

"You want to give me the inside story on the, uh, fun you had with me?" I say to him once his mouth is cleared of debris.

"Sure," he mumbles, eyeing the nearly full dish of peanuts on the far side of the table. "Anything you wanna know."

"Okay. How soon after I started negotiating with American did you have Leo working for you? Did he approach you or did you approach him?"

"That's a good question, Macallan. But wouldn't you rather start with the rumor campaign? Or however did it happen that MFI had no records for *MD Office* and like a good scout reported it to ABC?"

"I already know that. You bought MFI through a shell company, that's how."

"Good work, buddy. I liked that touch. It was purely accidental, though. I was in the market for a fulfillment house, anyway. When we discovered we'd bought Jack Parsons's old fulfillment house, the rest was just obvious."

"That's what I figured."

"And the Jack Parsons tape," Mackey says, taking another fistful of peanuts. "Aren't you gonna ask me about that?"

"I'm pretty sure I know that, too." I think back on that moment of horror and confusion, hearing Woodcock play the tape of a conversation I never had. "It was the time you called me with all those stupid questions about your party. You were recording me, weren't you."

Mackey nods proudly.

"But how exactly did you dummy up the tape?" I ask.

He smiles with great pride. "I own a couple a radio stations. The big one's got one a these new digital sound processors. Just take a recording and put it on a disk. The computer can cut it up, take out the breaths, put in breaths, reverse the order, do anything you want to it. You can't tell it from the real thing. All I had to do was get your voice on tape saying a few things like, 'A dollar a name.' The rest was easy."

I remember that day in Leo's office. Mackey calling out of the blue, asking me to ask him stupid questions, over and over. And I remember the smell of House of Lords on the phone that day. And the same smell on the day Woodcock had me hauled out of the office like a criminal. "Which brings me back to Leo," I say. "How soon did you have Leo on your payroll? Did you recruit him? Did he come to you? When did he tell you about my negotiations with American? How much did you pay him to plant the cassette in my desk? Tell me all about you and Leo."

Mackey looks at me earnestly and then begins to smile.

"Tell me," I ask, pressing the point, "how much longer was Leo supposed to stay at *Elixir*? Did I fire him too soon? Or was that on schedule, too?"

Mackey starts to laugh.

"I just figured out why I like you so much, Macallan." He nudges me playfully. "You make me feel smart, that's why. I mean, look at me— common as dirt, no education, no couth. And look at you, good-looking, educated, all the advantages. You fit right in here with these elegant media candyasses. You've even made enough money to call yourself rich—in a little sorta way. And shit if I don't feel smart sitting next to you. I like you, Macallan. You come around any time you want. Any time, you hear."

He laughs again, diabolically. It is a laugh that seems somehow familiar.

"Come on," I say. "Tell me about you and Leo. It's only fair. Let me have it."

"I'll tell you, Macallan. But not right now. You see, I want you to have a reason to come see me again. I think we can still do business together. We'll talk about that later, next time. Okay? That way, I'll be sure we'll have a next time."

A booming, amplified voice from the dais announces that dinner is about to begin and would everyone please go back to their assigned seats. Mackey pretends to prepare himself. He sits up straight and picks up his Pierce dinner program as if to study it. "Go on back to your table," he says to me. "Go finish your contract and then we'll talk. I think we can still have a lot of fun together. I got plans for you, Macallan. Now run along. I'll be seein' you."

Mills reappears at the table without Leo. The ballroom becomes very noisy as people everywhere start milling back to their seats. Mackey is through talking with me. He leans across the table to chat with his returning publishers. I get up and head back toward the *Elixir* table. On the way, it hits me why I seemed to recognize Mackey's evil laugh. It is the same laugh from the dream that haunted me. The mysterious towering figure who laughed and said, "I will make you lose it all." I feel a little shiver of recollection. Then, poof! The specter vanishes. It was only a dream. I am going to fight it, I tell myself. And win.

I can see the *Elixir* table in the distance. Suddenly, out of the crowd, a hand grabs me by the arm and yanks me aside. It is Leo. His eyes are angry slits, his face puffy and flushed with aggression. "I'm gonna get even with you, Macallan. You fucked me over. And now I'm gonna return the favor."

"I didn't fuck you over. I found you out. Now get your hands off me." I pull my arm out of his grip. I turn to walk away from him, but he grabs me again, this time with both hands. He holds me so that we are standing face to face.

"You don't know shit from apple butter, kid. But then you never did. You see, I know what you're up to. You think you got an ace up your sleeve. But I know what it is and I'm gonna ruin it for you. I'm gonna show you just how much better at this game I am. Better than you'll ever hope to be. I'm gonna see to it that you lose. That's right. I'm gonna make you lose. I'm gonna make you lose it all!"

Suddenly, I feel myself gasp for breath. The coincidence of the words of his final threat sends deafening echoes through my head. I am shaken. Not by Leo but by the mental shock waves his remark unleashes. "What the . . . ?" I mutter, trying to bring the room back into focus. I stare at Leo, through him, trying to constitute what he really is. And isn't.

"You're going after stockbrokers, Macallan," he whispers in my ear. He leaves a cloud of his scent in my face. "I know all about it."

CHAPTER THIRTY-FOUR

"There's someone else I'd like to sit in on the meeting with us," Al Tully explains. "The guy we just brought on board to head up investment banking." Al and I are readying the Greenthal/Peck conference room for my big presentation. "Let's put him over here," he says, taking another one of my bound leave-behinds and putting it carefully, like a dinner place setting, in front of the chair next to where Adam Wahl, the company's new president, will sit. So far, it looks like I will be serving up special issue for six, including Wahl, two other senior vice presidents, the man from their ad agency, and this new guy.

Al Tully, a fifty-five-ish bear with graying red hair, is one of the most likable of guys, and he knows it. A stockbroker who went upstairs into management, he has a natural gift for pleasing. He gets his way by focusing totally on the person he is with, charming, disarming, making his own ego disappear into his very evident admiration of you. Until you realize that he has led you into doing exactly what he wanted in the first place. In my case, Al extracted freebie after freebie in exchange for his full-price sponsorship of the special issue. I will be giving away (rather, American will be giving away on *its* budgets after I'm gone) free booth space at medical conferences, customized mailings, financial planning kits, tax-planning desk blotters, and, possibly, Greenthal/Peck calculators, just like the Zentane one Marie found for me.

"You all set?" Al asks. I am straightening my tie.

"All set," I reply, giving him a thumbs-up.

"I'll round up the boys," he says and leaves the room. I walk to the flip chart at the head of the conference room table and review my main points one last time. This is a simple, straightforward media sale. All I'm doing is delivering my *Elixir* readers into the hands of an advertiser who would love to get their undivided attention. The struggles of the past few weeks have reminded me, more powerfully than ever, that a magazine is nothing more than a vehicle for advertising. The editorial content, the design, the attitude, the journalistic passion, everything human and creative that I or anyone else can pour into it, is nothing more than bait. It doesn't matter whether the content is scientific monographs, analysis of world politics, movie star gossip, or close-up shots of female genitalia. It's just bait. The percentage of edit versus advertising is always calculated to achieve a certain balance. Not to please the reader, but to be sure that the ads are not bunched together in a jumble. The true value of having riveting, prize-winning editorial is to reassure advertisers that their ads will be read.

Part of me is glad to be getting out of this game.

The door to the conference room opens. Al leads in the troops. In the usual blur of handshakes and greetings, I meet Adam Wahl, the president, a coldly handsome man with slicked-back hair and a very expensive hand-tailored English suit. He must be ten years younger than Al, mid- to maybe late forties. There are two paunchy, jacketless men in white shirts and loud suspenders—Jay Mosier, head of sales, and Stan Potter, head of the portfolio management group, both Greenthal/Peck old-timers. And there's Burt Prager, the man from the ad agency, whose appearance and manner contradict each other. He has the body of a big, powerful bruiser, yet he acts like a terrified, obsequious fawner who can't grovel enough to please others. Burt's handshake is clammy and soft.

"Tim'll be along in just a minute," Al says in an aside to me. "He's quite a catch for us. We've always been weak on the origination side." He means investment banking, originating the pieces of paper brokers sell to investors.

"More like nonexistent," Wahl adds snidely, making a point of over-hearing and not looking up from the legal pad on which he is scribbling.

"Yeah, nonexistent," Al continues, accepting his boss's contribution graciously. "But Tim's gonna change all that."

"He'd better," Wahl mutters under his breath. He looks at his watch, then at the empty place beside him. "Let's get started."

Al nods eagerly at me to begin.

"Gentlemen," I say, approaching the flip charts, "I want to talk to you this afternoon about some medicine for Greenthal/Peck. This medicine is going to be good for you and very easy to take." I peel back the first page to reveal my first chart. I point to the big block letters as I announce, *"Elixir* magazine. RX for Growth for Greenthal/Peck." So begins my presentation. I am in great form today. Confident, friendly, articulate. As I speak, I make sure to make eye contact, sincere and direct, with each individual member of my audience. Except for Wahl, who refuses to look up from the notes he is making on his legal pad.

I move from my general introductory outline to my first mini-essay. " 'Smart Doctors, Dumb Investors,' " I announce as I peel back that chart. That gets the little laugh I had hoped it would. "We at *Elixir* make it our business to know our medical readers even better than they know themselves. To prove my point, I want to show you some exclusive research we did on their attitudes toward money in general and their own competence as money managers in particular."

This data plays well. So does my delivery. "So you see," I say, wrapping up the final "Smart Doctors, Dumb Investors" chart, "doctors say, on the one hand, that they are perfectly capable of managing their own money themselves and don't need any help. And on the other hand, upon further probing, they admit they do not have the time, expertise, or talent to maximize the investment potential that their high incomes create. This is a very human response, especially when you consider, as we at *Elixir* do every day, that the key to communicating with doctors is getting past the doctor's big ego to the human being underneath. Because if you can locate that vulnerability, that's where the selling opportunity is. Especially for a company like Greenthal/Peck."

The words are flowing out of me effortlessly. But they sound somehow strange, a little off. I mean them, I believe them, and I know they are true and valuable. These are the words and thoughts with which I have built this business. But suddenly, to another part of my brain, a part I am just beginning to meet, my words sound false. I am spewing farcical bullshit. I vow to keep this feeling to one side and not let it interfere with my performance.

Just then the door opens.

"Tim!" Tully announces, welcoming the latecomer and motioning him toward his assigned place at the table. I can't believe what I see. Tim is Tim Conover. *The* Tim Conover. He is as shocked to see me as I am to see him. Or at least he seems to be.

"Jesus! Bob Macallan!" he says, recovering a fraction of a second ahead of me. He bounds across the room to shake my hand. "Al, when you told me this was a media presentation, I didn't put two and two together."

"You guys know each other?" Al asks.

"Know each other? I sold this man's magazine to American Communications. That was my deal. And," he says, giving me his best grip, but avoiding eye contact, "a very fine magazine it is, too."

"Gee thanks, Tim," I say, disengaging my hand from his. I inspect Conover for an instant. He looks the same physically—prep school superhero MBA—but the edgy arrogance he used to project is gone. He must have been turned down for partnership at Hale Hadley. No successful Hale Hadley man would deign to set foot in a place like this otherwise. The defeat must have taken him down a few pegs.

"I haven't been holding things up, have I?" Conover asks as he walks toward his seat beside Wahl.

Suddenly it all comes together. Conover. Conover! The keeper of secrets must also be the betrayer of secrets. Who was having dinner with Atwood and Howie Marcus? Who was in a position to know everything all along? American, Mackey, and all the rest. Conover. Only Conover.

"Geez, Adam," he says, looking at his watch. He is trying not to sit down. "I've got a call I have to make. I'm afraid I really can't stay."

Does Conover have it in mind to call his dinner companion, Atwood? Or even Atwood's boss, Elton Mackey? Conover has already sold my company, and it didn't help get him a partnership at Hale Hadley. Therefore, I am of no further use to him. What he needs now are people who can supply him with fodder for new deals. People like Mackey.

Maybe Leo was just a pawn in all this, after all. Maybe it was Conover who leaked my negotiations with American to Atwood last spring. Maybe Elton Mackey was his client then. Maybe he's a client of his now. Or, worse still, a prospect he is trying to woo. How better to curry favor with the owner of *Panacea* than to tip him off about a potential sales coup by its one and only rival?

Conover must not leave this room until I have a sale. I must get a yes out of this meeting before Conover can get to the phone.

Before Wahl answers, I jump in. "Come on, Tim, you may know the financials of the magazine business, but you've never heard the fundamentals. This information'll help you be an even bigger wheeler-dealer. It's the heart and soul of the magazine game. Come on, you can wait, can't you?" Don't you dare leave this room, Conover. Don't you dare!

"Yeah, Tim," Al agrees with me. "This is an interesting presentation."

"So far," Wahl mutters, still not looking up.

"Uh, give me just a couple of minutes," Conover says, stalling by his chair.

"Keep it moving," Wahl says to the room, waving things along with his free hand. Conover uses the impatient signal to dash for the door.

"I'll be back," he says as he exits, closing the door.

I am shrieking inside. Panicking. If I could leap across the room, I would. I'd stop him, strangle him with my bare hands, smash his head against the metal corner of the table until his brains popped out, drink his blood, tear out his liver, anything to stop him. But I cannot. Instead, I flip to the next chart.

I must not let the Conover incident throw me. Try not to think about a white elephant, I tell myself, recalling the psychological parlor game. Just try. What the hell is he up to? Who is he calling? What can I do to block him?

As I continue my canned presentation, I pray that my preoccupation does not show. Let me tell you how much doctors enjoy *Elixir* and trust what they read in it. I proceed with the charts that define the readership of *Elixir*. Chart by chart, I dissect our 250,000 physicians. Chart by chart, I strain not to think about Conover. Just look at these doctors. Let's examine who they are, how old they are, where they live, where they work, what types of practices they have, and, of course, how much money they make. From the way I've set up the data, the message is clear. These are 250,000 prime potential customers just waiting for Greenthal/Peck.

There are nods around the table, culminating in a grunt from Wahl.

I can continue.

My mind wonders what Conover is doing right now while my mouth says, "I don't want you to think that *Elixir* is the only way to reach this audience. But I can prove to you that no other vehicle is as efficient or as cost-effective as *Elixir* in doing the job. Now, please bear in mind that all the data I'm about to show you comes from independent third-party researchers and other media vehicles themselves. There are no stacked decks here. Let's start by seeing what Simmons and MRI tell us about reaching doctors."

This part of the presentation is designed to convince these quantitative types once and for all. Numbers, numbers, more numbers.

"So you see," I say, bringing the big research section to a close, "you *can* reach doctors with your message in other ways. But you'll also spend a lot more money than you have to and waste your message on millions of people you don't want to reach. You see the proof on these charts, and you can find more complete abstracts from their original studies in the appendix of the leave-behind. Proof that no other vehicle reaches as many of the doctors you need to reach as cost-effectively as *Elixir*. Bar none."

There's a natural pause as I let that point sink in before going on to the next. Where the hell is Conover?

I flip to the next chart, which deals with the special merits of our special issue. I flash a confident smile and charge ahead, reading the first heading aloud. " '*Elixir* special issues,' " I say, " 'special advertising that *lasts.*' " I hear myself blabbing onward toward the conclusion. More charts, more data. Finally, the wrap-up arrives.

"Gentlemen, this is an opportunity to be first. To be exclusive. To carve a place in the minds and pocketbooks of an important, hard-to-reach market. An opportunity to do it smarter, more efficiently, and way ahead of all your competitors." I flip to the final chart of the easel. Reading its contents aloud, I say, " 'For growth at Greenthal/Peck, we prescribe *Elixir* and its upcoming special issue.' "

I pause and look around the room. The faces all look positive, all except that of Adam Wahl, who still has not looked up from his legal pad. "Any questions?" I ask.

"Yeah, I got one," says Stan Potter, taking off his half-moon reading glasses and leaning back in his chair. "But first, I gotta tell you I like it. I like it a lot."

"Me, too," says Mosier, Potter's matching bookend. Potter nods and continues, "Do you really think we can do any business with a booth at a medical conference? I mean aren't these guys gonna be running around to the next lecture on cardiopulmonary atomic reactors and like that? They're coming for medicine. Are they gonna sit there and let us show 'em how small-cap stocks have been performing relative to the S and P 500?"

"That's a good question, Jay," I reply, moving away from the easel to a more conversational mode. "I'll tell you what we've learned from five years of talking to doctors, five years of digging to discover what's really on their minds. What we've found is that for over ninety percent of them, the last thing on their minds is medicine. Do you know what our most successful articles have covered? Not cancer, not heart disease, not the latest miracle cures. Our biggest successes, the material that has generated the most interest, gotten the most letters and the most requests for reprints, were our articles on food, wine, and foreign travel. It's true. The good life, that's what's on their minds. I'm convinced that if Greenthal/Peck positions itself as *the* financial expert to make the good life easier to get, you're going to be swamped with doctors ready to do business. I'd make sure it's your best brokers manning the booths, not just trainees there to gather leads. After the impression you make appearing on every ad page of the special issue, they are going to be very predisposed to listen carefully and seriously to whatever Greenthal/Peck brokers have to say."

"Sounds good to me," Mosier says. "But I've got a concern about the breakdown of fixed-income products versus equity products that we advertise. I really think these guys are better prospects for me than for Jay. They're more conservative, they're tax-conscious. Now, in the chart, your breakdown of fixed-income ads against equity was—"

Al jumps in for me. "That's our call, Jay. They'll do whatever mix we want."

"Yeah," I say, "what we're hoping for is the chance to work closely with you"—I nod at Prager—"and your agency to present the product emphasis you think is right." Prager nods back at me.

"Don't worry, we'll work it all out together," Al says to the room, trying to bring the matter to a close. "Any other questions?"

"Just one," says Prager. "Let me begin by saying that this was a very thorough presentation. Well thought out and professional. Our agency has never dealt with a publication in your area before, as you might well imagine. As you know, we specialize in financial accounts. We see ourselves as the strong right hand of all the great Wall Street firms, and no agency can touch our ability to place space in the financial press. So while this medical thing is a little off the beaten track for us, I want you to know that I agree with our clients here. I totally agree. And I want to say that I'm very favorably impressed. Very favorably." Wahl looks up from his pad for the first time and stares quizzically at the gaseous ad man. Prager prattles on, oblivious. "But I would be remiss in looking out for our client's interests if I did not ask this question. I'm interested in the shelf life of your special

issues. My concern is that Greenthal/Peck get maximum bang for its buck."
He looks pleased with himself and his oration.

"Well, Burt," I say, "perhaps we should compare it to the leading financial books. I'd say the shelf life for an edition of the *Wall Street Journal* is a little less than one day. For *Barron's* or *Forbes* it's three to five days, a week at most. Would you say that's fair?"

Prager nods.

"Well, Burt, the shortest shelf life of all our special issues was one that we knew would be a little under six months. The one on laser medicine." Prager smiles to hide his embarrassment and begins studying his thumb. I pick up my copy of that issue from my pile of props on the table in front of the easel. "The technology in that field completely turns over twice a year, the developments are coming so fast and furious. It was a trade-off for us and our advertiser." After holding up the issue for all to see and flipping through some pages, I hand it across the table to Prager. He takes it and skims it politely while I continue. "In that case, we knew that the issue would be very, very hot for half a year and then it would be forgotten. New developments, a whole new ball game. *But* during that six months it was *the* reference work on the subject. And it had an impact on all sorts of specialties." Prager hands me back the laser medicine issue. I replace it with my other papers and turn to face Wahl. He does not look up.

"Now in the case of hypertension," I say at Wahl, "the field is not technology-driven and it does not turn over anywhere near as fast. And what we've done is assemble the best and latest developments from a very broad range of research specialties. The lasting value of this special issue is really this 'whole patient' approach to a very complex, specialized subject. We see it, therefore, as a reference work that a whole spectrum of specialists will keep at hand for, oh, realistically, a year or more. I'm trying to be conservative, mind you. But I think we're creating a classic reference source here. Which will translate into a very long-lasting bang for what is really not that many bucks."

Prager nods solemnly. Al motions to me to sit down and pats the empty chair beside him to indicate where. I do as instructed.

"Any other questions?" Al asks.

"Nope," Potter says.

Mosier shakes his head no.

"Well, at Greenthal/Peck, we've always prided ourselves on decisiveness. Jay, Stan, I take it your answer is yes."

They nod affirmatively.

"Willing to kick in your share of the budget?" Al asks.

They look at each other, then nod again.

"Okay," Al continues. "Adam, you've got our votes. Are you ready to give us a decision?"

Adam takes a deep breath, clearly for dramatic effect, and puts his pen down. Very slowly, he gives up his legal pad and lays it down on the table. He takes another deep breath and slowly arches his neck back to look up, as if his answer were written on the ceiling. The rest of us get a panoramic view of the underside of his jaw and larynx. He studies the ceiling for what seems like too long. At last, he starts to speak.

"What I think is." Then he stops as if that were a complete sentence. Just then, the conference room door bursts open. It is Conover. He dashes over to Wahl without even acknowledging the rest of the room. He gets down on one knee to be level with Wahl's head and starts whispering in his ear. He cups his hands over his mouth and Wahl's ear to make sure no one can see or hear what he is saying. Conover spills out his message in a big, excited rush. Wahl, having lowered his head back down to a normal position, listens impassively, nodding slightly.

"Then we won't," Wahl says vacantly, only half to Conover.

Hearing this, Conover heaves a sigh of relief and stands up.

"Sorry," Conover says, apologizing to the room. "I guess I missed your presentation, Bob." He picks up the binder at his place on the table and remains standing.

Who has Conover been on the phone to? What is he trying to pull? For a flash, I see everything of mine crashing down in flames. I lean forward in my chair about to say something, what I do not know.

"This is a, uh . . ." I hear myself say. I feel Al's hand clench my arm tightly and push me back into the chair.

Wahl looks absently at the blank wall on the other side of the room.

"Adam," Al says to get his attention. "I thought we were—"

"Huh?" Adam asks, turning and focusing on Al, as if seeing him for the first time. He then looks back at Conover, who offers a little shrug. "This looks fine. But let's wait till after the holiday to commit."

"After which holiday?" I ask rudely and out of turn in my clients' internal discussion. Tully shoots a surprised glance my way.

"Right after Thanksgiving," Wahl says matter-of-factly. "Couple of other things floating around. Gotta weigh the options. Don't worry. We'll give you an answer." With that, Adam Wahl clicks his ballpoint pen shut, stands up, and heads for the door. "Conover," he says as he passes behind Tim's back, "my office." Conover follows on the boss's heels, saying no good-byes. The meeting is over.

CHAPTER THIRTY-FIVE

At this point, the road back into Bayport opens onto a brilliant stretch of coastline. It is three in the afternoon; the late November sun is already descending behind us. Wendy is tapping her feet on the dashboard of the Ford we rented Wednesday night at Boston's Logan Airport. "Yeah, I took him aside and filled him in while you were unpacking the car. I said, 'Clint, please don't bother him about business this weekend. Everything's on hold. But it's going to be fine. The biggest favor you can do him is leave it alone.

Just let Robert relax. I can't tell you anything more about Greenthal/Peck because there's nothing more to tell. When there's news, believe me; you'll be the first to know.' He said okay and we went back to talking about the weather."

"Aha!" I exclaim. "So that's why Dad and Jimmy barely spoke to me through that whole Thanksgiving dinner." Yesterday we had the Macallan family feast at one of Bayport's favorite old-time restaurants, Dom Valley's World of Steak 'n' Potatoes. The food was plain and leaden, just like the conversation between the Macallan men. At the end, Clint grabbed the check in an act of paternal magnanimity. With his grudging, halting way of extracting bills from his wallet, he ended up shorting the waiter with a mere 10 percent tip. "Just roundin' it off," he said, unembarrassed at his parsimony. Pretending I had to go to the men's room, I went back to the table and left more money.

"Geez, this is gorgeous," Wendy says, looking out over the expanse of water and rocky shoreline. "How come your family never took advantage of all this beautiful scenery?"

"Because in Bayport," I say, "the water was only for two kinds of people. The poor who worked on it. And the rich who played on it. We were too proud to let ourselves be part of the first group and too broke to be part of the second."

"But there's no charge for coming out to admire it," Wendy says, turning this way and that in her shoulder belt to admire the rocks and the sea. "Why not come out here just because it's a beautiful thing to do?"

"In the Macallan household? A pleasure for its own sake? Unheard of."

Wendy wrinkles her nose.

"How do you like the name Lisa?" she asks, changing the subject to baby imagining. "Do you like Lisa if Swee' Pea is a girl?" Wendy has temporarily named our baby after Popeye and Olive Oyl's infant charge because, she says, nobody could say whether it was a boy or a girl, either.

"Lisa," I repeat slowly. "Nice. But a little ordinary."

"Just think about it," she says.

Returning to Bayport this time with my baby-focused Wendy has triggered a very distant, almost forgotten memory. Great-grandmother Macallan, Isabelle. "Eyesa," she and everyone else pronounced it. I remember Isa carrying a baby in a big shawl wrapped around her waist and over one shoulder. I may even have been the baby. It was a pouch, a swing, the way she wrapped it, a perfect habitat that enveloped the baby in her warm peasant strength and kept her hands free to keep on working at whatever needed to be done. I remember Isa sang a little ditty as she bounced the baby against her breast.

> "You can come 'n see the baby any time you care to call,
> He's lying with his mammy in a wee white shawl,
> And he looks so cute and spanky,
> Like a dumplin' in a hanky.

And the name I'm going to give him
Angus Jimmison James McCall.
Too-ta-ta-too-ta-too-ra-lay,
Too-ta-ta-too-ta-tar-ree-oh,
There is a baby in the house
And I am his daddy-oh!"

Great-grandma Isa, who died when I was a little boy, came south from Nova Scotia to work in the fisheries as a girl. She brought old tales of misery told to her by her great-grandmother, who had made the journey from Scotland early in the nineteenth century. She told of the Clearances. The Scottish Holocaust. When tens of thousands of crofters were ripped from their ancestral lands, stripped of their cottages and all their possessions, herded like cattle onto wagons bound for the ports, and thrown into ships like slaves, to be sent to places like Canada and Australia. And why? To free the land for large-scale sheep farms. To help pay for the lavish London life-styles of other Scots, their own clansmen. The aristocratic ones. The superior, educated kin who knew how to buy paintings and big houses and run up gambling debts and drink French claret—and use legal maneuvers and fancy language to overturn centuries of communal landownership and steal what was not rightly theirs. The Clearances were an act of family betrayal on a mass scale.

My people were among the simple, ignorant victims who were "cleared." Isa retold the tales of that awful day. No, the agents told them in the morning, they did not need to bring anything from their houses, for they would not need it where they were going. And by evening they were on their way. Gone forever.

That remembered outrage gave my ancestors a deep mistrust of anything that smacked of the fancy, learned, and sophisticated world. The mistrust survives to this very day. I saw it in Isa and her children. I see it in my father. I see it in my brother. I even see it in myself. It is a sense of bitterness and defeat and hopelessness in the face of an unjust, overpowering world. The Macallans never really recovered from the injustice. They never prospered in the New World. They stuck to their peasant pride, kept their peasant minds and eyes closed, and refused to learn or change. For change and learning would be a treason, a defection to the side of the slippery, sophisticated villains who caused all the misery in the first place. No, for the Macallans, poverty and stupidity became badges of pride and honor. It is a troubling heritage to carry.

"And I am his daddy-oh!" I find myself singing idly.

"What?" Wendy asks, dropping something in the glove compartment.

"There is a baby in the house," I sing, "and I am his daddy-oh!" She knows the song now, too.

"You sure are," she says, hugging my arm. "Or will be."

"I just don't want to be anything like *my* daddy-oh. I think that's why I've been so afraid of all this baby stuff."

"Do you mean that?"

"Yeah, I think that's been the root of my problem."

"Does that mean you've gotten over it?"

"Maybe."

"You mean you're afraid of being too much like your father?"

"Afraid of being him, becoming him. Know what I mean?"

"Oh, Robert, you are nothing like him. Nothing. Look at the two of you."

"That's precisely my problem. I do look like him. Genetics is very powerful. I'm starting to get jowls like his. These blue eyes are his and his father's before him. My performance in the face of adversity this year was, well, mixed."

"Oh, come on. So is everybody's. You think you're Superman or something? You will pull it off. I have complete confidence in you. You've accomplished ten times more in your life than he ever thought of trying in his. Sweetie, look at you. You're smart, you're sensitive, you're articulate, you're worldly, you're—"

"Wendy, don't you see? Those are all qualities I have been taught to mistrust. Everything I ever learned from that man tells me I should absolutely not trust people like me. And there's a lot of heredity behind that. Hundreds of generations of dumb, proud victim peasants telling me through my DNA that I have no right to be what I am. Don't you see? I am a self-canceling proposition."

"You are not. Robert, you are not your grandfather or your father. You are you. You are very different. And, I might add, better. Evolution, you know, does occasionally move forward for the better. Think of yourself as a favorable mutation in the gene pool. The first Macallan fish that was somehow equipped to crawl up on land and walk around. You're starting a whole new set of possibilities. You're not limited by your ancestors. You've got some new and better material you can pass on to your offspring to make them more adapted for survival. That's what Darwin would say."

"Geez, a new species."

"New and improved. And Darwin proved that the good traits get passed on." She takes my hand and pats her unpregnant tummy with it. "Now tell that to Swee' Pea."

"Swee' Pea, your dad is a positive mutation of the Macallan species."

"That's more like it."

"I just want to feel I have something good to pass on. It scares me to think I might take after Clint and give a kid a heritage of doing the same."

"Don't worry," Wendy says, "not possible."

Coming back into Bayport, I don't have to think about directions. I drive down Danforth Street, past the triple-decker houses and out to the patch of modest single-family houses that is my old neighborhood. The car seems to guide itself down Parsons Avenue and finally onto Monroe Street.

"I hope I'm nothing like him," I whisper to myself. "God, I hope so."

Every time I revisit the Macallan house, it seems to get smaller. All the houses on Monroe Street do. They are ordinary, middle-of-the-middle-class houses, two-story, two-bedroom, one-bathroom. Our house looks like any smallish suburban house anywhere, innocuous and wholesome. But to me it represents a prison of the spirit. A place where I searched in vain for confidence and acceptance of a self no one else could imagine. A place that almost destroyed my faith in the future. A place with an infinite capacity for creating fear, guilt, and paralyzing self-doubt.

Our house is still the one in the worst repair on the street. Peeling paint, shabby roof, and scruffy balding lawn peeking through the snow. No doubt the neighbors still talk behind Clint's back. He does not and never did care. As I pull up in front of the house, everything is as I remember it. Except for Jimmy's rented Lincoln Town Car—gold, gaudy, fat, and tinny—pulling out of the garage.

As we come to a stop at the snowy curb, the Lincoln pulls out of the driveway and into the street. It is Jimmy behind the wheel. He steers the gold boat alongside my car, heading in the opposite direction. He rolls down the front electric window on his passenger side. Wendy rolls down her window. Cold air pours in.

"Hey, Brother," Jimmy says above the Lincoln's engine noise. He looks uncomfortably past Wendy. All women seem to make him uncomfortable.

"Hi, Jimmy," Wendy says cheerily.

"Uh, hello there," he says, acknowledging her but lowering his eyes momentarily.

"You look pretty good behind the wheel of that piece of iron," I lie, complimenting Jimmy on his car with the phrase Clint always used. It is the first time we have seen him in this chariot in the daylight.

"You betcha, Bro'. This is just like the one I drive in Tucson. You know, when a guy gets used to a little class, he's gotta have it all the time." He smirks at the plain sedan I have rented. I think it is a Tiempo or a Taurus, some Ford or other with a *T*.

"You're not leaving, are you?" I ask as I turn my motor off and unbuckle my shoulder harness.

"Be back tomorrow, Bro'," he sneers, as if imparting a piece of valuable and possibly confidential information. Wendy sits back in her seat, pretending she is not there, trying not to block the brothers' view of each other. "Piece of business," Jimmy says, "an old deal I gotta finish up with a guy in Nashua."

Jimmy has not even shifted his idling Lincoln into Park. He means for this to be a brief conversation. "Listen, Brother." He taps the steering wheel impatiently. "I forgot to tell you. I was cleaning out the attic on Tuesday, before you got here. Found a few boxes a your old shit, high school stuff I guess. The garbage truck was downstairs and charging by the hour, so I made an executive decision and had him cart it away along with some other useless shit. You hated high school anyway, didn't you? Like everything else around here. Wasn't good enough for you. Right? So I figured I might as well pitch it." He gives me a smug grin. "You don't mind, do you?"

"No," I say, feeling at a disadvantage in this impromptu setting. In fact, I had been looking forward to sorting through those boxes of mine. I had made a mental list of items I wanted to bring back to New York, most from those very boxes. I was planning to reclaim my share of memories. I feel stung by what Jimmy did. And cheated.

"Listen, I got business to do. But I'll be back to say good-bye." He raises his electric window and is about to peel away. Then he remembers something and lowers it again. "Hey!" he shouts. "Why don'tcha go sell some ad space while you're here? Write the trip off as a business expense. That's what I'm doing." His window hums up into place, and the fat gold Lincoln rumbles away down Monroe Street.

Wendy opens her door and starts to get out. "Come on. Let's just get this weekend over with and get on with our own lives. Remember, Swee' Pea is listening to everything we say and do."

I make a shhh gesture as I open the car door and step out into the cold.

Saturday afternoon, Clint and I are in the kitchen sorting through canned goods after spending the morning packing moving boxes. He is a smaller, slightly stooped, older version of me. Same sandy hair, his gone to gray and white. Same blue eyes, his now sunken and more sad-looking than mine. Same jowls, his fully blown, mine just starting. Our biggest point of difference is evident when he speaks.

"How much you pay for canned corn in New York?" he asks in his thick New England accent, a can of store brand corn in hand. *Payfuh canned conn in Noo Yawk.*

"I don't know, Dad."

"Come on, how much you pay?"

"Uh, I don't think we eat canned corn."

"Well, guess how much I pay. Come on. Guess."

"I don't know. Dollar seventy-five."

"You guessing for the ten-ounce can or the sixteen-ounce can, 'cause this is a ten-ouncer in my hand."

"Okay," I say, having neither interest nor inclination for this game he always plays. "I'll guess a dollar seventy-five for the ten-ouncer, two-fifty for the sixteen-ouncer."

"Jesus, Son, is that what you're used to paying for canned corn? You sure know how to piss away your money down there. Son," he says, holding up the canned corn like an important object lesson, "I pay eighty-nine cents for this. The sixteen-ouncer'd only cost me buck and a quarter. It's a good thing you're rich. You gotta be to live down there."

The cramped little kitchen looks the same as it did when my mother died more than a decade before. A few pieces of decorative crockery on top of the plain white Sears cabinets, touches that she put in to express her blunted aspirations to a more genteel life-style than she could afford. They will be the next items to be wrapped and packed up.

"You know, Son," he brags as he puts the last can into the cardboard packing box, "no one can live as cheap as I do." I have been hearing this as long as I can remember. We went through a whole string of financial disasters when I was twelvish and just discovering the transcendent importance of fathers' cars to budding adolescent boys. I was injured by the shiny new Pontiacs and Mercurys I saw other dads drive. While my father happily toodled along in his noisy fifteen-year-old Chevy with rust so bad you could see the road through holes in the floor. I was mortified. He seemed proud. "Why can't we have a nice new car like the other guys?" I would ask. "Hmmph," he would snort, "guys like Buddy Austin, they *need* a fancy car like that." He said it accusingly, as if it were a weakness, a vice, a shame. "I can drive 'em and drive 'em long after nobody else'll go near 'em," he would say, never guessing why his very words embarrassed me to death.

"Nope," he says, pouring himself a glass of ice water, "I don't need much. Never did. Never will."

"But, Dad," I say, taking plain tap water for myself. "You don't have to live like the cheapest guy in Bayport. Not anymore. How many times have I told you that I—"

He cuts me off. "Son, like I always told you, I take care a myself in my own way. I pay my own way. And I don't take handouts, not even from my own flesh and blood."

We have been over this before. But this time, I try coming at it slightly differently. "You accept free plane tickets from Jimmy. You don't mind staying under his roof?"

Suddenly he is defensive. "That's different. That's part of our deal." He stops himself uncomfortably. He looks like he did not mean to say what he said.

"What do you mean, 'part of our deal'?"

He looks down at the floor. "Well, uh, I, uh, mean, your brother needs my help. He needs me to be his partner. I helped set him up in the business."

"Really?" I ask. Clint has no capital to speak of. Just enough insurance money from my mother and savings to support his very modest life-style. He is still avoiding my glance. "How did you set Jimmy up? Tell me."

"I helped him the only way I know. With my hands. And with what I learned in my own years. I never made a big score like you did, but I been in a lotta businesses. It's true I made mistakes. But you know, some guys who never do it wrong never know what it was they did right. They just stepped in shit and don't know how or why. But not me."

He turns and heads for the den. We pass through the living room, now almost empty of Macallan family effects.

"Let's watch the news," he says. What he means is the weather report. He sits patiently through wars and terrorist waves and world financial panics, paying no attention whatsoever, waiting for the Bayport weather forecast. Two, sometimes three times a day. Nothing penetrates Clint's consciousness except the frontal system coming in from the west or the storm blowing up from Cape Cod.

He drops into his stuffed reclining chair in front of the old television. The tiny den with worn easy chair and stiff couch is, as usual, dark. He keeps the curtains drawn in winter to save on heating and in spring and summer to save on electricity for fans. "So what's that pretty wife a yours doing downtown?" he asks, settling into his habitual half-reclining position.

"Looking at pottery. You know the crafts shops in the Old Town section? They've got some nice stuff from local craftsmen. You ought to take a look. You could get something for your new place."

"Nah, I don't need any dishes. Last time we bought any china was just after your brother Jimmy was born. Don't need any more. Prices are probably outta this world."

The local news report comes on. It is a provincial, scaled-down version of the New York network station format, NEWSDESK 12. The same jittery theme music, the same bouncing electronic logos. But the local anchorman's loud plaid jacket and long sideburns are quite different from the look of his big-city colleagues. Clint goes into his news show trance. He will sit frozen for the next thirty minutes, until he has heard the local weather.

"I think I'll take a shower," I say. "I feel a little dusty from all this packing." Clint grunts. I might as well be talking to the wall.

"Say, Dad, are the extra towels still in the little closet upstairs? Wendy used up all the ones you left us drying her hair this morning."

"Sure," he says, not looking up from a report on Bosnia he will never remember. "Everything's still the same."

I head up the narrow stairway Jimmy and I used to slide down as kids and open the door to the small linen closet. There are piles of old sheets and towels, holding memories from before I was born. On the middle shelf are some toiletries stored for future use or just abandoned and forgotten. I see what looks like a bath towel on the bottom of the middle shelf. I have to slide the bottles to one side to get to it. As I move the unused mouthwash, deodorant, and aspirin bottles, I see one bottle that stops me dead.

It has a silver crown, elaborate Gothic letters, and a phony royal seal. It is all too familiar. "House of Lords," it proclaims. "The aristocrat of scents. For the man born to power."

Suddenly, Leo invades my nostrils and my memory. His threat at the Pierce dinner, the telephone handsets, a thousand encounters in the men's room. Agitated, curious, and a little angry that someone of my blood would have this in common with the enemy, I charge downstairs for some answers.

"What's this?" I ask the transfixed Clint.

"What's what?" He does not look away from the sports. He has never been to or participated in a sports event in his life.

"What's this?" I repeat, holding up the bottle of House of Lords.

My angry tone gets him to look away from the TV, but only for a second. "That's perfume. Cologne, isn't it?" He goes back to the sports.

"Yours?" I ask.

He mumbles.

"Is this yours?"

Still looking away. "Nope."

"Then how did it get here?"

"It's Jimmy's."

"What's it doing here?"

"He left it. Musta forgot it when he moved to Tucson."

"Jimmy uses this stuff?"

"Every day." I have finally distracted him from the television. Jimmy must be more interesting than the baseball scores. "Yeah, he tried to get me to use it. 'Come on, Dad,' he said. 'It'll make you feel like a million bucks.' But I just can't put on perfume, know what I mean? Jimmy slaps it on right after shaving. Stings like a son of a bitch. Jimmy says it wakes him up." Clint goes back to the TV, now featuring a local home electronics save-a-thon.

I stare at the House of Lords bottle in my hand. A sickening, impossible, horrible thought crosses my mind.

"Jimmy been using this a long time?" I ask.

"I dunno."

"Look at me, Dad. Please." He looks up. "Has Jimmy been using this stuff a long time?"

He is annoyed and puzzled at my pointless interruption of his ritual. "I said I don't know, Son. He brought it with him when he moved back home last year. I don't know when he first started usin' it. What's a matter, anyway?"

"Did Jimmy bring it with him when he visited New York last summer?"

"I dunno."

"But you say he liked to use it every day, right?"

"Yeah, every day. Said it made him feel like a million bucks. He's got a new brand now. Musta left that one. What's bugging you, Bob?"

I see Woodcock playing the incriminating cassette at my desk, his accusing finger waving in the air at me, his self-righteous rage and smug delight at my downfall. I try to sort out my recollections. Jimmy handled my phone that morning, too. Just minutes before the big blowup. But how could my brother Jimmy, the small-time New England car salesman, get a doctored cassette from magazine magnate Elton Mackey? And how, I ask myself further, did Jimmy suddenly come into some muffler shop franchises in Tucson?

I remember the cold I was suffering from, my stuffy nose and sneezing. Then the rush of adrenaline as the world collapsed. The rush that restored my sense of smell and filled my head with House of Lords.

I walk over to the television and switch it off. Clint looks up at me with distress. The weather was just about to come on. I place myself between his chair and the darkened TV.

"Dad, exactly how did Jimmy get set up with the Mister Muffler franchises?"

I am studying my father carefully.

"I told you, this big shot down in New York set him up."

"Was this big shot, by any chance, a big shot by the name of Elton Mackey?"

Clint looks uncomfortable.

"Uh, I don't know who the guy is."

"You ever heard of anyone by that name?"

"What name?"

"Elton Mackey."

"No. I don't think so."

"You sure?"

"Yeah," he says, fidgeting a little. "I'm pretty sure. Son, I'm missing the weather."

"The weather will be on again at eleven." I remember the late night phone call I got from Clint right after American made me their offer, right after Atwood set up my meeting with Mackey. I remember the pep talk Clint gave me about listening to whatever Mackey was going to tell me. I remember telling Clint everything, everything since the first hint of the deal with American.

"You do too know who Elton Mackey is," I say, keeping my voice low and controlled. "You told me you read an article about him in the paper, that he was salt of the earth and a fine man and how I ought to be proud to do business with him. That's what you said."

He is silent.

I remember Atwood's ESP about my movements and the progress of negotiations with American. No, I did not tell anyone at *Elixir* anything about the talks. But I told my father everything. I interpreted his interest as a combination of loneliness and excitement for the big doings in my life.

I feel confused and lucid all at once. I put the House of Lords down on the coffee table.

I look at my father. My father looks at the floor.

"Dad, I want you to tell me the truth. The truth."

"About what?"

"About what you know about Elton Mackey."

"I don't know shit about Elton Mackey."

"Well, you must know something about him to have praised him so highly to me."

"I don't know shit about the man. Only talked to him a couple a times on the phone."

"What?" I am stunned. "When?"

"Long time ago," he mumbles.

"What on earth were you talking with Elton Mackey about?"

No answer.

"What did you two talk about?"

314

He looks at the floor again.

"Come on, what?"

"You." I can barely hear him.

"How did you and Elton Mackey come to have phone conversations about me?"

He keeps his head down.

"Tell me, goddammit. Tell me!"

"Well, it was your friend called me. That kid Marcus, the one who helped unload the car when I brought your stuff to New York."

"Howie Marcus?" Things are beginning to come clear. Marcus was still shopping me around after I told him to stop shopping my company.

"Yeah, him. Said you two were still asshole buddies. Said he was lookin' out for you in the big city like he always did, 'cause sometimes you didn't know enough to get outta your own way. I said, 'Boy that's true.' He explained all about the companies Mackey owns and everything. Asks would I like to talk to Mr. Mackey about making a good deal for you. I said sure. Then Mackey gets on the line himself. Starts tellin' me about how he got started with nothing and all that. Then he tells me that he'd like to buy your magazine and give you a real good deal. He wants to know more about you so he'd be sure you guys would hit it off in your meeting. Said it would be a real good deal for you. Be the best thing you could do in the magazine business."

"And you believed him?"

"He said it would be the best deal you could make. And I already seen what four-flushing bastards those guys at American are. I was just trying to help you, Son."

"You were? So that's the only reason you talked to Mackey. Was to try to help me. Are you sure that's all?"

"Uh-huh."

"Really? There was nothing else? Absolutely nothing else? Come on. Level with me, Clint." Without thinking about it, I have stopped calling him Dad.

Clint looks over at the closed curtains.

"That's all there was?" I ask.

"Well, he did say—" Clint is mumbling.

"I can't hear you. Speak up."

He clears his throat. "He did say that if I could, you know, help move the deal along, uh, there'd be a little something in it for me."

"For *you*?"

"He just wanted to know a little bit more about you, and he seemed like he was good people. I never trusted those guys at American, and you shouldn'ta neither. Look at the trouble they gave you. Both times."

"Jesus, Dad, you sold me out."

"I was trying to do what was right for you, honest. That's all."

"How much did he offer you?"

"I just wanted the best for you."

"How much did he offer you? Tell me, goddammit."

Clint looks at the blank television. "Fifty thousand."

"Fifty thousand!" I shriek. "You sold me down the river for fifty grand. You want fifty grand, you want fif—"

"Son, I can live on that for five years. It's not a lot of money to a guy like you. But to a guy like me . . ."

"I'd give you money any time you want, you know that."

"Son, you'll give me money because you look down on me, because you think I'm washed up and no good. Mackey said this was a deal I could help him with. How often does a big guy like Mackey want to talk to a guy like me? All of a sudden, I got something to offer. All of a sudden, I'm worth listening to. Guys get finder's fees for doing nothing in deals all the time. They don't do shit. This was a helper's fee for doing something. A consultant, that's what Mackey called me, his consultant. Son, I was trying to do what was right for you. And along the way there'd be a little something in it for me. There's nothing wrong with that. That's business. That's a good deal all around, you gotta understand that."

He leans forward in the chair as if he might reach for the television.

"Don't you dare turn that on," I command. "I want the whole story. All of it."

He sits up straight in his chair, preparing for the next round of questions.

I begin again. "Now I didn't sell to Mackey, did I? So you didn't get your fifty grand consulting fee. No wonder you sounded disappointed when I told you I went with American." I remember that phone call, too. I thought he was just in a bad mood. "So give me the whole story. You tried to help Mackey do his deal and it fell through. Then what?"

"Well, Jimmy came home and was looking around for a deal of his own. Jimmy was awful down back then, awful down." He looks up at me for the first time, pleading in his eyes. "They forced him outta the dealership. He was their top guy, made money for 'em like crazy. The more he made, the more they hated him, those goddamn sons a the owner. They had it in for him." He looks ahead again, switching back to his storytelling. "So I was telling Jimmy how Mackey had wanted help and all. And Jimmy listens to me and he says, 'I got an idea, Dad.' Tells me I gotta get in touch with Mackey again and let him talk to him. Jimmy says his idea is gonna help everyone. Everyone. So I call Mackey back. I had to do some real talking to get through to him. He didn't want any part of me after you went with American. Anyway, I got through finally and Jimmy gets on and starts talking to Mackey. He can be a helluva good talker, your brother, once he gets started. You know, you're not the only one with the gift a gab in this family."

"Evidently."

"So he gets on with Mackey and starts talking. Then he and Mackey tell me I can get off the call. So I do. I don't know what they talked about, the two of them. But they talked a long time."

"I can imagine," I sigh. I think of Jimmy, hostile, hateful, angry—mostly at me. I can just see him licking his chops and getting even for everything. "So what happened after that?"

"Your brother comes downstairs—I was on the phone down here; he was upstairs in the bedroom—and says he's got a deal with Mackey that's gonna help all of us, including his big brother, who doesn't always know what's best for him. Jimmy says we're all gonna come out ahead. All of us. I just gotta do what he says and he and Mackey'll take care of the rest."

"And you believed him?"

"We were all gonna get something. Mackey was gonna buy your magazine from American and give you a big job, and Jimmy was gonna get financing for his muffler shops."

"And you?"

No answer.

"And you?"

"I got a piece of the muffler business. Ten thousand a year, like I was gonna get before, only better 'cause it'll be every year. You know, a real piece a the action."

"I see."

Mackey had already started his rumor campaign when Jimmy must have fallen unexpectedly into his hands. Mackey was looking for ways to throw me off and get the foothold he wanted. And suddenly Jimmy offered himself as an inside agent of destruction whom I would never suspect. How perfect for Mackey.

The lights go on all at once. If I had eyes inside my brain, they would be blinded by the flash. Leo didn't compromise my secret negotiations. My father did. Leo didn't plant the incriminating cassette. My brother did. In all likelihood, Conover didn't call Mackey to say that I was close to a deal with Greenthal/Peck. Jimmy did. Probably just now while I was safely out of the house. "What exactly did Jimmy tell you he was doing for Mackey?"

"Son, you got it all wrong. We were all trying to help each other, that's all."

"What did he tell you he was up to?" My voice is controlled but strident.

"He said he was going to arrange for you to make a better deal with Mackey. He said you didn't know what was best for you. So he'd help you do it in spite of yourself. He said this was a big chance for all of us and that you wouldn't get hurt."

"Oh shit. And you believed him? You honestly believed him?"

"Jimmy needed a chance, too. You got any idea what your brother's been through? He'd been down on his luck so bad. Jimmy needed a break and I could help him get it. *I could help him.* He said nobody could touch you anyway. You made all that money. You've had nothing but green lights ever since I can remember. Your brother kept getting the rug pulled out from under him. Believe me, I know what that's like. It's been happenin' to me ever since I can remember. Jimmy needed a chance, Son. And with that shit luck an' ignorance a yours, I figured nothing could—"

"Don't you ever—ever—say that to me again!" I am screaming now, drowning in realizations and memories I now have to completely revise. I cannot even begin to think of what I must do to stop Mackey from spoiling the possibility of a deal with Greenthal/Peck. I yell at him, "You idiot! You fool! You dupe!" But I know that I am not screaming at him. I am screaming at me. I am raging at my blindness. Why couldn't I see? My stupidity. How could I not figure it out? My innocence. How could I not suspect?

"You told Jimmy everything I told you about my business? As soon as I told you, you told him, and he told Mackey. That's what happened, right?"

No answer.

"That's why you were so interested in me and my business, wasn't it, old man?"

He looks straight ahead at the blank television.

"Oh, by the way. Did you give Jimmy the name of the brokerage house I'm having negotiations with? Wendy told me she mentioned it to you the other day. Did you pass that tidbit on, too?"

Still looking away from me, he gives his head a faint little nod, barely visible, but a nod all the same.

I think I hear myself mutter aloud, "I hate you." But I might have only been talking to myself. I look at the stupid bottle of House of Lords sitting on the coffee table. I feel like throwing it against the wall and watching it shatter. But that would only foul the room with more of its sickening presence.

Clint looks at the floor with hands folded. I stand silent, facing him.

The sound of a car pulling into the driveway breaks the moment, then the sound of the back door to the kitchen opening.

The sound of footsteps.

Then Wendy's cheerful holler pierces the air of the den.

"Hey, one of you big, strong Macallan men want to give a girl a hand?"

I am at the wheel, driving us away from Bayport. Leaving Bayport for the last time. The last time. The sky is black with the afternoon darkness of early winter. The highway to Boston is almost empty. The rest of the world won't start coming home from this big family weekend until tomorrow.

"I think that's a good strategy," Wendy says, the concern in her voice reaching deeper than the business issues we are discussing. *"Elixir* is still the original, the one the doctors care enough to pay for. *Panacea* is just a copycat book and they mostly give it away free. It's less than a year old. It's still unproven. You've got a very strong case. Especially for an investment that'll cost as much as the special issue. That should squash whatever promises Leo makes to them."

"It's the only strategy I've got." I feel myself biting my lip. "It's got to be good."

We retreat into our own thoughts for a while. We have not discussed what just happened at the house. I grabbed Wendy and told her we were leaving. I told her why and what I had found out. She went ashen and hugged me. Then everything was a blur of rushed packing. I don't remember whether Clint was watching the TV or whether he was just sitting in the den, but he stayed put through it all. We left without saying anything more.

"I'm also going to unleash Crosby and all the rest of the reps on Wall Street," I say after more road has whizzed by. "If Greenthal/Peck falls through, I won't let—"

Wendy touches me softly on the shoulder. "Don't worry. It won't, it won't."

"You know, if it all falls apart, if we start losing more advertisers again and I can't pull off this special issue, you know, American could claw back the first half of the money they paid me. It's in the contract, you know. It could happen."

"I know it could. But it won't happen. It will not happen. I believe that, honey. And so should you. You've got to believe it. You've just got to."

"I do. And I'm not just saying that. The good news is there are no more leaks. It's all in the open now. So I can fight it. And believe me, I know how to fight. There are no more dirty tricks they can play. I can win it in a fair fight. I am goddamn sure of that. Goddamn sure."

"Me, too, Robert. Me, too."

"I'm gonna fight for all I'm worth. And win. Just watch."

"I know you will."

A tollbooth plaza appears ahead on the horizon. I let up on the gas to begin slowing down. As we pull to a stop under the concrete canopy, I toss the quarter into the bucket. We are lit by the ghostly yellow glow of the sodium lights overhead. The open window lets in a blast of cold air. There is no one behind me. I lean back in my seat for an instant, still gripping the wheel with both hands. I close my eyes for an instant and take a deep breath.

"Wendy, would you mind driving for a little bit? I don't know what it is, I'm just having trouble getting my eyes to focus on the road. It keeps getting blurry. I don't know why."

Wendy leans forward to look more closely at me.

"I guess I must be more tired than I thought," I say.

She removes my right hand from the steering wheel and takes it in hers. "You're not tired, honey," she says. "You're crying."

DECEMBER

CHAPTER THIRTY-SIX

"Yeah, that'll be Roni's turf," I say, "and the regional brokers will belong to George." We are at the blackboard in my office, dividing up Wall Street firms into territories for my *Elixir* salespeople. We haven't been together this way like a real team since . . . since before American first offered to buy me out.

"Now as to whether it becomes open season on prospects for the special issue," I say, feeling like a football coach with chalk in hand, reviewing plays, "you'll have to wait for my phone call from Greenthal/Peck. If Wayne and I pull it off, Greenthal/Peck becomes your big endorsement for ads you sell in later issues. If we don't get them, it's like you never heard of Greenthal/Peck and may the best man or woman get the extra bonus points for a new special issue sponsor." I look directly at Wayne, who is half-sitting on the corner of my desk, the place of honor for my right-hand man. This is my chance to make things right with him after lying to him before. "If we win, Greenthal/Peck becomes Wayne's client. He spotted them first. But no matter how this afternoon turns out, he still has dibs on Merrill, Dean Witter, and Shearson. After all, it was his insight to go after investment houses in the first place." Wayne returns my gaze with a satisfied smile.

This is a new beginning. I have managed to gather my troops back together and rededicate them to a common purpose. It was no small feat. After all the deception I used on them over the past months, I had to find a very drastic and shocking ploy to regain their trust and commitment. Indeed, I was forced to resort to the most drastic and shocking ploy of all: I told them the truth. Exactly the way it happened to me: secret meetings, attacks of paranoia, family betrayal, and all (minus, of course, the personal parts with Wendy and Laura Chasen).

To my astonishment, they bought it. Or me. Or whatever. So here we are, with a newly sweetened bonus plan and a new determination to play and win together. And now, I find myself entertaining thoughts of staying on, asking Harry to renew my contract, running *Elixir* and maybe building it into something even bigger and better.

"It's funny to think that Leo is making his presentation to them," Roni says, waving a perfectly manicured index finger in the air and pointing it directly at the floor, "right this very second."

"Dueling medical books," I say, nodding. "Leo presents to Wahl this morning; Wayne and I go this afternoon. Decision promised at the end of the day. Winner take all."

"Cool, isn't it," Wayne says, relishing the thought of the *mano a mano* competition.

"Cronyism versus content," George adds, based only on the things he has heard about Leo's way of doing business.

"Okay?" I ask. "Everybody's clear on who's doing what to whom?" I get a round of affirmative answers and the meeting breaks up. "Wayne, I'll come pick you up around one o'clock." I rest my hand on his shoulder as I walk him out of my office.

"One o'clock it is," he says.

"Oh, by the way, there'll be a limo waiting to take us downtown. Gotta match the enemy, weapon for weapon." Wayne gives me a thumbs-up and heads down the corridor for his office. I stand for a minute in my doorway, thinking.

"So," Marie says, turning herself toward me in her swivel chair, "it's really do-or-die with this presentation this afternoon."

"It is for me, at least. *Elixir* can get on without it; the book'll be fine. But I don't know if I'll be able to make up *my* numbers in time, if they say no."

"If the worst happens, what then?"

"Then I get screwed. Big time."

Marie sighs.

"Don't worry," I say, trying to sound chipper. "I think the guys are going to get a lot of sales; they're really fired up."

"Yeah. Bob Macallan, cheerleader."

"It's what I'm supposed to do here."

"Bob, can I ask you something that's out of line?"

"Marie Padrone," I say, walking over and sitting on the edge of her desk, "I don't think there's anything you could ask me that would be out of line. Next to Wendy, you're—"

She brushes away my last comment with a sweep of the hand. Her face takes on a serious cast. "Bob, are you going to renew your contract with American for another year?"

Hmm, the big question.

"Gee, a while ago I would have said absolutely not. But suddenly, we're all back in the saddle and having so much—"

"Bob," she says, looking me straight and deep in the eyes, "I think you should get your money and get out. I don't have a good feeling about where all this is going."

"What do you mean, I—"

"Bob, you're a real nice guy. Probably too nice. Know what I mean? You built this up, and you profited from it. But I think it's all over here. I think it's just a matter of time. And if you're lucky enough to have your freedom, if you can just, uh, well then you really oughtta, well, you know what I mean."

"Yeah, I know what you mean."

"Bob," she says, taking my hand and squeezing it, "good luck this afternoon."

"Thanks, Marie." Without thinking, I lean down and kiss her on the cheek.

"And that's what the original can offer you that no copycat publication ever can," I say, turning down the last of my flip charts. I stare directly at cold, handsome, slicker-than-slick Adam Wahl. This time in this meeting, he returns my look. But there is nothing in those gray-green eyes to connect with. His look is as dispassionate as an auditor's report, his indifference as profound as that of the most hardened guard at Auschwitz. Adam Wahl is the perfect man for business.

He kept us waiting all afternoon. We were supposed to go on at two. He did not appear until well after four. It did not matter if he was really tied up or not. It was all part of the test. Maybe sometime later I can find out if he did anything similar to mind-fuck Leo this morning.

I glance for an instant at Wayne, sitting at my side. He nods. Yes, this really was a stellar presentation in its conception, execution, and delivery. We have done everything we can possibly do and done it as well as it can be done.

I look at Al Tully, the only other Greenthal/Peck man privy to this magazine salesman shoot-out. Tully nods appreciatively. I'm the guy he brought in in the first place, and I have not let him down. But the tentativeness of his smile and his nervous body language make it clear that the power to make this decision does not rest with him.

Adam Wahl sits, thinking, calculating, weighing.

"Any questions I can answer?" I venture nervously.

"No," he says, letting himself smile. Not to be friendly, but to celebrate the fact that his reticence has made me squirm. "No questions. I think I got it. This business of yours isn't exactly brain surgery." He turns to Tully. "Potter was gonna come down for the end of this meeting. Where is he?"

Tully jumps to his feet and goes to the wall phone. Just as he asks the operator to connect him with Stan Potter, the conference room door opens and Potter, again with electric suspenders and no suit coat, walks in.

"Hi there," he says graciously to me, "wonderful to see you again. Sorry I couldn't be here to listen." He looks in Wahl's direction and gives him an "okay" sign with thumb and index finger. Wahl nods his acknowledgment.

Suddenly, Wahl says to no one in particular, "I think this is the magazine that can help our portfolio management business grow."

I am shocked at this positive, highly prejudiced remark.

"That your judgment, too, Stan?" Wahl asks of his chief of portfolio management.

"Yeah," Potter says. "I definitely think it's the one that can do that."

"Then it's a done deal," Wahl says as he stands up and prepares to leave. "We go with this *Elixir* or whatever the hell it's called." Wahl heads directly for the door. He has no intention of making polite chitchat to wrap up his decision. "And, Tully," he says as he is halfway out the door, "get that windbag from the ad agency over here and have him chisel this guy down a little more."

That's it. I can hardly believe it. I feel Wayne patting me on the shoulder. I see Al Tully come up to me and start shaking my hand up and down. But my mind is elsewhere. Everywhere. It is screaming, Fuck you, Leo Sayles. I beat you on your own turf, and I beat you fair and square. With no whores and no kickbacks and no logrolling and no bullshit. I finally beat you, one on one. And you, Mackey. And you, Woodcock. And you . . . Before I allow my mind to wander to Clint and Jimmy, I turn to face Wayne and Tully and redirect my full attention and focus to this victorious transaction here and now.

"Wayne," I say, giving my favorite salesman a mock punch to the arm, "do you want to phone the good news back to our friends at the office?"

"I can't imagine anything giving me more pleasure, Bob."

A few minutes later, Prager arrives from the ad agency. He and Tully and Wayne and I spend the next half hour sending for papers and working out the details of the deal. I let Wayne lead our side in this negotiation. Greenthal/Peck, after all, will be his client, whether I remain at *Elixir* or not. We emerge from the conference room with a letter of intent from Al and an insertion order from Prager. I have accomplished everything I set out to do. Rather, Wendy and I, Wayne, and all my colleagues at *Elixir* have.

"Bob, you guys did a fine job," Al says to me out in the hall.

"Thanks, Al," I say. "Wayne and I are going to make you a happy and very regular advertiser."

"That's what we're here for," Wayne adds, playing his role as the temporary second fiddle faultlessly. He takes the precious documents and puts them into his attaché case. I can see that he is ready to go. I take him aside for a moment.

"Our limo, Mr. Crosby, is still waiting downstairs. Why don't you take it back to the office and process this paperwork?"

"You bet." He turns to walk away.

"And, Wayne," I add, "keep the driver for tonight. You shouldn't have a problem finding one of your young lady friends to help you enjoy it for a night on the town, should you? Especially if it's on the company."

"No, Bob, I don't think that'll be a problem." I watch him as he heads down the corridor, a definite spring in his step.

"Say, Al," I ask, returning my attention to Tully, "can you point me in the direction of Tim Conover's office? I'd love to catch up with him a little before I go back to the office."

"Sure. Isn't it a small world? I had no idea you knew each other, no idea. Let alone that he sold your company." Al takes me by the shoulder and points me toward the southern end of the corridor. "See that corner office down there?" I nod. "He's right there, one flight up. You know where the stairs are."

"I sure do. Thanks again, Al."

"Be seeing you."

I head for the interior stairwell and the next floor up.

At the end of the corridor I spot Conover's corner office. The secretary's desk across from his door is unattended. I walk up to the side of his open door and stop, hoping I might hear him on the phone with Atwood or Mackey or even Howie Marcus. The only sound I hear from the office is the tap-tap-tapping of something on a hard surface.

I stick my head in the door. Tim is sitting at his desk, jacket off, tapping his pencil and looking annoyed.

"Can I visit?" I ask.

"Sure, come on in." He gestures toward the chair in front of his desk, trying to cover his unease. Conover's new office is much bigger than the noncorner one he had at Hale Hadley. The decor is different, too. Gone are the hunting prints and the phony English antiques. This look is classic modern design. Sleek, simple pre-Memphis Milanese, all blacks and grays.

"Did I catch you at a bad time?" I ask, knowing that I did and not giving a shit. I want some answers from him. Now.

"No," Tim lies politely, "it's okay. Just stuck on a point in this deal. I'm waiting to get through to the client. He's tied up with something else."

"Gee, that's too bad," I lie in return. There is a silence. I wait. Conover broods about his problem, then remembers why I came to Greenthal/Peck.

"I'm sorry I had to screw up your presentation the other day. I had to get Wahl's okay on this deal we were bidding for." He winces slightly at the recollection. Apparently that deal did not go so well. "Oh, geez, I forgot to ask, Did you get the order? Are we going to sponsor the issue?"

"Yup. Signed, sealed, and delivered."

"Well, congratulations." He offers a preoccupied little smile.

"And congratulations to you, too," I say, trying to sound social and chatty, "on your great new job. They say downstairs you can walk on water."

"Oh thanks," he says, still distracted. "Yeah, it was time to leave old Hale Hadley, break out of the womb." I look around the office for the portrait of himself framed in gold-edged leather. It is not here. On the corner of the desk is a smallish photo in a silver frame. His wife and two kids. Very blond, very cute.

"So," I ask, "you, uh, been doing any more deals in publishing since *Elixir*?"

"Nah, been scratching away," he says with frustration instead of subterfuge, "but nothing that's come through."

I could almost like this new self-effacing Conover.

"Deal market is close to dead, but I hear there are a few acquirers still on the prowl. NewsCo, Becker, Tavarnier." Then I add, as deadpan as possible, "Mackey."

"Oh yeah," he sighs, "I've been out there courting them all. No takers that I could find, unfortunately."

"NewsCo?"

"No."

"Becker?"

"No."

"Mackey?"

"Not them, either. Or Tavarnier. I've been calling everybody." He makes a zero with thumb and forefinger. "But what's weird is that my sixth sense tells me there's a big publishing deal out there waiting to happen. A really big one. I just haven't been the one to ignite it. At least not yet. Say, you got any ideas? There are at least six different combinations of major players that make potential sense to me. Maybe we could have lunch next week. I'll show you some of my ideas, where I think I can create some action. Tell me what you think. What do you say?"

This Conover is indeed a changed man, soliciting another human being's opinion about anything—and investment banking, no less.

"Sure," I lie again. "My calendar's back at the office. I'll give you a call." Pause. "So, uh, you don't think Mackey's a good candidate for some action? I hear he wants to become a real player."

"Nah," he says with real exasperation, "not as far as I could tell. I really tried with the Mackey people. But I got nowhere. I must have had dinner three times with his head New York guy, and all he did was stonewall me about their plans." He stops for an instant, then smiles. "Interesting, though, he kept trying to pump me for details about your deal with American. Yeah, wanted to know all about *Elixir*. One time there was a little guy there, had a mustache, claimed he was an old buddy of yours."

"Howie Marcus?"

"Yeah, that's him. He really kept pushing to find out what I knew. That guy just won't quit."

"And you told him?"

"Nothing, of course." He puts one hand over his heart and makes a Boy Scout salute with the other. "The Hale Hadley code of client confidentiality. The secrets of my clients I shall take to the grave. It's very deeply ingrained in us all, I'm afraid. Besides, I knew that Mackey was starting a book to compete with yours."

"Panacea."

"Yeah, *Panacea.* How are they doing with it?"

"Too soon to tell. These things take time."

"Yeah, I know. Well, anyway, I wasn't about to compromise you and American."

"Unless he was going to offer you a big, fat deal."

"And he wasn't about to do that."

"So you held fast to your principles."

"Sadly."

We both laugh.

"It's good to see you again, Bob. Glad that Greenthal/Peck is working with your book."

I could try to pump him more, but my instinct tells me that he's really okay. He's telling it straight. I know now who betrayed me. I just try not to think about it. I get up from the chair. "Say, Tim, I see that your secretary's desk is vacant right now."

"Yeah, she's out sick and we're shorthanded in this department. Temporarily, at least." He seems a little embarrassed; this kind of sloppiness would never occur at Hale Hadley.

"Tim, would you mind if I made a couple of calls before I leave?"

"Not at all. Make yourself at home."

"Thanks." I turn to leave.

"Oh, Bob," I hear from behind, "just leave a quarter on the desk."

I chuckle politely and head for the secretary's station diagonally across from Conover. My first call is to Truedale and Wolfson.

Before Iris can announce the firm's name, I blurt out, "Hello, Iris, it's Bob. Is Wendy there?" My excitement is finally coming out.

"No, Bob, she's not."

"Is she reachable? I gotta talk to her."

"Is this an emergency? Did something bad happen?"

"No, no. Quite the opposite. Is she reachable?"

"Afraid not. She and Liz called about ten minutes ago from Paint It Black, so they're either in the subway or a cab on the way up here."

"Okay, I'll be in transit by the time they get back. Can you give her a message?"

"Of course. You been running or something? You sound all outta breath."

"No, just selling. Tell her they said yes. Yes!"

"That all?"

"Yes, just yes. That's all. Thanks, Iris. Bye-bye."

I hang up and sit for a moment on pins and needles. It really is going to happen. It really is going to be all right. I feel adrenaline or joy or something pulsing, pushing, gushing through my veins. My limbs are lighter than air. I know what to do next. I'm going to get Woodcock off my back once and for all. I'll tell him that the special issue is saved and he can leave *Elixir* the hell alone. I dial the number almost without looking; I know it by heart.

"Mr. Woodcock's office." It is Miss Boardman, sounding uncharacteristically frazzled. I hear other phones ringing madly in the background behind her.

"Hello, Miss Boardman, this is Robert Macallan. Is Harry there? I've got something that will be of tremendous interest to him. Is he there?"

"Oh, I'm, uh, can you call back please? Mr. Woodcock's not available just now." More phones ringing. "Excuse me, could you hold, please?" The line goes silent for twenty, maybe thirty, seconds.

She comes back on. "Uh, yes, I'm sorry. I'm sorry, who is this, please?"

"It's me, Miss Boardman. Robert Macallan from *Elixir* magazine. I've got an important message for Mr. Woodcock. Really, he'll want to take this call. Please put me through."

"Oh, Mr. Macallan, he can't take your call *now.*" Phones still ringing out of control behind her.

"Say, what's going on up there? Hello? Miss Boardman? Are you there?"

"Mr. Macallan, could you please call back? I'll try to get your message to Mr. Woodcock, but my guess is he won't be able to return it for some time. Please, can you call back later? Sometime. But not today."

"What's going on? You got terrorists in the lobby or something?"

"Please. Mr. Macallan, I really have to go now. Good-bye."

I hang up, utterly mystified. What on earth could be creating all that chaos in Miss Boardman's orderly life on the forty-eighth floor? That puzzling phone call has brought my body back under the power of gravity. What a letdown. I try to recapture my feeling of elation, but it is gone. I still feel great, but I have definitely returned to earth.

Just then, Conover comes tearing out of his office, shrieking at the world.

"Jesus Christ! Jesus Christ! I told you it was in the air, I told you I could smell it. I knew it! Jesus Christ, Bob, I was just telling you there was gonna be a big one!"

"A big what, Tim?"

"A big publishing deal. It just came over the tape!"

I try to ask him about it, but he keeps on raving.

"Jesus, Bob, you're not gonna believe this. This combination was number seven on my list of six, I can't believe it."

"Who? What?"

"You're gonna love this, you of all people."

"So tell me."

He stands still for an instant and takes a deep breath before speaking. "American Communications is being taken over."

"American?" I ask. "By Grubman?"

"No. National Entertainment."

"What? That guy Kristatos, who owns the movie company?"

"And records and video games and pinball machines and fast food and so on."

"Wow," I say, not yet even trying to measure the possible impact on me.

"Jesus, what a deal! I can't believe I wasn't in on it." He pounds the side of his head in not-so-mock frustration.

"How'd it happen? What's the deal, Tim?"

He stabilizes himself momentarily to explain. "American was in a hammerlock by Grubman and the Belsky brothers." He is jabbering at very high speed. "Rather than fight it out, they caved in and took an easy way out with Kristatos. He ran circles around them. Offered them an even stock swap with National. Supposedly a merger of equals. Ha! Details are sketchy, but it looks like they gave away the whole fucking store. Just gave it away. Those wimps! Jesus, I gotta make some calls!" He darts back into his office and starts dialing frantically.

JANUARY,

THE NEW YEAR

CHAPTER THIRTY-SEVEN

"I think you should do it today. This morning," Wendy says, scurrying barefoot around our bathroom in bra, panties, and half-slip, her hair still wet from the shower. "I think it's important." She reaches into the big plastic shopping bag from the discount toiletries store to extract the last of the items she bought last night. "You've got to set the record straight with Leo. You accused him unfairly and you punished him unjustly." She grabs the big jar of Tylenol and the tube of baking soda toothpaste and lines them up on the bottom shelf of the medicine cabinet.

"Now hold on a minute," I say from back in the bedroom. "Even if Leo didn't actually betray me, I'm sure he would have eventually, if he'd been smart enough or been given the opportunity." I am standing in front of the mirror that's over Wendy's dresser, in my boxer shorts and white shirt, wrestling with my cuff links. "I say the hell with him. I have no moral obligation to Leo Sayles."

"Ro-bert." She turns from her unpacking and stands in the bathroom doorway to get my full attention. "It's about making things right with *you*. The moral obligation is to you, not to him. Yes, Leo is a crummy bastard. But that's not the point. You fired him, you dishonored him in public, you—"

"That part was all true and documented. Leo is a low-level white-collar crook."

"And you were happy to look the other way when it suited your purposes."

I lower my head in order to concentrate more closely on getting my left-hand cuff link inserted through all four layers of cloth.

"Ro-bert," she says insistently. I look up. She is standing with arms crossed over her chest, one bare foot tapping silently on the tile floor. "The difference is that you are picking up a check for five million dollars this morning and Leo isn't. You're the one who should be able to be a little

329

magnanimous. You've won. And you won cleanly, on content. Make it a victory you can be proud of all around."

"So what do I say to him? That I'm sorry? I hear he's making more with Mackey than he did with me."

"I wouldn't exactly call it an apology. I'd say it's more an acknowledgment, setting the record straight."

"Okay, all right." I get the left cuff link in place, finally. "But he'd never take a call from me. I can't imagine taking him out to lunch."

"Isn't *Panacea*'s office just a couple of blocks away from American Communications?"

I nod.

"Doesn't Leo have a regular morning ritual? A buttered kaiser roll and a large light coffee that he buys and eats at his desk?"

"Yeah, I can't imagine that he's changed that habit."

"Then ambush him on his way into work. He must stop at a coffee shop or something. Chances are it's the one that's closest to his building. Catch him on the street, make your peace with him, then go to American, get your check from Woodcock, and close the book on this part of your life. Then come back home and we'll start making babies."

"I just don't see the point."

"Yes, you do."

"No, I don't."

"It'll make you feel better."

I give her a skeptical look.

"It'll make *me* feel better," she says.

"Oh, all right."

She turns and motions for me to follow her into the bathroom. "Can you come in here a second?" She reaches into the shopping bag and holds up a carton about the size of a large Kleenex box. "Do you know what this is?"

"The label says 'ovulation kit.' "

"Uh-huh. Can you move your shaving stuff off the shelf over the sink? I have to keep this handy."

"So that's the little chemistry set, eh?"

"That's it. From now on, we can't have sex without it."

"Is there some kind of device in that box I don't know about?"

She ignores my sarcasm. "During those four or five days, we have to do it when *it* says when. You've got to conserve your, uh, energy to be ready when duty calls."

"At your cervix," I say, giving her a little salute.

"Wiseguy," she says and puts the ovulation kit down on the sink and pulls me to her in a hug. "Do you have any idea how proud I am of you?"

"I think I do." I lean down and kiss her lightly on the lips.

She waits for our lips to part and kisses me in return. "I don't think you do."

I kiss her back. "Maybe you're right. I can't imagine how proud you are."

"You got through it all," she says, kissing me again.

"Correction," I whisper. *"We* got through it all. And we will get through it all."

"You . . . me . . ." Wendy says, punctuating each word with a kiss.

"And Swee' Pea," I add, closing the discussion with a deep, long kiss.

Leo is easy to spot coming out of the Athena Coffee Shop, briefcase in one hand, breakfast bag in the other. In his double-breasted camel's hair topcoat and homburg hat, he is an elegant anachronism. Leo's look is a throwback to the glory days of American business, when everyone believed and obeyed without question. He could be a member of Dwight Eisenhower's cabinet or the executive in charge of marketing the Edsel or the PR man selling bomb shelters in home basements.

This morning is bright and chilly. You can see your breath.

Leo is walking east along Forty-sixth Street. The rays of the morning sun are shining right into his eyes as he approaches the tower where *Panacea* has one-half of a lower floor. I intercept him just before he turns for the revolving doors.

"Leo, I just want a minute. Please."

Between the glare of the sunlight and his morning reverie, he is caught completely off guard. He stammers for an instant, then snaps, "Jesus Christ, what the hell do *you* want?"

"Just a minute of your time, Leo. That's all."

"I've already had more of you than I need, thanks." He turns to go into the building. I take his arm to hold him back.

"Leo, I'm sorry. I fired you wrongly. I accused you of spying and conspiring and I was all wrong. All wrong. I just wanted to set the record straight."

"Jesus." He smiles. "Would you say that to my lawyer in a deposition? With an admission like that, I could slap you with the biggest open-and-shut lawsuit in history." He pauses for dramatic effect. "Good thing I'm not litigious by nature."

Yeah, I say to myself, by the time I got through documenting your sleaze in court you couldn't sue for cab fare. Instead, I say to Leo, "Look, I'm getting out of publishing and I just wanted to, uh, well, you're very well situated now . . ."

"With Mackey," he says, the edginess easing out of his voice.

"Yes, with Mackey." Suddenly I feel uncomfortable. "And, uh, that's good for you, uh . . ." I've done what I set out to do. He has heard me admit my wrongdoing. We're not about to kiss and make up. "The important thing is you've, uh, ended up, well, uh . . ." I can think of nothing more to say.

Seeing me fumfering puts Leo at ease. He smiles. "So, you all set to collect the rest of your big score? Eh, kid?"

His nastiness helps me regain my equilibrium after the discomfort of apologizing. "That's right, Leo, my big score. The one I got by defeating you on the issues. It's an area you might do well to explore. It's called content."

Leo looks at me quizzically. Instead of being irked at my burst of righteous arrogance, he looks slightly amused. "What do you mean, content?"

"Just what I said. The issues. Substance. Value. You know, meat. The real stuff, whatever you want to call it. I won at Greenthal/Peck because I proved we had the goods and we could deliver. No favors, no goodies from the butter and eggs man. It was one of those rare occasions where the truth actually made a difference and took the day."

Leo's amused look has grown into an ear-to-ear grin.

"You know, kid, it's a good thing you're getting out of this business. You better take your money and go retire somewhere with your illusions."

"What are you driving at?"

"Jesus, Macallan," he continues, "just because you made a lot of money in this business doesn't mean you're any good at it. It just means that you grabbed a few things and pulled 'em together in the right way. Once. And you got away with using a lot of genuinely talented people like me, just long enough to get what you needed. But try it again, buster, and I'll give you odds you'll fall flat on your fucking face. I don't care how big your bank account is; you'll never hold a candle to me in this business. And that smug little speech of yours proves just how much you don't know."

"What are you talking about, Leo?"

"Jesus, kid, am I supposed to spend my whole goddamn life educating you? It was bad enough when I was working for you. But you don't pay me, anymore." He turns and starts to walk away.

"Leo," I say urgently, "what the hell are you talking about?"

He stops and turns around.

"Don't you know?"

"Know what?"

Leo emits an exasperated sigh. "Know what got you the Greenthal/Peck account." He inspects my confused face. "Shit, you don't know! I figured you were just faking. You really don't know."

I refuse to give him the satisfaction of saying again that I do not know.

"Some society broad called up and said she'd dump two million in their asset management group if they bought your special issue instead of mine."

I stand there in silence.

"It must be nice to have friends like that, Macallan. That's one broad you musta stuck it to extra good. Two million worth! Yeah, you won. But don't give me any of that high and mighty horseshit."

"Leo," I stammer after him, "what else do you—"

"Look, I'm busy. Why don't you give Marie a call. I hear she knows more than she's letting on." With that, he turns and walks away. I can hear him muttering to himself, "Not a clue, not one fucking clue."

"How does Dudley like my old office?" I ask Marie. I am standing in the bank of phone booths in the lobby of American Communications. I don't think it's the same phone I used a year ago, when I got a quarter from Conover to call Wendy with news of American's offer, although it could be.

"Oh, Dudley is still Dudley," Marie says, "you know. Dudley." She sounds preoccupied, troubled.

"Marie, what's wrong?"

"Oh, Bob, it's nothing. I—"

"Come on; out with it. This is me you're talking to."

"Bob, I just have a bad feeling about what's going on here. There are all sorts of rumors going around."

"What kind of rumors?"

"Oh, you know. They're going to fire everyone or move the magazine to another part of the country. There are a bunch of them. I just have a bad feeling about it. Just between you and me . . ." Her voice turns low and confidential. "I've been looking for another job. I don't want to wait around and get—"

"Marie, nobody in his right mind would ever—"

"Bob, it's going to get ugly. I can just feel it coming. I don't want to be here when it happens."

"Marie, any company would be lucky to have you." I feel helpless. "Remember, if you need any kind of reference use my name."

"Believe me, I will."

I can't help feeling unsettled. However stupidly, I imagine Marie sitting at her desk at *Elixir* forever, one of the constants of the universe, ballast for an unstable world. "You know, the place just won't be the same without you."

Pause. Here it comes. I can visualize one of those knowing looks forming on her face. "Bob," she chides me, "the place hasn't been the same since you sold it."

I can think of no adequate comeback. I wait a moment to allow for a change in climate.

"Marie, can I ask you a question about the recent past?"

"How recent?"

"Last month."

"Shoot."

"Did anybody call for me while Wayne and I were making our pitch at Greenthal/Peck?"

Pause. I can almost hear her thinking. "No."

"You sure?"

"Of course I'm sure.

"No, nobody called you." She is stonewalling.

"Marie, there's something you're not telling me. Something that went on that day."

No answer.

"Something to do with Laura Chasen. Laura Chasen got involved with Greenthal/Peck. Somehow. Come on, Marie, give it to me straight. What happened?"

Pause.

"Come on."

Nothing.

"You're holding out on me, Marie. Somehow Laura Chasen found her way to Greenthal/Peck that Thursday afternoon. That was no accident. And the only other person on this planet who might possibly have made a connection between Laura Chasen and my meeting, Wendy, would never in a million years have done it. Come on, Marie, what did you do?"

"I'm sworn to secrecy."

"Marie Padrone, you've got to come clean. My mental health, emotional balance, and ability to function as a whole person are at stake. I must know what happened. Please, Marie. I have to know."

Another pregnant silence.

Finally, she speaks. "I called her."

"You *called* her? On the phone? How did you know where she was?"

"I got hold of her in Hong Kong," she says, very matter-of-fact.

"I don't think she has a permanent address beyond the offices of her lawyers and trust officers. Why, she's just—"

"When she was here waiting for you that day, we got to talking."

"I guess so. If I remember, she was regaling you with stories of Bangle Bay."

"We talked about a lot of things, Bob. But mostly about you." I wince. "That's when she gave me the numbers of a couple of friends of hers. She said one of them would know where to reach her, no matter where she was traveling. She told me to keep those numbers in my Rolodex for you, just in case."

"Just in case of what?"

"In case you ever decided you needed to reach her."

"And so?"

"So when you said that the Greenthal/Peck meeting was do-or-die, I made an executive decision. I knew that Gene Merritt was her friend and all. And those types have all this power and influence that they use to help each other. At least, that's the impression I always got from reading. I figured there's gotta be some truth to it. So I said, What the hell? Maybe her friend Merritt can pull some kind of strings or something. So I called the first number and there was nobody home. But I got the second woman and she knew just where Laura was staying. Reaching her was actually pretty easy. It was the middle of the night in Hong Kong, and she was asleep in her hotel room."

I almost ask Marie if Laura was alone when she called her, but I decide not to. "What did you say to her?" I ask.

"I just explained the situation, you know, and before I could say much more, she got all excited and asked for the telephone number of Greenthal/ Peck. She told me she would try to make a little magic. That was her word. She told me to stay by the phone and wait for her to call back. A little later, just after you guys left for the meeting, she called and said she had one of her Swiss bankers working on a little piece of magic. After another couple of hours, she called to tell me that her banker had worked it out and that you would soon find yourself pulling a rabbit out of your hat." Adam Wahl wasn't playing waiting games that afternoon; his people were negotiating with Laura's people. That's why Stan Potter came in grinning. That's why Wahl said he thought my book would definitely help his asset management business grow. "She was so happy, almost giggly like a little girl. We talked for a while about a bunch of things, apart from you, that is."

"I see. Did Laura tell you how much money she invested with Greenthal/Peck?"

"Bob, she swore me to secrecy. I mean, really."

"Marie, you've come this far."

"Two million was what she mentioned. She said it was a nice round number."

I should have remembered that Leo is always to be trusted when it comes to gossip. Should I call Greenthal/Peck for more information? No, something tells me I don't want to hear it from them. Do I ask Marie for the telephone numbers that can help me reach Laura? No. Not now. "Is there anything else?"

"She told me that if you ever did find out, I should tell you this: she wanted 'to make sure you got your taste of the big injustice.' That's what she called it. 'The big injustice.' "

"Marie, I, uh, don't know what to say." I glance at my watch. I am due upstairs in Woodcock's office momentarily. "I'm sorry, but I've got to run off to an appointment. I just don't know what to say."

Pause.

" 'Thank you' would suffice."

"Marie, thank you." I take a deep, deep breath and exhale. "Thank you."

"You take care, Bob."

"You, too."

As I walk toward the bank of elevators that go to Woodcock's floor, I inspect the scene. Things look normal in the lobby of the American building on this ordinary Thursday morning. But the month-old merger with National Entertainment has already started changing the company drastically. There are rumors of huge sell-offs and layoffs, all to pay off the astonishing mountain of debt used to finance a deal that will give the shareholders little beyond highly diluted shares in a dubious new company they never asked to own.

Woodcock is to be liaison officer between American and National, the only executive from American on Kristatos's private staff. Apparently, he won the mogul's loyalty early on, having conspired with him weeks before the merger. It was Woodcock who helped to strong-arm his old friends Dillon Edwards and Walt Drummond out the door to make room for the vending machine tycoon's absolute rule. He also led the investor relations publicity campaign that herded the shareholders, like the proverbial lambs, to an overwhelming yes vote. And if that does not send Andrew Henderson spinning wildly in his grave, Woodcock is creating an office of "Corporate Synergy." Its official mission will be to cross-pollinate projects between the two companies. Its actual mission will be to compromise the editorial independence of American's publications in order to promote National's entertainment projects.

As I enter the elevator, I brace myself to meet with the old Harry Woodcock in the new American Communications.

"Good morning, Mr. Macallan," Miss Boardman says, extending her hand. She is so warm and welcoming as she escorts me toward Woodcock's office, all smiles and human interest, it is as if she were reminding me that we are dear, dear friends. How, I wonder, could I ever have forgotten?

At the doorway to Harry's office, she leaves me. Harry is on the phone. He looks up and waves me in to have a seat by his desk.

"No, no," he says into the handset. "I agree. You're absolutely right. . . . Uh-huh. Right. I agree wholeheartedly. . . . Yes. Thanks. Bye." He puts the phone down and leans back in his chair. In the far corner of the room are packing boxes, some filled. Harry must be moving again.

"Well, Bob," he says cordially, heartily, "here we are." He looks around the room, inspecting it, as if this were the magical destination that together we have sought and finally arrived at.

"Yeah, here we are," I say, nodding at the stack of boxes, "but it looks like you are on your way someplace else. May I ask where?"

"Oh, just down the hall," he mumbles with false modesty and makes a little pointing gesture over his shoulder to indicate which direction down the hall. The only other office in that vicinity is the airport-sized corner office that just a couple of weeks ago was inhabited by Woodcock's dear friend and mentor, Walt Drummond. "So, Bob, how are we these days?" he asks in the tone of a family doctor questioning a dotty octogenarian.

"Well, Harry, *we* are fine," I reply with a let's-cut-the-shit edge in my voice. "But *we* were a little pissed off that American unilaterally decided not to consider renewing my employment contract with *Elixir*. We were thinking that there were some interesting and valuable things still left to do there."

Harry leans back in his chair, makes a little steeple with his hands, and leans his chin against it. "Couldn't tell you then. Can tell you now."

"Tell me what?"

His eyes narrow, he starts to smirk. Here comes the dagger. "Your little magazine is going away. It doesn't fit our plans, never did as far as I'm concerned. We're getting rid of it. At a loss, I'm afraid. But that's just a short-term blip. What's important is we're getting rid of it. I couldn't possibly have told you that until we had a deal."

Marie is right. Again.

"But you're here to pick up your check, not to reminisce about a dead medical publication. That is the only reason you are prepared to endure this meeting. Isn't that right? Ordinarily, we could simply have wired your money to your bank and completed this transaction. But I wanted you to come here so I could see you one last time. I wanted to see your face when I told you that your little magazine is about to vanish from the face of the earth, leaving not a trace. Everything you worked to build will be gone."

I am angry at the news. And disappointed. But I'll be goddamned if I'll let him see. "Just who are you selling it to?"

"A certain company based in Cleveland wants *Elixir* removed as a competitor. EMC. They're going to fold it into their own medical life-style book. And, poof, they'll be alone in the category. Isn't that interesting?"

"I suppose so," I say icily.

"I told you long ago, didn't I? You're not a builder. You're just a taker. You'll leave nothing behind you. To you, it's all for money. You don't understand what is demanded of people in order to make a company great, to create an institution that can last. That's why I wanted to see your face when you found out that everything you made will be erased. And I wanted to be the one to hand you this."

He takes a plain envelope out of his top drawer and holds it up between thumb and forefinger. "This is it, Macallan. Everything you worked for. Everything you ever wanted. Everything that matters to you. Come and get it."

He tosses the envelope to his right. It floats through the air and lands on the carpet a few feet from where I sit. I will have to get up, walk over to it, and bend down in front of Harry to get it.

"Your money, Mr. Macallan." He sits up formally in his chair and reaches for a memo in the top of his "in" box. "Take it and get out of this company," he says out of the corner of his mouth. He begins reading, making a theatrical display of his interest. "Now," he whispers without looking up, "or I will call security and have you forcibly removed." He flips to the second page of the memo, pretending to be absorbed in his reading.

I stand up and walk to the side of his desk. I can feel his eyes on me. I bend down and pick up the envelope off the floor. I stand there without moving, within the arc that defines the personal space behind Harry's desk. I am standing inside his turf. Slowly, prolonging each motion, I slide my finger into the sealed envelope, tear it open, and extract the check. I hold the check in one hand, the torn envelope in the other. It is a certified check to the order of Robert Macallan in the amount of exactly $5 million and no cents.

Harry clears his throat. I do not move. He reaches for his phone and pushes the intercom button. He pauses. Still, I do not move. "Miss Boardman, would you . . ."

I put the check back in the envelope, slide it into the inside breast pocket of my suit jacket, still not budging.

". . . would you call corporate secu—"

I turn and start walking toward the doorway.

"Never mind. Thank you. Please see Mr. Macallan out."

Walking through the grand and dreary lobby of American Communications, I feel removed from immediate sensation. The world around me feels dreamlike and tentative. I pass through the revolving doors. I feel cold air and bright sunshine, but distantly, as if they were touching someone else who was telling me how they felt.

Harry has fired me again, wiped out my purpose, erased my achievements. For an instant, the events of the last five years evaporate, and I feel just the way I did six years before. I stand on the sidewalk with no place to go. Just as I did then.

Then I put my hand to my chest. Through the layers of topcoat and suit jacket, I feel the thin envelope with the single sheet of paper within. I look around me at the people coming and going about their jobs. I pat the envelope. It has healed old wounds and slashed open new ones. It has changed everything. And nothing.

Laura yanked the strings of fate and granted me the bounty of the big injustice. In doing so, she robbed me forever of moral certainty, my sense of earning and deserving. She knew exactly what she was doing. What she wanted me to understand was not just the unfairness of money, but the ambiguity of it.

Just like six years ago, I will walk through these crowds unnoticed. Just another human animal in this overcrowded colony. Just as I did six years ago, I will go off to start something new. What, I don't know; where, I can't say.

But this time, it will not be a flight from anything. But a journey to something.

I am ready. To begin a new life with Wendy.

To become a good father to a brand-new person. Like a child. Like myself.